PRAISE FOR

Dust of the Damned

"*Dust of the Damned* is a damnably fun ride through a West that never was, in the company of fine folks who should have been. When the West gets weird, Peter Brandvold is the best trail guide a reader could ask for."　—Jeff Mariotte, author of *Desperadoes*

"Supernatural, .45-caliber Western mayhem at its best! Brandvold delivers a no-nonsense, blood-and-guts foray into the unknown."　—Shannon Eric Denton,
Harvey Award–nominated coauthor of *Graveslinger*

"A rip-roaring, weird Western adventure, told with Peter Brandvold's excellent eye for detail and bristling with action. If you start reading it at night, you'll probably be too scared—and too caught up in the story—to sleep. Brandvold is one of today's top Western writers, and he's better than ever in *Dust of the Damned*."　—James Reasoner,
Spur Award–nominated author of *Redemption, Kansas*

"*Dust of the Damned* is a breath—or should I say 'dragon's breath'?—of fresh air. Part Western, part fantasy, part adventure, and all action, it shoots off like a comet and never lets up. Its conclusion leaves you wanting more. Well told and action-packed, *Dust of the Damned* is an invigorating read and another winner for Peter Brandvold."　—Tom Roberts, publisher, Black Dog Books

"A full chamber of horrors and .45 slugs for things that go bump in the night."　—Beau Smith,
author of *Wynonna Earp: The Yeti Wars* and *200 People to Kill*

Dust
of the
Damned

PETER BRANDVOLD

BERKLEY BOOKS, NEW YORK

THE BERKLEY PUBLISHING GROUP
Published by the Penguin Group
Penguin Group (USA) Inc.
375 Hudson Street, New York, New York 10014, USA
Penguin Group (Canada), 90 Eglinton Avenue East, Suite 700, Toronto, Ontario M4P 2Y3, Canada
(a division of Pearson Penguin Canada Inc.)
Penguin Books Ltd., 80 Strand, London WC2R 0RL, England
Penguin Group Ireland, 25 St. Stephen's Green, Dublin 2, Ireland (a division of Penguin Books Ltd.)
Penguin Group (Australia), 250 Camberwell Road, Camberwell, Victoria 3124, Australia
(a division of Pearson Australia Group Pty. Ltd.)
Penguin Books India Pvt. Ltd., 11 Community Centre, Panchsheel Park, New Delhi—110 017, India
Penguin Group (NZ), 67 Apollo Drive, Rosedale, Auckland 0632, New Zealand
(a division of Pearson New Zealand Ltd.)
Penguin Books (South Africa) (Pty.) Ltd., 24 Sturdee Avenue, Rosebank, Johannesburg 2196, South Africa

Penguin Books Ltd., Registered Offices: 80 Strand, London WC2R 0RL, England

This is an original publication of The Berkley Publishing Group.

PRINTING HISTORY
Berkley trade paperback edition / January 2012

Library of Congress Cataloging-in-Publication Data

Brandvold, Peter.
    Dust of the damned / Peter Brandvold.
        p. cm.
    ISBN 978-0-425-24517-0 (pbk.)
    I. Werewolves—Fiction.   2. Supernatural—Fiction.   I. Title.
    PS3552.R3236D87   2012
    813'.54—dc23
                                            2011038301

PRINTED IN THE UNITED STATES OF AMERICA

10 9 8 7 6 5 4 3 2 1

With a tip of the hat
to the cross-genre pulpsters of old
who published their yarns in the pages of the great
Weird Tales.
And in memory of cover artist
Margaret Brundage,
1900–1976.

Dust
of the
Damned

Chapter 1

DEVIL'S LAIR

"Sun'll be down in an hour, Uriah." The old prospector's voice had a tremor in it.

The big man riding the rangy palomino stallion he called General Lee slanted a hazel eye at the sky vaulting over the towering canyon walls. "An hour and a half, I 'spect."

"That ain't enough time," said the prospector, Junius Webb, riding a mouse-brown burro along a narrow trail meandering through a deep, high-mountain, stream-threaded canyon in the Sawatch Range of central Colorado Territory.

The big man, ex-Confederate ghoul hunter Uriah Zane, glanced at him skeptically. "You said the cave was just over the next rise."

"We still don't got enough time. It's too damn late in the day, Uriah."

"Stop whizzin' down your leg, Junius," Zane said, his voice

low and gravelly and pitched with the soft, rolling vowels of his North Carolina origins. "This ain't my first spin on the ole merry-go-round."

"You ever spin on it so late in the day?"

"Later," Zane said as they topped the rise. "Keeps the fear up, and that's a good thing in this business." He drew back on General's reins.

Zane was a tall, dark, powerfully built man with thick arms and shoulders. A little past thirty but with a hard wiliness that made him appear older than his years, he wore smoke-stained buckskin pants and a tunic, a long, charcoal-colored wolf vest, and knee-high wolf-fur moccasins. He had a handsome but rough, square face that from a distance appeared hand-hewn from knotted oak. Closer up the lines and planes looked finer, less severe, but the eyes, not without tenderness, gave the impression of great age.

His cheeks and jaws were carpeted in a thick, black beard. His long, hazel eyes, slightly slanted and owning a wry intelligence, turned color throughout the day—green, gold, yellow, brown, sometimes the blue of a high mountain lake. His hair was long and nearly black as an Indian's though he himself was of Scotch-Irish and French Huguenot descent. He'd been born and raised in the red-dirt heartland of North Carolina. He'd been born into the Southern gentry, his people having arrived on the New World's shores in the 1750s, then traveling to the savage, Indian-teeming North Carolina wilderness via the Pioneer Road. His family had grown wealthy raising bright-leaf tobacco, a skill handed down from father to son.

Even as a young man, Uriah Zane had betrayed his singular, solitary nature. He had preferred stalking the surrounding mountains, hunting bears and panthers and fishing remote streams alone for sometimes days or weeks at a time. He found such activities far more fulfilling and exhilarating than bedding down in the tobacco barn to gauge the furnace temperature during the long, painstaking process of preparing the rich golden leaves for market.

Neither had he cared for the debutantes' coming-out balls and large gatherings so characteristic of his moneyed, socially conscious class. Early on, he'd earned a reputation for taciturnity and reclusiveness but also one as a formidable backwoodsman, acquiring hunting and survival skills equal to those of the Amerindians he often found himself fighting and killing, though he felt nothing but respect for the natives, knowing he and his kind were the interlopers on their territory.

A necklace of wolf claws dangled from a rawhide thong down the hunter's broad chest, which was clad in buckskin that a Ute woman he'd holed up with one winter had beaded in sun, moon, and star designs across both breasts.

Horn-handled bowie knives jutted from sheaths strapped inside the tops of his moccasins, and on his shell belt he wore two Colt Navy pistols, while a stout, savage-looking LeMat pepperbox revolver jutted from a shoulder holster under his vest. He wore two cartridge belts, one appointed with lead slugs, the other with silver. Down his back hung a quiver and a heavy wooden crossbow that Zane had fashioned himself not long after the War, when he'd headed west to hunt ghouls for his personal satisfaction as well as for a living.

Ghouls ran amok on the western frontier, and a man who could bring in a few werewolves or blood-swillers or the infernal living devils known as hobgobbies and collect on the bounty the

U.S. government was offering could make a fair living for himself. If he lived, that was. Or wasn't transformed into the very beast he hunted, which was always a risk.

Zane knew that risk better than anyone.

The same curse had befallen a few friends of Uriah Zane, and Zane himself had undertaken the unenviable task of running them down. He'd thought that was only right. In their places, he'd have hated being taken down by a lucky shot from a thirty-a-month-and-found local badge toter, say, or, worse, allowed to live forever in a form he'd once shunned. Cursed for all eternity.

All in all, a man like Zane, broken by the civil strife and the ghastly tools that Lincoln had used to win the War at Gettysburg, could do worse for himself.

He had no home, no family. The plantation at Rose Hill had long since been taken over by carpetbaggers, and those of his family who hadn't fallen under tooth and claw at Gettysburg were battered and broken husks of their proud former selves, defeated not only by the deaths of so many of their own but by the way those soldiers had died . . . or been cursed to live forever like those who'd cursed them.

Now Zane stared out from beneath the brim of his black, bullet-crowned sombrero banded with woven eagle feathers. His eyes, set deep in leathery sockets, narrowed slightly at the corners as he surveyed the canyon before him with the keenness of a raptor's gaze.

He sniffed the breeze, wolflike, listened closely to every weed rustle and branch squawk, to every tumbling pinecone. It was hard even for his keen ears, however, to hear much above the river rollicking down its rocky bed to his left, chugging, churning, and spitting white foam over its pine-clad banks.

But he hadn't made it nearly ten years in the ghoul-haunted West by striding wildly into swiller-haunted canyons. His friend Junius Webb, who'd been prospecting here in Colorado for nearly thirty years, had informed Zane of the swillers holed up here high in the Sawatch Range. Webb had stumbled on the lair when, picking and shoveling along the banks of the Taylor River, he'd sought refuge from a violent summer thunderstorm in a cave at the base of the northern ridge wall. He'd shared knowledge of his grisly find with the stipulation that once the swillers were sent back to the hell they hailed from, Zane would pay his old friend half of the money doled out by the nearest government bounty office.

Detecting no sign of danger—though one never knew what besides swillers was lurking in these dark canyons—Zane touched his heels to the palomino's flanks and continued on down the rise. His makeshift wagon clattered along behind him, and Junius Webb found himself eyeing the contraption grimly, for it was far from your usual buckboard or spring wagon. In fact, it wasn't really a wagon at all but a coffin, of all things, on wheels!

Yessir, a pine coffin showing the wear and tear of many ghoul-hunting jaunts, with a heavy hinged lid with a stout cross carved into its top. Webb shivered and looked away, saw the sun hovering near the crest of a distant western ridge wall, angling dark shadows down the steep, pine-clad canyon walls, and shivered again.

"Yep, gettin' damn late," he muttered, though he was well aware his protestations were falling on deaf ears.

Zane glanced over a bulky shoulder at his unwilling partner. "Lead the way, Junius."

"You sure know how to torture a feller, Uriah," Webb said, batting his heels against his burro's sides and riding on ahead down the narrowing, darkening path between ridge walls that bulged and knobbed and sometimes leaned inward, sometimes backward.

Ten minutes later, Zane followed Webb off the trail to the right, and climbed the steep slope spongy with forest duff and fragrant with balsam and spruce. The cave appeared at the base of a bulge in the granite cliff that jutted two thousand feet straight up into the slowly darkening sky. The cavern's ragged opening was just high enough for a man of Zane's height of six and a half feet to enter bent forward at the waist.

Zane halted General Lee and, patting the palomino's long, gold neck soothingly—the General always got his blood up around swillers—slung his two-hundred-and-thirty-odd pounds out of the saddle, walked over to the cavern mouth, and dropped to his knees to get a look inside, one gloved hand on the edge of the opening. The darkness was too dense to penetrate much farther than a few yards.

He sniffed. Cool smells of damp stone, mushrooms, and the fetor of bird shit. A bear had investigated the cave's opening some time ago—Zane could still smell its rank sweetness. But it hadn't ventured far inside. The faint tracks led away from the opening.

He turned to where Junius Webb stood in front of his burro, holding the beast's bridle up close to the bit. "How far does this go into the mountain?" Zane asked him.

"Deep. About sixty yards to the swillers' lair."

"What compelled you to venture that far in, Junius? I never would have suspected you of bravery."

"I'm a prospector, Uriah. Might be a mother lode of silver in there . . . though I'd never mine it now, after what I seen in there. Got some good color in the walls, though. I reckon that's what lured me in so far."

Webb's Adam's apple bounced in his turkey neck as he slanted another cautious eye to the west. "You sure you wouldn't rather we got an early start tomorrow?"

"It's ten miles back to your cabin." The big ghoul hunter strode resolutely toward his wheeled coffin. "And I for one don't cotton to bivouacking in swiller country after dark. Nope, we'll take care of this situation right here an' now. Why don't you hold these torches?" He pulled a couple of relatively straight cedar branches, their ends wrapped in burlap and soaked in coal oil, out from the storage rack beneath the casket, and tossed both to his sallow, patch-bearded, weak-kneed partner.

He flipped the hasp on the casket lid and opened it to reveal a brass-canistered Gatling gun nestling among its wooden tripod and other tools of the ghoul hunter's trade—wooden arrows, steaks, hammers, a spare LeMat, a shuriken that Zane was still learning to throw and that worked well against the nasty hordes of hobgobbies that roamed certain regions of the West. There were several coiled bandoliers containing .45-caliber shells for the Gatling gun, which Zane had managed to swipe one night, drunk, his pockets emptied by a run of hard luck at craps and red dog, from an Army paymaster's storage shed.

He'd chewed himself out the next morning for resorting to common, albeit federal, thievery, but the shed was open, and after he'd stumbled into it and passed out on a pile of flour sacks, the gun was there in all its potential ghoul-killing glory—glistening and attainable—so he'd appropriated it and hadn't looked back.

He needed the gun worse than the Army did, as they'd proved next to worthless at running ghouls to ground. Mostly, the blue bellies turned at the first sign of a yellow fang or wolf snarl, and ran like hell back to their fort, soiling their drawers.

Junius whistled. "Whoo-ee, look at all them silver bullets. Good Lord, Uriah, you must have a couple thousand dollars there, with silver prices as high as they've climbed in the past few years!"

"I got a secret source. And sometimes Uncle Sam pays my bounties in silver and I have it melted down for bullets."

Zane slid a few stakes aside and lifted the Gatling gun from its grisly housing. As he did, a burlap sack spilled its contents into the nest the gun had occupied. Junius gasped at the head with its ragged, bloody neck staring up at him, pale blue eyes glassy in death, fangs bared beneath a curled upper lip. The ears were large and porcelain blue.

"Christ!"

"Ah, shit. Here—hold this."

Zane handed Junius the Gatling gun, which the old prospector accepted after he'd dropped the torches. The vampire head was already beginning to smoke where the sun touched it, the flour-white skin turning waxy and ready to melt, as Zane opened the bag and nudged the head back inside with his fist, saying, "Get back in there where you belong, Mortimer."

"Nasty damn business," Junius said, scowling down at the bloody sack.

"Tell me about it. Gotta keep the damn swillers' heads covered good till you haul 'em in for bounty, because Uncle Sam don't pay for ashes." Zane scowled and shook his head, and then grabbed the Gatling back from Junius.

"Wasn't that Mortimer Quinn?" asked Junius.

Zane nodded as he rested the Gatling on one shoulder, slung a sack of arrows over the other one with his crossbow, and headed for the cave. "Caught him in Leadville some days ago, cavortin' after dark with fallen women in back alleys. That old stage robber died nasty, but I got him."

He ducked into the cave, then dropped to one knee and lit a match. He glanced out the entrance at Junius, who stood there holding the two unlit torches in his arms, looking stricken. "Come on. You started this thing; now we gotta finish it. And if we dillydally much longer, we'll have to wait till morning, and I don't think you want to camp out here with the beasts in here huntin' out *there*."

Junius gave an agonized groan and lurched into the cave. While Zane lit one of the torches, the prospector said, "I been wonderin' why I been losin' cattle of late. I bet it's these swillers in here been takin' 'em. Thievin' bastards."

"Yeah, well, I reckon swillers livin' this remote have a hard time keepin' their larders filled. Usually live close to towns like that coven they found livin' in that old whorehouse in Aurora near Denver."

"Uriah?"

Zane had begun moving back into the cavern as Junius walked along beside him, holding up the flaming torch. Zane kept his voice down.

"What is it?"

"My Bonnie's one of 'em."

Zane jerked a look at him. "You sure?"

"She disappeared a couple months back. She done me that way before, but I think she musta got bit one night when she was out skinny-dippin' in the creek by moonlight, and they took her. She was always fascinated by 'em, always talkin' about how manly the males were."

"I'm sorry, Junius." Zane wanted to say that Bonnie had been a good woman, but he knew Junius would see the lie. Bonnie was twenty years Junius's junior and had taken up with the man when he'd been flush with gold and silver and bought a herd of cattle with which to start his own small ranch. But she was wild—anyone could have seen that. She'd have slept with a billy goat if he'd been flush with poker chips and had flexed his biceps at her.

The prospector shook his head, smacked his thin lips, which were cracked and stained from tobacco chew, the wind and sun of the mountains, and camp smoke. "If we run into her, let me drill the arrow through that bottom-dealing bitch's heart my ownself, all right, Uriah?"

Zane continued on into the cavern, hiking a shoulder. "I reckon it's the least I could do, partner."

Chapter 2

. . . .

BLESSED BULLETS

"We're gettin' close," said Junius, his voice echoing faintly off the stone walls.

Zane could hear water dripping and a faint vibration in the ceiling, feel it in the stone floor beneath his boots. The cave smelled of pent-up air, bat guano, and a bitter, coppery substance that Zane recognized as blood. Even after all these years chasing ghouls, his heart quickened, and the short hairs stirred faintly along the back of his neck.

The floor dropped suddenly, and the vibration grew to a dull roar that then bounded into a louder cacophony until he could feel the moisture in the air against his face and smell the mineral aroma of underground water. Junius walked a little ahead of Zane, sort of sidestepping, holding the torch aloft and sliding the flickering illumination farther and farther into the corridor, pushing shadows back and away and to each side, angling his and Zane's own silhouettes onto the wall to their right and behind them.

"River ahead," the prospector said. "With a bridge acrosst it. I figured some old prospector built it, so I ventured on across."

The floor continued to drop steeply until the torchlight showed the walls falling away to each side and a large, cold, dank area opening ahead. The roar here was almost deafening, and Zane could feel water droplets spitting at him.

"Easy, now," Junius said loudly enough to be heard above the tumult.

He stopped and extended the torch out over a deep, narrow ravine, water coursing through it—white and wild and chugging over submerged boulders. The river's trench was about twelve feet deep and twice again that wide. Straight out from Zane and Junius stretched a bridge constructed of rope and pine planks. The planks were well worn, varnished by countless crossings.

"I crossed it once," Junius said, his voice trembling in earnest now as he nearly shouted above the water's roar. "It's sound. We'd best get a move on, huh? Them swillers'll be wakin' up soon."

"They are in a ways, ain't they?" Zane said, feeling Junius's apprehension at the lateness of the day. Last he'd seen the sun, though, it had just been starting to dip down behind the western ridges. They likely had a good half hour before it fell beneath the horizon.

Zane lowered his Gatling gun to the floor, wincing as the blood flowed back into his shoulder, reawakening numbed nerves, and nodded for Junius to continue. The prospector stepped onto the worn planks and, holding the torch high with one hand, held on to the other torch as well as one side of the rope bridge with the other. He took mincing steps until he was on the opposite bank, and Zane was right behind him.

"Just beyond here," Junius said, walking ahead more slowly now between the cave's narrowing walls, his eyes fairly glittering with terror.

They came to an opening in the left side wall. Junius stopped, holding the torch high. Zane stopped beside him and stared into what appeared to be a library or smoking parlor outfitted by folks of class and culture. There was a red plush fainting couch, heavy, deep chairs upholstered in wine-red and lime-green crinoline, a large scrolled liquor cabinet, and several heavy bookshelves stuffed with well-worn tomes. There were a number of small tables where drink glasses and ashtrays sat. A Tiffany lamp glowed on one, its wick turned low.

By far the largest chunk of furniture in the room was a shiny black grand piano over which a Union flag was draped.

"This job just got a whole lot easier," Zane said.

"Wonder how long they been holed up here," Junius muttered.

"What I wonder is how they got that piano in here."

"Not the way we came—that's for sure. Must be another way in." Junius nodded at a low door on the room's far side, flanking the piano. "They're back in there. You think we could pick up the pace a little, Uriah?" The prospector made a gulping sound as he breathed heavily through his nose.

He continued forward, crossing the room. Zane followed him, glancing down as he passed the piano, to see an ashtray in which a half-smoked cigar rested, its coal cleanly removed, saving the stogie for later. Zane wasn't sure why, but the image made the nerves along his spine twang as he ducked through the doorway to find himself in a long room, even danker than the others, in which seven mahogany coffins sat on pedestals draped in red, purple, or pink velvet with gold tassels.

"Let's set to it," Zane said, moving to the first coffin and unslinging his crossbow from his shoulder.

The coffin had varnished wooden handles carved in the shapes of lions' feet. Zane grabbed one of the feet and raised the lid to stare down at a pale, silk-suited man with gray hair and a carefully trimmed gray beard and handlebar mustache. He slept with his thin-lipped mouth closed. Wrinkles at the corners of his eyes made it look as though he were smiling. A leather-bound copy of *Ivanhoe* lay open on his chest, as though he'd been reading just before he turned out the lamp on the table beside him and drew the coffin lid closed.

Zane lowered the crossbow in both hands and triggered an arrow through the swiller's chest, just above the book. The eyes and mouth snapped open. The large, powder-white, beringed hands jerked as though to grab the arrow, but they didn't come up even halfway before they relaxed, and the light left the swiller's eyes.

Blood oozed out around Zane's arrow, which he'd bought from some Hunkpappa Sioux up in eastern Wyoming—he preferred Sioux arrows because they used the tough, reliable wood of the chokecherry shrub—to stain the silk shirt behind the black silk double-breasted jacket. That was a lot of blood for a swiller, which meant he must have drunk recently—a bedtime snack, perchance?

Zane moved to the next casket, Junius following him closely, wringing his hands. As Zane opened the next lid, the prospector plucked a battered old railroad watch from a pocket of his baggy duck trousers and flipped it open.

"Oh, Jesus . . . damn near six, Uriah. The sun sets around six in these parts this time o' the year!"

"Don't get your bloomers in a twist," Zane said, as he fired another arrow, mortalizing the immortal, red-haired gent in his crossbow's sites. As the beast's jade eyes opened in shock, Zane said, "Nighty-night, pard," and hurried over to the next casket.

Nocking his crossbow again, he opened the lid. His eyes widened in surprise. The female's eyes were already open and staring up at him, fear trickling into them and causing the pupils to widen. Her red-painted lips began to spread, as though she were preparing to scream. Zane quickly aimed the crossbow straight down at her chest, and thumped an arrow between her breasts that were all but revealed by her low-cut, green velvet gown.

"Oh!" she cried, lifting her head sharply and closing both slender hands around the arrow, groaning and grimacing. "Oh, you dirty . . . *shit*!"

"Holy hobgobbies!" Junius exclaimed, leaping back. "Your fear up now, Uriah?"

Quickly plucking another silver-tipped arrow from the quiver down his back and nocking the crossbow, Zane hurried to the next casket, finding another swiller coming to life before he hastily killed it forever. The next two were also beginning to awaken before Zane drilled arrows through their hearts, then turned to the final coffin.

Junius stood beside the casket, facing Zane, who yelled, "Look out!"

Too late. The suited, black-haired beast leaped out of the open casket and kicked Junius hard in the side of the head. Junius yelped and flew sideways into one of the other coffins, he and the casket tumbling in a heap from the pedestal and hitting the floor with crunching thuds.

The black-haired beast—a young man in shiny black cowboy boots that had never been near a cow pie, and an Indian-beaded, fringed elk-skin jacket stained snow-white and fancily trimmed with whang strings along its arms—bolted, snarling, toward Zane.

The beast's fangs were fully extended, its eyes red as it sprung off its shiny black boots. Zane triggered the crossbow a half second before the beast slammed into his chest. Zane flew straight back into another casket, knocking the casket off its platform and following it down to the cave floor, the snarling, slithering, red-eyed beast on top of him clawing at his throat and trying to bury its jaws in Zane's neck.

Zane released the crossbow, managed to snake his arms up and close his hands around the beast's throat. He wasn't trying to kill the thing—he knew strangulation wouldn't work—but only to keep those damn fangs from tearing into his neck.

No need. The beast's jaws stopped snapping. His body relaxed. The pale lids did not close down over the red eyes, but the eyes lost their savage light.

Wincing at the pain of the casket under his back, Zane shoved the swiller off him and lay there against the coffin, catching his breath. Junius was on all fours, breathing hard and groaning and shaking his head as if to clear the cobwebs. Blood dribbled down from a cut on his earlobe.

Zane heaved himself to his feet and grabbed his hat and crossbow. "You all right there, partner?"

"Ah, hell, Uriah." Junius winced and cupped a hand to his ear. "I don't know how you do this for a livin'. Let's get outta here. I need a drink. I need a drink bad, hoss!"

Zane grinned and was about to inform Junius of the bottle he had in his saddlebags outside the cave, but closed his mouth and frowned. He heard a distant squawking sound, as though of creaky hinges, and the scuffs of shoes across the cave floor behind him. There were groans and what could only be described as muffled, savage snarls.

Junius's torch was almost out. Uriah scooped up the second one and touched it to the first. Fire caught the kerosene-coated burlap with a *whoosh*, and Uriah swung around to face the direction the sounds were coming from, fear making his heart skip beats.

It skipped more beats when he saw that this anteroom of sorts led to others, and from those others, more well-dressed swillers were stumbling, bleary-eyed and a little disheveled, still waking up from their naps, but, realizing the lair had been invaded, were hissing and starting to run toward Zane.

The ghoul hunter swung around and grabbed the prospector's arm, pulling the man to his feet. "Let's pull our picket pins, Junius!"

"What the hell is that?"

"More!" Zane shoved the torch into Junius's hand and pushed him toward the door. "Run—I'm right behind you!"

He swung around as the first swiller sprinted, snarling and cursing in some language Zane didn't recognize, and Zane quickly nocked his crossbow and buried an arrow in the center of the beast's paisley vest. That slowed the throngs of others that were jostling shadows behind him, but not by much. There were too many for Zane's crossbow.

Cursing under his breath, he dropped the crossbow down his back and grabbed the stout LeMat snugged into his shoulder holster. He triggered the shotgun shell under the main barrel. The shell was filled with crushed silver dimes and nickels, and it laid out two or three of the oncoming horde, before Zane, striding awkwardly backward, flicked the LeMat's lever toward the main cylinder and squeezed off a silver .44 round, dropping a fat, blue-fanged woman in a gaudy pink dress. He bolted out of the room behind Junius, who was sprinting as fast as his old, bowed legs and creaky ankles as well as his heavy hobnailed boots would allow, the torch flaring above his head and showing his long, thin hair bouncing across his shoulders as he ran.

"You're a dead man, Uriah Zane!" one of the swillers shrieked behind him.

"Damn," Zane said, not breaking stride as he headed toward the rush of the underground river. "I didn't realize I was famous in these parts."

"Oh, you're famous in all parts, Uriah!" a male swiller shrieked behind him.

Through his moccasins, he could feel the vibration of the stream as well as the pounding of running feet behind him, and just a glance over his shoulder showed the jostling shadows of the horde catching up to him—at least a few. One made a dive for his feet, tripping Zane, who nearly went down but regained his balance and momentum after firing the LeMat into the swiller's head, and continued chasing Junius.

Ahead, the torch dropped, and Zane saw Junius's crumpled frame on the cave floor beside it, about ten feet in front of the bridge.

"Goddamnit, Junius!" Zane shouted above the river's roar. "Get up an' *run!*"

"Twisted my ankle," the old prospector grated out.

Zane grabbed the old man's arm, and Junius tried putting weight on one ankle. He cursed as it gave out beneath him.

The ghouls were too close, their shadows lurching across the floor around the torch. The hissing sounded like an awakened rattlesnake nest. Zane aimed the LeMat and fired, the report sounding like a hammer rapping an empty rain barrel in the close confines. That gave the running horde momentary pause. Ten or fifteen of them were behind him. Except for their blazing eyes and bared fangs, they could have been a moneyed, well-read group of civic boosters just now leaving a natty opera house on Larimer Street in Denver. Despite their slight dishevelment upon waking, the ladies were immaculately coifed and gowned, the men suited and well-groomed, pomade glistening atop several combed black or sandy heads.

Zane shoved the LeMat at them, and they lurched back. He triggered a silver round into the chest of one who looked especially determined, and then, as the dead, snarling swiller fell back against several of the others, Zane reached down and pulled Junius up and over his shoulder, leaving the torch where it lay, heading for the bridge.

Not to be thwarted, the howling vampire horde jerked back to life behind Zane. As he gained the bridge's other side, he could feel the jostling of the planks. He set Junius down near the Gatling gun, palmed his Colt Navy from the cross-draw holster on his left hip, and drilled the first swiller on the bridge in the chest while triggering his LeMat into the swiller behind the first.

The second swiller yelped indignantly and clutched his breast, from which blood issued as well as several white smoke tendrils.

"Well, I'll be goddamned," Zane said, his face brightening.

"I believe Father Alejandro's blessing gives these slugs an extra pop!"

"Huh?" Junius asked, incredulous.

"Never mind."

Zane emptied both the LeMat and the Colt, then holstered both pieces. He scooped up the Gatling gun, quickly spread its three legs, and directed the canister toward the nattily dressed figures once again making a dash, Indian-file, across the bridge. The first one was ten inches from the end of the Gatling's six-mawed barrel when Zane began twisting the wooden crank.

Bam-bam-bam-bam-bam-bam-bam-bam!

The first slug tore a big hole in the belly of the nearest ghoul, who stumbled back and down while the next slug tore into the gent he'd fallen into. That gent screamed and fell sideways over the bridge and into the raging river.

As the Gatling gun continued roaring, the shots sounded like massive empty barrels tumbling down a rocky ridge, causing Junius to drop to his knees and clamp his hands over his ears. The other ghouls on the bridge were blown back onto the planks or thrown over the sides and into the stream.

Junius whooped and hollered as the blasts continued, cutting into the hordes still coming, so enraged at the invasion of their lair that they'd sacrifice themselves to the Gatling gun in an attempt to get at the big man in wolf furs crouched over it, cranking the flashing, hammering cylinder.

Three rounds ripped through a stringy-haired woman in a plain muslin dress, and Junius whooped louder. "There's Bonnie. Woo-hoo! You drilled her good, Uriah!"

Suddenly, the torch on the other side of the bridge sputtered out, probably under a swiller's boot, but Zane kept cranking the

Gatling gun, hearing the screams and the splashes as the bodies dropped into the river and were washed on out of the cave. He'd fashioned his own cartridge belt, which held a hundred rounds of ammunition, so it took a while to empty it.

When the crank clicked on an empty chamber, Zane unsheathed his second Colt Navy and aimed it out over the dancing bridge. He listened as the Gatling's roars faded beneath the rush of the river.

In the inky darkness he could spy no movement. He wished he had another torch. Suddenly, the stygian blackness before him moved, and he heard the bridge squawk on its worn ropes. A persistent ghoul was marching toward him. He triggered the Colt. There was a squeal, but he could smell a sickly sweet perfume as the bitch continued toward him.

He emptied the Colt. The squeal came sharper this time, and there was the thud of a body slamming down on the bridge.

He waited, listening, quickly reloading the smoking Colt from the shell belt around his waist. Finally, he fished a match out of his shirt pocket, scratched it to life on his thumbnail. The glow spread well enough that he could see no more ghouls heading toward him. Four or five lay twisted atop the bridge. Several more lay with their heads and arms dangling off the opposite bank. He couldn't see any farther than the bank beyond, but he could detect no other movement.

He heard nothing but the river.

Junius lit a match, too. He held it up and looked around warily. Finally, he cast his glassy gaze to Zane. "That was a fine mess o' Yankee swillers, Uriah."

"Yeah, we cleaned up," Zane said after a while. "Sorry about Bonnie."

"No need." The prospector paused. "I sure am glad you came loaded fer bear, Uriah."

"Blessed bullets."

"Huh?"

"I had an old friend bless the silver bullets. Gives 'em a little extra punch." Zane gave the old prospector a wolfish grin. "Don't tell no one, Junius. I want it to be my own special secret."

"Blessed bullets. Whatever you say, Uriah."

Zane dismantled the Gatling tripod, hefted the gun onto his shoulder, and rose. "Come on—I'll buy you a drink."

Chapter 3

. . . .

GHOUL HUNTER'S LAMENT

Zane and Junius Webb spent the night in the canyon, on the other side of the river from the cave, drinking coffee liberally laced with busthead from the bottle in the ghoul hunter's saddle-bags, and roasting a jackrabbit buck that Junius had shot earlier in the day, near the start of their excursion.

Junius had no liking for bivouacking this close to the swillers' cave, and Zane had to admit, if only to himself, to a buzzing along his own nerve endings. He'd never encountered so many swillers shacked up in the same place before. He and Junius had come close to being torn to shreds, the blood sucked out of their bones, in the cave over yonder.

Worse yet, they might have been transformed, though he couldn't imagine himself and Junius fitting in among that crew of fancy swillers.

Good to know the blessed silver bullets worked so efficiently, however. Next time he ran into a sky pilot, he'd be sure to have him bless a few more boxes of .44s for his Colts and LeMat and his Henry repeating rifle.

Zane and Junius took turns throughout the night keeping watch, though it wasn't really necessary. Neither slept except in short spurts, awakened by every owl hoot and falling pinecone, expecting to see a flour-faced demon glaring down at them, saber fangs flashing in the firelight.

They rose early the next morning and returned to the cave, where Zane set to work with a hand ax, cutting the heads off as many dead swillers as he could find. As each head dropped away from the ragged neck, Junius gathered it up by its hair and dropped it into a croaker sack, muttering sour lamentations under his breath. When he'd filled four sacks, and Zane had accounted for twenty-three heads, they tied the tops tight, making sure no sunlight could get in and spoil their work.

"Nasty damn business," Junius complained once more as he and Zane draped the four croaker sacks across the wheeled casket in which the trusty Gatling gun nestled.

"Yeah, well, someone's gotta do it," Zane said for the seventh time that morning, doffing his hat and running a big hand through his thick mane of tangled black hair. "You're glad to have them swillers gone, ain't ya? Might have turned you into one of 'em."

"I doubt a swiller'd care for the white lightnin' I got runnin' through these old veins, but I'm damned tired of 'em feedin' on my cows. The neighbors' cows, too. And I been wonderin' why all the game disappeared from this neck of the Sawatch."

They had a last cup of coffee, then broke camp, and, Zane straddling General Lee and Junius Webb in the saddle of his burro, they headed back to the main trail and began following it west along Taylor Canyon, the wheeled coffin rattling along behind, the croaker sacks swaying to and fro down both sides. It was a nice day in the high country this late in the year, the sun a warm caress, the leaves of the aspens well on their way to turning their vibrant yellows and golds.

They stopped to rest and water their horses in a horseshoe of Taylor River, and Zane stepped into the trees to evacuate his bladder. He took a deep breath, leaned back a little on his hips, and glanced at the sky. He glanced away, then lifted his eyes once more to the rim of the granite and sandstone ridge rising on the opposite side of the river.

A bird was winging around up there, likely hunting the ridge crest for jackrabbits or cottontails. Zane squinted. One hell of a big bird.

As he watched the raptor, or whatever it was, wing out over the canyon from the ridge crest, he vaguely detected a slight tightening in his shoulder blades and a thinning of his piss stream. He lifted a gloved hand to shade his eyes and scrutinized the winged beast just now flying over him, about two thousand feet in the air and beginning to bank as it gradually headed back toward the ridge. Massive lime and gold wings, like giant bat wings, swatted against the air while a long tail, spiked on its top side, curled like a ship's tiller. The head owned the shape of the alligators Zane had once seen on a tobacco-selling journey to southern Georgia, only this head had large triangular ears, like a dog's ears.

Green and gold scales along the winged beast's reptilian body flashed in the sunlight as the beast careened back over the top of the ridge and disappeared behind it.

Zane stood staring, incredulous. He blinked his eyes as if to clear them, wondering if what he had spied was really only a large hawk or eagle but a trick of the light had given it the shape of a dragon.

He stared at the sky over the ridge, hoping the beast would appear once more. After a time, Junius called from behind him, "Uriah, if you're havin' trouble in the peein' department, I know a fella in Gunnison. Sells an elixir that'll have you streamin' like a Belgian plow horse!"

"Did you see that?" Zane said, buttoning his pants and striding back toward the prospector.

Junius was holding the burro's halter and waving blackflies away from his own long, wart-stippled nose. "See what?"

"That bird up yonder?"

The prospector lifted his gaze. "What bird?"

"Ain't sure it was a bird." Zane brushed past the man and grabbed General Lee's reins. "Do me a favor. The rest of the way to Gunnison, keep an eye on the sky for me, will you? Don't laugh or spread it around the saloons till I know for sure, but I think I seen a dragon."

Junius had turned, wincing a little on his twisted ankle, to follow Zane with his gaze. He arched a skeptical brow. "A what?"

The ghoul hunter swung into the leather and felt his bearded cheeks warm with chagrin. Was he going mad? "Just keep an eye skinned upward and let me know if you see anything you ain't used to seein'. Now, come on, goddamnit. We don't have all day to burn out here. I wanna turn these heads in before we start attracting mountain lions!"

He neck-reined General Lee around and, the casket wheeling along behind him and the croaker sacks swishing like grisly ornaments down its sides, headed back up the western trail. They wound around through the canyon until the steep walls gradually lowered and they were on a broad open flat, the river to their left now, distant mountains jutting like storm clouds in all directions, several peaks already snow mantled.

They crossed the river, wide and shallow here on the sage flats, and entered the cow and mining town of Gunnison. The rough little prairie oasis was so high in altitude that the sun literally appeared to be raining gold out of a vast cerulean sky upon the log shacks and shanties and tent saloons and corrals and leaning privies and stock pens.

Gunnison had a broad main street, its crown jewel a turreted sandstone opera house at a hitch in the road. The log and frame false-fronted businesses around it were more than humbled by its gaudy opulence, though there was a three-story brothel painted red and deep purple, with balconies on the upper two stories, that tried its damndest to compete.

Gunnison was bustling, as it always was this time of the year, with drovers driving beeves to be shipped out on the railroad to Denver or Salt Lake City and prospectors making their gradual way out of the extreme high country around Crested Butte and Tincup to lower altitudes for the winter. And since Gunnison was sandwiched between two known ghoul hideouts—one of hobgobbies, the other of werebeasts, of which there were several known varieties including bobcats and pumas—there was the ever-present and generally unheeled bounty-hunting crowd as well.

A couple of pianos were being hammered in saloons up and down the street. Cutting through the patter as well as the rumble of conversations rising from clumps of waddies and frontiersmen of all shapes and sizes all over the street, a man's angry voice shouted, "Goddamn your vermin hide, McCreedy! I want you outta here *now!*"

Boots clomped. A man yelled. Spurs rang. The batwings of the Wolf's Howl Saloon on the street's left side belched out a burly gent in a short bearskin coat, duck trousers, and brown bowler hat. He stumbled across the gallery, arms akimbo, and continued on down the three steps to the street where he fell and rolled, kicking up a sand-colored dust cloud, and lost his hat.

A dapper-dressed, mustached gent wearing a five-pointed copper star and a ten-gallon Stetson stomped out the batwings, descended the gallery steps, and drove the point of his right, black, hand-tooled boot into the ass of the man in the street. His victim yowled and leapfrogged forward, cursing bitterly and holding one hand against his ass. The badge toter kicked the pilgrim's ass again, through his hand, and again his victim leap-frogged forward and twisted around, red-faced, blond hair hanging in his pain- and fury-pinched eyes. One hand flew to the six-shooter on his right hip.

The mustached badge toter laughed and stood with his boots spread, both hands on his hips shoving back the tails of his charcoal-colored frock coat. "Go ahead, McCreedy. Jerk that toad, if you've a mind. Never know; you just might be as fast as you *think* you are!"

McCreedy stayed his hand but kept it on his pistol butt, glaring up at the tall gent with the badge who dared him with his mocking blue eyes. Men had come out of the saloon behind the town marshal, holding beer mugs or shot glasses, some smoking, eyes glittering their appreciation of the show before them. McCreedy cut his wounded gaze to the onlookers, then shuttled them back to the town marshal, veins bulging in his forehead as he jerked his Schofield out of its holster.

The lawman slapped leather, his hand a blur as the steel-blue Colt came up in a flash, and roared, smoke and flames stabbing from the barrel. McCreedy's head jerked back as the . 44 round drilled through his temple and plunked into the dust about two feet behind him, spraying blood, brains, and bone into the grit.

McCreedy's quivering hand opened. His six-shooter tumbled into the street by his right knee, and he sagged back in the dirt, shivering as though he'd been struck by lightning.

The crowd fell silent.

Zane and Junius Webb had stopped in the street about thirty feet before the saloon from which the ruckus had erupted. Zane clucked as the lawman, whose name was Wayne Lomax, strode toward the still-shaking carcass.

"That's a mighty fast draw you got there, Marshal," the ghoul hunter said.

Lomax stood over McCreedy but turned his head toward Zane and Junius and grimaced. "Oh, Christ. Not you, Uriah. As if I don't have enough trouble." He picked up McCreedy's gun and turned to Zane once more. "This son of a sow been leadin' up a gang sellin' busthead to the hobgobbies out on Eagle River. You ever confront a drunken hobgobbie, Uriah?"

"A time or two. Like takin' down a bear with a slingshot. I see now why you were so contrary, Wayne."

Lomax beckoned toward the saloon veranda, and three men came down and started to pick up the dead McCreedy and haul him off to the undertaker's. The lawman shoved the dead man's pistol behind his black cartridge belt and sauntered over to Zane and Junius, canting a skeptical eye to appraise the wheeled casket behind the bounty man.

"That's some outfit you got there, Uriah."

"Thanks."

"What's in the sacks?"

"Swiller heads. Ran into a cave teemin' with the vermin, like bedbugs in a Mexican brothel, about ten miles up canyon." Zane arched an admonishing brow. "Ain't that your jurisdiction, Marshal Lomax?"

Lomax's nostrils flared, and he hardened his jaws. "Sundown."

"What's that?"

"That's your deadline for hauling your crazy ass, your crazy friend, and your ghastly casket the hell out of my town, Zane. Sundown!"

Zane's broad, bearded face darkened. His voice was pitched low with an almost affable menace. Darkly, he smiled. "Now, you know better than to tell *me* what to do, Wayne." He splayed his right hand across his thigh, near the Colt Navy jutting on his right hip.

Chapter 4

. . . .

U.S. BOUNTY OFFICE

Town Marshal Wayne Lomax looked pained and frustrated.

He cut his eyes from side to side to see who, if anyone, was witnessing his confrontation with the notorious ghoul hunter Uriah Zane. Since most of the onlookers had drifted off after Lomax had killed McCreedy, Lomax looked vaguely relieved.

But he kept his voice low as he said in defeat, "Goddamnit, Uriah. You bust up any more saloons in my town, I'm liable to get voted out of office. Now, will you "—he paused to look around once more, then stepped up so close to General Lee that the horse nickered nervously, and through gritted teeth Lomax said quietly—"kindly finish whatever business you have here, stock up on the supplies you need, and all the firewater you can hold, and move on out? Plenty of ghouls up in them mountains yonder. You have a way, Uriah, every time you're here, of makin' me look bad. Weak. And it ain't a good thing for a lawman to look weak in the eyes of those he serves."

"Ah, shit, Wayne—you're fast enough. Why don't you just go ahead and shoot me? You been wantin' to since we was six years old."

Lomax ran a frustrated hand across his mouth and rattled a sigh. "You know I can't shoot my own blood. 'Specially since there's so few of us Lomaxes and Zanes left in the world. But believe me, if we weren't kin, they'd be hauling you off to where they're taking Lyle McCreedy even as we speak."

"I'll be damned," Junius said with awe, raking a hand across his patch-bearded face. "I didn't know you two was kin."

Lomax turned his agonized eyes on the wizened prospector. "Hold your tongue, Mr. Webb, or I will fabricate a reason for incarcerating your rock-breaking ass!"

"Double cousins," Zane told the prospector. "We're *real* close, Wayne an' me. Least we were till I won a turkey shoot when we was tit-high to a sow's belly, and Wayne had to take my turns in the tobacco barn that summer 'stead o' sparkin' Constance Summerfield, who ended up my brother's betrothed."

"So help me, Uriah, if this ever gets out . . ."

"Ah, don't worry. I won't ruin your reputation," Zane said, touching heels to General Lee's flanks and starting forward, his indignant cousin scrambling aside. "Just don't go thinkin' you can tell me what to do. Gravels me, and you know how we Zanes get when we're graveled."

As he and Junius rode forward through the blood splotch that Lyle McCreedy had left in the street, Lomax called behind him, "Marshal Angel Coffin was in town earlier . . . inquiring about you." His voice owned a faintly mocking tone.

Zane sawed back on General Lee's reins and looked over his shoulder. The marshal stood grinning at him, a fist on his hip, one boot cocked with self-satisfaction. Zane worked a corner of his broad mouth pensively and said with a wolfish growl, "Have I ever been tied to lace panties or apron strings, cousin?"

Undefeated, Lomax chuckled. "Just passin' along a little news, is all."

The marshal turned and started to stroll away.

Zane burned. "What'd she want?"

Lomax stopped, turned back toward him, his cheeks above the upswept ends of his mustache dimpling in delight. "She was goin' after a gang of train-robbin' hobgobbies down around Montrose; was hopin' she'd find you here, since you're familiar with the area, an' all. I told her I hadn't seen you in a month of Sundays, thank the good Lord, so she rode on toward Montrose." His mocking grin broadened. "Alone."

Zane's brows furrowed.

"Hope she don't run into no trouble out there. Me, I woulda backed her play, but I got no deputy, so of course it wouldn't be right to desert my post here in Gunnison. Oh, she'll probably be fine. I hear the girl can take care of herself."

"That's right—she can," Zane said and heeled General Lee ahead once more.

Riding off his right stirrup as they continued along the street, meeting broad-wheeled mountain wagons and horseback riders, some of whom Zane nodded to, Junius said, "Who's that your cousin was talkin' about, Uriah?"

"No one," Zane said curtly and began angling the palomino toward the right side of the street, where the low-slung, shake-roofed U.S. Bounty Office hunched beneath the glaring sun.

Smoke issued from the place's tin chimney pipe and slithered forward over the brush-roofed gallery.

He dismounted General Lee, wanting to keep his mind off Marshal Coffin. Not that he figured he could. He and the red-headed marshal from Denver had thrown in together a few times to hunt ghouls—once in the Indian Nations and once in Dakota Territory, another in eastern Wyoming. She was the daughter of a famed senior U.S. marshal, and Zane, who didn't normally cotton to badge toters, had found himself liking the young woman's sand. She was pretty as a desert dusk, an Amazon straight out of a boy's fairy tale with her straight, rose-red hair that fell to the middle of her back, and her curvy, high-busted figure decked out in black leather and a soft, butternut, doeskin vest.

Somehow Angel managed to wear the scar she'd incurred from a wolf's claw at an angle across her right cheek as well as any man would. It not only didn't mar her beauty but somehow heightened it by adding a touch of danger to complement the smoldering green eyes that were in heart-skipping contrast to her hair.

She was a few years younger than Zane, who was older than his years, and they'd ended up sharing each other's blankets a few times, here and there in camps about the frontier. It had seemed a natural thing, them both being alone and naturally hot-blooded. They'd kicked up quite a storm, those nights. Kept the coyotes quiet, as the saying went.

The only problem was, after he'd shared the woman's hot roll, she'd somehow gotten stuck in the back of Zane's mind. He wasn't used to women staying with him long—in his mind or anywhere else. Such a distraction wasn't safe out here, where it served a man to keep his mind clear.

Besides, Angel Coffin was as much her own woman as he was

his own man. Hell, she was a deputy U.S. marshal. She could take care of herself even in known ghoul country.

But she had asked about him. . . .

Zane tossed General Lee's reins over one of the two hitchracks fronting the bounty office, and mounted the front gallery, Junius Webb falling into step behind him and batting dust from his buckskin shirt and baggy trousers with his hat. Zane punched the latch and stepped inside.

"Pete?"

There was no one in the office, though Zane could hear a man and woman laughing together behind a door in the opposite wall. The woman gave a little squeal, and leather bedsprings squawked raucously.

"Sounds like Pete's bein' entertained," Zane told Junius. "Come on in." He glanced at the bullet-shaped stove in the middle of the room, fronting the cluttered desk of the local U.S. bounty distribution agent, Lieutenant Pete Borgland. A battered black coffeepot chugged quietly atop the warming rack. Zane headed toward a crude wooden cupboard near the stove and grabbed a couple of relatively clean coffee mugs off a shelf.

"I've learned not to disturb Pete when he's doin' the mattress dance. He can get surly as an old squaw and find a reason to short your bounty money." He filled both cups from the pot and thrust one at Junius. "Might as well enjoy his mud while we wait. Hasn't killed me yet."

Zane sagged down in one of the two visitors' chairs fronting the desk. Junius sat in the second one, his eyes glittering, lips quirking a devilish half grin as the sounds of lovemaking continued emanating from behind the closed door that directly flanked the desk.

"Oh . . . oh, God . . . !" said the woman.

"Shut up, Dixie—I'm tryin' to concentrate here," said the man.

The woman laughed throatily. "Relax," she said just loudly enough for Zane and Junius to hear through the door. "You're doin' just fine, hon. Much better than last time."

"Goddamnit, Dixie—you gotta talk so much?"

Leather springs sighed. The headboard of Pete Borgland's bed slammed against the wall with the regularity of a metronome.

Beside Zane, Junius snickered. He tried to sip his coffee but ended up choking on it for laughing.

Uninterested—even a little revolted—Zane sipped his own coffee and stared at a large map of the western territories to the left of the door behind the desk. It had been printed by the government offices in Washington several years ago, and it delineated the Ghoul Lands, the scattered chunks of the western frontier where the main ghoul populations were known to reside throughout the West.

The swillers' main territory occupied a good portion of western Utah and southern Idaho—though any hunter worth his salt knew they could be found in and around any major town or city—while the hobgobbies dominated a large, egg-shaped portion of western Colorado Territory starting just outside of Montrose, where, according to Lomax, Angel was headed. The main packs of werewolves had spread onto two smaller chunks of land, one in the Anvil Mountains around Tombstone, Arizona, the other west of Laramie, Wyoming—though they, like the swillers, were known to haunt portions of every territory west of the Mississippi. According to untrustworthy Washington reports, their numbers were supposedly dwindling.

That was merely propaganda meant to keep President Sherman in office. Zane didn't believe a word of it.

The ghoul hunter sighed and turned away from the map. He knew better than any map where the ghouls resided. He'd just been trying to keep his mind off what Deputy U.S. Marshal Angel Coffin was up to, because he wasn't her damn keeper, and even if he started out after her now—which he couldn't do until General Lee had had several hours of good rest and plenty of oats and water—he likely wouldn't catch up to her before she caught up to the train-robbing hobgobbies she was after.

What plucked at him, however, was the fact that she was asking around for him. She was a proud woman, and she rarely asked for help even when she needed it. That must mean she really thought she needed it now.

"Ah, hell," Zane said as the seemingly never-ending love cries continued behind the closed door.

Beneath the ruckus, he'd been hearing a rat scratching around in the room's rear corner, behind Pete's desk. The rat was still there, scuttling along the wall and munching up what looked to be the remains of a venison sandwich.

Zane's heart thudding impatiently, he wrapped his right hand around the big Colt Navy conversion revolver holstered high on his left hip and raked the hammer back. "Stick your fingers in your ears, Junius."

"How come?"

Zane answered with a thunderous blast of the .44. The rat disappeared in a spray of blood and fur, then landed in two quivering halves.

Chapter 5

. . . .

VERMIN CONTROL

Behind the door, the woman screamed.

"What in God's name . . . ?" came Borgland's indignant cry from the same room.

Zane let a devilish glint spark in his eyes as he holstered the hogleg. Bare feet slapped the bedroom floor. The door jerked open and Pete Borgland poked his wide-eyed, unshaven, double-jowled head into the room. He didn't have a stitch on, and his pale belly curved forward like a big water bladder carpeted in curly black hair.

"Sorry, Pete," Zane said. "Just doin' a little vermin control. Hope I didn't disturb you and Dixie back there!"

Borgland followed Zane's glance to the dead rat that had fallen still amid its own spilled blood and innards against the wall. His eyes popped wide in his broad, round face. "Goddamn you, Uriah!" Then he slammed the door and, cursing and stumbling around, started dressing.

He and Dixie spoke a few words in hushed voices, and then the door opened again, and Pete Borgland was stomping into one boot, his blue cavalry bib-front tunic half-buttoned, as he stumbled into the main office and slammed the door behind him.

Borgland, a rotund man with thinning, curly dark brown hair and bulging blue eyes, stopped and pointed. "You've gone too far this time, Uriah!"

"Ah, sit down and have a cup of your rotgut mud, Pete. Besides, you said the same thing last time."

Borgland scowled, his breathing slowing gradually, and pressed his hair against the sides of his head with both hands. He glanced at Junius. "What's this drunkard doing here?"

"I bet I don't drink no more than you do, Lieutenant." Junius grinned, showing about four discolored, misshapen teeth. "I threw in with Uriah. Showed 'im where a devil's lair of swillers was holed up. We got us over twenty heads out yonder—don't we, Uriah?"

Borgland scowled as he drew up the suspenders of his cavalry trousers. "Where in the hell did you find that many swillers all in one place?"

"There were more than that," said Zane, taking another sip of the bitter coffee. "Lost a whole passel in a river."

Borgland continued to stare skeptically at Zane. Finally, he said, "Let me see these heads, so I know you two ain't been on a bender the last few months."

Zane led Borgland and Junius outside. He slid the staghorn-handled bowie knife out of his right moccasin and cut into one of the four bags draped over the casket holding his Gatling gun. One of the severed heads spilled out, hit the street with a thud, and immediately started to smoke and sizzle until the skin melted and curled away from the bone. Flames licked out of the growing black hole in the head's temple, where the sun hit it directly.

The fire exploded with a *whoosh!* and almost instantly the head was turned to a pile of gray ash from which a few lingering flames licked before dying.

The head hadn't completely burned up before Zane was holding the cut bag up by its bottom and shaking out the four other heads in it, all of which hit the ground and rolled and burst into flame.

"That's five there."

Zane summarily cut into and emptied the rest of the bags while Pete Borgland watched ruefully from the veranda. Junius stood one step down from Borgland, letting his injured ankle hang lightly over the step's edge, thumbs hooked behind the cartridge belt wrapped around his concave waist and bony hips, grinning gleefully.

When all twenty-one heads had hit the street and flared up like Mexican fireworks, quickly turning to dust, Borgland swung around and headed back into his office. "All right, all right. Quit showin' off. Get in here and I'll see if I got enough cash to cover the bounty."

"He'll come up short," Zane said with a fateful sigh, cleaning the blade of his bowie on Junius's ragged shirt as he mounted the veranda.

As he ducked through the door and into the office, Borgland was crouched over the safe abutting the back wall, to the right of the door, which just now opened. A pretty though tired- and disheveled-looking redhead with sandy eyebrows appeared. Borgland looked up as Dixie came out and started toward the front of the room.

"Hey, where you goin', honey?" Borgland said, spreading his arms. "I done told ya—I'll be back in a minute."

"You paid for an hour, Pete. That hour was up pret' near two hours ago."

Dixie, dressed in a low-cut, cheap, pleated dress with a red sash to match her hair, and taffeta flowers pinned to one thin shoulder strap, rolled her hips as she approached Zane, who stepped to one side, making room. She blinked slowly and spread her thin lips in a smoky smile. "Hi, there, Uriah. Long time, no see."

Zane removed his hat and dipped his chin. "How you been, Miss Dixie?"

At the door, she swung around and slid a slender lock of hair behind her ear, caressing the doorframe with her rump as she raked her eyes across the big ghoul hunter's tall, brawny frame. "Come on over to the Wildcat later, and we'll discuss it." She cut a wry glance at Borgland. "I'll give you a good deal."

She rolled on out the door and pulled Junius's battered canvas hat down over his eyes as she stepped down off the veranda and headed out into the street.

Borgland sighed as he removed a small canvas sack from the safe, whose only other content was an old Civil War–model Colt Army, straightened his back with a slight crunching sound, and, wincing, tossed the sack onto his desk.

"Twenty-one ghouls," he muttered, shaking his head and tipping up the sack to allow a mess of gold coins to spill out onto the blotter half covering the scarred top of his desk. "And here I thought we were runnin' them ghouls to ground, cleanin' 'em out good. Ain't that what the Army's been tellin' us—that we're winnin' the goddamn war against those creatures?"

"That's what the Army says," Zane said, digging a small hide makings sack out of an inside pocket of his wolfskin vest. "But I been out there in them mountains and canyons as much or more than any Army patrol, and I can tell you, you can't ride from Bozeman City up Montaway to Denver without runnin' into more than I got bullets and arrows for. Everywhere you go, settlers are havin' a time of it—losin' stock to the swillers' and werewolves' night raids and bein' attacked right out in open ground by the hobgobbies."

Thoughtfully, Zane dribbled chopped Mexican tobacco onto a sheaf of wheat paper troughed between the first two fingers of his left hand. "And I don't know if the altitude's gettin' to me, or what, but I think I saw a dragon on the way into town."

The government paymaster stopped counting and sliding coins around with his index finger to glance up at the bounty hunter skeptically. "What'd you say?"

Zane rolled the wheat paper closed around the quirley and stuck the cylinder in his mouth to seal it with spit. "You heard me right."

Borgland studied him for a time, then went back to sliding gold coins away from the scattered group on his blotter. He laughed and shook his head, as though Zane had told him an especially funny joke. But his expression soured suddenly, and, still counting under his breath, he said, "I just hope you're as mad as you must be. The swillers, werebeasts, and hobgobbies are all the monsters I need. Don't need no more."

He reached into a desk drawer and pulled out a small canvas pouch, which he held open beside his desk while he slid the counted coins into it. "At least Charlie Hondo's all sealed up tighter'n a tick on a dog's ear in Hellsgarde Pen."

Zane frowned over the match he'd lit to fire his cigarette. "Hondo's in Hellsgarde?"

"Sure as shit in the hogpen." Borgland smiled though he had only two gold coins left on his blotter. The rest were in the burlap sack he now set down hard on Zane's side of his desk. "They run him to ground two weeks ago in Denver, playin' faro if you can believe it. Drunk as a damn English lord. A barman recognized him from a wanted dodger, sent over to the federal building for marshals, and eight of 'em came in, snugged their rifle barrels up against Charlie's neck, and dragged him away, howlin' like a fork-tailed devil, in chains. They had a quick trial and, since it was obvious they really did have the fearsome leader of the infamous Hell's Angels in custody, hauled him out to Hellsgarde in one o' them armor-plated jail wagons accompanied by an entire company of federal soldiers, three cannons, and four Gatling guns."

"What the hell they go to all that work for?" Zane said, anger burning in him as he remembered that horrific night in the green hills around Gettysburg, when he lost not only a brother, three cousins, and an uncle, but nearly every Confederate soldier bivouacked in the area that night excepting a few wise and desperate enough to throw up a white flag with General Lee's own tearful blessing.

Lee had been mangled and would later take his own life with a silver bullet, just as Abraham Lincoln did a few weeks later, disgraced by his unforgivable sin.

"Shoulda taken his murderous hide out and shot 'im! Course, they shoulda shot Abe right alongside him—if he wasn't already dead, that is—but the least they coulda done is killed the sonofabitch!"

Zane's face was swollen with rage, veins standing out on his forehead. He clenched both fists tightly at his sides until his knuckles nearly popped. Tobacco from his crushed quirley sifted between his fingers. Borgland backed away from the enraged hunter, genuine fear bleaching his pasty features.

"Christ almighty, Uriah—I myself personally had nothin' to do with it. You know what the policy is—those ghouls they think might be more dangerous dead than alive, they lock up in Hellsgarde and throw away the key. They don't want none of 'em comin' back even stronger than they was when they was alive."

Jaws hard, eyes blazing, Zane said, "The superstitions of foolish old men. You kill a werewolf, he's dead. That's all there is to it." He oughta know as well as anyone, Zane vaguely reflected with a moment's feeling of dread.

"Well, some Europeans more experienced with them vermin than even we are seem to think the most powerful of 'em gain more strength if they're killed by humans. Takes a werewolf to kill the most powerful werewolf and keep him dead." Borgland shook his head. "I reckon after the big mistake they made at Gettysburg, trusting those devils *who just seemed so honest and sincere*, they ain't takin' no more chances. It's Hellsgarde for the worst."

"Ah, hell, Uriah," Junius said, standing near Zane, looking apprehensively up at the big man towering over him and Borgland. "It ain't like Hellsgarde's a Sunday picnic along the river. They don't treat 'em none too well there. I hear they cage the werebeasts up tight in stone-walled cells without windows and with stone, iron-banded doors that need to be opened with three keys."

The prospector whistled his appreciation of the government's thoroughness. "I say it's a fate worse than death."

Zane drew a deep breath but he still looked swollen up and ready to rain. "They get the rest of 'em—the other three still on the loose?"

The original band of Hell's Angels had been comprised of forty-five mercenaries, most of whom had been run down and killed by bounty hunters, including Zane himself, who'd personally taken care of a half dozen. Last he'd heard, four remained on the run somewhere in the West, keeping low profiles, including Hondo himself.

"Ain't heard nothin' about them." Borgland sagged down in his chair and pocketed the remaining two coins on his desk. "All I got to say is folks everywhere is gonna be sleepin' a whole lot sounder now that old Charlie Hondo's been run to ground and locked away at Hellsgarde on a diet of cornpone and piss water."

Borgland blew a deep sigh of genuine relief.

"Well, that's somethin', anyway." Zane, calmer now, stuffed the coin pouch into a pocket of his wolf vest and cuffed Junius lightly on the shoulder with his hat. "Let's get us a drink and split the winnin's."

As Junius followed Zane to the door, Borgland said, "Ain't you gonna count it?"

"Why?" Zane said, not looking back but striding on out of the office, the little man limping along behind him. "I'd feel cheated if you didn't short me."

Chapter 6

. . . .

WELCOME TO HELLSGARDE

"Hey, Curly Joe!" summoned the uniformed driver of the prison wagon making its way along the scruffy, two-track Hog Wollop Trail in the shadow of the snow-dusted San Juan Mountains in southern Colorado Territory. "You know what smells worse than you and your amigos, Lucky and One-Eye?"

"No, what's that?" yelled Curly Joe Panabaker above the jail wagon's incessant rattling and clattering. He slouched in the modicum of shade provided by a bobcat hide tied over the cage's top.

The driver winked at the man riding shotgun beside him and glanced over his shoulder at Curly Joe and the other two men riding in the cage, their hands cuffed, their ankles shackled to the strap-iron bars. "Nothing stinks worse than you boys. *Nothin'!*"

The driver threw his head back and laughed. The shotgun rider laughed as well.

Curly Joe looked at his cohort riding directly across from him. One-Eye Langtry returned the dull stare as he jerked and lurched with the wagon's pitch and sway. The other man—the third prisoner in the wagon—rode with his back against the rear door.

Lucky Snodgrass was a tall, rangy redhead with a face nearly covered with tan freckles, and a braided ponytail that slithered down his back before it coiled up from the wagon's hard, plank floor to slither onto his buckskin-clad lap, showing the diamondback rattle wrapped into it with cracked rawhide.

"Is that right?" Lucky said to the driver, bunching his broad nose, his pale blue eyes searing into the driver's back, which was clad in a dark blue cavalry tunic, the shoulders of which were mantled in clay-colored dust. "When's the last time you had a bath, Murphy?"

"Me?" said the driver. "I had me a bath last night in Sapinero. Me and Jimbo here both did; didn't we, Jimbo?" He grinned over at the shotgun rider beside him—Sergeant James "Jimbo" Schwartz. "Us and the two whores we bought for ourselves in Missus Dyer's House of Unbridled Badness!"

Murphy and Schwartz elbowed each other and giggled like schoolgirls, both men staring straight ahead toward a high sandstone ridge standing up tall in the desert, a steep arm of the San Juans looming cool and blue behind it.

"You sure there was girls present?" asked One-Eye Langtry, blinking his one brown eye against the dust roiling up from the wagon's right front wheel.

Schwartz looked over his shoulder. "What's that s'posed to mean?"

"It means," said Curly Joe, flexing his right forearm and staring down at the naked dragon-girl tattoo dancing through the thin curtain of fine, light brown hairs, "we think you two Nancy boys mighta been entertainin' each other in that washtub. No girls present at all!" He grinned wickedly. "Accordin' to the rumors we been hearing across the whole Southwest, you two wouldn't know how to please a woman even in the unlikely event you was fortunate enough to bed one!"

"So, instead of women, you boys prefer to play grabby-pants with each other." Lucky Snodgrass squirmed around on the wagon floor, lifting one buttock and then the other, and mocking, "Oh, Jimbo, reach down there for the soap, would you, please? Oh, you naughty rascal, that wasn't the soap and you *know* it!"

The three prisoners laughed and yipped like wolves.

Murphy and Schwartz looked at each other, their faces flushing behind the dust and windburn on their bearded cheeks. Finally, Schwartz flexed his fingers on the shotgun he held in both hands before him. "Tough talk for doomed men, eh, Murphy?"

"It is, at that," said Murphy, loudly enough for the men behind him to hear above the wagon's clattering. "We'll see how tough these fellas are once they get to Hellsgarde."

"Hellsgarde won't hold us," announced Lucky Snodgrass. "No, sir—I'd bet the seed bull me and my pards'll be bustin' outta there in a few days. Maybe a week, since the layout's new, an' all. But a week at the most."

Murphy and Schwartz looked over their shoulders at Lucky, as though the man had just sprouted horns and a forked tail, and they roared in exasperation. Murphy slapped his thigh.

"Son," he said as the ridge wall grew higher and sheerer before them, so that the men in the wagon could make out the pits and fissures in its towering face, "ain't you never heard of Hellsgarde before? No one—and I mean *no one*—breaks out of Hellsgarde. Not even the *ghouls!*"

Schwartz was still looking incredulously back at the three scruffy, dusty prisoners, the long, curly, seed-flecked hair falling from the man's tan cavalry kepi blowing in the breeze. "No, sir, not even the spooks the place was built for even try it!"

"Hey, you know what, Schwartz?" said Murphy. "I wonder if they'll house these fellas with ole Charlie Hondo himself. Hah! Wouldn't that be *fun?*"

"Charlie Hondo'd have these three for a saloon-sized meat plate, first full moon." Schwartz winked at Curly, One-Eye, and Lucky.

Curly Joe feigned a puzzled air, and said, "Who's Charlie Hondo?"

"You mean you ain't never heard of Charlie Hondo?" asked Murphy, staring straight ahead over the backs and bobbing heads of his four-mule hitch.

"Don't recollect I have," Curly Joe said, shrugging a shoulder and looking around at his partners. "You boys?"

One-Eye and Lucky also feigned befuddled expressions and shook their heads.

"Charlie Hondo's the meanest goddamn son of a shape-shiftin' demon son of a bitch in all the West," said Schwartz. "How could you never hear o' Charlie Hondo? Why, he was the leader of that pack of werewolves those two geniuses, Lincoln and Grant, brought over from Russia or Prussia, or wherever the hell they found 'em. You know, the leader of the pack those crazy Yankee bastards used to win the War with." He narrowed a skeptical eye. "You fellas sure you never heard of Charlie Hondo?"

"He only became Charlie Hondo when he came west," said Murphy, flicking his reins over the mules' backs and turning off the main road onto the secondary trail that rose gently toward a dark oval in the sandstone cliff wall. "I believe his name over the big water was Ludwig somethin' or other. Three or four names strung together like freight cars." He gave a mocking snort. "Who the fuck needs more than two names? Someone please inform me."

"Oh, that's right," Schwartz said, nodding. "When this Hondo feller—his real name I can't pronounce—and his yellow-fanged werewolf amigos came west, they took American names, don't ya know? So they'd fit in, you see? And lost their accents, and dressed like us normal folks so they could wreak all sorts of blasphemous, ass-ripping havoc."

Schwartz gave a shudder.

"Well, I'll be damned," said One-Eye, shifting his lone eye toward Curly Joe and quirking his mouth corners ever so slightly. "Learn somethin' new every day, don't we, Curly Joe?"

"I'll say we do," said Curly Joe, glancing at Lucky Snodgrass sitting at the rear of the jail cage, showing a gap-toothed, tobacco-brown grin.

As the wagon approached the cliff wall, Curly Joe saw that the black oval he'd seen was in fact a tunnel mouth. One just large enough to fit a wagon the size of the one he and his compadres were riding in.

As the wagon drew to a stop while a man walked out away from the ridge, Curly Joe saw the blue steel bars over the tunnel mouth. They winked darkly in the late-afternoon sunlight that was touched with salmon and saffron hues, pulling dark pools out from cedars and clumps of rabbit brush.

To each side of the tunnel mouth was a high, wooden, brush-roofed platform. On each platform, a guard in infantry blues sat behind a brass-canistered Gatling gun, which together looked like twin giant, golden mosquitoes. The muzzles were turned toward the wagon, both guards flexing their gloved hands over the guns' wood-handled firing cranks. Long cartridge belts draped down from the gun's brass barrels.

The man walking toward the wagon was large and hairy and sporting a striped serape instead of the customary government-issue tunic. A long, stout cigar protruded from one corner of his mouth. He wore bandoliers crisscrossed on his chest, two pistols in hip holsters, and a third in a shoulder holster.

"Hello, Pablo," hailed Schwartz. "You wouldn't spare another one o' them stogies for an old friend, would you?"

Pablo scowled at Murphy and Schwartz as he sauntered back to the jail cage, the dust just now catching up to the rig and making the big Mexican blink and swipe at the air with one thick, brown hand. He told Schwartz to go fuck his mother. Then, "Who you got here?"

Schwartz reached into his tunic and extracted a bulging manila envelope. "Here's the orders. Bringin' one Curly Joe Panabaker, One-Eye Langtry, and Lucky Snodgrass to Hellsgarde for incarceration under order of the—"

"They spooks?" Pablo asked, ignoring the envelope, standing well back of the cage and cocking his head to one side as he inspected the contents of the jail wagon.

"Nah, hell, they ain't spooks," said Murphy, leaning forward with his elbows on his knees, lightly holding the reins of the stamping, blowing team. "They killed a coupla federals down in Arkansas. You know what happens when federal marshals get beefed."

"Might be against the law to jail humans with spooks," Schwartz said, hungrily eyeing Pablo's big cigar, "but I reckon we won't tell on ole Judge Parker if you boys don't. Besides . . ." He gave a devilish leer to the three slouched, bored-looking prisoners. "We think it'd be kinda fun to see how long these fellas'll last at Hellsgarde, jailed with the likes of Charlie Hondo. Or maybe they'll feed 'em to Avril Wiggins or that crazy bloodswiller Hannibal James." He blinked slowly and held his narrow-eyed gaze on Curly Joe.

"Damn!" Curly Joe feigned a look of bald horror. "You didn't tell me you not only got ole Charlie Hondo housed here, but Hannibal James, too! Law, law, pards, I think I just pissed down my leg!"

The prisoners hissed through their teeth and hammered their backs against the cage walls, making a racket.

Scowling, Pablo turned and walked back to a small, brush-roofed shed that abutted the cliff wall, just right of the steel-banded door over the mouth of the cave. He threw up a hand. "Take 'em in!"

He ducked into the hut. A cranking sounded along with the clinks of large links looping around a winch, and slowly the steel door rose and disappeared into the cliff face over the cave. When Murphy had flicked the reins over the mules, and the team and wagon had disappeared into the cave, heading toward the light on the other side, Pablo shouted, "You three amigos have a nice time in our fair little prison, now, you hear?"

Pablo and the two men manning the Gatling guns grinned at one another.

From inside the tunnel, above the wagon's loud rattling and the mules' clomping hooves, Curly Joe shouted, "Thanks for the warm welcome, Pablo. But we ain't fixin' on stayin' all that long!"

The prisoners' echoing wolflike yips and howls dwindled slowly. Pablo rolled his cigar from one corner of his mouth to the other and scowled darkly into the tunnel.

Chapter 7

· · · · · · · · · · · · · · ·

THERE BE DRAGONS

"House o' ghouls—that's what this place is," Curly Joe said as the wagon rattled out of the hundred-foot tunnel and into the light of the canyon beyond.

Curly Joe, Lucky, and One-Eye stared up at the giant, castle-like dwelling that must have occupied a half square mile of the canyon floor. There was a moat around the place, complete with a drawbridge, and American flags buffeting from the six or seven tower turrets. The castle had been fashioned after the medieval castles in Europe, because not only were they impregnable from the outside; they were damned hard to escape from once you'd been locked up inside.

"What's that?" Schwartz asked as Murphy headed the mule team toward the castle's giant wooden door constructed of complete red oak logs and which, drawn up tight against its casement, appeared wide enough for at least two broad wagons to safely enter in tandem.

"I said this place is a damn house of ghouls," repeated Curly Joe.

"You got that right," barked Murphy, waving to one of the several blue-clad guards standing sentinel in one of the two turreted towers on each side of the drawbridge. "This house o' ghouls is you boys' last resting place. Don't worry, though. There's more like you here. The warden likes to keep a good supply of blood for the swillers—don't ya know? President Sherman says out of one side of his mouth that the swillers ain't s'posed to dine on nothin' but chicken and hog blood, thus the barns way on the back side of the canyon. But out the other side, he says we can do as we see fit, 'cause nothin' quiets a howlin' swiller like human blood."

"Yeah," added Schwartz, widening his eyes in mocking delight. "Fresher, the better." He glanced at the greenish sky arcing over the canyon and the giant hunk of carved granite housing more than two hundred spooks of all known varieties— from werecats to witches—and whistled. "Gonna be a full moon tonight, too. Charlie Hondo, he loves nothin' more than a human thrown into his cage on the night of a full moon." Schwartz elbowed Murphy. "Don't he, Murph?"

"Sure 'nuff," the driver said, having stopped the team and now watching the drawbridge slowly drop down toward the moat. "Keeps him busy for a while. Keeps him from howlin' all night. There's a ranch a coupla miles from here, and we get complaints the day after every full moon. The Chain Link's foreman says Charlie's caterwaulin' stampedes his cattle!"

"Hell," said Murphy. "I hear him down in the quarters by the creek; wakes me up of a night dripping in a cold sweat and streakin' my drawers. Sounds like a hundred million ghouls all howlin' at once. But I reckon it's only Charlie Hondo himself and the two or three other hairy bastards housed here. And the swillers. Plenty of them here, and thank God they don't raise the racket the shapeshifters do."

Lucky Snodgrass wrinkled his nose as he sat inspecting the giant castle from which ribbons of smoke curled through two separate chimneys visible from this vantage. "Smells worse than we do. Even worse than Schwartz."

Murphy chuckled. "You house a few hundred ghouls together, and that's the smell you get. Nothin' stinks worse than a blood-swiller's shit. Like blood sausage left out in the sun—oh, *Lord!*"

"You got that right," said Schwartz as the drawbridge dropped lower, the great ratcheting sounds from a winch inside the castle sounding like the rumble of near thunder. "Some say a werewolf smells worse, but I say hog scat to that. A werewolf's a werewolf, and I have no love for the breed—even though they did help us win the War, by God—but a vampire's shit smells like a whole privy full of well-seasoned dead rats with a couple of dead skunks and adders thrown in to really make you sick!"

The drawbridge dropped to the turf, and the mules brayed and jerked in their harnesses as dust wafted from the platform's impact with the ground on the near side of the moat. The giant chains squawked like the heavy timbers of clipper ships moored to harbor wharves.

"Well, what you fellas might think of doin'," said One-Eye, wrinkling his nose against the almost palpable stench, "is *haul* the shit *outside* and bury it *deep.*"

"Done thought of that," said Murphy, shaking the ribbons over the backs of the mules and putting them up the ramp. He cackled and cut a cunning glance at Schwartz. "Why you think you boys are here?"

He cackled some more as the wagon lurched and thumped onto the drawbridge and headed on over the deep, black water of the moat from which sharpened silver blades protruded at irregular intervals. Schwartz said, "Charlie'll probably feed on one of ya tonight, but that leaves two of you to haul his shit out of the place . . . at least until the next full moon! Charlie's shit ain't as bad as the swillers' shit . . . less'n he's been feedin' on human flesh. Oh, gawd!"

Both men tipped their chins back and laughed as the wagon clattered between the castle's four-foot-thick stone walls. Once inside a broad, open area littered with straw and horse shit, where several cook fires added the smells of roasted meat to the latrine and rancid sweat smell of the place, Murphy halted the wagon.

Soldiers clad in Army blues and fur coats—the sun had fallen behind the western ridges now, and the autumn chill was fast descending—sat around on benches with bored, lazy expressions. Some were playing poker while others whittled or cleaned rifles or, in one case, fed strips of jerky to a three-legged cur that rose on its one back leg, dancing in a circle and howling for dried bits of parched beef or venison.

There were women here, too—broad-bottomed wives or whores of the noncommissioned officers, likely—clad in shapeless skirts and jackets or animal skins, stirring clothes in black kettles suspended over dancing fires. From somewhere unseen came the clangs of a blacksmith's hammer. From a long row of stables to the left of the wagon came the whinnies and brays of horses and mules while a limping soldier in a bobcat skin forked hay into a small corral abutting the stable, where an empty jail wagon sat, tongue drooping.

While the drawbridge began rising back toward the castle's outer wall, Gatling guns atop the twin towers on either side of it were swung around, the soldiers behind them hunkered low and aiming, menacing looks in their eyes beneath their kepi brims. A man moved down the steps from the left tower—a portly, middle-aged man clad in a long bear coat and wearing a blue cavalry hat. The bear coat was open to reveal his blue wool cavalry trousers, a single yellow stripe running down the outside. He puffed a meerschaum pipe, and his tall, black boots flashed in the waning light, the heels clicking on the stone steps.

"Who do we have here?" he asked, removing the pipe from his thin lips and scowling at Murphy and Schwartz, who'd climbed down out of the wagon's driver's box to walk around to the cage's rear door. Murphy pulled a key threaded on a rawhide thong out of his coat.

"Three prize turkeys, Major Mondrick. Sent out here from Arkansas by Judge Parker with President Sherman's signed blessing."

"Spooks?" asked Mondrick as he neared the bottom of the steps, scrutinizing the men through frosty blue eyes set deep in suety sockets. His nose was long and stitched with crinkled veins like knots of blue thread.

"Not these three. Killed a coupla U.S. marshals out Arkansas way. For non-spooks, they're a savage bunch; I'll give 'em that. They had the choice of being hanged last week in Fort Smith or getting hauled out here." Murphy gave a cockeyed smile.

"Good, good," said Major Mondrick, the warden of Hellsgarde Penitentiary. He slipped the stem of his pipe between his lips and puffed as he approached the jail wagon. "Maybe I shall pit them next Sunday against a couple of the feistier ghouls in our boxing league."

"Maybe oughta feed one o' 'em to the blood-swillers tonight. Or . . ." Murphy grinned at the warden. "Maybe you oughta throw him in ole Charlie Hondo's cage."

"Why?" The warden bunched his wiry brows and loosed a couple more smoke puffs as he gave a condescending gaze to the jail wagon driver. "So you and your lowly ilk can watch the bloodletting, hear the screaming, bet on how long it takes Charlie to clean up his mess?"

"Well, hell, Warden," said Schwartz, his features creasing indignantly. "Ain't that what we'll all be doin' come Sunday?"

Mondrick stretched his lips back in a faintly abashed smile. "Touché." He looked into the wagon, where Curly Joe, Lucky, and One-Eye slouched as before, returning the warden's glare. "Oh, well, I suppose I could let you boys have one for this evening. But save the other two for Sunday. You know how Mrs. Mondrick and I and the Considines from the Chain Link Ranch enjoy our Sunday festivities."

"Warden Mondrick!" an English-accented voice called from high above. "Come on up here, Warden. I wish to speak to you about your bathing facilities! Not quite up to the Freeman-Johnson Regulatory Agreement Regarding the Incarceration of Non-Humans, are they?"

Mondrick lifted his head to one of the casement windows in a tower high overhead, in the main part of the castle.

"Shut up, Hannibal. You just got here two weeks ago, and you're already getting on my nerves!"

"Send up one of your big-breasted peasant bitches, will you?" Poking his head out the one-foot-by-one-foot window casement, the swiller named Hannibal James jerked his round, pale face toward where the washerwomen were boiling clothes. "I'm thirsty—and *horny!*"

He snapped his fangs, snarling.

Several of the washerwomen looked up at the castle wall with expressions of great revulsion.

Warden Mondrick glanced at one of the men crouched behind a Gatling gun in the tower to the right of the closed drawbridge. He jerked his chin toward the swiller, and the Gatling gun belched, spitting smoke and flames from the end of its six-barreled canister. The bullets hammered the stone wall around the swiller's window a quarter second after the immortal beast had pulled his head inside. The rocketing lead blew up rock slivers and dust.

The Gatling's swivel squawked as the gun was again aimed down at the jail wagon. Warden Mondrick turned his attention back to the new prisoners then, too, and the pipe fell out of his hands to bounce off his right boot, gray tobacco ash smoking.

"Holy shit!" cried Murphy and Schwartz at nearly the same time, widening their eyes at the jail wagon in which all three prisoners continued to slouch as before.

But, unlike before, they were no longer men slouching with their hands cuffed and ankles shackled.

They were wolves.

The blazing wolf-red eyes and the fangs curving down like sharp, miniature sabers from their upper jaws set the warden's heart to pounding so hard he thought it would literally explode from his chest.

All three sets of pulsating red eyes and grinning teeth were focused on him.

Murphy was slapping the covered holster on his right hip, trying to get his gun out, and screaming, "Holy Christ, they're *spooks*! They're spooks, Schwartz—*shoot 'em!*"

As the warden stumbled backward, swinging his gaze toward the Gatling guns in the guard towers and trying to find the words to the orders he was trying to shout, Schwartz fumbled his Henry rifle up.

Wolves? he was thinking beneath the thundering of the blood in his ears. *It ain't even dark yet!*

Levering a shell into the chamber, he pressed the butt to his shoulder and took aim at the wolf you could still recognize as Curly even if you didn't know where he'd been riding in the wagon—something about the facial features and eyes.

Schwartz fired too quickly, and the first slug ricocheted off one of the iron straps on the door and hammered Murphy's right shoulder, tearing his coat and squirting blood from the driver's back. As Murphy stumbled backward, grabbing his shoulder and grunting, Schwartz fired two more shots into Curly Joe, merely puffing dust from the outlaw werewolf's shirt and pin-striped vest but not appearing to penetrate the tough, hairy hide.

In fact, the lead bullets merely seemed to tickle Curly Joe, for the outlaw tipped his wolf head back and loosed a near-deafening howl, kicking his wolf legs and hammering his paws against the wagon's wooden floor in jubilation.

The others were howling and doing the same, kicking up a tornado in the warden's head. Mondrick finally found the words he'd been searching for and shouted at the Gatling gunners, "Shoot! For Christ's sakes, shoo—"

The air was sucked out of his throat as a weirdly shaped shadow swept over him. A half second later there was a roar like that of a hundred steam valves being released at once.

Varooooooossssshhhhhhhh!

The tower right of the drawbridge, and the man and the Gatling gun on top of it, were suddenly consumed by a great ball of black-stitched, red-orange flames. As the gunner in the other tower turned his head toward the conflagration, he disappeared, too, in a second ball of fire that licked down over the sides of the tower, leaving charred rock in its wake.

The burning gunners' horrific screams were barely audible above the fire's roar and the great creaking of enormous, flapping wings.

Mondrick, who had fallen on his butt at the base of the steps rising to the guard tower, now lifted his eyes to the sky. As it had been threatening to do for the past twenty or so seconds, his heart exploded like dynamite in his chest, not killing him but paralyzing him and filling him with as much hammering pain as the increased horror he felt when he saw the shiny-scaled, locomotive-sized, winged creature sweeping over the castle and favoring him with one large, copper-colored eye, like a small, leering sun.

"Oh, no," he rasped. "Don't tell me there's dragons now, too!"

Chapter 8

. . . .

THE HOBGOBBIE TRAIL

The silhouettes of mesquite branches shone like witches' fingers on the rocky slope in the light of the full moon rising over the West Elk Mountains near Sapinero, just north of the San Juans in Colorado Territory.

It shone like a giant, sun-bleached skull—so clear and vivid in the lens-like desert air that Angel Coffin could have surveyed the lunar plains and mountains if she'd lifted her head. But the deputy United States marshal out of Denver had no time to marvel at the night sky.

She kept her head down, eyes forward, as she scrambled up the side of the rocky knoll in a shallow, cedar-rimmed canyon, hearing the drunken, jubilant singing of the Mexican hobgobbies down the other side of the rise. Several were singing badly while another strummed a mandolin. Other sounds rose on Angel's left—strange grunting noises.

Angel stopped suddenly and crouched down behind a boulder, holding her Winchester carbine straight up and down in hands clad in black gloves from which she'd cut out the fingers. She was dressed nearly all in black leather excepting a sleeveless, low-cut doeskin tunic that was drawn tightly across her full breasts, her deep cleavage exposed behind rawhide drawstrings. She didn't wear the revealing attire out of vanity, but only because it was comfortable in most climes and gave her nearly six-foot but willowy and graceful frame ample ease of movement.

Over the tunic she wore a Spanish-style deerskin charro jacket stitched in red. Tall, black, lace-up boots rose nearly to her knees. Her skintight leather breeches were shoved down into the tops of the low-heeled boots.

Doffing her black Stetson, shaking her rose-red hair out, and setting the hat down beside her, she peered over a jumble of black volcanic rocks humping up on her right, and narrowed her jade-green eyes. On her smooth, tapering cheek, beneath her right eye, lay the sickle-shaped scar she'd incurred several years ago from a wolf's decisive swipe a half second before she'd blown the beast to hell.

Angel studied the two human-shaped shadows moving among a few mesquites and desert willows.

About fifty yards away from Angel's position, she realized they had to be part of Rafael Ortiz's band, who'd been robbing banks and raiding ranches throughout Colorado Territory for months. The living demons, who could occasionally pass themselves off as humans despite their long noses and close-set eyes and the fact that they were no more human than a rattlesnake, which made them particularly hard to run down, had left clear signs south of Leadville. Some said the hobgobbies were the offspring of the Devil himself, and Angel, who'd had plenty of experience with the wretched vermin, had found no reason to contradict the theory.

There they'd robbed the second bank in their monthlong raid, after enjoying a show at the opera house, oddly enough. Judging by their southward bearing, they were probably intending on returning to Mexico, where the devils were welcome if they had pocket jingle, and if they limited their desecrations to the Apaches and relatively defenseless peons, both a bane to the current Mexican government. Also, the Mexicans were more tolerant of hobgobbies because they were natural enemies of the werebeasts that were as nettling south of the border as north of it, and they were more effective than Mexican bounty hunters at thinning the renegade packs.

Angel had tracked them along with her partner, Deputy Dwight Curry, who had been gunned down six days ago. Angel and Curry had been so intent on the hobgobbies' trail that they'd made the mistake of not keeping a close eye on their own backtrails, and several of the band had swung back and flanked them, killing Curry but not before he'd taken out one of the devils and wounded one other. Angel had dispatched the other two before burying Curry and getting back after the main band comprised of the remaining five riders, heading as due south as possible in this demon's playground of towering ridges, slanting mesas, and the maze-like, rocky, snake-infested slashes of canyons.

Angel Coffin had been a deputy U.S. marshal for six years and was as respected as any of the men in a profession that, since the War, did not discriminate against women because, due to the depredations of the ghouls, women outnumbered men on the frontier nearly two to one. There simply weren't enough men any longer to fill all the traditional male occupations, which gave women the opportunity to fill them. Angel had honed her skills and was confident, though not overly so, that she could handle the Ortiz bunch well enough solo.

Still, she didn't like that moon coming up. Not only was it too damn bright, but she should have known better than to night hunt during a full moon when anyone with any sense was holed up in a werewolf-proof cabin. She'd been so eager to run Ortiz's bunch down, however, that she'd lost track of the lunar calendar—an embarrassing, tinhorn mistake that was too damned dangerous to make twice.

Ortiz was out here, though. Maybe he knew something about the hunting habits of the wolf packs in this area. Maybe the werewolves were sticking close to their home country again and dining mostly on Indians, wild horses, and ranch cattle.

Just thinking about one of those spooks getting on her scent out here made Angel shudder—something she took pride in rarely doing. The deputy marshal was no hothouse flower, but even a man like the notorious Uriah Zane, her sometime lover and trail partner—a moody loner who hunted the devils for a living—shied from the thought of a pack of the howling hordes cutting his trail. Werewolves were hardly ever outrun or dissuaded. In fact, Angel had never heard of anyone surviving a werewolf attack unless they were somehow able to make it to a stout-walled shelter with a wolf-proof, iron-banded door.

The deputy marshal pressed her tongue to her lower lip as she peered over the rocks to her left, trying to get a fix on whoever was over there. Finally, wanting to keep track of all members of Ortiz's gang, so she could corral them all later, she pushed out from behind her covering boulder and made her way slowly, weaving among the rocks, toward where the two were grunting and groaning together and making belt buckles and spurs jingle. And then, when she found a nook in the rocks with a good view of the pair, she quirked her mouth corners knowingly.

The demons were fucking like back-alley curs. Not surprising. Male hobgobbies were even more randy than human men, but they were seldom not outshone by the females of their species.

One of the two shadows among the moon-silvered mesquites was bent forward over a flat-topped boulder while the other shadow rammed his pelvis against her round, naked bottom. The bell-bottomed charro slacks of Ortiz's hobgobbie sister, Leonora, were bunched around the young female's ankles while one of the males from the gang rammed her from behind so hard that he had to hold her hips taut in his gloved hands to keep her from sprawling to the ground.

Leonora cackled nastily, wildly.

"Damn fools," Angel muttered, staying low among the rocks and tufts of Spanish bayonet. "Liable to call the wolves down out of the hills, put us all in one helluva bind."

She began to pull her head behind the boulder, but couldn't quite get her eyes down behind the rock. Something about the pair hammering against each other, the male grunting savagely and the female cackling and hissing Spanish curses, gripping the sides of the rock in front of her, pulled at Angel's own loins.

She caught herself, rolling her eyes. Christ, she reckoned it had been too long since her own last tussle. A girl needed a roll in the hay from time to time to keep her mind clear for more important things, like staying alive in known ghoul-haunted lands.

She studied the pair just finishing now in the mesquites not fifty feet away from her.

"*Mierda!*" Ortiz's sister said with an angry snarl. "I was nearly there, fool!"

The male—oddly tall, not so oddly humpbacked, and wearing a wagon wheel sombrero—backed away from her, awkwardly reaching down to pull up his pants, which had been bunched around his boots. "You take too long, Leonora," he whined in Spanish, in the bizarrely hoarse and high-pitched voice of his kind. The females spoke more like their human counterparts, slightly throatier.

"You don't take long enough, Rubio!"

"Shh! Keep your voice down, woman! You want to let every wolf in the territory know we're here?"

Leonora stumbled back, tripped over her slacks, and fell with an indignant yelp and rattle of spur chains. The small gold amulet that she wore around her neck glistened in the velvety moonlight.

"Leonora!" Rubio reached for her, but she pulled her arm away.

"Leave me, boy! Who is afraid of a fucking wolf, anyway? I'd like to roast one over the fire tonight. Go back to your friends!"

"But, *chiquita* . . ." he whined. He did not leave but stood back in the shadows a ways, his rounded shoulders set with chagrin while the woman dressed, the hump on his back adding to his air of grave defeat as it canted his head downward.

Finally, Leonora got her slacks pulled back up and her belt buckled, and wrapped her cartridge belt and pistols around her waist. Muttering angrily, she donned her black sombrero, adjusting it carefully on her black-haired head, then stomped through a crease in the hills, heading off toward Angel's right and out of sight.

Rubio followed, stumbling drunkenly, hanging his head in chagrin. They were heading in the direction of the singing and the strumming of the mandolin.

Angel waited. She wanted the entire gang together and in one place before she bore down on them, started planting beads with her Winchester '73, and commenced blowing their black hearts back to the particular hole in Hell they'd all slithered out of—though some said each hobgobbie was master of his or her own hell.

A wolf's howl rose and circled the night sky. It silenced the mandolin and the drunken voices from the direction of the hobgobbies' camp. Angel drew a sharp breath and hunkered low behind her covering boulder, feeling chicken flesh rise along her spine.

She waited, breathing shallowly, as though the beast could hear the breath rake in and out of her lungs. Relief loosened her shoulders when no other howls followed the first. There was only silence save for the faint crackling of the demons' fire and the beating of Angel's own heart.

Finally, the strings of the mandolin were strummed once more. They were not tentative strains but challenging ones. Angel ground her teeth. The males and lone female spoke loudly, as though intentionally drawing the werewolves in.

Angel looked down at her cartridge belt, saw the lead and silver bullets housed there in the leather loops for such nights as this. The Winchester was loaded with lead cartridges, ready to go. She had more than enough. No need yet for the precious silver, because hobgobbies could be taken down the same as men. Her silver-chased Colt Peacemaker was holstered low on her leather-clad right thigh, fully loaded as well, and her ancient but well-preserved, razor-edged, silver Spanish sword, a gift from her father when she'd followed in his footsteps and joined the ranks of the U.S. Marshals, was sheathed in a matching black scabbard on the outside of her right leg. Jutting from a boot was a ten-inch Mexican dagger she'd pulled off a swiller bathhouse owner in San Antonio.

In addition, she had three ninja-style shurikens with five points of thinly shaved silver tucked into two separate pouches inside her cartridge belt, over her belly. She'd trained herself to throw the discs nearly as well as a twelfth-century samurai.

She was well armed and well skilled, a formidable foe against even hobgobbies.

How many wolves could be out here, anyway? To avoid leaving a too-clear trail for hunters, they usually ran in fairly small packs.

Finally, when the music and voices dwindled and it seemed the hobgobbies were settling down, Angel rose from behind the boulder and began following the trail Leonora and Rubio had followed, moving quietly in her boots and keeping her eyes and ears skinned for a possible night guard. She doubted the demons would post a lookout—for all their savagery, they were a drunken, arrogant lot—but she hadn't climbed the ranks to deputy U.S. marshal by being careless. Moving as gracefully as a puma, she stole up and over a low rise, following the game path through the scattered trees and desert shrubs.

Ahead, the fire's pulsating glow shone—a circle of umber light in a slight clearing. The strummer had put away his mandolin and was at the far edge of the firelight, his back to Angel. By the set of his head and shoulders and position of his arms, he was relieving himself in the brush.

Leonora was arranging a bed for herself a few yards to the right of the mandolin player and casting jeering glances at Rubio. Her unsatisfactory lover was keeping his head down, scowling as he poured coffee from a black-speckled pot into a dented tin cup. The two other males in the group, one of whom was the leader, Rafael Ortiz, were resting back against their saddles, grinning mockingly at Rubio, their near-lipless mouths stretched wide beneath their long, pointed noses.

Angel heard the murmur of their voices, but she couldn't hear what they were saying. They seemed to be speaking to both Rubio and Leonora, who grunted her responses while keeping her dark-eyed, incriminating scowl on Rubio, who said nothing.

Good. They were all distracted.

Angel hurried forward, moving on the balls of her feet. She'd learned to tread quietly on the quietest of desert nights, always leaving her spurs in her saddlebags and wearing no ornamentation on her clothes. She gained a cottonwood about thirty feet from the clearing, crouched behind it, and drew the Winchester's hammer slowly back to full cock.

Chapter 9

. . . .

SOMETHING SNORTED

Angel had just started to take one final gander at the camp, hearing one of the men say, "You know, Leonora, back in Rio Juarez, the senoritas all marvel at my love skills," when Leonora's brother yawned suddenly, and said, "Forget it, Pedro. No one can satisfy my sister's goatish lust. No one. Not even I—her brother!"

He laughed and began to haul himself to his feet, casting his eyes toward the tree behind which Angel was hunkered. She drew her head back behind the cottonwood and gritted her teeth as Rafael continued to laugh his menacing, high, squeaking laugh, and said in slurred Spanish that it was time to drain his dragon.

Leonora said, "Thank God I was that drunk only once, Rafael!"

"As I remember, *mi hermana*, you came pretty close to enjoying yourself."

Spitting sounds of revulsion rose from the other side of Angel's tree. At the same time, she heard Rafael's laughter and saw a long shadow stretch across the ground to her left. The hatless silhouette continued to angle off through the trees in the direction from which Angel had come.

Rafael followed it, passing so close to the cottonwood that Angel could smell the sour tequila sweat mixing with the typical death stench of the hobgobbie. The smell filled her nostrils and brought tears to her eyes, nearly making her choke.

Rafael stopped about ten feet beyond her, facing away. Angel held herself as still as possible. She could hear her heart pounding and hoped the demon neither sniffed nor heard her, as a hobgobbie's senses were nearly as keen as a wolf's. Rafael growled, hiccupped, and gave a grunt. His piss streamed down before him, steaming slightly on the cool ground.

Angel gritted her teeth resolutely, her heart racing, and raised her Winchester, flipping it end for end. So much for keeping the gang corralled. She stepped toward Rafael, and, closing her upper teeth over her lower lip, smashed the rifle's butt solidly against the back of his neck, just up from the hump on his back. She heard his neck crack, saw his head tilt at an odd angle just before he staggered forward, appearing even drunker than before, and wheezed.

"What the hell was that?" said Leonora. "*Mi hermano*, you all right over there?"

Rafael gave a long, last sigh and fell face forward on the ground with a thud and a fart.

Angel swung around with the Winchester, dropped to one knee, raised the rifle to her shoulder, and aimed into the clearing, drawing a bead on Rubio sitting on his saddle, knees spread, holding his steaming cup to his lips but scowling over it toward Angel.

She squeezed the Winchester's trigger. The rifle roared, punching a hole through Rubio's wool serape and causing his eyes to widen suddenly. He dropped his coffee cup. Angel quickly racked another shell into the Winchester's breech. There was no arresting ghouls, only dispatching them.

Before her, the others, including Leonora, had all reached for weapons, but only the male nearest Angel, a fat, bearded Mexican ghoul with one milky eye, had wrapped his hand around the Schofield jutting from the holster beside the saddle he'd been reclining against. Angel calmly drilled a bullet through the dead center of his forehead and was ejecting the spent, smoking casing, when the fourth man bounded off his heels with the agility the hobgobbies were known for, and dove like a demon missile toward the marshal. Angel nimbly threw herself to one side, rolling up off her right shoulder and springing back to her feet, but not before the fat ghoul was on her again, bulling into her chest with his head and shoulders.

Angel dropped the rifle and hit the ground hard on her back. She groaned. The hobgobbie half snarled like a wolf and half hissed like a diamondback, his eyes glowing red as coals as he peeled his nearly nonexistent lips back to show the fangs that, when the ghouls were aroused, became even longer and more savage-looking than a swiller's.

The light in his eyes dulled, and his fangs retreated a little. Angel withdrew her ten-inch Mexican dagger from the ghoul's side, feeling his hot, piss-yellow blood wash over her hand. She stuck it into him again, angling upward toward his heart. He made a gurgling sound and, staring incredulously at Angel, shook his head and closed his eyes.

Leonora had frozen halfway to her feet and was staring at Angel with her lips bunched, a knife in one hand while she raised a Colt with the other. Her pointy-nosed face with close-set, dull brown eyes was twisted with near-hysterical rage, showing her curved yellow fangs, but she held fire.

In her right hand, Angel held her cocked, silver-chased Colt around the shoulder of the ghoul still sprawled and death-spasming on top of her. She narrowed an eye as she aimed down the barrel at Leonora, crouched as though ready to spring.

Leonora said throatily, just above a whisper while narrowing her devil's eyes, "What did you do to my brother, Scar Face?"

"He was resisting arrest."

"He was taking a piss!"

"Got me."

Leonora screamed and triggered her pistol with one hand, then threw the knife with the other. The male atop Angel jerked as the slug and the bowie ripped into his back. The Colt in Angel's hand roared once, twice, three times. It barked once more, flames and smoke streaking across the camp.

Leonora was sent staggering backward with the first shot, and the following rounds kept her moving and screaming like a wounded hyena, hair flopping around her head.

Somehow still on her feet, she turned around and, holding her arm across her belly, staggered off toward the edge of the firelight, dragging her boot toes and howling. Several yards beyond the light, under a drooping willow, she dropped to both knees, screamed once more, and fell flat on her face.

Angel shoved the body off of her and gained her feet, breathing hard, chest rising and falling heavily behind her doeskin vest. She stooped to clean the dagger on the dead male before her.

A wolf howled.

Angel froze.

The high-pitched wail was louder than before, and Angel jerked her head up toward a ridge forming a saw-toothed, black velvet silhouette against the stars about a half mile away. Her heart shuddered. The hobgobbies' horses nickered and shifted uneasily off in the trees to Angel's right, about thirty yards away.

Something snorted.

There was a thud of something heavy hitting the ground behind her. Dropping the dagger and the empty Colt, Angel wheeled, automatically plucking a five-starred shuriken from the pouch in her cartridge belt. Her eyes had just skimmed the shaggy, gray-black wolf standing crouched before her, hackles raised, before she threw the deadly silver disc with a flick of her right wrist.

The beast's shrill scream sounded like a train whistle as the shuriken cut into its chest, instantly stopping its heart. The beast itself lurched up on its back legs and twisted around before tumbling in a heap, quivering.

She couldn't be sure it was a werewolf, but the way the shuriken had stopped it was a pretty good sign. . . .

Angel picked up her Winchester. On one knee and looking around wildly for more beasts, she quickly loaded the Winchester with silver cartridges. Off in the darkness beyond the fire, the horses danced and nickered. Brush snapped, and faint snarls and mewls rose. They didn't seem too close yet.

Angel racked a live round in the Winchester's chamber, then

set the rifle aside and loaded her .45, plucking the silver cartridges from her shell belt without looking but keeping her eyes
on the darkness beyond the fire. Quickly, she decided to make
a run for it. Probably, the wolves would linger over the bodies
of the dead hobgobbies, devour them first before they came after
her. If they did, and if there were only five or six in the pack,
she'd be able to hold them at bay with her rifle.

Having made up her mind, she holstered the Peacemaker,
fastened the keeper thong over the hammer, grabbed her Winchester, and ran. She'd run about fifty feet before the snarling
rose from the hobgobbies' camp, and she could hear quick, padded feet moving toward her from both sides of the trail.

Shit.

She might have made the wrong decision.

She kept running as fast as she could on the treacherous
terrain, holding the Winchester in her right hand, pumping her
left arm. Her black Stetson blew off her head and flopped down
her back by its horsehair chin thong.

A cold stone dropped in her chest when she heard the thuds
of the running pack growing quickly louder, and she could hear
the throaty, slathering snarls. She didn't look back, knowing it
would break her stride, but kept running until, when she sensed
at least one beast getting too close, she stopped, swung around,
dropped to a knee, and raised the Winchester to her shoulder.

A big wolf nearly as black as the night but limned in silver
moonlight was twenty feet away and closing by fluid leaps and
bounds. His eyes glowed yellow red. Angel raked the Winchester's hammer back and fired.

The beast snarled and yipped, dropped, and rolled, piling
up on itself four feet in front of Angel's knees. She cut a glance

around, saw at least three more shadows bounding toward her from both sides of the trail, their strides now slowing in light of what had happened to the black.

"Come on, you bastards!" Angel shouted, angrily racking a fresh round into the chamber. "Come and get it!"

The shadows sort of hunkered low to the ground, making them hard to see even with the milky light radiating from a big, round moon hovering about a quarter of the way from its zenith and casting the night in an eerie twilight.

One of the silhouettes moved. Angel snapped a shot at it, heard the precious silver round spang off a rock. She ejected the cartridge, heard it clang onto the gravel behind her.

"Shit!"

Levering a fresh round into the chamber, she rose slowly and began backing away, sliding the rifle from right to left and back again. She couldn't tell if the beasts were following her or not. When a werewolf had turned completely into a wolf and not some man-wolf amalgam, it was especially cunning and danger-ous. These might be trying to get around her and cut her off.

That thought fired adrenaline into her veins. She twisted around, took the rifle in one hand once more, and broke into a full-ahead sprint. She'd seen a cave near the place where she'd tied her horse. If she could get in there, she could hold off the wolves till morning if she had to.

Liquid breaths rumbled in wolf lungs behind her. Padded feet thudded. Sage branches snapped and gravel crackled. She glanced over her shoulder, saw what must have been a whole dozen of the shadows lunging toward her, several pairs of eyes glowing fiercely in the moonlight.

She dug her heels into the ground, pushing harder, her heart racing now, blood flowing hot through her veins. She ran past the place where she'd stumbled onto Leonora and Rubio fucking, and followed a path down a steep incline. The wolves were on both sides of her now. One was lunging toward her so quickly he almost appeared to be slowing so he wouldn't overtake her. Another was coming hard on the other side, fangs showing pale between gaping jaws.

Angel wanted to stop and shoot but she couldn't. Something told her that if she did that, she'd be dead almost instantly. Even if she got one of the beasts, the others would be on her in seconds.

"Oh, Christ," she heard herself nearly sob aloud.

She should have stayed by the fire.

Ahead was the sand-bottomed draw she'd crossed on her way to the hobgobbies' lair. The wolves would get her down there. The deep sand would slow her. She glanced once more over her shoulder. One was so close to her now that she could smell the rancid stench of his breath, see the foam flecking from his jaws as he breathed.

Angel bolted into the draw. A strange resignedness overtook her as she felt the deep sand grabbing at her boots, slowing her.

On the draw's opposite bank, she glimpsed something that she only vaguely registered as odd. A hatted figure silhouetted against the sky hunkered over something that appeared mounted high up off the ground and that flashed like gold sequins in the lunar light.

At the same time that she recognized the bullet-crowned hat, she heard a man's voice shout, "Down, Red!"

Angel probably would have gone down, anyway, as the sticky hands of the sand were grabbing at her heels. She hit the draw, rolled, and buried her face in the sand as a great cacophony shattered the night's bizarre silence.

Bam-bam-bam-bam-bam-bam-bam-bam-bam-bam!

Beneath the din, wolves yelped and yowled. A furry, rancid-smelling body hit the ground beside Angel and rolled beyond her until it piled up against the base of the draw's opposite bank. She heard the thuds of several others, and the wild thrashing of brush as a couple of the wounded tried to crawl away.

When the gun had hammered away for nearly twenty seconds, Angel lifted her head and glanced up to see the flash of the revolving maws and the quicksilver of its bullets streaking out over her head and off across her backtrail.

After another fifteen or so seconds, the din died suddenly, leaving only swirling echoes growing softer and softer, as though the moon were swallowing them piecemeal.

The gun blazed once more, causing Angel to jerk with a start and again mash her cheek against the sand, watching her backtrail with one eye. Several more streaks of silver flashed across the draw.

A final, agonized yip rose. A body thumped to the ground.

After a few more seconds the Gatling gun fell silent.

On the chill night air, Angel smelled the coppery stench of hot, flowing blood.

The silence was broken by a scratching sound. Angel gained her knees as she looked up the bank before her. The silhouetted figure crouched over the smoking Gatling gun mounted in its open casket, touched a match to a cigarette protruding straight out from between his lips.

Blowing gray smoke, Uriah Zane said, "Damn, that's a lot of 'em."

Angel drew a deep breath, the blood only just now beginning to slow in her veins. The terror was still there, but it was mixed with embarrassment and an automatic defiance. "I hope you're not thinking I needed your help, Uriah."

"Oh, no," Zane said, a ghostly silhouette smoking atop the casket. "They were just about to turn tail and run in the other direction."

Chapter 10

. . . .

"NOT YOU, TOO, URIAH!"

When Angel said nothing, only stared up in anger and with a sickening feeling of humiliation at the giant wolf-killer towering over her, Zane gave a disgusted grunt, leaped out of the casket, and strode down the slope to drop to one knee beside her, puffing his cigarette. "Where you hurt?"

"My pride."

"Fool woman."

She could smell the musky horse-and-sage scent of him as he bored his gaze into her, blowing smoke in her face. Only vaguely did she admit to herself that she was relieved to see him, that, in fact, she wanted to throw her arms around him and bury her face in his chest. It wouldn't do for him to know that, however. She'd never been a damsel in distress, and even though she'd come to within inches of being wolf bait, she wasn't about to start now. There was a bone-deep need in her to be respected . . . especially by Uriah Zane, for some damn stupid reason.

Not going easy on her, he said, "What in blue blazes are you doin' out here on a full moon?"

Tears of fury oozed from her eyes, and she felt a great convulsion in her throat. A wave of rage as well as frustration and befuddlement exploded within her, snuffing expressible words from her racing thoughts and emotions. How was it only Uriah Zane could make her—*her*, a deputy federal marshal, and a damn good one!—feel like a silly, little, pigtailed schoolgirl hysterical over a harmless spider crawling across the floor?

"Fuck you, Zane!"

The ghoul hunter snorted. "Don't take nothin' for granted. Where ya hurt? And don't mince words. We ain't got all night. I'm out of silver bullets for the cannon yonder, and I don't doubt other spooks are on the way."

Angel heaved herself to her feet, wincing at the pain shooting up her leg from her right ankle, which she couldn't put much weight on. She glared at Zane, who straightened his big frame that stood about five inches over hers, the quirley dangling from a corner of his mouth. He was the only man she felt physically dominated by, and she hated that about him despite being so infernally attracted to him. "I made a mistake. Leave me alone, damn you."

He stared at her in fatherly admonition, and she found herself averting her gaze from his and giving in a little. "I twisted my ankle." She lifted her arms, saw that her elbows were bloody and sandy. "Scraped my elbows."

"That it?"

"Yes, that's it," she returned scornfully. "You asked, and I told you. Sorry my throat's not cut."

"The night's still young."

"What're you doing?"

"Gonna help you up."

He gave a grunt, and then suddenly she was in his arms, snaking her hands around his neck with a gasp. As though she weighed no more than a straw stock, he carried her up the side of the ravine and set her down on a rock beside the wheeled casket, the Gatling gun jutting up from it.

Zane's horse, General Lee, glanced at her over his shoulder and gave his tail a swish in greeting. Tendrils of white smoke were still unraveling from the machine gun's six nasty maws.

"It's not worth all that," she said, feeling the heat emanating from the Gatling gun beside her. At least, she thought the heat was coming from the gun. She had a soft feeling in her belly as she watched him standing before her, his broad-shouldered frame silhouetted against the moon. His long, coal-black hair hung down from his bullet-crowned sombrero to flow over the shoulders of his wolfskin vest. "I could have walked, saved you a backache. How'd you know I was out here?"

He crouched, picked up her right foot, wrapping his hands around the boot and pressing slightly against her ankle. "Lomax in Gunnison said you were looking for me."

The truth was he hadn't planned on searching for her till the next morning. But he hadn't been able to keep her off his mind, so after a few beers and whiskey shots with Junius Webb in the Ace of Diamonds in Gunnison, he'd paid the old prospector his share of the bounty gold, retrieved General Lee from the livery stable—the horse had enjoyed sufficient rest, water, and feed— and headed out well before sunset.

As the pain shot up into her shin, Angel winced and dug her

fingers into the rock she was sitting on. "Figured you was on the grub line again and might need a job. I lost Curry two days ago."

Zane straightened and started walking away from her into the brush and low, rocky buttes. "I'll fetch your horse. You hear any more wolves, give a holler."

Angel barely heard that last, because he was just then disappearing through a notch between the buttes, moving as soundlessly as a jungle tiger in his high-topped fur moccasin boots from the tops of which bowie knives jutted.

"How did you find me *here*?" she called after him, receiving no reply. "I mean, this is big country, Uriah . . ."

She sat there, angry again and feeling frightened because he'd left her and hating the feeling, because she was a marshal, goddamnit, and she had no business fawning over the likes of some unheeled wolf killer.

Damn Lomax for letting Zane know she'd inquired about him. She must have been drunk. When he was around she sometimes lost her confidence, found herself feeling dependent on his admittedly superior hunting and tracking skills, and that graveled her no end.

"Seen your horse," Zane said later, when he'd retrieved Angel's paint mustang, and they were heading along a faint Indian trail to some cabin where the wolfer had said they'd find safety from the creatures of the full moon.

"What's that?" she said.

"Seen your horse."

"I got that much, Uriah. You saw my horse."

"That's how I knew you were out there. Tracked you up to that little box canyon you tied ole Cisco in."

She looked at him riding off her left stirrup. He rode easily in the saddle of the big golden stallion, trailing the wheeled casket.

"You didn't have to come."

He didn't look at her but stared straight ahead and didn't say anything.

"One thing about shootin' wolves during a full moon," he offered after a time, "is they're sure to stay dead."

"Yes, I remember." Angel lifted her gaze to the full moon that had shrunk down to the size of a newly minted dime and was riding straight above her head. "If you kill them when they're men, their souls will haunt you, depending of course on the strengths of said souls. But if you kill them when they're in bad need of a shave, like the bunch back there, they *stay* dead."

"They go back to Hell where they come from."

She looked at him again in the darkness. "You really believe all that hillbilly lore?"

"I surely do, Red."

She couldn't keep the admiration from her voice as she said with a tender smile for him, "You're one of a kind, Uriah. I'll give you that." She hardened her eyes at a remembered slight. "You son of a bitch."

He widened his eyes innocently. "Now what'd I do?"

"Why didn't you wake me before you left last time? In Nebraska. Coulda said you were pulling out, said, oh, I don't know, maybe *good-bye*? You know how stupid and cheap that makes me feel? Goddamnit, Uriah—I got a reputation to look after the same as you, and you know how many folks in that relay station knew you left me sound asleep up there in the dark after you rode out, like I was your six-peso *puta*?"

Zane hiked a big shoulder. "Sorry, Red. I reckon I shoulda

woke everybody up and told 'em I told you I was leaving and didn't pay you for your services." He arched a skeptical brow at her, emphasizing the irrationality in her thinking.

"And I—*I*, Uriah—led you to those three spooks! Because I knew you were riding the grub line and in need of a stake! And that's how you repaid me, by making me look *cheap!*"

"I ain't no grub-line rider, goddamnit!" He'd raised his deep voice with its rolling accent, and it caused Angel's paint to jerk its head up with a start.

Uriah's fury, and the way it made his eyes turn a dark shade of amber, always took her aback. She'd seen him furious—raving mad—and it had caused her to close her hands instinctively over her Colt's butt, in case his fury would turn toward her. It never had. But it always made her ill at ease. She'd always figured it was his brooding nature and violent temper that held him back from others, that kept him riding his own lonely trails.

"That's not the point, Uriah," she said finally, softly, turning her head forward in silent supplication. He'd saved her hide tonight, and she had no good cause to rile him. Besides, she knew that what she'd really wanted back in the Nebraska relay station was for him to have stayed with her another day or two. She hadn't wanted him to leave so soon. Waking and finding him gone—his side of the bed cold—had hurt her feelings, and that, in turn, had embarrassed her.

Since she was a girl, her embarrassment had always turned to anger. And her anger, like Zane's, held her aloof.

For another half hour, they followed the trail between steep sandstone ridges, the one on the right curling out over the canyon like a massive stone tongue, blocking out the moonlight and the feeble starlight.

"Good Lord! Where are you taking me? We'll be in Wyoming before long," she said as they climbed a low rise, having to ride single file now as the trail pinched down to only a few feet between piles of boulders that had fallen from both ridges, nearly blocking the canyon in places.

"Here." Zane stopped the big golden and stared under the overhanging ridge where a small cabin hunkered, seeming to glisten, as though outfitted with jewels of some kind. "It ain't the Larimer House in Denver, but I reckon it'll do for a full-moon night."

Angel heeled her horse off the trail's right side and into the massive shadow of the canyon wall. Out of the moonlight, she gained a clearer view of the cabin—an incredibly stout hovel constructed of what appeared to be full pine timbers, with a slightly peaked roof also of pine. The door was two pine trees joined by a heavy Z-frame and bearing a stout iron latch. On either side of the door were steel brackets apparently for locking the cabin from the outside.

The shiny ornaments on the cabin's outside walls were not sequins but silver-chased horseshoes and deer and elk antlers. There was even a silver-chased bear skull mounted over the door, under the overhanging roof.

Angel turned to Zane, who'd ridden up beside her and swung heavily down from the stallion, shucking his Henry repeater from his saddle sheath and racking a shell into the chamber. "Wait here, Red."

The big man strode to the cabin and tipped an ear to the door. He pulled his head back, and called just loudly enough to be heard from inside, "Hello, the cabin. Anyone here?" His deep voice sounded bearlike in the heavy silence.

He waited a few seconds, tipped his head to the door once more, and then tripped the steel latch and drew the door open with his rifle barrel. The heavy door shuddered, its hinges squawking like red-winged blackbirds.

He stood in the black opening for a time, holding his rifle across his chest, then ducked under the low doorframe and disappeared inside. Angel remained aboard her paint, watching, looking around this cool, dark side of the sheltered canyon, the moonlight washing over the ridge above her to fill the canyon beyond with liquid pearl.

Inside the cabin there was the rattle of a lantern mantle. A match scraped, and a dull, gradually intensifying glow leeched out the open door. The mantle pinged again, and then Angel saw Uriah's big frame move just inside the door, where he laid his rifle across a table before ducking back outside.

"How'd you know about this place?" she asked him.

"Belongs to a friend of mine, Abel Lundquist. We're on his ranch. Leastways, it was his ranch."

She stared at the hovel's silver trimmings. "Abel's a spook, isn't he?"

"Yep." Zane stopped in front of the cabin door, hooked his thumbs behind his wide shell belt, and stared out over the canyon. "*Was* a spook. Got bit just after the War, when the Hell's Angels first come west."

After a long, brooding pause, Zane said, "Abel built this cabin for nights like this one here." He tipped his head to look at the moon kiting across the gray-blue sky. "He was worried he'd kill his family and the men who worked for him. One of those men, his *segundo*, put a silver slug in him last month when he refused to lock himself in the cabin before the moon filled out. Mary, his wife, gave the order. But only because Abel had told her to if he ever got too weak, too savage, to seclude himself here."

"I'm sorry, Uriah."

"Ah, hell, it's the same old story, ain't it? Hell's opened its doors, and there's no closin' 'em now."

"They've always been open. At least, as long as I can remember."

The big man gave a dry chuckle. "Keeps my larder filled, anyways, I reckon."

Angel stepped out of her saddle, forgetting the nasty twist in her right ankle, and sucked a sharp breath against the pain shooting up her leg.

"Ah, hell, I'm sorry, Red." Zane left his horse and strode quickly over to her, grabbing her arm. "Here I was woolgatherin' during a full moon when I should have been getting you inside."

"I have to unsaddle—"

Again, she was in his powerful arms before she could finish protesting, and she wrapped her arms around his neck as he carried her toward the cabin. "Uriah, *please!*"

"Hush, now, damnit."

He carried her inside the sparsely furnished hovel, turned left, strode past an eating table on which the lantern flickered, and laid her down on a large, high bed covered with bobcat hides. He sat down beside her, shucked out of his gloves, and picked up her ankle, gently probing with his thick, brown fingers.

"Where's it hurt exactly?"

She looked down her legs at him, his soft eyes merely hazel now and filled with concern as they stared at her. She looked from his broad shoulders and the hard expanse of his chest under the wolf vest and his tight buckskin shirt to his flat belly, then returned her gaze to his hands.

They were large and thick and brown from years of the frontier sun. Powerful. A killer's hands. But she could feel the warmth of them seeping into her twisted ankle, assuaging the pain. The heat oozed up her legs and into her belly, ensconcing her heart, which quickened.

She swallowed as she lay back on the pillow and stretched her arms toward him, flexing her fingers desperately. "Goddamnit, Uriah."

He removed his hands from her ankle, crouched over her, lowered his head, and closed his mouth over hers.

Her body turned warm as summer honey. She opened her mouth for him, welcomed his hot tongue with her own. She rose up a little, pressed her breasts against his chest, squirmed around, feeling her need for him growing in her loins, and groaned for him.

He pulled away from her, stared into her eyes, and pushed her back down onto the bed. "I'm gonna tend the horses. I'll be back."

He swung around and ducked out of the cabin. She lay there, feeling desolate, hearing him outside tending the horses, leading them away, likely to some hidden corral.

She squirmed around with the need for him, hating herself for feeling this way about one man when the frontier had plenty. Not that she hadn't sampled others, but it was this burly, hillbilly ghoul hunter from Carolina who stuck in her craw, who made her want him and need him when she wanted to need no one.

When he returned, he closed the door, shutting out the moonlight, and walked over to the bed and began shucking off his clothes. Angel's breasts swelled under her tight vest as she watched him slip out of the wash-worn balbriggans that clung to his brawny, towering frame like a second skin. Naked, his big member flopping against his thighs beneath his hard, corded belly, he turned to open a window shutter, and stare out into the night.

"No one followed us, Uriah," she said, appreciating his white, muscular buttocks and the backs of his bulging thighs. "I'm sure of tha . . ."

She let her voice trail off as she stared at his broad back, the right shoulder blade protruding slightly as he crouched to peer out the window. Angel's lips parted as she gazed at him, awe-struck. At the bottom of the wing-like blade was a mass of knotted flesh about the circumference of one of Zane's own hands.

It was jagged and ridged with scar tissue. The scars were teeth marks—two larger than the others.

Fang marks.

Angel gasped.

"Don't hurt to be careful," Zane said before straightening and closing the shutter. He turned to her, his black-bearded face twisted in a wry grin, eyes spoking at the corners, his member jutting with raw, masculine desire.

He frowned. "Figured you'd be out of them duds by now." He moved toward her. "Never knew you to be shy, Red."

She had risen up on her elbows. Her heart throbbed. Her voice was too dry for speech.

She stared at his eyes, in which she could detect little amber sparks, like the coals of a burned-down campfire, and her belly twisted with horror. As he sat down beside her, making the bed's wooden frame creak under his weight, part of her wanted to bound up off the bed and run away from him, to go screaming and crying into the night.

No, Uriah, not you, too!

But he had her out of every stitch of her clothes in a minute, his breath raking her naked, tingling skin as he breathed harder and harder with his passion. He buried his face between her full, ivory, pink-tipped breasts, raked his thumbs across her nipples, and drew a deep breath as though to capture the raw essence of her in his lungs.

And then he flung himself between her legs, which her own raging desire spread for him. He cupped her breasts in his big hands, mashed his mouth down on hers, sliding his hot tongue between her lips as her hands closed over the taut, hard slabs of his buttocks.

And then nothing in the world—not even that he might be one of those he himself hunted—seemed to matter anymore except their two bodies toiling and writhing together.

Chapter 11

. . . .

THE BURNING WAR PARTY

"Shy last night and quiet as a church mouse today," Zane said the next morning, as they followed a wagon road northwest, in the general direction of Denver. "Red, what's got into you?"

She turned toward him. Her eyes were troubled beneath curved, red brows. Her hair, tinged with orange in the midmorning light, blew around her tapered, fine-boned cheeks in the cool breeze. She turned away from him and brushed her knuckles across her scar, as she did from time to time, mostly when she was upset about something.

She didn't say anything but he could tell that her head was filled with unexpressed thoughts and emotions.

Zane reined General Lee up sharply. "What's got your neck in a hump? You haven't said one word since breakfast, and then you only said 'no' when I asked if you wanted more coffee. If I was a self-doubting man, I might think you didn't enjoy yourself last night, Red."

Angel doffed her black Stetson and ran her gloved finger around the sweatband inside the crown, not looking at him. "How is it you know so much about the wolves, Uriah?"

"What're you talkin' about? Haven't I been huntin' 'em since I came out here ten years ago?"

"How do you know you have to kill 'em while they're changed or they'll come back and haunt whoever killed 'em?"

Zane studied her beneath ridged brows shaded by his sombrero's broad brim. "Hell, that ain't no big secret. The Injuns have known that for a long time. I heard it from a Crow medicine man up in Montana, when I first came out here lookin' for the Angels."

She slanted a skeptical eye at him, holding her hat in her hands. "That's how you learned it? The only way you learned it?"

Zane sighed and poked his hat up his forehead. "How else would I . . . ?"

He let his voice trail off, and then a sourness settled in his gut, like a swig of bad milk.

"I saw your back." She set her hat on her head and looked away from him, staring off at a distant dust devil. "Why didn't you tell me, Uriah?"

"Ah, hell."

"Why?"

"I didn't see the point. You'd just see me as different and there'd be no convincing you otherwise." Zane gestured behind them as though to indicate the wolves they'd killed last night. "I'm not one of them, Angel. I'm still me. I have it in me, true enough. But I've learned to control it."

She shot a cold, incriminating look at him. "Like hell."

"I've told it straight, Red. I am one of them, but then again, I'm not. I talked to a Comanche shaman down in Texas. He taught me how to keep the devil on a leash." Zane paused, studied her as she studied him with that cold look of accusing. "But if you want to ride out, go ahead. I won't stop you."

She continued to study him but her expression had gradually changed to one of utter befuddlement. "There was a full moon last night, and you . . ."

She remembered the frantic grabbing, clutching, caressing, sucking, grunting, the throbbing light in his wolfish red eyes as he'd brought her several times to heights of passion she'd not only never before experienced but never even realized were attainable. Even now, despite herself, a wave of near-savage desire washed over her just thinking about it. If he rode over to her now, grabbed her, thrust himself against her, she'd have a hard time stopping him, because she wouldn't want to.

But she had to. She'd never share his bed again.

He was one of *them*—one of the demons they hunted.

He was reading her mind. "I didn't tear your throat out, did I?"

"Why didn't you?"

"I told you. I can control it." He looked at her pointedly. "It's not like your father, Red."

She'd just opened her mouth to respond when a stone rattled down an escarpment behind her.

"Down, Red!" Zane clawed the Colt Navy revolver from the holster positioned for the cross draw on his left hip.

Angel threw herself sideways out of her saddle, hitting the ground on her left hip and shoulder as an arrow whistled through the air where she'd just been sitting, to clatter among the rocks on the trail's other side.

Zane's pistol quickly roared three times. A shrill cry sounded from the escarpment, and Zane leaped off the palomino's back, hitting the ground running as the Apache rolled down from the niche in the scarp where he'd been drawing back a second arrow nocked to his painted ash bow.

As the Indian in deerskin leggings and calico shirt piled up against a boulder at the base of the scarp, the wolfer dropped to a knee and aimed his Colt up the slope, sliding the barrel from right to left and back again, ready for another flat brown face to appear among the rocks and crags.

Behind him, Angel rose to her butt, palmed her Peacemaker, and rocked the hammer back. She'd lost her hat, and her hair hung in a mess about her shoulders.

"Any more?" she asked.

Zane squinted one eye as he aimed up the slope. His heart thudded, but his hands wrapped around the gun were steady.

"Not yet."

He drew a deep breath. One advantage—maybe the only advantage aside from slightly keener vision—of having been bitten by the raggedy-heeled stage robber Alden Woodyard, north of Laramie, was having a heightened sense of smell. Like his magnified vision and hearing, he didn't always have it, but when he needed it most it came to him, and he could smell the wild musk and blood scent of the dead Indian lying nearby.

But in the slight breeze wafting over the top of the escarpment he could detect only sage and cedar, maybe the cucumber smell of a snake den up there among the boulders.

Lines cut across his broad, sun-leathered forehead.

No. There was more. And he could hear something else now, too—the clomp of unshod hooves.

"Wait here."

He straightened and, lowering the rifle, bounded up the slope, leaping from one boulder to another until he'd gained the crest of the ridge. Hunkering low and doffing his hat, he peered between two boulders and through a scattering of gnarled cedars, down the slope's other side and to his right.

Dust rose about a quarter mile away. Beneath the sun-burnished cloud was a string of galloping horses ridden by small, brown men in calico shirts and bandannas, long, black hair flying out behind them in the wind.

Some were armed with bows and arrows, spears lashed to the sides of their mustang ponies. A couple had what appeared to be repeating rifles—both Winchesters and Spencers, Zane could see now, squinting—jostling down their backs by rope lanyards. The Apaches—Lipans, judging by the design of the war paint on their cheeks and foreheads and on the withers and rears of their galloping horses—were cutting across a sage-stippled flat on an interception course with the trail that Zane and Angel had been following.

Through the roiling dust, Zane counted fourteen braves. The pack had heard the reports of the wolfer's pistol, and now they batted their moccasined heels against their ponies' flanks, heading toward the scarp.

Zane doffed his hat and ran back down the escarpment, leaping from one rock to another, moving easily, with a light-footed grace and agility that was a by-product of his new condition. "Mount up," he told Angel, who was holding the reins of both their horses. "War party behind us."

She tossed his reins to him and swung up into her saddle, wincing a little at the ache in her ankle. "Apaches?"

"Lipans."

"Wolves on the prowl last night must have stirred 'em up." The Indians held the white-eyes responsible for increasing the werewolf activity in their native lands, since they also blamed the whites for driving the beasts west in the first place.

"Yeah, a full moon will do that."

Zane hammered his heels into General Lee's loins, and the big palomino bounded up the trail, the casket clattering along behind. Zane glanced over his shoulder as Angel galloped up beside him. He could hear the thudding of the Apaches' unshod horses as they approached the scarp from the far side.

"How many?" Angel asked, pulling her hat low on her forehead.

"Too damn many, and they're well armed. If we can make it to Cimarron, a couple miles ahead, we should be in the clear." Zane holstered his Colt and shucked his Henry from the saddle boot, cocking it one-handed.

"Cimarron's farther than that, Uriah. It's a good five miles from here."

The ghoul hunter shook his head as he held his reins in one hand, his rifle in the other, its barrel resting across his saddlebow. His crossbow jostled from where it hung from his saddle horn. "Don't think so."

"I think so!"

"You got no sense of direction, even less of distance."

Angel said something that Zane couldn't hear because just then a war whoop rose behind him, above the thudding of the hammering hooves and the cracks of rifle fire. A bullet spanged off a rock just left of the trail, and General Lee shied slightly.

The wolfer ground his heels against the palo's flanks once more, urging more speed. Angel followed suit, reaching forward and sliding her Winchester from the sheath lashed to her saddle beneath her right thigh. "We're gonna have to make a stand, Uriah. They're comin' fast, and those mustangs are built for speed!"

Zane glanced behind. Angel was right.

He nodded in reluctant agreement as they followed the trail around another escarpment. When the Indians were out of sight on the scarp's other side, though their hooves continued thudding, their savage war whoops rising, Zane pointed over his horse's head toward where two mounds of volcanic rock humped on the left side of the trail. The dykes lay side by side with what appeared a twenty- or thirty-foot-wide crease between them.

"See them rocks?" he shouted. "Pull in there. They'll have to swing back, and that's when we'll take 'em!"

After three more strides, they checked their horses down suddenly. Both gave indignant whinnies as they spun on their back hooves and were sent storming into the gap between the two volcanic dykes pocked with solid bubbles and streaked with bird shit. Ahead along the crease, Zane saw a ragged fox leap across the path and disappear into a hollow at the base of the right-side lava mound.

He and Angel reined their horses down at the same time. They swung out of their saddles, Angel cursing when her right foot touched the ground. They'd both just raised their rifles and started running back toward the trail, when a weird rumbling sounded and a windy whooping noise that was much louder than anything the Indians had voiced earlier issued from overhead.

A foul-smelling wind picked up dust and weed seeds, and there was a rumbling like that of a distant twister. The air warmed instantly.

Screams cut the air above the thudding of the loudening horse hooves, and then the war party was riding past the mouth of the gap in which both Zane and Angel crouched, rifles raised to their shoulders. Instead of aiming down the barrels, they were both looking around with incredulous, haunted looks on their faces.

The entire pack of Indians and horses galloped past the gap as a large ball of licking, crackling, smoking orange flames consumed them. Men and horses screamed shrilly, raising gooseflesh across the wolf hunter's broad back. The stench of charred flesh and horsehair filled Zane's nose as he heard Angel gasp beside him.

A half second later, a vast shadow passed over them, and they both looked up in time to see what appeared to be the striated belly of a giant fish fly over them from about twenty yards above the rounded tops of the two dykes. A snakelike tail of scaled, burnished bronze flicked and curled. The creature was so huge that it made a rushing sound, kicking up its own wind, lifting another small twister around the ghoul hunters.

"What the hell was that?" Angel asked, looking wide-eyed up at Zane and blinking against the windblown grit.

The ghoul hunter was startled out of words. He blinked as he stared out the mouth of the gap between the escarpments, where he'd just seen what he couldn't possibly have seen—the entire war party, men and horses, galloping inside a great ball of orange fire. He could still hear them screaming, smell them burning, though he could no longer see them behind the dyke.

Lowering his rifle, he ran forward, then stopped at the mouth of the gap and looked to his left, the direction in which the burning riders had been galloping.

Slowly, he moved out from the gap and into the trail, still blinking in disbelief at what he was seeing—all the Indians and horses now strewn in ragged black mounds along the trail and in the desert to both sides. A few of the horses thrashed as they continued to burn, but they and the braves were all down, scattered as though they'd fallen from the sky.

Most of the braves appeared dead. One was crawling into the desert off the trail's right side, shrieking while orange flames licked up around and over him. He was fried to black cinders. Finally, he stopped, rose to his knees, lifted his head, shrieking still louder and raising his arms as though in supplication before flopping to the ground and falling still.

Zane heard Angel's spurs ring as she walked up beside him and stared at the burning horses and fallen braves.

"Law," Zane muttered in his soft Southern drawl, running a hand down the black stubble on his face, his eyes glassy with shock. "Seen it once. Hoped I'd never see it a second time."

"In case you weren't paying attention," Angel said, her voice rising as she lifted an arm to point at the sky, "you're about to see it a third time."

Zane followed her finger. The dragon had banked and, flapping its great jointed wings and flicking its long, kitelike tail, was headed back toward them, narrowing its snakelike eyes as it homed in on its prey, black smoke licking from its nostrils.

Chapter 12

. . . .

WOLVES AT HIGH NOON

The four wolves ran as one across the mesa, long, thick hair of varying shades of gray and brown ruffling at their necks and glistening in the high, dry Colorado sunshine. They ran side by side, none breaking stride until the willowy, square-headed beast on the far right was distracted by a jackrabbit and swerved away from the main group to give brief chase until the jackrabbit dove into a hole among some rocks and prickly pear and stared out, quivering.

The wolf gave a taunting howl, snapping its jaws, and raced after the others who were just now approaching the mesa's edge.

Tongues hanging, panting, mewling and yipping eagerly, the four wolves stopped and looked over the lip of the ridge. The stage trail angled around the base of the mesa, and just now a coach was fast approaching from the southeast, the team running full out under the driver's blacksnake, which cracked over their backs with the sounds of pistol shots. The sweat-lathered team appeared bathed in silver under the high-noon sun.

The driver cursed and yelled. The shotgun rider sitting beside him held on to his seat for dear life, his double-barreled shotgun wedged between his legs. The coach rattled and clattered. Dust roiled up to glisten like burnished copper.

"Got a timetable to keep, Lucy!" the driver shouted through the bandanna drawn up over his nose, jerking his arm up to crack the popper at the end of the whip once more, making one of the wolves give an instinctive start, leaping up off its front paws and groaning.

"Get up there, Jeremiah!" the driver bellowed. *"Lift some dust, Abilene!"*

One of the other wolves nipped another in its eagerness, then all backed a few feet away from the lip of the ridge, so they wouldn't be seen by the shotgunner or driver, and hung their heads low. Their eyes darkened in hungry anticipation. They snapped their jaws and licked their chops.

The thunder of the approaching coach grew louder and louder until the stage was nearly directly below the wolves. The largest of the beasts glanced at the others, giving the signal, then hurled itself over the side of the ridge, plummeting twenty feet in an arc of gray-brown fur and glowing red eyes, to land on its front paws squarely atop a long steamer trunk lashed to the top of the stage, behind the driver and shotgun messenger.

Two others landed on the roof, as well, while a third—the lightest colored of the four wolves—came to rest directly upon the shotgun rider and went immediately to work, snarling loudly and savagely as it tore the unsuspecting man's throat out.

The shotgunner screamed as he dropped his Greener and

reached for his bloody throat while the wolf shook him like a bone.

The driver's eyes nearly popped out of his skull as he watched the attack, his wide-open mouth pushing a circle out from behind his red bandanna.

Blood sprayed, covering the driver, who then commenced screaming, kicking his feet as though to run, until one of the three wolves closed its jaws around the back of his neck from behind and, with the strength of six common wolves, jerked the man up and out of the driver's boot and onto the coach roof. The wolf promptly tore the driver's throat open, silencing the man's hysterical screams, then rolling him off the coach to hit the trail and tumble, limbs akimbo, blood flying.

A woman inside the coach screamed.

One of the other wolves atop the coach grinned at the wolf who'd killed the driver, then pivoted off its back legs. It grabbed the edge of the roof with one paw while throwing the rest of its body over the side.

When it had its back feet inside the coach window, it removed its paw from the edge of the roof, and the coach bounced as it landed inside the carriage. Screams rose in earnest below the other three wolves, who hunkered together on the roof, turning at nearly the same time back into One-Eye Langtry, Lucky Snodgrass, and their particularly savage leader—Charlie Hondo.

There they were—three of them fully outfitted in their Western trail garb complete with six-shooters and battered hats, as though they'd never been wolves at all. Charlie Hondo, born to Romanian nobility, was tall and thin, with bulging, crazy eyes and long, sandy hair hanging down from the sides of his head, while his pate was as pink and bald as a baby's rump. Gold hoop rings dangled from his ears. In mockery of the Lutheran church, having been sent to an orphanage after his family had banished him for raping and chopping two serving girls up into tiny bits that he then dumped in the castle's well, he wore on each cheek two dull green tattooed crosses. They were in grisly contrast to his bulging, glittering, light brown eyes.

Due to a fairly common shape-shifting magic, the Angels' clothes worn while in their human forms had not materialized in their wolf forms but had come back through the second shifting of their shapes. Now wearing the blue Army uniform of Warden Mondrick of Hellsgarde Prison, complete with cavalry sword, holstered Colt Army .44, and even the pocketknife, matches, and other paraphernalia the man had had in his pockets when Charlie had eaten out his heart and then beheaded him, the leader of the formidable wolf pack gave a tooth-gnashing rebel yell.

He leaped down into the driver's boot and took up the reins that the driver had dropped on the floor. He almost lost the warden's blue hat on the wind, but grabbed it and stuffed it under the seat.

The horses had heard the screams and smelled the blood and were still smelling it now as Curly Joe Panabaker was hard at work inside the carriage, raising shrieks and bone-splintering screams from the two drummers, one doctor, and two women riding in there, on what had been, only seconds before, a pleasantly eventless midday trek between Dead Horse Gap and Wild Rose, in the far-southwestern corner of Colorado.

The team was running wildly and trying to leap out of its hames and harnesses, but Charlie Hondo, hoop earrings thrashing and flashing, got them back on their leashes, holding them steady to the trail. One-Eye climbed onto the box beside Charlie, while Lucky Snodgrass remained on all fours, grinning delightedly over the side of the carriage roof as the savagery continued below.

Presently, one of the now-headless drummers flew out the coach's right-side door to hit the trail rolling, and Lucky whooped and clapped his hands maniacally. The doctor, also headless, was thrown out the opposite door, where his blood-geysering corpse bounced off a boulder beside the trail. Lucky glanced over his shoulder as the sawbones disappeared in the roiling dust cloud behind the carriage.

He whooped and hollered and pumped his fists in the air. "Wolves at high noon! Can't beat *that!*"

The wolfish growls and snarls and angry yips intermittently drowned the screams until the throatless, disemboweled women were both rolling like rag dolls in the trail behind the coach, quickly lost in the distance.

A loud snarl rose, followed by a howl. And then the carriage jerked, and two hairy human hands appeared at the edge of the coach roof. Curly Joe lifted his head up above the roof, his funnel-brimmed hat snugged to his head by the rawhide thong secured taut to the underside of his chin. His red eyes turned blue, and the hair on his hands disappeared.

He grinned and gave another howl, this one belonging to a man, and hoisted himself up onto the roof where he sat with his legs raised, arms wrapped around his knees, grinning and looking around at the sunlit afternoon sliding past the carriage.

"I like this," he said, slowly shaking his head in awe-filled appreciation of his new abilities. "I really do like this a lot, pards."

Charlie Hondo glanced over his shoulder at Curly Joe, looked away, then looked back again, widening his pale, lifeless eyes under the brim of his dusty blue cavalry kepi with the gold braid around the crown. "Curly Joe, you keep smilin' that hard, you're liable to break your face in two!" He loved being a "Westerner" as much as the others.

One-Eye had his Schofield out of its holster. He broke the piece open to check the loads. "Curly Joe's just enjoyin' his new abilities, Charlie. You should, too—since it's bein' able to turn whenever we want, day or night, full moon or not, that got you outta Hellsgarde."

"That and that dragon," added Curly Joe.

Hondo, the alpha wolf, shook his head and stretched his lips back from his rotten teeth in revulsion as he held the six-hitch team's reins deftly in his long-fingered hands and stared ahead along the trail. "Glad to be out of that fuckin' perdition. Wish I coulda killed that warden one more time. Ripped his head off with my teeth just once more!"

The former Ludwig Jurgen Abelard Kiesler grinned at his compatriots. "Much obliged, boys. Oh, I woulda got outta there eventually, but you and that fire-breather sure made it a whole lot easier. I owe you a round of ale . . . if there's anything excepting coffin varnish to be found out here."

Dubiously, he studied the parched desert terrain sliding past the coach, and batted his lashes against the dust.

"Where'd the dragon come from, Charlie?" asked Curly Joe. "Don't recollect anyone mentionin' dragons."

"I reckon," said Charile, planting his cavalry boots on the dashboard and leaning back in the jehu's stiff wooden seat, "the dragon was a little something extra provided by our lovely, bewitching benefactor, Senorita Ravenna." He grinned in delight, remembering the beguiling, crotch-stirring image of Ravenna sprawling nude on a corn-shuck mattress in a Dodge City flophouse, the day after he'd met her in the Long Branch Saloon. "I suspect she'll be catching up with us soon."

"Ah," said One-Eye eagerly, snapping the Schofield closed, spinning the hogleg on his finger, and sliding it back into the holster thronged low on his denim-clad right thigh. "Miss Ravenna."

"Senorita Ravenna de Onis y Gonzalez-Vara," said Charlie, letting the long and regal Spanish name roll lovingly off his tongue. "A fitting name for that Mex piece of horny ass."

"You sure we can trust her?" Curly Joe said, trying feebly to roll a cigarette in his thick, brown fingers, despite the stage's violent jostling and the hot wind. "I never have known a Mex—male or female—I trusted any more than I could throw uphill against an Oklahoma cyclone."

"Oh, we can trust her," Charlie said with a self-satisfied air. "The girl's powers might be as strong as that cyclone"—he glanced over his shoulder at the others, winking assuredly—"because she needs us as much as we need her. Besides, she fancies my pecker!" He threw his head back and howled, snapping his jaws.

Curly Joe gave up on the cigarette and let the wind take the paper and tobacco, brushing his hands on his patched, checked wool trousers. "And once we get to Mexico?"

"She'll be sharin' in our newly acquired fortune, Curly. Once we find it, that is. You don't think she and her spells helped you spring me from Hellsgarde just for my pecker, do you?"

"I reckon not," said Lucky Snodgrass, who sat back with his

hat tipped over his eyes, trying to catch a few winks. "But you never know about a witch. Ever'one I ever known has made me nervous. They're a selfish lot, I tell you. And their powers make 'em dangerous. I hope she ain't just toyin' with us."

Charlie slapped Lucky's knee, fairly teeming with confidence. "You let me worry about Senorita Ravenna," he said, shaking the ribbons over the team, urging more speed as they started up a long, easy grade. "Ravenna needs us as much as we need her. She followed me to Dodge City for some reason. If I hadn't gotten drunk and careless in Denver and thrown in Hellsgarde, I might have found out." He paused, sucked at a gap in his upper teeth. "Oh, she's got somethin' wicked on her pretty little mind, all right. But I think it's to our benefit." He grinned at the others. "Besides, I got her eatin' outta my pants!"

Again, Charlie howled.

The others glanced at one another uneasily as the stage shot up and over the hill, then moved even faster down the other side. Ahead, at the bottom of the grade and in a broad horseshoe amid a jumble of high boulders piled on the trail's right side, the Sandy Wash relay station appeared—a low-slung, L-shaped cabin with a broad-roofed gallery angling off its front, a barn and two corrals, and a windmill spinning lazily in the warm fall breeze.

One-Eye sniffed the air in the direction of the cabin. "I do believe I smell beer, Charlie!"

Hondo worked his nose, then shook his head. "You've been too long in America, One-Eye. That's not beer. That's a flooded hog wallow tainted with alkali and stinkweed. But just what the doctor ordered!"

Charlie pulled the stage up between the barn and the cabin,

and the horses had barely settled back in their collars before the cabin's timber door squawked open, and a short, potbellied old man in ragged pants and suspenders came out, blinking his eyes sleepily and tucking his shirttails into his slacks.

Two other, younger men came out behind him, and as the old man stepped off the wide gallery shaded by a brush roof, the younger men angled off away from him toward the team and began unbuckling straps while casting wary eyes at the men atop the stage. The old man ambled, limping slightly on his right leg, toward the coach. As he did, he glanced at the driver's boot and slowed his pace, frowning.

"What the hell . . . You ain't Mike 'n' Rascal. . . ."

He stopped, staring up at the four men riding the coach's roof, blinking as though to clear his bleary blue eyes. The tip of his red nose was nearly as large as an apricot, and badly pocked and pitted.

"You're an observant son of a bitch," said Charlie Hondo, throwing the brake and wrapping the ribbons around it. The other three Angels glanced around at one another, grinning and chuckling. The two young hostlers, working quickly and automatically, well versed in their profession, continued unharnessing the team, casting wary glances from the newcomers to each other and back again.

The fresh horses in the holding corral off the barn ran around with their tails humped.

"Hey, old-timer," said One-Eye, waving his hat at the dust just now catching up with the coach, "you got any beer in there worth drinkin'?"

"I . . . I don't see no passengers," the old man said, tentatively, as he took a few more steps toward the coach, lifting his chin to peer in a window.

"And you won't, neither," said Lucky, as he stepped down to the left front wheel, then dropped to the ground. "'Cause they're all wolf bait litterin' the trail back yonder."

The old man made a face as he turned away from the blood-coated interior of the stagecoach. "Oh, Jesus!"

"Jesus won't help you now!" Lucky said, suddenly back in his sleek wolf form.

Lucky the wolf leaped atop the old man and had him flat on his back and dying in seconds, while Charlie and One-Eye, also in wolf form, leaped down from the front of the driver's boot and onto the backs of the two horses nearest the stage. In seconds, they ran up across the backs of the other horses that had only seconds ago been released from the hitch, and leaped on the two young hostlers who could only stand there, lower jaws hanging, as the two wolves pounced on them under a high, copper sun.

Just as the old man's had been, their screams were short-lived.

The terrified horses, still strapped to each other but free of the wagon tongue, ran off across the yard, dragging the double tree and kicking their back legs in horror.

Charlie Hondo changed back into his cavalry-suited man form. Then both Lucky and One-Eye changed into their more soiled but well-armed frontier visages. They stared down at Curly Joe, who lay facedown in the dirt beside the recent wheel ruts made by the stage.

Lucky ran to him, placed a hand on his arm. "What the hell happened, Curly? The stage run you over?"

Curly grunted and pushed up onto his knees, snatching his hat off the ground beside him. He looked at Charlie. "I didn't change!"

Charlie scowled back at him, confused. "Say *what?*"

"I didn't change, Charlie. I was just about to—I could feel the hairs pushing out and my hands and feet growin' big, and just as I was about to jump off the coach, I went back to myself so quick I couldn't catch myself. I was expectin' to land on all fours, and . . ." He winced as he hauled himself heavily, painfully, to his feet.

"Same damn thing almost happened to me, Charlie." One-Eye adjusted his black eye patch and rubbed the slight paunch pushing out his blue wool shirt, the V-neck of which was held together with strips of braided rawhide. "I felt a little hesitation, sort of a weakness. And now . . ." He made a face and continued to rub his belly. "I don't feel so good. This never happens during a full moon. Of course, I don't change so quick then. . . ."

Charlie snapped his head at Snodgrass. "What about you?"

Lucky shrugged. "I didn't have no problem. What about yourself, boss?"

Charlie had just opened his mouth to speak when the cabin door, which had been standing open, closed with a *bang!* A girl's voice shouted from inside, "You mangy wolves pack up and fog the dusty trail. I got a shotgun loaded with silver dimes, and I'm just itchin' to use it!" Her voice grew shrill. "Wolves at high noon—I never seen the like."

The four killers looked around at one another. Their moods lightened. Charlie smoothed his long, shaggy mustache with the index finger and thumb of his left hand.

Smiling wolfishly, he began striding toward the cabin. "Fellas, I smell purty young female flesh."

Chapter 13

. . . .

RAVENNA AND THE DRAGON

"She sounds like she's got some spunk," said Lucky as he and the others followed Charlie to the cabin. "I like my wenches spunky."

They stopped just off the edge of the ten-foot-wide gallery as Charlie mounted it, stepped to one side of the door, and hammered it three times with his fist, causing dust to leap from the cracks.

"You, in there," the alpha wolf called. "You'd best open this door and toss the gut-shredder out. You got me mad already, callin' us names who you've never met. And you had the nerve to threaten werewolves with silver? Come on, you little bitch, what's got into you? I'm so mad now, I'm liable to suck your throat out your asshole and spit it back in your face!"

"Might just do that, anyway," said Curly Joe, bending his knees slightly and adjusting his crotch. "After I drill her, I mean.

I ain't had me a mattress dance in a month of Sundays." He grabbed his crotch and lurched hungrily up and down, bending his knees. A thoughtful cast entered his gaze. "I wonder if I can do it changed. . . ."

"You mean as a wolf?" Charlie asked.

"Why not?"

Charlie shrugged as though the idea hadn't occurred to him but was worth considering.

"Best proceed with caution," advised Lucky, sliding his long-barreled Remington and rolling the cylinders across his forearm. "You heard—silver."

"Where in the hell'd she get silver out here?" One-Eye wanted to know. "Silver dimes, no less!"

There was no mineral, not even gold, more precious than silver. The only thing more sought-after on the entire frontier was blood-swilling girls with Indian blood—especially blood from the most savage tribes like the Crow up in Montana, the Utes in Colorado, and the Comanche, Apache, and Yaqui in the Southwest and Mexico. They were ferocious as well as rare, and it was said that if a man survived a night with one, no other woman could ever satisfy him again.

"Mr. Jipson done stored 'em up," the girl obliged One-Eye's inquiry. "And I got two loads snugged down in both these ten-gauge barrels, so you take your hairy, foul-smelling asses and vamoose!"

Her shrill voice broke on that last.

"'Hairy, foul-smelling asses'?" Charlie said, gritting his rotten teeth and glaring at the door, blood vessels bulging in his forehead. "Listen, you fuckin' little bitch, you open this door or I'll break it down. If I have to do that, I'm gonna be even madder than I am now!"

On the other side of the door, the girl sobbed.

Charlie grinned.

He licked his lips, absently massaged the cross tattooed on his right cheek, and gentled his tone. "Honey, look. Werewolves, we are, indeed. You got us pegged. But, while we are werewolves and we did kill your employers merely for the enjoyment of a bloody kill, we're tired now. We'd just like food, beer, and rest. We got money. We'll pay you."

He paused, taking a deep breath as though speaking so gently, suppressing his rage, was sapping his energy. "Best yet, we'll let you live. Now, won't you please open the door?"

The girl's strong, defiant voice was gone. Weakly, befuddledly, she asked, "How in the hell'd you fellas change into wolves right here in broad daylight? The full moon was *last* night!"

"Let us in, honey, and we'll tell you all about it," said Curly Joe, voice pitched with lust.

"You'll turn again," the girl said, "and you'll do me like you did Mr. Jipson and Eb and Leonard."

"No, no, no," said Charlie. "But I'll tell you what we will do if you don't open this door." He calmly removed his hat, inspected the gold braid, flicking bits of dust and weeds off it with his fingers before lowering the hat to his side, and, face swelling up and turning as red as an Arizona sunset, shouted, *"We'll burn this bloody place right down to the ground, and you along with it, you defiant little whore!"*

Silence.

Curly Joe snickered as he and One-Eye and Lucky stood just off the gallery, thumbs hooked behind their cartridge belts, Lucky holding his Remy pointed at the door, in case the girl should storm out firing.

From inside, the girl's frightened voice: "You promise you won't kill me."

Charlie swallowed. "I promise," he said as gently as he could, his voice quavering.

Another stretched silence. Then there rose the scraping of a locking bar being removed from over the door. The steel and leather latch clicked, and the door squawked as it drew inward a few inches to reveal a young girl's pretty, freckled face staring through the crack. Deep furrows cut across her freckled forehead, and her eyes were suspicious, fearful. "Remember, you promised."

She screamed as Charlie rammed his shoulder against the door. As the girl fell back into the stage station's thick shadows rife with the smell of grease, tobacco, and woodsmoke, Charlie bounded inside and grabbed the shotgun out of her hands. The girl hit the floor on her butt with a yelp, and Charlie stood just inside, his long shadow falling across her body clad in a low-cut flour-sack dress.

She was barefoot, and her pale blues eyes sparked with fear between wings of her long, straight, tawny hair.

The other men sauntered into the station behind Charlie.

"She's purty, all right," said Lucky, swallowing hard and glowering down at the girl.

"Right well set up, too." Curly Joe doffed his hat and started forward, tossing his hat onto the table. He glanced over his shoulder at Charlie. "You want her first, boss?"

Charlie scowled, his fists still balled in fury at his sides. "Nah. You boys deserve first turns with her. I reckon I owe you that. Besides, I think she stinks worse than we do."

Curly Joe turned back to the girl and began unbuckling his cartridge belt. "You an' me, girl, we gonna have us some fun."

"No!" The girl jerked her arm away from him and heaved herself to her feet. "You promised!"

"Promised we wouldn't kill ya," said Lucky as he and One-Eye followed Curly Joe after the girl, who scrambled, stumbling and falling and trying to run barefoot on the scarred wooden floor. He gave a whoop. "You ever tumble with a werewolf before?"

As Curly Joe, One-Eye, and Lucky went after the girl, Charlie walked back out onto the veranda, at the edge of which he stood and, tipping his face to the softening sunlight and a slight breeze wafting down from the high country in the northwest, dug a long, black cheroot from the breast pocket of the warden's rough wool shirt. From behind him came the girl's curses and sobs as the men apparently cornered her in the cabin's north corner.

Charlie scratched a match to life on the warden's black cartridge belt and touched the flame to the end of his cigar.

A whirling sounded in the far distance.

Charlie passed the sound off as merely a gust in the freshening breeze, but as he blew his match out with a puff of cigar smoke, he curled a dubious brow as he stared into the rolling rock-, sage-, and cedar-stippled desert beyond the station.

The whirling grew louder and louder, and for a moment Charlie wondered if the station wasn't about to be hit with one of those infernal cyclones that plagued the flat, less arid country a little to the east, when a large, dark cloud slid into view, its fishy white belly raking the top of a high, northern ridge. Charlie scrutinized the shadow as he blew more cigar smoke out his broad nostrils, and felt his lips part as his lower jaw sagged slightly.

The cloud had enormous, flapping wings and, all alone in the cobalt sky gaining a darker cast as the afternoon waned, was fast approaching the stage station. It wasn't a funnel cloud. It wasn't a cloud of any kind, Charlie saw now as the sunlight winked off the lime-green and golden scales, and the dragon's wagon-sized head, like the head of a deadly, giant diamondback rattlesnake, turned toward him, eyes like burning green and red coals.

Flames shot out of the dragon's nostrils—two slender jets of orange fire flicking out like twin tongues merely testing the air before receding again into the bizarre beast's antenna-adorned head. The flames' black smoke was torn away on the wind.

"Yeeeee-HAWWWWWWWW," came a cry beneath the whirling sound of the dragon.

Charlie looked away from the fast-approaching winged beast then, realizing that the sound had to be coming from the dragon itself, turned back to it as its great, bat-like wings rose and fell while its finned tail curled out behind it, propelling it along from behind.

The cry came again, and as the dragon approached the station from a mile out now, dropping and coming on fast, Charlie made out a slender figure astride the dragon's back, throwing one arm out and whooping as though the fool were riding a bucking bronco in a Fourth of July rodeo in Abilene.

Charlie squinted his eyes incredulously.

A *female* fool. Long, black hair flew out behind the woman's head in the wind. Her willowy, curvaceous body was clad all in black and brown, with a red sash and matching red boots angling back against the dragon's broad body. In contrast to the dragon's girth—the beast was the size of a small barn—the girl appeared little larger than a cat as, yipping and yowling and throwing up her arm, she held in her other hand the leather ribbons of a braided gold harness of sorts that curved around the beast's stout neck. Beneath the woman was a red velvet blanket trimmed in gold, with gold tassels fluttering in the wind as the beast now made its final approach, the sage and cedars shivering in the wind of its sinewy wings.

Charlie tipped his brim low against the ground fog of dust, straw, and horse shit. He couldn't help chuckling then, as he recognized the woman astride the dragon, and stepped down off the veranda and walked across the yard as the dragon set down between the crazily spinning windmill and the cabin.

"What the hell's that?" shouted one of the men from inside.

The girl's cries had died to mere whimpers and occasional snapped curses.

Boots thumped on the worn puncheons behind Charlie, as the pack leader strode several yards out from the veranda and stopped, grinning around the cheroot smoldering between his teeth, crossing his arms on his chest, and rocking back on the heels of his polished cavalry stovepipes. Sitting atop the now-idle dragon, who blinked its copper eyes slowly at Charlie, short bits of fire curling from its nostrils and its wings flexing slightly as they settled against its sides, Ravenna de Onis y Gonzalez-Vara pinched her black hat brim in salute.

The pretty Mexican *bruja*, or sorceress, swung her right leg up in front of her, where a saddle horn would have been had she been using a saddle, and dropped spryly down to the dragon's left wing. From there, spreading her arms out for balance, the red sash and the tails of her long, black leather duster fluttering out around her, she dropped straight down to the ground.

Striding toward Charlie, the witch glanced over her shoulder at the idling dragon, and said, *"Siente y comportese, Chico!"* *Sit down and behave yourself.*

"You are even a better witch than I imagined," Charlie said, letting his flat brown eyes roam lustily across the woman's exquisite, black-and-brown-clad, well-armed figure.

"How's that, *mi amigo?*" Ravenna asked as she stopped before him, smiling and showing all those perfect white teeth though his eyes were lingering on the black vest, which was all she wore beneath the duster and which revealed more of her full, enticing, olive-hued breasts than it hid. The top of each one was tattooed in black with a weirdly shaped symbol—a totem of some kind.

"I was just thinking of you before I saw . . ." Charlie glanced past her at the dragon, whose sides expanded and contracted slowly, heavily, as he breathed, his scales sparkling as the light dashed across them with each expansion and contraction. "Your crazy bird there . . ."

"Be careful, Senor Charlie," Ravenna said, lifting her chin to smile up at him while waving a finger in good-natured admonishment. "Chico does not like to be called a bird." She glanced over her shoulder at the dragon. "What the hell, Chico. *Va la causa un cierto apuro, huh!"* *Go wreak some havoc!*

Eagerly, Chico flapped his great wings, rising up on his giant, birdlike legs, and heaved himself into the sky. The wind of his wings lifted dust and grit against which Charlie and Ravenna closed their eyes and held their hats down tight to their heads.

"What are dragons, anyway?" Charlie asked when the bird was winging off to the west and banking north, as if suddenly sensing prey in that direction.

"They are dragons, fool." Ravenna rose up on the toes of her fancily stitched, red, black-topped boots to plant a kiss very lightly on his lips. "You were thinking of *me, Major Charlie*?" she said, running her fingers over the shoulder straps on his greatcoat, obviously surprised and flattered.

"Encountered a little problem we need to disc—"

He stopped when one of the men inside the cabin cursed loudly. Running footsteps sounded, emanating out the open door until the girl, looking frantic, a torn strap of her dress hanging down to reveal a wash-worn camisole behind which her right breast jiggled, dashed across the veranda and bolted past Charlie and Ravenna. As the girl headed for the barn, leaping the stage driver's bloody carcass, One-Eye came running out of the station house, flanked by Lucky and Curly Joe, whose lower lip was bleeding.

"Bitch bit me!" he raged.

The three stopped when they saw Ravenna with Charlie. "What the hell is that?" said Curly, slowing as he came down the steps and pointing at the dragon now winging back over the stage station. The other two were casting incredulous looks between the dragon and the beautiful senorita in the black duster and revealing fawn vest from behind which her ample breasts swelled invitingly.

"My horse!" said Ravenna delightedly. "I've put him out to pasture for the time being." Looking at Charlie, she said, canting her head toward the barn, "Who's the whore? You haven't been cheating on me, have you, Charlie?"

She nudged one of her round hips against Hondo's crotch, stuck a finger through one of his gold earrings, and gave it a gentle, chiding tug. "I've been saving myself for you ever since Dodge City!"

Charlie tittered. "The hell you say!"

"Be careful or I'll send you there," she admonished with just enough of an edge to rock Charlie back on his heels. "You know I have the magic for it."

Glancing again at the dragon just now fading from sight but obviously more compelled by the prospect of toiling between the station girl's legs, Lucky bolted away from Charlie and Ravenna, heading for the barn.

"Hey, slow your horses!" shouted One-Eye, sprinting for the barn.

Curly Joe wiped blood off his lip and took off after the others. "I git her first, goddamnit! She drew my blood!"

Charlie watched the three, hearing their spurs chinging, shaking his head and chuckling.

"Were they so depraved in the Old Country?"

"Oh, I reckon." Charlie looked at the witch and necromancer and gave her low-cut vest a commanding tug. "We best talk business, *chiquita*. We got problems. "

"Business?" Ravenna stuck her two index fingers behind the waistband of Hondo's pants and returned the tug. "But I just got here, and I smell like Chico. I must have a bath. *Vamos!*" She grabbed his hand and jerked him along behind her as she mounted the veranda. "We'll take one together, Charlie! It'll be fun. *You'll see!*"

She laughed and dashed into the cabin. Unable to resist such a delectable creature, and forgetting for the moment that she could send him to the devil's own Hell in pieces, he ran in after her and closed and locked the door behind them.

One-Eye and the others could sleep in the barn.

Chapter 14

. . . .

HATHAWAY

As the dragon careened toward him and Angel, Uriah Zane raised his Henry repeater to his shoulder, took hasty aim, and fired.

He didn't wait to see if his paltry round had any effect on the beast, but swung around and followed Angel back into the crease between the rounded mounds of ancient lava. He'd only just pulled his left foot behind the cover, when a great rumbling and *whoosh* sounded and orange flames licked over the top of the dyke, curling down its sides to within a few feet of Zane and Angel.

The heat was like that of blacksmith's fully stoked bellows, and it smelled like brimstone.

"Uriah!" Angel shouted, ducking into a two-foot-high notch cave at the very base of the dyke.

Zane threw his big body down and rolled into the notch

behind the redhead just as another stout, roiling lance of fire hammered into the ground behind him. He rolled away from the flames that curled a few inches into the gap. He half rolled on top of Angel, shielding her body with his own. There was a great rushing of wings, and as the smell of scorched earth permeated the cave, what sounded like the squeals of an enraged pig rattled Zane's eardrums.

He gritted his teeth against it. Her face turned toward his, Angel did the same.

The squeals dwindled into the distance, as did the rushing of the wings.

"Christ!" Angel said.

"Not even close."

Zane started to roll away from her. She grabbed his arm. "Wait. It might be circling."

"I'll see."

Her face reddened in anger, making the hooked scar beneath her eye turn pale. "Give it another minute, goddamnit, Uriah! We know nothing about those . . ."

She let her voice trail off. Zane, ignoring her as he usually did, had rolled out of the notch cave and, on one knee, holding his Henry in his hands, surveyed the skies. All clear. The ground around him—the sand, gravel, sparse tufts of sage and Spanish bayonet—were black and smoking.

"It's clear."

Angel rolled out and climbed to her knees, looking around. Zane remained there, too, scowling up at the blue sky, wondering if he'd really seen what he thought he had.

He'd heard the legends, of course. What kid hadn't? A few people claimed to have seen such winged dinosaurs, but none of the stories had ever been corroborated. But then, when he'd been a kid growing up on his father's plantation west of Charlotte, blood-swillers and shapeshifters had been legends, too. They'd been thought to exist only in Europe and isolated pockets here and there about the West, but few white men had yet seen them.

For him, tales of the shapeshifters from faraway lands had dissolved in a cold rush of bloody reality that night in the hollows of the hills near Gettysburg, when Grant and Buford had turned loose their recruited horde of werewolves.

Zane gave a shudder, remembering that awful night, seeing the man-beasts—wolves twice the normal size and with vaguely man-shaped heads but wolflike fangs and claws—running upright and storming into the Confederate bivouacs even as the pickets screamed and fired on them with their crude trapdoor Springfields, and soldiers poured out of their tents in terrified confusion, thinking it was the blue bellies attacking at night.

In just a few hours, every Confederate soldier save a lucky few, like Zane himself, wounded earlier that day by a Union minié ball to the neck, had been ripped to bleeding piles of viscera steaming in the full moon's pearl light. Zane's own brother, Zachary, had been one of those piles. . . .

"Where are the horses?" Angel said after a time, breaking the pregnant, eerie silence.

Zane heard her as though she were a half mile away. He was still staring at the sky, hearing the howls, snarls, and squeals of his doomed Southern brethren.

Angel placed her hand on his forearm. "Uriah."

He turned to her sharply, startled. "What?"

"Did you see the horses?"

Zane looked around. He'd forgotten about them. He didn't

think they'd been in the crease between the dykes before he and Angel had fled from the fire-breathing demon. "Must have run off. Good thing." He ran a big hand down his bearded face, pressing away the horrible memories aroused by the beast who'd nearly burned him and Angel to cinders. "I'd hate to be stranded out here afoot with that winged devil flying around."

She closed her fingers a little tighter about his arm. "You okay?"

The question annoyed him. In his line of work, a man didn't have time for the distractions of memory. Furling his brows angrily, he pulled his arm away and said, "Yeah."

He heaved himself to his feet, walked out the opposite end of the notch, and looked around. General Lee and Angel's paint, Cisco, stood a good half mile off, reins dangling as they nervously looked around, twitching their tails, as terrorized by the winged beast as Zane and Angel were. The wheeled casket was still in the palo's tow, looking none the worse for wear.

"What's going on, Uriah?" Angel came up to stand beside him. "You've been hunting spooks longer than I have. You ever see anything like that before?"

"Not since yesterday. Caught a brief glimpse of one, maybe the same one, on the way into Gunnison."

Zane was still squinting up at the sky. A winged giant that spat fire would be one hell of a formidable foe. He doubted even the Gatling gun would be of use against it, unless he could get it in close. But then you had the fire to worry about.

"Till then, I never seen one. Heard somethin', though. . . ."

He tried to remember the story he'd heard a couple of years ago in Mexico.

"Somethin' about a young girl from a wealthy hacienda down

Sonora way . . ." Again, he let his voice trail off and jerked his head to the north, in the direction he and Angel had been traveling. Beyond a low jog of brown hills sounded the muffled snaps of gunfire. In the sky careened a winged figure, a column of orange light angling groundward.

Angel said tonelessly, "It's after somebody else."

Distant screams sounded amid the shrill whinnies of terrified horses.

"Let's go," Zane said, jogging in the direction of his and Angel's horses, resting his rifle on his right shoulder.

He moved fleetly for a big man, and it was all Angel could do to match his long strides. When they gained the horses, they quickly went over the tack, tightening latigo cinches and pack straps that might have come loose when the mounts had fled the dragon. When he was sure that the wheeled coffin was still harnessed properly to General Lee, Zane swung up into his saddle and slid his Henry repeater into its sheath, which was angling forward across his right stirrup, and touched spurs to the palo's flanks.

General Lee had great power in his legs. The stallion bounded off its rear hooves with a shrill whinny, it and the trailing coffin angling northward. Zane stayed wide of the burned Indians and their dead horses, knowing his own horse would be repelled by the stench.

He glanced over his shoulder to see Angel galloping about twenty yards behind him. The woman was a wonder to him. She could be as much female in bed as a man could ever need or want, yet she had the sand of a seasoned frontiersman to boot. He knew she was afraid, because she wasn't crazy—hell, his own guts were pulled in a hard knot—but as she crouched over her paint's neck, her hat brim pulled low against her jade eyes, red hair flying out behind her, she looked more determined than anything else.

But what did Zane expect from the daughter of the famed lawman? She wore his boots well. At least, the boots he'd once worn.

Ahead, as Zane and Angel headed for a notch in the brown, boulder-strewn hills, the shots grew louder but then dwindled as Zane saw the dragon pull off to the northeast. The flapping wings and body merged into a single dot, and then the dot was swallowed up by the sky, leaving Zane to clench his belly tight as he wondered what devastation it had left in its wake.

Rising smoke told him where to head, and, following a crease between the rocky hills, he came to a broad bowl cut into the side of a high bluff. Here, horses and men lay scorched and sizzling, strewn about the rocks and brush of the bowl as though, like the Indians, they'd been dropped from the sky. Zane rode ahead, and Angel followed suit, widening the gap between them as they both surveyed the carnage.

Most of the horses and bodies were charred beyond recognition, but Zane saw a sleeve on one of the cadavers that was burned down to the charred bone, smoke slithering out its eye sockets. The sleeve was blue wool and had a cavalry sergeant's three bars worn point down on it. Elsewhere, Zane saw a blue cavalry kepi and a mule-eared, low-heeled, stovepipe cavalry boot with a smoking black leg bone sticking up out of it. On a horse's wither he saw the customary U.S. brand.

Zane had ridden only halfway through the carnage before his eyes were aching from the stench of burned flesh, leather, and horsehide combined with the dragon smell of brimstone he'd noted before.

"There must be twenty soldiers here, Uriah." Angel's voice was muffled by the red neckerchief she held to her mouth and nose. She stopped her paint beside a boulder near which another horse, its burned rider's right leg poking from beneath it, smoked and sizzled, the belly expanding and contracting from the gases inside. "They must be out of Fort Saber near Socorro."

"This is Abner Dean's command."

"Who?"

"Buddy of mine. Captain of the first cavalry who rides patrol around here." Zane looked at a horse and a charred black skeleton several yards to his left. "A good man, for a blue belly. Poor bastard didn't know what hit him."

"Hold it right there!"

Zane snapped his head around, trying pinpoint the owner of the burly voice. His eyes stopped on a short, portly black gent in buckskins and blue cavalry hat standing in a deep notch in an escarpment against the base of the bluff. He was round-faced, and his woolly black beard was liberally sprinkled with gray. He held a Sharps carbine to his shoulder and was squinting as he aimed down the barrel.

"One wrong move out of either one of you, I'll drill ya good, kick ya out with a cold shovel!"

Zane studied the black man. "Who the hell are you?"

"Scout. Ride over here, both of ya." He added with menace, "*Slow.* And keep them hands where I can see 'em."

Zane and Angel shared a glance, then moved their horses forward across the hollow. They halted near the mouth of the ravine where the short, stocky black man stood, aiming his cocked carbine, coffee-brown cheeks bunched as he squinted against the sun.

Angel glanced in revulsion at the carnage around them. "Put the gun down, mister. You overestimate us if you think we did this."

Zane, within twelve feet of the man with the rifle, could see that despite the rough features and smoke-stained buckskins bespeaking a man of a long career on the Western frontier, the officer was as stunned by the bizarre happening here as Zane and Angel were. His chocolate eyes were rheumy and uncertain—an uncustomary look for the man, obviously. Like the wolfer and the marshal, he was as frightened as a kid just run out of a haunted house by an ax-wielding blood-swiller.

"I seen it." The black man mashed his lips together inside his thick, curly beard. He seemed a little incredulous about the rifle, but he was too stunned to lower it.

Vaguely, he wanted to put human or known ghoul form to the killings. Humans, swillers, and the like were more easily understood, more easily held responsible for their actions than that winged, fire-breathing, man-incinerating creature known only in fairy tales.

He said in his deep, quavering voice, "Don't know if I believe what I saw. I take it you seen it, too?" The skin above the bridge of his freckled, wedge-shaped nose wrinkled.

"We saw it," Zane said. "Saw it a while ago, too. It took out a passel of Apaches on our trail. Torched 'em just like Abner Dean's boys."

The black man lowered his rifle to hip level, keeping it aimed in the general direction of Zane and Angel, canting his head to one side. His buckskin shirt was sleeveless, and his black upper arms hung like slabs of charred beef at his sides. "You knew Dean?"

"That's right. When he was stationed at Fort Bowie, I rode scout for him against a pack of Injun swillers in the Chiricahuas. I'm Uriah Zane. This here's Angel Coffin, deputy U.S. marshal out of Denver."

"I'm done having that carbine aimed at me, mister," Angel said tightly.

He depressed the Sharps's hammer and raised the barrel, pressing the stock against his double cartridge belts from which several knives and pistols jutted. A thin smile parted his cracked, pink lips, and his weary eyes flashed in recognition. "You got your father's disposition, Marshal Coffin."

Angel frowned.

"You don't remember. I don't blame you. I was your father's deputy when he was sheriff o' Julesburg." He patted his hard, black belly angling roundly out from behind his worn buckskin shirt trimmed with Indian designs that Zane recognized as Coyotero. "And I was, oh, about fifty pounds lighter."

"Alpheus Hathaway!" Angel's face lit up, white teeth flashing, as she swung down from her saddle and ran into the broad arms of the burly Army scout.

He laughed and held her tightly, patting her back. His face sobered quickly, and he glanced from Zane to the burning shrubs and charred bodies around them, the stench not so bad here as the breeze was out of the north. "Sorry place for a reunion, huh, girl?"

Angel pulled away from him, following his gaze, her own smile fading quickly, as well. "At least twenty men, Al."

"Twenty-three. I rode with 'em as chief packer and scout. I was ridin' ahead, as the Lipans been on the prod of late, though it wasn't the 'Paches we was after. We was headed for Hellsgarde

Penitentiary over in Devil's Canyon." He canted his head to indicate southwest, talking to Zane now, too. "I was up there on the saddle, headin' back this way, when I seen the bird."

He shook his head and looked truly befuddled, almost out of his mind in confusion and bereavement. "A fire-breathin' bird."

"A dragon," Angel said softly, as though to herself, as she looked around.

"Yessir. As real now as the blood-swillers and shape-shiftin' wolves from across the ocean. What's the frontier comin' to?" Hathaway looked at Zane, furling his brows. "It's almost like Hell's doors done opened again, just like they did back in sixty-three, lettin' ghouls from our worst nightmares out."

He paused, grimaced sadly. "I'd like to bury these boys. But there's no time. We was headed for Hellsgarde. Been a break there."

"Nah," Zane said. "Not possible. Hellsgarde's an impregnable castle. Hell, Devil's Canyon itself allows no way in or out except through a stout steel-mesh door."

"That's what I said when Major Dean told me about it, and signed me up to scout the expedition." Hathaway studied Zane. "You're Uriah Zane."

"That's right."

"I'd recognize you anywhere, Mr. Zane." Hathaway walked over and extended his hand, and Zane shook it. "Pleased to make your acquaintance. You'll be interested to know that the four survivin' Hell's Angels broke out of Hellsgarde. Three broke in, broke Charlie Hondo out."

Zane straightened in his saddle, stared at the man as though he'd spoken in a foreign tongue. Rage bit him like an Apache arrow. Rage and fear. That the man who had led the wolf pack that had wiped out several Confederate companies including his brother and several cousins and an uncle was free, was beyond belief.

He hardened his jaws and shook his head. Suddenly, he neck-reined General Lee around, ground his heels into the horse's flanks, and bounded off at a dead gallop toward the blue, serrated ridges of the San Juan Mountains rising in the west.

Chapter 15

A BREED OF FLYIN' CRITTER

Zane checked General Lee down after a quarter-mile sprint, realizing that killing his prized horse wouldn't get him to Hells-garde. Gradually, Angel and Hathaway, who rode a tall and surprisingly quiet gunmetal-gray mule, caught up to him and kept pace to either side of him.

"How'd it happen, Hathaway?" Zane asked the cavalry scout.

"Don't know the answer to that question, Mr. Zane. All I know is most of the guards was killed, but they sent a telegraph message to the fort yesterday, asking for help to track the killers down and manpower to keep the rest of the ghouls in their cages."

"Any others get away?"

"Don't believe so. Three Angels were hauled through the gates in a jail wagon, though no one knew they was Angels. Didn't even know they was ghouls. Killed some federal badge toters to get themselves hauled to Hellsgarde, then shapeshifted soon as they got inside the main door, sprang Charlie Hondo, killed the warden and a passel of guards."

"They changed in broad daylight?" Angel was dubious. No ghouls were ever hauled by night. Not on any night.

"That how I understood it, Miss Angel."

Zane said, "How'd they get out the tunnel? You couldn't drive a Baldwin locomotive under full steam through those bars. And not even a ghoul could climb those canyon walls."

"Don't know the answer to that, Mr. Zane. The message that come in didn't tell us much, just to fog the trail out to Hellsgarde as fast as we could."

"You can call me Uriah."

"All right. An' I'm Al. What do you suppose ole Charlie's intentions are now that he's free?"

"No tellin'," Angel said, riding on the other side of Zane. "But I'd bet the seed bull he's not aimin' to start a church."

They pushed their horses hard toward the steep ridge wall behind which the appropriately named Devil's Canyon and Hellsgarde prison lay.

The ridge stood tall and dark and fittingly ominous, owning the shape of a black-scorched sawtooth blade. While they'd spotted the ridge not far from where they'd met Hathaway, the formation rose before them slowly across the cedar-stippled flat scored with sudden arroyos and pocked with low bluffs. Slowly, the pits and troughs and fissures in the ridge's sheer wall gained shape and dimension.

The October sun hammered down, and the day grew hot.

The air smelled of greasewood and sage, and there were occasional tinges of blossoming autumn wildflowers. The sky, to the group's relief, remained free of dragons.

When the trio had slowed their mounts after a long lope, giving them a rest, Angel swung her paint up beside Hathaway's mule, which the black scout called Annabelle and which he'd been riding for nearly six years, preferring the mule's bottom and sure-footedness over what he called the clumsiness and unreliability of horses.

"Sure is nice to see you again, Al," Angel said. "Though I wish it were under better circumstances."

"Them boys didn't deserve to die like that. Personally, I'd like to give that bird about twelve rounds of twelve-gauge buck, if I ever see him again." Hathaway patted the long, double-barreled shotgun that rode in a saddle sheath on the opposite side from his rifle. Like most frontiersmen, he also had a cross-bow lashed to his saddle, draped across one of his saddlebag pouches, the flap of which was stamped u.s. He frowned apprehensively. "Why is it I have a feeling I will?"

"Why is it I have a feeling that twelve rounds of twelve-gauge buck won't bring it down?"

Hathaway glowered, then, as he studied the young woman he'd known long ago, gave a low whistle. "Look at you. The last time I seen you, you was in pigtails and tendin' chickens behind you and your pa's house when you weren't out trying to bring down sage hens with your slingshot. Now . . . why, you're a full-grown woman."

He grinned brashly, showing a nearly full set of large, white teeth. "With all the curves to prove it!"

Angel colored with embarrassment.

Hathaway glanced over at Zane. "Ain't she a fine-lookin' woman?"

Zane glanced over at Angel, who did not look at him. "About the finest I've seen."

"I know it ain't none of my business, but are you two . . . ?"

"Hell, no," Angel said too quickly. Then, to soften it: "You best get yourself under rein, Mr. Hathaway. I'm also a federal marshal and I do not cotton to bein' harassed by an old saddle tramp."

Hathaway shifted his questioning gaze between Zane and Angel, then chuckled uneasily.

After a time, as they rode straight toward the ridge, following the wagon trail they'd picked up several miles back, he said without looking at Angel, "Again, this ain't none of my business, but any word about your pa?"

"No."

Zane hadn't expected her to elaborate, as she rarely spoke of her father since the respected lawman James Coffin had been turned into a swiller by a pack haunting the Missouri River breaks up in Dakota. They had attacked him and two other federal marshals when they were investigating illegal shipments of whiskey to the Sioux reservation near Bismarck. So he was surprised now to hear her say, "Last I heard he was spotted in Montana. That was two years ago. He sent me a letter once, but I didn't open it."

"Why not?"

"He's a killer, Al. There's a high bounty on his head. Like most, he just can't resist human blood. Even if he could, once they've changed, they're no longer the people they were." She turned her head slightly to give Zane a quick, sidelong glance.

He was glad when they saw the tunnel mouth at the bottom of the ridge, and the six or seven soldiers milling around a Gatling gun on a tripod aimed straight into the hand-hewn and dynamite-blasted cavern. Two others were hunkered in rocks on both sides of the trail, sitting smoking against the rocks until one swung his head toward Zane's group and whistled at the guard on the other side of the trail from him. Both soldiers jerked to life and grabbed their carbines.

"Who goes there?" shouted the young soldier on one knee atop a boulder on the trail's right side. They were skittish as hell.

Angel called, "I'm a deputy United States marshal. We got word of the attack on the prison and are here to investigate. Who's in charge?"

The rifle-wielding guards glanced at each other. Another swung the Gatling gun around on its wooden tripod, and aimed the six-barreled weapon at the group.

"You're not gonna need that, fellas," Angel said. "I have stamped papers in my saddlebags. With me are Uriah Zane and Alpheus Hathaway, and I'll vouch for both."

The guards lowered their rifles only slightly, glancing at one another nervously, and came skipping down the rock piles, leaping onto the trail. One was tall and skinny, a quirley smoldering between his lips. The other was medium tall, paunchy, with curly orange hair puffing out from beneath his tan kepi.

He waved the group over, and Angel took the lead as she, Zane, and Hathaway rode up to the young guards. Angel slowly reached back to dig around in a saddlebag pouch, and showed the guard her papers encased in a small leather portfolio.

When the guard seemed satisfied with the documents, he

gestured to the others to stand down. Zane rode up to the cave mouth, where the other soldiers were slowly, almost reluctantly lowering their rifles. They were all young and bright-eyed, and their muscles seemed to jerk under their ill-fitting uniforms.

Zane turned to the soldier manning the Gatling gun. "How in the hell did those ghouls bust through the tunnel?"

"Didn't bust through it," said the guard in a faintly sulking tone, turning toward the tunnel mouth. "That flyin' devil melted the door."

Zane swung down from General Lee's back and, ground-reining the palomino, walked over to the tunnel mouth, gazing at the ground. His heart skipped a beat.

When he'd first seen it, he'd thought that the material littering the cave mouth was a large mud puddle from a nearby spring. But now he saw that the hardened, twisted sheets of melted steel were all that remained of the door that the government had promised was absolutely indestructible to any and all forces, be they men or beasts. It had been built of the stoutest grade of steel found anywhere in the world. Stronger even than its own density in stone.

Hathaway and Angel rode up behind Zane and looked down at the mass of melted minerals.

"Holy hob," said Hathaway, removing his floppy-brimmed black hat and scratching his head slowly. "I guess we know what kind o' flyin' critters done that—don't we, pards?"

"I reckon we do," Angel said, casting an anxious glance at the sky.

Chapter 16

. . . .

THE COVEN

Lieutenant Andrew Jackson McAlpine, assistant warden of Hellsgarde Penitentiary, scratched a match to life on the surface of the late Warden Mondrick's broad desk and, with fingers shaking as badly as if he were aboard a train traversing a stretch of bad track, touched the fire to his long, black cigar.

Leaning forward in the late warden's leather-upholstered swivel chair, he planted his elbows on the desk and blew smoke out his nostrils as he tossed the stove match into an ashtray carved in the form of a bear's open paw, and thumbed his spectacles up his long, slender nose.

"You have any idea what it's like here now?" he said, his voice quaking as badly as his hands. "I have just barely enough men to run this place, let alone keep the two hundred and fifty ghouls housed here under lock and key."

"I'm sure you're under a lot of stress," said Angel.

"Stress?" Warden McAlpine chuckled without mirth and lifted a brandy snifter to his lips. He swallowed, making a pained expression. "No, it's far from stressful wondering when one of the bastards is going to get loose and suck your blood and turn you into one of them. 'Horrifying' is a better word. I just hope, when it happens, and it will surely happen if I don't get some *fucking support out here, goddamnit!*"—he punched the top of the warden's desk so hard his spectacles slid down his nose and the Tiffany lamp rattled—"that they just tear my throat out and let me die!"

"Easy, partner," Uriah said from where he stood at a casement window, one elbow propped atop the coping as he smoked a tightly rolled quirley of strong Mexican tobacco and sipped the late warden's whiskey from a water glass. "Givin' yourself a heart stroke ain't gonna make the situation any easier."

"Sorry the soldiers didn't make it, Lieutenant," said Hathaway. "Sounds like we ran into the same winged devils that attacked the castle." The black scout sat in an overstuffed leather couch near the oak door at the back of the large room outfitted with game trophies, maps, and heavy, exotic wooden furniture acquired during Warden Mondrick's hunting adventures throughout the world. He'd been a prominent member of Lincoln's and then Sherman's cabinets and, since he had no wife or family and didn't mind living beyond society's fringe, had volunteered for the warden position at Hellsgarde.

Zane doubted that that was the case with McAlpine. The young assistant warden looked ready to resign and gallop back East just as soon as he could.

A fire danced and crackled in a fieldstone hearth. Mondrick had tried to make the office as homey and familiar as he could in an attempt, most likely, to assuage the fact that he was surrounded by screaming devils, any one of whom who would send him to Hell if they ever got their talons or claws into him.

And one eventually had. . . . Hondo had even taken the man's clothes.

"If the courier gets through," Angel said, sitting in the visitor's chair angled in front of the desk and turning her own brandy snifter in her fingers, "Major Dean will send more men. I'm sure more will be coming from Fort Reynolds, as well. We'll find a way to handle those dragons, just like we've found ways to handle everything else."

"Yes, everything else." McAlpine curled his upper lip and, drawing a deep, calming breath, sagged back in his chair. "I know this isn't the ascribed view, but why the hell not kill them all? Kill them all now before they all get away!" He threw back the last of his brandy and, fumbling with the cut-glass decanter on his desk, refilled it.

"Don't want to make the situation any worse than it already is," Hathaway reminded the man. He sucked on a fat stogie from the warden's humidor, blowing a large smoke ring. "Part of me wants to agree with you, though, Lieutenant. Especially after what happened to my detail. Sooner or later, somethin' real bad's gonna happen because we got so damn many o' 'em all over the West. And now we got some we didn't even know we had."

His heavy, rounded shoulders jerked as he chuckled fatefully, shaking his head. He was thinking, of course, about the dragon.

"Look, we can discuss politics all we want," Zane said, blowing a lungful of cigarette smoke out the open casement window, looking out over the scorched yard that had only recently been cleared of charred, dead soldiers, "but what we really need is to haul ass out of here and try to cut Charlie's sign."

"It's too late in the day, Uriah," Angel said wearily, showing her own frustration. "We're gonna have to hole up here for the night whether we like it or not. The sun'll be down soon."

Zane blew a smoke plume out the window over the darkening yard. Angel was right. It was too late in the day to start out. They and their horses needed food and a good night's sleep.

But he had a dark feeling, whether due to his recently acquired and troubling condition or not, that something bad was going to happen, and the chance of that occurring grew by leaps and bounds with every minute Charlie Hondo and his men were running off their leashes. If he'd had hackles at that moment, they'd have been raised.

"You have somewhere we can bunk?" Angel asked the lieutenant.

"Sure, sure. We have an entire wing for visitors, if you'll pardon the ghouls' screams, which tend to pick up after midnight but begin to fade slightly after three." McAlpine blinked slowly. "I'll send someone to make sure the beds are made. You can dine with me, if you like, in the warden's quarters. Thank heavens none of the cooks were burned to ashes. Little good they'd do if we were under siege again—most being women."

"You'd be surprised what a woman can do with the right weapons, Lieutenant," Angel said crisply, throwing back her brandy.

McAlpine, a pale, light-skinned man with large ears and pomaded hair, looked chagrined.

Zane took another puff of the pungent Mexican tobacco he liked so well for the peppery tang it left in his throat, and blew the smoke into the room as he said, "Does the name Elaina Baranova ring a bell with you, Lieutenant?"

McAlpine looked at him, the lines of weariness in his fore-head cutting deeper. "Of course. Our resident black sorceress, one of three we have imprisoned here. We call her 'the queen' because she acts like one and seems to carry the respect of nobil-ity among the other ghouls. Oh, God, why bring her up now?"

"I'd like to speak with her privately."

Angel threw back the last of her brandy. "Why? Who is she?"

"Oh, that won't be possible, I'm afraid, Mr. Zane. No one speaks privately with any of the prisoners here. All conversations must be overheard by second and third non-ghoul parties out of fear, of course, of spells being exchanged or imparted." He spoke that last as though reading the words out of a regulation manual.

"All right, you can join us. But I would like to speak to her."

"Uriah . . ." Angel said.

"I'll tell you later."

"If you're to speak with 'the queen,' Mr. Zane, we'll need a third party in addition to a couple official jailers. I'll summon them in the morning."

Zane flicked his cigarette butt out the window. "We're pul-lin' out first thing in the morning. I'd like to speak to her now."

Angel hiked a shoulder. "I'll be that third party, Lieutenant. If Zane thinks it's important to talk to the witch, I'd like to hear what she has to say."

"You don't want to go in there," Zane said.

"Why wouldn't I?"

"Look, look," said McAlpine, looking pained. "I would rather do this tomorrow, Mr. Zane. My nerves are all leaping up and down my spine, and—"

"I need to talk to her tonight, Lieutenant."

"Good God, man, *why?*"

"She could save us a whole lot of time and make a big difference to whether we catch up with old Charlie Hondo or not."

They all stared at him.

Hathaway broke the silence after blowing another smoke ring. "Well, hell." He stubbed his stogie out in an ashtray on the sofa beside him. "I reckon I'll trail along, too. Me, I'm partial to witches myself. Had one put a hex on all three of my ex-wives."

Half-drunk, he grinned.

McAlpine summoned a couple of jailers armed with carbines and stone talismans draped around their necks, which some believed would ward off spells and incantations of doom founded in the darker forms of known magic.

They were a burly pair, tough-nut soldiers who'd survived the War and who obviously prided themselves on having the courage it took to guard the ghouls at Hellsgarde. They wore sweat-stained sombreros with the brims turned up in front and fastened to the crowns, cavalry-fashion. Each carried a Model '67 Winchester carbine, and in addition to the talismans, they wore bandoliers of both brass and silver, though there were no werebeasts of any stripe in the Witches' Wing of Hellsgarde.

Crossbows dangled from their hips. Several knives of different shapes and sizes bristled about their uniforms.

The wing was on the opposite side of the castle, and the two gravely silent guards, holding flaming torches aloft, led Lieutenant McAlpine, Zane, Angel, and Hathaway down endless stone cavern-like corridors lit with flickering torches. Their boots clacked and chinged on the cracked, heaving stones. The warden shamelessly cradled the cut-glass brandy decanter to his chest, as though it were a suckling baby, and took occasional pulls directly from the bottle.

No cells opened onto this main, circuitous artery through the bowels of the castle, but eerie sounds of all pitches emanated from the thick stone walls, almost as though the walls themselves were making them. Occasionally, Zane could feel a vibration in the floor beneath his boots.

Once, he put his hand on the wall and felt the shudder there, as well. He remembered the cave in which he and Junius Webb had found the high-brow swillers, and the hair on the back of his neck pricked. He almost wished he'd fortified himself with one more shot of whiskey. Odd, he vaguely thought, that as a ghoul himself he'd be so squeamish.

He gently closed his fist, shutting away the thought as he believed he'd closed off that dark side of himself, forever able to keep it from reaching the light of a full moon as it had but only once in the year since he'd been bitten.

When they came to intersecting corridors, they stopped in front of two broad, timbered, iron-banded doors. Overhead lay a wood sign on which WITCHES COVEN had been burned. While one of the guards fumbled with a key ring, Zane glanced to his left and saw several barred doors opening off both sides of the corridor. Cells, most likely.

What else could they be? He looked down the right corridor and saw the same thing—more doors.

Ghouls of some sort must lurk inside, though there were no sounds here but the murmurings in the rock walls and the clatter of the keys on the heavy iron ring. There was also the gurgle of liquid as Lieutenant McAlpine threw back another slug of the brandy. Chairs on either side of the door the guard was unlocking said that guards were customarily posted here, but due to the sudden lack of manpower at Hellsgarde, they were probably all out guarding the canyon to make sure no spooks got out.

Or in again.

The locking bolt clicked. The guard opened the heavy door that rocked back slowly, like the door of a vault, on stout hinges. Unexpectedly, a pleasing odor, a homey odor, wafted into the dank hall from beyond the door, and as one of the guards led the company into the room beyond while the other closed and locked the door behind them, Zane was surprised to find himself in a large room outfitted much like the first floor of a cozy albeit modest house in your typical frontier town.

One in which supper was being cooked. The smell of fried liver lay thick in the pent-up air.

There were two rooms partitioned off from each other by a crude-hewn set of stacked cupboards, a sitting area with comfortable chairs and a fainting couch to the left, and a kitchen with a cloth-covered table and a black range to the right. Two lumpy old women in shapeless dresses, heavy shoes, and aprons were cooking in the kitchen while—Zane blinked and felt his hand edge toward the butt of the Colt Navy slanting across his belly—a sleek black puma lounged on a braided rope rug before a snapping fire in a fieldstone hearth.

In front of him and the warden, the burly guard stepped back, pivoted on his hips to face the cat, and cocked his Winchester loudly.

The deputy warden made a gurgling sound in his throat and pointed at the beast sitting there as though on a sunny slope, slowly flicking its tail, yellow eyes shiny with reflected fire and lamplight. "She . . . G-goddamnit! She's not supposed to do that!"

The old woman forking beef liver around in a sputtering pan turned to see the cat, and said in a scolding tone, *"Elain-ahh!"*

Throaty laughter sounded a half second before the cat on the rug sort of melted, waxlike, shifting its shape to become a beautiful, blue-eyed brunette with gold hoop earrings and a high-busted, full-hipped figure in a green velvet dress trimmed in wolf fur. Lounging on the rug before the fire, her long legs curled beneath her, Elaina Baranova threw her head back and laughed her hoarse, husky laugh, showing all her white teeth glistening like porcelain between full, red-painted lips. Her blue eyes, which owned a Slavic slant in a heart-shaped face, shone like polished marble.

"Miss Baronova, you've been warned countless times against shape-shifting, and if this . . ."

"I do apologize, Lieutenant McAlpine," Elaina said, though her exotic eyes were riveted on Zane with the zeal of a stalking huntress, "but a girl gets bored, you know. I don't shift my shape regularly but just to get the guards' goat."

Her lips stretched pleasingly. "Zane." She almost whispered it, scrutinizing him as though he, too, were a figure that might shift and be suddenly gone or merely a figment of her imagination.

"Hello, Elaina," Zane said. "Been a while."

Her bosom heaved behind the dress, the cleavage-baring neckline of which was fringed with wolf fur as black as the puma she'd just been. She slid her eyes from Zane to the others, her gaze lingering on Angel.

"Well, you certainly bring a crowd, don't you?"

"Yes," Angel said coolly, her own eyes appraising the strangely beautiful woman before her. "He does."

Chapter 17

· · · · · · · · · · · · ·

ELAINA BARONOVA

Elaina's long, slanted eyes narrowed with a feline-like knowingness as she said, sliding her gaze from Angel back to Zane, "She's jealous."

Angel snorted. "Like hell. Uriah and I are after Charlie Hondo and the ghouls who broke him out of here. We'd just like to ask you a few questions, if—"

"Red." Zane looked at her sharply. "Let me handle this."

"Handle what? I certainly never expected to see you again, not after I ended up here on a handful of rumors and innuendo that spread like a wildfire around New Orleans." Tears shone in Elaina's eyes, and her lip trembled a little as she said, "Crowd or not, it is good to see you again, Uriah."

McAlpine turned to Zane. "How well do you two know each other, anyway?"

"Lieutenant, let us have a minute, will you?" McAlpine began to object but Zane interrupted him with, "I know it's against regulations. But I believe Miss Baronova has some information about the folks who busted Hondo out of here, and if we want him back in his cage, I need a moment alone with Elaina. It could be the difference."

McAlpine slid his eyes between the pair, then drew a sharp, resigned breath. "All right, all right. It's against regulations but I don't hope to be here much longer, anyway. And I reckon things couldn't really get much worse than they already are."

He canted his head toward a curtained doorway in the middle of the back wall. "You have five minutes. No weird stuff. If she were to loose some spell she's privy to, it wouldn't do much good for us to have her locked up in the first place, would it?"

"Elaina?" Zane said.

"Anything you want, Uriah. Just wish we had more time." She quirked her lips devilishly as she glanced at Angel, who regarded the witch blandly.

Elaina walked to the curtained doorway, her long, green crinoline skirts rustling softly across the floor carpeted in a deep, plush, wine-red rug without any design whatsoever, due, most likely, to the government's fear that Elaina and the other two sorceresses might turn one into a talisman of sorts.

Zane followed the Russian witch through the curtain and found himself in a room not nearly as well outfitted as the two he'd just left. In fact, it was a jail cage with two large cots in it, all appointed with heavy skins and furs. There were only two windows, hardly larger than rifle slots, high up in the walls.

The curtain had just barely fallen back into place before Elaina spun around, hair and skirts flying, and flung her arms around Zane's neck, pressing her soft lips to his. At first, he resisted. But even with Angel in the next room, he couldn't resist an embrace from his old lover Elaina Baronova, witch that she had turned out to be. A deadly witch, he well knew. But one who he hoped was still in love with him.

They'd met when Zane had taken a riverboat to New Orleans hunting Cajun ghouls and ended up spending the long, rainy winter there.

As he mashed his own lips against hers, feeling her suck at him gently, her saliva warm and tasting as he remembered it had when they were about five years younger and holing up in one of the brothels owned by Elaina's father, himself a medium, who had built a nice stake before the War operating a circus and traveling carnival show throughout Louisiana and Texas that specialized in fortune-telling.

She pulled her head back slightly, then rubbed her nose against his. "Did you come to spring your witch, Uriah Zane?"

"I came to ask for your help."

Vaguely, he was wondering if she'd noted the change in him, but nothing registered in her eyes, and he thought that a good thing. Maybe he'd suppressed it so far that not even a witch of Elaina's caliber could detect it.

"Anything for you, Uriah." She leaned into him, pressing her breasts lightly against his chest and resting her wrists on his shoulders. "You know that. You tried to save me once, made a genuine effort to make an honest witch out of me, and I was too pigheaded to listen. Thus, I am fated to remain here with those two old crones whose powers can't hold a candle to mine, for the rest of my life."

She brushed her lips once more across his. "Or until you rescue me."

Zane placed his hands on her wrists, gave them an affection-ate squeeze. She was as wicked as they came. She'd wielded her powers with aplomb in New Orleans, gaining power over her father's competitors and even casting a spell to turn one into a spider, which she then crushed beneath her shoe. So she'd been incarcerated here in Hellsgarde, a prison reserved for only those most diabolical of witches who, unable to resist their own pow-ers, had proved beyond rehabilitation. She'd have been hanged if there'd been a judge brave enough to pass sentence on her.

Still, Zane felt a pull toward her. Before he'd known what she was, they'd had a wonderful couple of rainy months in each other's arms.

Knowing he didn't have much time, he leaped to the point of his visit. "Who helped those three wolves rescue Charlie Hondo, Elaina? Who's the dragon-speaker?"

"Something tells me you already know the answer to that question, Uriah."

"Ravenna?"

"That's right." Admiration shone like guttering candles in Elaina's long eyes. "The god Elyhann has taught her very well. Makes me jealous."

"Oh, you didn't do too bad."

She stepped back and crossed her arms on her breasts. "Dragon conjuring. Even I have to admire such gall. Elyhann never cast such spells my way, and that truly does gravel me, Uriah. Oh, the fun I could have had!"

"Maybe you didn't ask."

"I shouldn't have had to ask. Ravenna . . . I have to admit that her harsh upbringing in Mexico, where witches are tolerated even less than here, made her riper pickings for Elyhann. Whatever the reason, if you're going after Charlie Hondo, Uriah, tread carefully. Ravenna has used the black powers of the meanest demon in Hell to her best advantage. There will be more tricks up her sleeve besides dragons."

"Why? Why would Ravenna help the Hell's Angels?"

"Charlie Hondo, you know, is a rakish ole devil. There's just something about a man who gets a nasty need for a shave every full moon. But Ravenna is a girl of opportunity, if she's anything, so I doubt it's merely sex or love. I really couldn't tell you, Uriah. But if he threw in with Ravenna to get him out of Hellsgarde, I'd bet my papa's last whorehouse that their partnership goes beyond the prison break. They've partnered up for a good, dark reason. She needs Charlie, and he needs her."

She dug her fingers into her arms. "It give me the shivers just thinking about it. So much power in a vessel even less restrained than myself."

"You know that Charlie and his pards turned several hours before the full moon rose, don't you?"

Elaina winked. "Like I said, Ravenna has some mighty powers, Uriah. Takes quite a woman to haze a dragon around the skies and to allow shapeshifters to shift at will. I'm betting that her powers are a little sapped, however. If you're going to catch up to them, it had better be soon, before she has time to replenish herself. No witch in human form, not even Ravenna, can stay strong forever."

"You have no idea where they're headed or why?"

Elaina's eyes became oddly uncertain as they dropped to Uriah's chest. The skin above the bridge of her nose wrinkled. "I tried to tap into that, but without my cards and amulets it's very difficult. The guards even scour this place for spiders! I did get a feeling, though, Uriah." She looked up at him, her eyes still apprehensive.

He waited.

"I felt that she's been sent by Elyhann herself. That Elyhann wants something . . ."

"What?"

"I don't know—maybe his favorite, dead son, Eurico—"

"Eurico?"

"Yes," Elaina said. "The Lord of Darkness. The long-dead werewolf god, slain by a demon even greater than himself. His death is what caused the werewolves on earth to lose their power—long, long ago—and for the humans to get the upper hand and run them into the proverbial hills."

Zane stared at her, wondering if she were mad as well as demonic.

She gazed back at him, her eyes owning an uncustomary graveness. "If they find what they're looking for . . . and if what they're looking for is the final resting place of Eurico . . ." The tip of her tongue flicked across her lower lip, and her eyes became so fearful that Zane felt a cold, heavy stone drop in his loins. ". . . And if it's true, as legend has it, that Eurico, with the right spell, could be reborn into another vessel, a werewolf vessel . . . it might not mean the end of the world, Uriah, but the start of so much darkness and chaos that we, all of us—humans, magicians, and even some ghouls—will be wishing it were."

Zane pondered this. "You think Hondo and Ravenna are out to resurrect the Lord of Darkness?"

"I don't know." Elaina pursed her lips. "Like I said, my resources are limited here. But if they do resurrect Eurico, it'll mean a return to the old days when the werewolves ruled the earth—night *and* day—and humans—even witches without the power to defy the snarling hordes—will be back cowering in caves."

Zane tugged at his beard. "Personally, I don't much care for cave life. Why, just the other day I found a whole cave full o' . . ." He broke off his own uncustomary nervous chatter. "Oh, well. 'Nough o' that." He kissed the witch's cheek. "Thanks, Elaina."

He began to turn away, but she placed her hands on his face and looked sadly into his eyes. "I'm so sorry, Uriah."

Zane frowned. Then he saw it in her gaze.

He hadn't buried the wolf in himself as deeply as he'd thought he had.

"But it's really not as bad as you think," she added.

A little later that same night but forty-five miles to the southwest, on a cot in the bowels of the Saber Creek Station, Charlie Hondo said as he closed his hands over the breasts of the witch bouncing up and down atop him, "Ravenna, dear, it's kinda hard to give you the full attention you deserve with your dragon staring in the window at me like he's fixin' to turn me into a pile of smoking ashes."

Ravenna stopped bouncing up and down on her knees and shook a thick tangle of hair from her eyes as she turned to the window. Two smoldering eyes shone a few feet beyond the open shutter, the beast's devil-like head silhouetted behind it.

She rapped her hand against the shutter and scolded, "Chico, you randy rascal. Get away! Go on! This is private business! Go find a hollow to curl up in, and I'll see you in the morning!"

The eyes blazed, then dulled, as the head lowered and slowly withdrew against the hulking body behind it. Charlie could hear the crunch of gravel and brush beneath the beast's taloned feet, smell the hot, stony breath and the general, indescribable sweetness and musk of the creature's ungainly body. Oddly, it sort of smelled like burnt squash.

There was a deep-throated groaning sound, and then the beast gained flight and rose up over the desert. The voices of the other three men could be heard in the near distance as they sat around a fire out there. They had finished long ago with the girl, though her screams had taken a long time dying and had added to Charlie's efforts at staying attentive to the rapacious Ravenna.

"Right protective, ain't he?"

"Shh!" Ravenna dropped her rump to his thighs and waggled around on him, sandwiching his face in her beringed hands, pressing her fingers hard against his temples. "Finish me!"

Charlie groaned and squeezed her breasts as she began pummeling him wildly once more.

After he'd brought her to the heights of passion, during which she mewled like a bobcat and fairly shredded his chest to ribbons with her fingernails, she kissed his nose and rolled onto her back beside him. "There is nothing like riding a wolf!" she said huskily, regaining her wind. "I love the savage in you, Charlie."

"I was about to return the compliment, Ravenna."

She chuckled and patted his thigh as she reached over to a crude wooden table beside the bed for two long, thin cigars, one of which she gave to Charlie. He rose up on his butt, adjusted the water-stained, corn-shuck pillow covered in blue-striped ticking, and stuck the cigar between his lips.

Ravenna fired a stove match to life on the table and slid the flame toward Charlie. It danced in her brown eyes. "You like your new powers? To be able to change at will—even during the day? Someday, you will change even when there is no moon to be found!"

As Charlie puffed his cheroot to life, Ravenna lit her own cigar, which was sticking out from between her perfect white teeth.

"Yeah, well, you see, that's what I been meaning to talk to you about, Ravenna." He inspected the cigar's glowing coal and blew smoke out his nostrils. "Ya see, a coupla the boys had a hard time changing a little earlier. Curly Joe made a complete fool o' himself jumpin' off the stage thinkin' he'd be landin' on four feet instead of two. The kid coulda hurt hisself."

Ravenna laughed.

Raw fury boiled up in Charlie. His face darkened, and his eyelids drooped. His jaw hinges dimpled, and he reached over the side of the bed and brought up a big skinning knife he'd found in the station, the blade flashing umber in the light from the little sheet-iron stove burning piñon pine in the corner.

Tossing his stubbed-out cigar on the floor, he rolled toward Ravenna, grabbed a fistful of her hair with one hand, using it to pull her head back hard against her pillow, and slid the knife up tight against her throat.

"Listen, you crazy little *puta* bitch, you make a fool o' Charlie Hondo and I'll be the last wolf you ever ride into ecstasy. You got that?"

Her two brown eyes stared up at him fearlessly.

The fury burned brighter behind Charlie's heart. He was accustomed to his threats evoking fear and trembling in women.

"Back in Dodge, you told me you knew where the Lord of Darkness is buried. You told me you'd not only get me there but see that his powers become mine." Charlie spat through gritted teeth. "Are you just bullshittin' me, Ravenna? Is this all just fun and games to you 'cause you're bored and lookin' to tumble with a werewolf?"

His brows bunched suddenly. A sharp fear shone in Charlie's eyes. He gulped and slowly relaxed his grip on the witch's hair. His palm gripping the horn handle of the skinning knife turned soft and spongy.

Beneath the covers and way down past his belly, there was a sharp pressure against his balls. He couldn't see what was causing such a minor but menacing pain, but he could picture the slender stiletto, no doubt as sharp as Charlie's own knife, snugged up taut against his scrotum.

One twitch of the witch's hand, and he'd be howling in the pitch of a she-bitch forever.

Chapter 18

. . . .

THE POWER OF EURICO

Ravenna kept her placid eyes on him and applied just a little more pressure to his balls.

"You've made a mistake, Charlie." She blinked, quirked her mouth corners menacingly. "Don't let it be your last."

Charlie's heart skipped a beat. He, of course, had been bluffing. He'd just wanted to put some fear into the girl. She, of course, was not bluffing, and appeared to be yearning to stick that pig poker clear through his pelvis till it was showing through his asshole.

What they had here was akin to a Mexican standoff.

"Now, now, *chiquita*," he cautioned, pulling the knife away and releasing her hair, "can't you take a little funnin'?"

"Sometimes my sense of humor is sorely lacking, Charlie." She grinned delightedly and kept the stiletto pressed tight against his balls for several more seconds, which felt to Charlie like hours, before withdrawing it, throwing her covers back, and dropping her feet to the floor.

Naked, full breasts jostling, her skin resembling varnished oak in the fire's umber light, she set the stiletto on the table and walked over to the stove. "I hope I haven't made a mistake about you, Charlie." She stooped to grab a piñon log off the floor beside the stove. "I chose you for this excursion as much as you chose me. In fact, I've been looking for you . . . or a beast like you . . . for years, ever since I learned about Eurico myself. I never wanted you for *you*, Charlie. You fool! I thought you were aware of that." She glanced at him in disbelief. "I wanted you for the *wolf* in you!"

Gruffly, she tossed the wood into the stove, then swung around so that her dark, magnificent body, all its womanly curves silhouetted against the crackling fire behind her, faced him. Gold hoop rings similar to Charlie's own dangled from her ears.

"If you knew the real secrets of Eurico, you would realize that. If you knew the kind of powers Eurico will unleash once we've found his last resting place and I use my powers given to me by Elyhann to awaken him, you would know I would not trifle with you, Charlie."

Charlie studied her, incredulous. He'd known about Eurico since he'd first been turned into a werewolf, when he was six years old, hunting in the forest with his father and brothers, and was bitten by one who lived near their Romanian estate. Most who changed gradually grew aware of Eurico. He was like a soft whisper in your ear, a dream you could never get ahold of.

The desire to learn more could become almost as strong as erotic passion, consuming, filled with the promise that if you could know Eurico—the Lord of Darkness, the *first* beast, the *ruler* of all beasts—the power of all the dark magic in the universe would be yours. That was all Charlie knew.

And now that he knew that the Lord of Darkness was real and could be found somewhere in the known world, he had to find him. This bewitching sorceress, whom he'd met in a smoky saloon in Dodge City during a drunken debauch just days before he'd been run aground by a passel of bounty hunters who recognized his face from wanted circulars, was going to take him to this formidable ruler of all.

He wasn't sure what would happen, but he felt he knew that at least part of Eurico's ancient, formidable power would be within his grasp, and he and his kith would no longer be at the mercy of mortals. Nor the cycle of the moon . . .

"Well, hell," Charlie said, abashed. "Why's our powers growing weaker?"

"Because *I'm* growing weaker." Bewitchingly cupping one of her pointed, upthrust breasts in one hand, she extended a finger at the window near Charlie. "*Cristo!* I conjured Chico up from twelve eons. That takes a lot out of a girl! I am sorry if the powers I provided you and your compadres are weakening, but I am in human form now, and the powers I derive from Elyhann must ooze through my human vessel—splendid as it is."

She walked toward the bed, rolling her hips, breasts and hair jostling as she moved, and sat on the edge of it, bringing one long, dusky leg up beneath her. She leaned toward Charlie, hair spilling over one breast, and smiled brightly in the dimness.

"But when we conjure Eurico, all the black magic in this world and many others will be yours, and you and your kind, Charlie, will not only shapeshift at will but will have the humans cowering beneath their beds for all ages to come. Your kind ruled once and lived in great cities together, before Eurico was defeated by a spirit even darker and more powerful than himself. But that spirit is long dead on a dead world turned to dust so long ago that even the oldest witches no longer remember its spells and hexes. Your kind will rule again. And if all goes as I've planned, you will rule supreme!"

Charlie grinned slowly and placed the cigar between his teeth, leaning back against the wooden headboard. "I like the sound of that." He frowned. "But . . . what do you hope to get from all this, *chiquita*?"

"A witch who can tap into the black magic of Eurico, Charlie, will be the most powerful witch in the world. Wolves and witches, Charlie, will rule the universe." She reached out and placed her hand on his crotch. "Won't we be stomping with our tails up then, *amigo*?"

Charlie started to reach for her but stopped when the rataplan of distant hooves sounded outside. Several horses, moving at a gallop, were hammering along the trail from the west.

Charlie sat up slowly, listening, hearing the voices of his own men grow as the hoof thuds continued getting louder. He looked out the window over the woodstove but could see only the glow of the other men's fire in the front yard and the stars showing faintly in the desert sky beyond.

The hoof thuds stopped, and now unfamiliar voices sounded.

Charlie smiled wolfishly as he leaned back against the headboard once more, crooking an arm behind him. "I reckon the fellas at the next relay station must've gotten around to missin' the stage. Not to worry. Curly Joe, One-Eye, and Lucky'll take care of 'em."

"*Sí*, but I hope they are not expecting to change. My powers are plumb sapped out, Charlie. The spell is weak and grows weaker. Even Chico might be heading back to where he came from soon."

"Shit!"

Charlie sighed as he swung his legs to the floor, pulled on his long underwear suit, and wrapped his shell belt around his waist, quickly securing the holster thong to his thigh. Ravenna lay back on the bed, drawing the covers up and pensively puffing her cigar as Charlie stomped into his boots. Hearing the voices in the yard growing louder, he pushed through the little sleeping quarters' curtained doorway and tramped into the main part of the cabin. He pulled the front door open and stepped out into the chill night air, stopping on the station house's rickety front stoop.

About twenty feet straight out lay his partners' fire, around which the boys' gear was piled and eating utensils were strewn. A coffeepot smoked as it sat on a hot rock near the dancing flames.

To the right of the fire, Curly Joe, One-Eye, and Lucky stood facing the three burly men sitting their snorting, nickering horses and pulling back on the mounts' reins to keep them in check. The butts of holstered pistols jutted from behind the newcomers' jacket flaps. Rifles were snugged down in their saddle boots. None of Charlie's own three men was wearing his pistol belt or even held so much as a pigsticker in his hand.

They were relying on their newfound and irresistible abilities to change at will.

The middle man in the group of newcomers was saying, ". . . All I can tell you fellas is we been waitin' on the stage, and there she sits, and we're just naturally wonderin' why in thunder it's still *here*."

The man on the far right neck-reined his horse away from the group and galloped off across the trail and into the desert beyond, where coyotes were howling and snarling. He'd likely soon come across the dead station men and the girl.

"All right, all right, there, fellas," Charlie said, stepping down off the stoop and making his spurs ring as he walked toward the newcomers. "I think I can straighten this all out, make it all real simple and clear."

"Is that right?" said the chunky man who appeared to be the leader, whose unshaven face shone red-brown in the firelight. He wore no glove on his right hand, and that hand was splayed across his wool-clad right thigh, near the handle of the big Smith & Wesson jutting up from the holster nearly concealed by his buckskin coat. "And how is it you're gonna be able to do that when these three can't?"

"Hey, Burt." The voice came from the desert, crisp and clear and sullen on the night air. "Think I found 'em."

Charlie looked at the man called Burt and grinned. Burt's eyes widened and shone like gold coins in the firelight as his right hand jerked toward the walnut butt of the big Smithy.

Charlie gave a howl as he snared his own Colt in his hands, clicking the hammer back and going to work, the blasts rising like cannon fire in the otherwise quiet night. Smoke puffed and flames spewed. In little more time than it took to blink, both Burt and the other man beside him were grunting as Hondo's lead punched them back in their saddles. They bounced off their horses' rumps and tumbled on down to the yard, the horses pitching and screaming and lurching away to gallop off in the night.

The boys looked at Charlie. One-Eye threw up an arm in exasperation. "We coulda handled it, Charlie. No need for all that commotion."

Hooves thudded. Beyond the boys, the third rider was a shadow galloping off to the west, his silhouette bobbing against the stars. Charlie took long strides as he crossed the yard and stepped into the trail, raising one of his pistols once more, narrowing one eye as he aimed.

The Colt leaped and roared.

Charlie listened. The hooves continued thudding. Then there was the gravelly thump of a body hitting the ground.

Charlie lowered the warden's Colt, turned, and headed back toward the fire where the other three were still regarding him doubtfully. "You boys ain't gonna be changing' for a while," he said as he continued toward the cabin and the lovely, insatiable witch awaiting him there. "So keep your nasty ole selves on a short rein, hear?"

Chapter 19

WOLF HUNT

Tracking the wolves out of Hellsgarde gave even experienced trackers like Zane and Hathaway fits the next morning.

Inside the canyon, the prints were sometimes men's boots and then wolf paws and then back to boots again—as though the four were still trying to get steady on their wolf legs. They had run down the tunnel as wolves, then sprinted along the Hog Wollop Trail for about a hundred yards before swerving off the wagon road and heading dead south across a high-desert bowl. The four were running all-out, obviously enjoying their new freedom.

They slowed their pace about halfway across the five-mile-wide bowl, milled around a long-dead deer carcass surrounded by coyote and bobcat tracks in a shallow dry wash, then followed another wash up through low hills stippled with Spanish bayonet, post oaks, and cedar. Here, the rough terrain made for slow going for Zane's and Angel's horses and even for Hathaway's mule. The wolf tracks were harder to follow, as the four spread out here across the hillocks and rocky knobs, but Hathaway found where they converged once more on a freshly killed elk.

They'd gutted the beast, ripping out most of the good meat and organs, including the liver and heart, and had a leisurely meal before drawing water from a nearby spring. Their prints were clearly etched in the mud rimming the moss-edged bowl in the rocks.

Refreshed, they'd continued southwest over a low jog of sandy hills.

The trackers had an easier time following the pack here but a harder time later on when they'd followed a rocky draw that rose up the side of a steeply shelving mesa. It was late in the day when they came to the mesa's lip, where all four prints simply disappeared.

Zane stepped down from General Lee's back, dropped to a knee beside the tracks, and looked over the edge of the cliff. A trail furrowed with narrow wheel tracks curved about fifty feet below, coming up an incline on the left and twisting and turning on down the grade to the right before straightening out and heading across a rocky flat. The sun was low, drawing shadows out from the sage and greasewood clumps, brushing the cedars with soft copper light.

"That's the Drier-Phelps Stage Company Road. Follows an old fur traders' route from Taos all the way to Tucson."

Zane looked at the trail, unable to see any wolf tracks in the finely churned, pale brown powder. He looked at Hathaway crouched beside him. "You reckon they hopped the stage?"

"I reckon I wouldn't put anything past 'em."

"That must be what they did," Angel said.

The marshal was holding a pair of field glasses to her eyes and looking south along the stage road. "Buzzards ahead. Feasting on something along the trail." She glanced at Zane and Hathaway as she dropped the glasses back into one of her saddlebag pouches. Then she reined Cisco around and trotted along the edge of the mesa, scouring the ridge face for a way down to the trail.

She found it a few minutes later, and Hathaway and Zane followed her down the perilous path twisting among red rocks and boulders. Zane brought up the rear, moving more slowly with the casket behind him, not wanting to crack a wheel or an axle. When they reached the trail, they scoured the area for more wolf prints.

Finding none, they decided to head south, the direction in which the stage's tracks said it was heading, and soon drew rein. Just ahead, buzzards were milling around a bloody woman's body dressed in a shredded dark red traveling suit. She lay parallel to the trail, hugging the right shoulder, one buzzard on her head, another on her belly.

The baldheaded, beady-eyed carrion eaters eyed the interlopers angrily, squawking their disdain and flexing their wings. Several more were hunkered down on both sides of the trail where they were dining on spilled entrails. A few more milled farther up the road, where Zane could see another body lying father off the trail about ten yards.

Zane stared down at the woman, whom he judged to be in her late forties, early fifties. A cameo pin was still stuck to her red jacket, which was spotted with the darker red of blood. Her limbs were stretched out to both sides of her, and she stared up at the sky through empty sockets.

Zane felt a keen revulsion. Murder for the sake of murder—that was the wolf's way. He thought of that vile predator lurking around inside him, and it made him want to throw his guts up.

"Take time to bury her?" Hathaway asked.

Zane shook his head. "Best not. Best to get on up the trail. She's dead. More'll soon be dead if we don't catch up to Charlie Hondo."

Angel gigged her paint on up the trail. Zane and Hathaway followed, stopping beside her near the other body, another woman, lying in the brush off the trail's left side. The shaggy black buzzards mewled and squawked in a half circle around her, one feeding on the navel exposed by the torn, spruce-green traveling suit.

Probably a sister of the other. Maybe a mother and daughter traveling together. Hard to say, with all the blood. Zane resisted the urge to shoot the buzzard off the woman's belly. Like the other woman, she was dead. And buzzards needed to eat, too. Even if he and the others buried these women, coyotes or wildcats would likely dig them up again.

"Let's ride." Zane mashed heels to General Lee's flanks, and galloped on up the trail, Angel and Hathaway falling in behind him.

He didn't slow when he spied several more bodies lying off in the sagebrush. He saw a blood-splattered coach gun, too, leaning against a sage-shrouded boulder as though it had been purposely set there. Most likely, that was where it had tumbled after the shotgun messenger had dropped it.

They rode hard for thirty minutes before rounding the base of a broad escarpment. At the bottom of the gentle grade before them lay a relay station—the Saber Creek Station, Zane knew from having crisscrossed this country several times in the past, hunting spooks. The stage sat in the middle of the yard, between the stock tank and windmill. In the holding corral off the barn, several horses stood like statues, heads hanging, a couple lazily switching their tails.

The group continued down into the yard, looking around cautiously, all shucking their rifles from their saddle sheaths and racking rounds into the chambers. They paused at the edge of the yard. Zane detected a sickly sweet stench in the desert off to his left and recognized it instantly. Putrefying human flesh.

They continued on into the yard, Zane edging away from the others and moving toward the stage whose wagon tongue drooped to the ground. Before he was twenty yards away from it, he heard the flies, and now as he approached he saw the clouds of them swarming around the carriage.

He rode up and glanced in the window. It was as though someone had taken a bucket of blood and sloshed it over both cowhide seats and walls and even the ceiling. There was more red than any other color in there. More blood lay thick in the dust beside the carriage, and as Zane gigged General Lee forward, he spied even more just ahead of the tongue. Men had been killed there, too.

He swung General Lee around and galloped across the yard and into the desert to the southwest, reining up when he saw the four bodies lying in the sage—dragged there and dumped unceremoniously. One older gent, two young men, and a young woman who wasn't wearing a stitch and whose pale body looked obscene in the harsh western light.

They'd been worked over by the carrion eaters, as well, until there were few distinguishing characteristics. Tonight, the coyotes and bobcats would return to fight over what was left.

Zane touched his moccasin heels to the palomino's flanks, and rode back into the yard, circling the holding corral twice and leaning out away from his saddle to inspect the ground etched with multiple sets of shod hooves. Angel and Hathaway were filing out of the cabin, holding their rifles and casting cautious glances around the yard.

As Hathaway dropped to one knee about thirty feet in front of the cabin, near the stock tank, Zane pulled General Lee back over toward the cabin, where Angel's horse and Hathaway's mule stood ground-tied.

"Nothin' in there," Angel said, grabbing Cisco's reins.

"No, they left early yesterday morning. They're long gone. Rode out on five horses."

Angel slid her rifle into her saddle boot. "Five?"

"Maybe one's a packhorse. Maybe they met up with someone else here. Ravenna Gonzalez-Vara."

"Got somethin' over here."

Hathaway was still down on one knee and staring at the ground before him. Zane swung out of the leather and set his rifle on his shoulder as he and Angel walked past a fire ring heaped with gray ashes, and over to the scout, slanting their long shadows across Hathaway and the track he was inspecting. It looked like the print of a large bird. Zane had seen such prints embedded in ancient lava in Utah and Arizona, and had figured them to be the marks of a winged dinosaur from eons past. Not only strange to see one similar in the finely churned dust and horse shit of the station yard, but also chilling.

Walking around, he saw several more prints just like it. As though one of those winged dinosaurs had been walking around out here recently. Or something akin to it.

A dragon, say.

Hathaway walked a few feet away from the first print and stooped to run his gloved hand over a sage shrub, crunching the blackened branches in his hand. "Burned."

"I have a feeling your friend Ravenna was here," Angel told Zane, lightly jeering.

"One good thing." Zane raked a thumb down his bearded jaw and stared at the corral. "They not runnin' as wolves. They're in the saddle. Ravenna must be tapped out, saving her strength."

"For what?" Angel asked, moving up beside him. "Where are they headed and why? Elaina have any idea at all . . . during your private conversation?"

Zane shook his head slowly.

Behind him, Hathaway gave a fateful sigh. "Hell, they're Hell's Angels. They're probably gonna run and kill awhile for fun, then try to slip in among the usual crowd again, just like they done before ole Charlie was caught in Denver."

"I don't think so."

Zane stared down the trail colored gray brown with the sun tumbling behind the western ridges, remembering the fear in Elaina's eyes that had pricked the base of his spine with the point of a cold, sharp nail. The memory of it did the same again now, and he felt the urge to hurry.

"Nah, I don't think so. Let's mount up."

"Dark soon," Angel said.

"We have another hour of light left." Zane slid his rifle into its saddle boot and stepped into the leather. "Let's make use of it."

He touched moccasin heels to General Lee's flanks.

* * *

They made camp that night in a box canyon south of Alamosa, and ate a meager supper of jerky, hardtack, and coffee. Wolves howled from the surrounding ridges and canyons. They took turns keeping watch from a scarp high over the camp.

During Zane's time on the scarp, he could hear the slightest rustle of burrowing creatures in the brush up and down the canyon they were in. He could hear the howl of a distant coyote, smell the blood of a rabbit killed by a hawk that the night breeze brought to him from the north, possibly far, far away.

Turning his attention to the camp below in which the fire guttered weakly, flames fingering up from a bed of umber coals, he could hear Angel's slow breathing as she lay curled in her blankets. From time to time, she gave a soft moan, and he wondered what she was dreaming about.

Him?

Her father, who had also broken her heart when he, too, had become a ghoul? James Coffin was a renegade now, running wild in the Montana mountains.

All Zane's senses were almost frighteningly keen and alive. The feeling made his limbs tingle thrillingly. At times, despite his trail fatigue, he felt a surge of raw power that made him want to run and climb and jump and . . . what?

Kill?

He tightened a fist against it.

No, he told himself, staring out at the star-capped night in which the waning moon climbed, relieved it was not full and feeling the fearful anticipation, as he always did, of the next time it would be full and high.

Would he once more be able to hold the wolf inside him at bay?

He and the others got started at first light. By midmorning they slipped across the Colorado border and into Arizona. Pushing the horses as hard as they dared, in the midmorning they followed the tracks of the Angels' five shod mounts into a small ranch headquarters.

There was a hay barn, two corrals including a breaking corral outfitted with a snubbing post, and a run-down, brush-roofed cabin.

They reined up near the windmill and stock tank, and Zane caressed the trigger of his Henry as he and the others got the lay of the place.

There wasn't much movement except four horses in the main corral off the barn, the lazily spinning windmill's rusty blades, and a tumbleweed bouncing off across the yard flanking the cabin from which emanated the squawls of a young child.

By the scuffed, windblown tracks in the yard—though with no sign of the dragon—the gang they were after had obviously ridden through here some time ago. Likely they'd moved on. But boot hills across the frontier were rife with men who'd banked too heavily on assumptions.

A child's face appeared in the window right of the cabin, two little hands closing over the window's bottom casing. A man's long face appeared over that of the boy, then just as quickly disappeared.

The cabin's front door opened. The man poked his head out, squinting his eyes, then drew the door wider and stepped out holding a .45/70 Springfield army carbine down low across his thighs. He was a gaunt, thin man with muttonchops and ragged pin-striped coveralls and a grimy undershirt. He wore stockmen's undershot boots, but both toes were nearly torn away from the soles. His shoulders were thick, his sun-browned hands on the Springfield large.

A wild horse hunter and breaker. Zane knew the breed. He eased his finger away from the Henry's trigger.

"We're friendly," he said.

The man had drawn the door closed behind him and haltingly stepped down off the cabin's dilapidated stoop and walked slowly toward the newcomers, squinting, a lock of gray-flecked hair hanging over one eye.

"Name's Zane," the bounty hunter said when the mustanger had stopped about twenty feet away. "The lady with the badge there is Deputy U.S. Marshal Angel Coffin, and on the other side of her is Al Hathaway, cavalry scout. We're after the gang that pulled into your yard sometime back—I'm guessing the day before yesterday."

The mustanger looked uncertain as he dropped his eyes to the ground as though looking for the tracks these newcomers had followed to his ranch. He looked back up at Zane, flicking his eyes across Angel and Hathaway, then said, "What'd they do?"

"Broke out of Hellsgarde," Angel said. "Leastways, the men did. The woman gave 'em a hand."

"When did they pull in and when did they leave?" Zane inquired.

"You had it right," said the mustanger. "Midafternoon day before yesterday. Pulled out the next mornin'. Hellsgarde, you say?" His facial muscles stiffened, and the lids drooped halfway over his eyes. "Why on earth . . . ?"

"Spooks," Hathaway said with a grunt, leaning forward to run a gloved hand down his mule's neck. "Shapeshifters. Wolves. They show you that?"

"There wasn't no such nonsense as that. I invited 'em to go ahead and camp behind the cabin, and Angeline cooked for 'em, and before they left they bought two beef haunches from me and gave me five dollars for 'em, though it weren't nothin' but a scrub cow."

Angel cast a wary eye to the sky. "The girl didn't come packin' a dragon, did she?"

The man's face colored up slightly, and his eyes gained an indignant cast. He thought he was being toyed with.

"I ain't seen no such nonsense as dragons," he said finally. "Good Lord. I have enough trouble keepin' a pack o' hobgobbies away from my cattle. Whole ranch of 'em in the next watershed to the north. They love beef—any beef that ain't their own, that is. Sometimes they even come after my hosses."

The mustanger shook his head as he stared in silent beseeching at Angel.

"When we've done run our current quarry to ground," she told the mustanger, "I'll look into it."

"I'd be obliged."

"In the meantime," Zane said, "mind if we water our horses?"

"The water's good. You can stay for supper, if you like."

"Thanks," said Hathaway. "We best keep movin', sir."

The mustanger nodded. "I gotta go back inside. Little one's sick, and the missus needs help with the others." His eyes acquired a sad look. "Too bad about Charlie and his pards and that girl. They was right friendly." He grinned bashfully. "That girl—she was an eyeful."

"I bet she was," Angel said.

The man turned and went back inside the cabin. Zane, Angel, and Hathaway watered their horses at the stock trough, loosening the latigos and slipping the bits from the horses' mouths. They fed them a couple of handfuls of grain, letting them eat it slow.

Resting in the windmill's shade, Zane and Hathaway each rolled a quirley. Angel smoked one of her long, black cheroots she bought for a nickel each in Denver and which, at one time, had been her father's favorite brand. Zane smoked only half of his cigarette. For some reason, the tobacco didn't taste as good as it once did. As the sun angled westward toward the White Mountains rolling up like severe clouds above the sage-stippled plain, they mounted up and headed along the trail once more.

After another hour's ride, they came to a right fork in the trail, the fork meandering up and over a distant rise among low buttes and mesas.

Zane halted General Lee and studied the trail with a speculative air.

"What is it?" Hathaway said.

"Gonna head up that canyon, see a man about a horse."

"What'd we need with another hoss?" asked Hathaway.

"I don't think he means a horse," Angel said. "Think he means silver."

Hathaway stretched a knowing smile. "Untaxed, I suppose?"

Zane shrugged.

Officiously, Angel said, "That's contraband, Mr. Zane."

"Nah, that's just affordable silver. Ain't much of it these days, with the increased demand since the War an' all."

Zane dismounted and quickly unharnessed the casket from General Lee. "I'm gonna make a quick run, leave this here. Don't need a busted wheel."

Grunting, he pushed the casket off into the dense brush and rocks along the trail.

"You sure you don't want us to go with you?" Angel asked.

Zane shook his head. "You two push on, find a spot to camp. If all goes well, I'll find you before sundown."

Zane remounted General Lee and galloped onto the forking trail, over the rise, and into a canyon between steep-walled table-top mesas.

Chapter 20

. . . .

A VISIT TO THE SILVER-BULLET PADRE

Zane lay atop a rise, focusing his field glasses on the lower canyon before him. The cut was abutted in the north and the south by steep cliffs leaning inward.

Up a brushy slope on the canyon's north side sat an old Spanish church flanked by a cemetery of tilting wooden crosses and engraved tombstones. A little ways down the hill from the church, and nearer Zane, lay a small mud-brick, brush-roofed shack from which a curl of smoke lifted. The sun's dying rays burnished the sandstone church above the shack so that it glowed like a new penny.

A thin stream flashed at the bottom of the canyon. On both sides of the stream were wood-frame shacks, seven in all. Sun-silvered and dilapidated, with brush growing up through the boardwalks fronting them, they were all that remained of a town built here by gold prospectors before the War and abandoned soon after. The stone ruins of an old Spanish pueblo could be seen around the newer buildings, only a few of them still sporting roofs.

There wasn't much gold in the stream, but the padre had found a healthy silver vein in a hidden canyon cut into the northern ridge behind the church. The Franciscan priests from Spain had been the first to exploit the vein, and they'd even processed the ore, a tradition that Padre Alejandro had been continuing for nearly thirty years with the help of his half-breed assistant, Tico Palomar. Few besides Zane knew of the silver cache, and he'd stumbled on it years ago when he'd holed up here to recover from an arrow drilled into his leg by a Coyotero Apache.

Despite Zane's lack of a spiritual bent, he and the padre had become fast friends. It was then that the padre had begun selling silver bullets to the ghoul hunter, as he did for a select few fighting the hard war against El Diablo, who would surely take over the world if not for the brave men who stood against him.

Spying no sign of danger below—he'd learned long ago to never ride into a place without scoping it out carefully beforehand—Zane returned his field glasses to his saddlebags, mounted General Lee, and galloped on down the hill and into the canyon. He cut away from the stream, mounted the northern slope, and drew rein before the humble shack.

"Padre?"

No answer but the breeze rustling the dead brush roofing the shack. An *ojo* hanging from the ceiling of the narrow front gallery twisted slightly in the breeze, its rope creaking faintly. The striped Indian blankets hanging over the windows from the inside fluttered.

"Padre Alejandro?" Zane called, louder. "It's Uriah Zane."

Still no reply from the shack. The door was closed. The padre was not in his garden to the shack's right, which the old Catholic watered each day from the stream, chanting and praying, as was his practice.

Zane gigged General Lee around the shack and up the well-worn trail to the church that stood like a hulking sandstone barrack. A cracked and tarnished bell crouched in an eroded belfry mounted high above the arched, wooden front door. Pigeons gurgled and fluttered. As Zane swung down from the saddle, they swooped into flight.

Zane dropped the palomino's reins, tripped the heavy oak door's latch, and shoved the door wide. His big frame filled the opening as the panel tapped the wall to the left, and he stared into the church's bowels that smelled of stone, wood, and candles.

"Padre?" His deep voice echoed.

The benches inside the place had long since rotted and crumbled and been hauled away. Now if any worshippers appeared—and there were damn few left in these hills—they simply knelt on the cracked flagstone floor. Beyond a dilapidated wooden rail and a rack of unlit candles lay the altar and a wooden cross.

Zane walked into the church, leaving the door open wide behind him, and followed his long shadow down the center aisle and around the altar to a small back door. He pushed the door open and peered into the cemetery.

Again, he called for the padre. Except for the breeze ruffling the brown, wiry weeds that had nearly overgrown the boneyard and the gurgling of the pigeons perched on the red-slate roof above him, there was no response. He raked his eyes across the cemetery. They caught on the large oak cross standing at the rear of the yard, and held there, his heart skipping beats.

Zane lunged into a run, leaping stones and small crosses until he stood in front of the large cross at the rear of the cemetery and stared up in horror at Padre Alejandro, who lay naked and spread-eagled and bloody, nailed to the cross just like his beloved Jesus.

Zane reached out and touched the man's thin, pale, blue-veined right ankle. Cold as stone. He looked at the gaunt face framed by long, grizzled, silver hair. The skin sagging against the concave cheeks was as dry as parchment. The man's brown eyes were half-open and staring almost tenderly down at Zane, his head canted to one side. The blood that had oozed down from the spikes driven through his hands and feet was dry. He'd been dead a day or two, his flat belly starting to pooch out away from his ribs from the putrefaction within.

Oddly, it appeared no buzzards had yet found him.

Zane backed away from his dead friend, the horror in his eyes hardening now to a keen rage as he lowered his right hand to the cross-draw holster on his left hip, and slipped the Colt Navy from its holster. He remembered the smoke lifting from the stovepipe jutting from the roof of Alejandro's shack.

Maybe whoever had done this was still here. Or was that too much to hope for?

He walked back through the church and out the front, swung up onto General Lee's back, and booted the horse down the hill. When he was fifty feet from the padre's shack, he slid down from the saddle while the palomino was still moving. He hit the ground jogging, and pressed his back against the shack's rear wall, near the closed back door.

He reached over and tried the metal latch lever. It clicked, and the door whined open a few inches. Zane gave a shove and stepped into the cabin. He was in the padre's kitchen, simply furnished with a small cookstove, eating table, and several plank shelves crowded with airtight tins and burlap food pouches.

Beyond lay the sleeping area with one rocking chair built of elk horns and hide and over which an afghan was draped that Alejandro used to wrap around his shoulders of a chilly night at this altitude and sip his home-brewed ale and stare into the hot fire provided by the small, mud-brick hearth in the left wall. The windows were covered by Indian blankets through which a dingy, washed-out light shone, casting the cabin in misty gray shadows.

The padre's cot lay before the hearth, in which a small fire smoldered. On the cot lay a man in threadbare long handles. He had long, obsidian-black hair and a long, sharp, upturned nose. The way he lay bespoke a hump on his back, neck bent at an angle. An empty whiskey bottle and a shot glass sat on the hearth on the far side of the sleeping beast. A cigarette stub lay on the floor a few inches below his sagging, knobby hand with finger-nails shaped like arrow points.

On the room's other side, two more figures lay on a straw pallet—a naked male and a naked female only partly covered by a green wool Army blanket. Lice flecked the hair of each. Two whiskey bottles, one empty, one half-full, and several of the padre's beer bottles lay or stood around them. The male was spooned against the female, cupping one of her small, pert breasts in his pale, gnarled hand. His face was buried between her shoulder and her neck, and he was snoring loudly.

The female opened her eyes and stared at Zane through sleep

fog. She blinked, recognition flashing in her pale blue eyes as she realized that she was not dreaming the big man in the room. She lifted her head with a start, stretching her lips back from yellow fangs.

A snakelike hiss rose from deep in her throat, and her eyes slanted devilishly. Zane's Colt roared, spitting smoke and flames into the dimness. The female tipped her head back and clutched her throat with both hands, making strangling sounds and staring wide-eyed at the herringbone pattern on the ceiling, quivering.

The male behind her lifted his head up, coming awake instantly, snarling, and reaching under the pillow they both shared. Zane's Colt roared twice more, blowing the male back off the cot, both slugs exiting his back with a spray of snot-colored blood and viscera, and painting the whitewashed wall behind him.

The female had fallen onto her back atop the cot, and was flopping around like a landed fish. Zane shot her again, through the heart, then turned toward the other side of the room where the other ghoul was reaching under his own cot for a sawed-off, double-barreled ten-gauge.

As the ghoul brought up the coach gun, Zane drilled him through his left shoulder. The man loosed a shrill falsetto squeal that felt like a slap to the ghoul hunter's ears, rattling his eardrums painfully. The black-haired hobgobbie dove forward off the bed, turning a complete somersault as he hit the floor, rolling toward the door. As he came to a standing position in his threadbare, filthy white balbriggans, he tried to bring the shotgun up once more, shouting in his bizarre old woman's voice, *"Fuck you, you red-blooded coyote!"*

Zane's Colt belched twice more, punching one slug through the top of the man's center chest, another through his other shoulder. The man squealed louder, and Zane threw himself hard to his left as the double-barreled barn blaster roared like a cannon in the close confines, spraying a pumpkin-sized load of buckshot across the kitchen and into the table and wall and through the open back door.

Zane rolled off his left shoulder and hip, dropping his empty pistol and shucking the one holstered on his right side, thumbing the hammer back, narrowing an eye as he planted the bead at the end of the barrel into the V over the cylinder, and fired.

The slug hammered through the ghoul's forehead, just below his hairline. As he flew back against the door with a high wail, he triggered his gut shredder's second barrel into the ceiling. He lolled against the door, which wobbled in its frame on weak hinges until it gave way with a crunching splintering sound, and both the door and the ghoul went sailing into the padre's front yard.

The ghoul piled up atop the door. He sighed heavily and lay still. Greenish-yellow blood oozed from the silver dollar–sized hole in his forehead.

Zane looked around the room, in which powder smoke billowed in blue webs, smelling like rotten eggs. The other two were down and still, oozing their putrid fluids onto the padre's hard-packed earthen floor.

"Sons o' bitches," Zane bit out, wincing at the pain his impact with the floor had caused in his left shoulder.

Slowly, breathing heavily, he gained his knees. He retrieved his empty Colt, then heaved himself to his feet, holstering the right-side gun, flipping open the loading gate on the left-side gun, spinning the wheel and letting the empty casings tumble onto the floor around his moccasins.

As he plucked fresh shells from his cartridge belt and punched them into the Colt's cylinder, turning it slowly, hearing each click, he walked through the open door and stepped over the dead ghoul. He looked around, expecting more ghouls from any quarter. They usually ran in packs, and it was odd to find only a few at a time.

He glanced up at the church, then toward a knob of rock looming on his left, then at the garden and clumps of brush and cedars all around the place. He heard a murmur of voices from the direction of the canyon, and stepped farther out away from the padre's shack to peer the hundred yards down the gradual slope into the deep arroyo.

Three figures were just now crossing the ghost town's single street and angling toward the base of the slope, looking up at Zane from beneath the brims of their battered hats. They were three ragged-looking hombres in worn trail garb. One wore a duster. He also walked with a limp and had a prominent hump on his back, giving him a twisted look. Zane inspected the other two more closely, saw that they, too, had humps lifting the backs of their shirts.

The one who wore a funnel-brimmed hat, red-and-black-checked shirt, and green neckerchief dropped suddenly to one knee and raised a pistol, aiming up the slope at Zane. The ghoul hunter wasn't worried about the hogleg. He was pretty much out of range of the short gun, unless the shooter was the best shot Zane had ever known. But ghouls were notoriously lazy and undisciplined, and it was hard to find a good shooter among them.

What had gained the brunt of his attention were the clumps of other ghouls just now spilling out of two of the other rickety, false-fronted buildings on the far side of the ghost town's narrow main street. They were all slouched and still pulling on shirts or denim jackets and checking pistols as they came on toward the slope. More movement caught Zane's eye, and he saw three more men filing out of the old Palace Hotel, and then three more men stepped out behind them.

And four more . . .

A pistol popped. Zane looked straight down below his position and saw smoke puffing in front of the hobgobbie in the checked shirt. The other two men were running up the slope now, taking long strides and casting savage looks up at Zane.

"Well, I'll be damned," the ghoul hunter muttered, swinging around and running over to where General Lee stood about fifty feet in front of the padre's shack, swinging his brown tail back and forth sideways and twitching his ears as he stared down the slope at the crowd headed toward him and his master.

"Easy, fella," Zane said, quickly shucking his Henry repeater from the saddle sheath.

He ran back to the brow of the hill and quickly, resolutely, dispatched the two ghouls running up toward him and laid out the pistol-wielding ghoul in the checked shirt. That didn't waylay the others a bit. In fact, it seemed to lure them on.

All twenty or so loosed a low roar and surged forward, filtering out between the dilapidated buildings and running up the slope. For all their sloth and the cumbersome humps on their backs, hobgobbies could run. It was almost as though they had springs in their ankles.

The group was coming on fast, triggering lead.

Zane lowered the Henry and ran back to General Lee.

"Hate to tell ya this, General," he said, catching up the reins and swinging into the saddle. "But I do believe we've done wore out our welcome here in old Dry Wash."

General Lee replied with a shrill whinny and lunged into a gallop, kicking up great gouts of clay-colored dust behind him.

Chapter 21

. . . .

A SNARLING HORDE

As Zane, atop General Lee, angled down the slope toward the creek threading the canyon's bottom, he looked to his right. Now the horde of hobgobbies in the grimy garb of thirty-a-month-and-found cowpunchers was running along the road paralleling the creek, on an interception course with Zane.

Holding the General's reins in his teeth and giving the horse his head, Zane shouldered the Henry repeater and snapped off three quick shots. The slugs puffed dust along the road and the slope and skipped away, screaming. That didn't stop or even slow the hobgobbie horde, as the ghoul hunter had known it probably wouldn't.

Once a hobgobbie had you in his sights, there was little stopping him except a slug or an arrow. They could be snivelingly nonaggressive when they weren't excited, but whipped up by the bloodlust, they'd chase you barefoot across a smoking lava field and gut you with the short, razor-edged knives they favored, or shoot you with a pistol or hogleg. They lacked coordination, and their eyes were bad, but they could shoot within ten feet as well as your average greenhorn who'd been practicing only a week or two.

The really bad thing about them was how fast on their feet they were. Zane had less ground to cover to the canyon bottom than they did running out of the ghost town, but as fast as they were all moving, as one yipping, snarling, cursing horde along the trail, he judged they were running nearly as fast as General Lee, and the palomino had been cut and gentled out of a bronco mustang herd in the rough country around Arizona's Chiricahua Mountains.

As he approached the canyon-bottom trail, Zane cursed and snapped off two more shots. One hobgobbie, within fifty yards and coming hard, running abreast of three others, yelped, grabbed his knee, hit the ground, and rolled, nearly tripping one of the others.

They all kept coming.

The front of the snarling, long-striding pack was only thirty feet from the intersection of the two trails when Zane hit the canyon bottom. General Lee gave an indignant whinny at the closing horde and swung hard left, faltering slightly before grinding his rear hooves into the turf and lunging forward until he was in full gallop once more.

Behind Zane, pistols and rifles popped above the hum and buzz of the frenzied ghoul pack. He heard the fast patter of running feet and glanced over his right shoulder just as the lead ghoul pistoned off his heels and made a mad dive forward, scissoring his arms as though to grab one of General Lee's hammering rear legs.

The ghoul missed by inches. He hit the ground with a shrill, enraged cry, and rolled off to the side of the trail, the one behind him wildly leaping over him, the others hammering on past him and after Zane.

Two of the front-runners were sporadically triggering shots, and several times the ghoul hunter felt the air beside his head curl warmly, saw the bullets plunk into the dust ahead of him. As he approached the rise atop which he'd glassed the canyon an hour ago, one bullet tore through his flapping wolf vest to kiss his right side, about a foot below his armpit. He felt little except the slight dampness of trickling blood.

He glanced behind once more. A few hobgobbies were slowing for the grade, but General Lee was, too, so the horde was continuing to gain on Zane in small increments. He could probably outrun them in time, because General Lee had more staying power than the hobgobbies, who could run like grizzlies for only short stretches, but this group was especially determined. He was beginning to feel the stony chill of the doomed in his bowels when, as he closed the gap between him and the crest of the hill, a familiar sight appeared between a boulder and a gnarled cedar right of the trail.

The Gatling gun's brass canister flashed as bright as a miniature sun, blinding Zane for an instant. As he snapped his eyes away, he heard the sudden ratcheting of the six-bored gun. Squeals and agonized cries rose behind him as the .45-caliber slugs tore and crunched through flesh, snapping bones. Zane rode on up and over the rise, leaped out of the saddle, and ran back up to the crest of the hill.

He dropped to one knee and raised the Henry to his shoulder. Now he could see Angel kneeling behind the Gatling gun and working the crank for all she was worth, wine-red hair spilling about her shoulders. On the opposite side of the trail, the bulky dark figure of Al Hathaway in his smoke-stained buckskins and blue cavalry hat knelt on a flat-topped boulder, levering rounds from his '67 Winchester, the empty casings flashing in the sun as they arced back over his right shoulder.

Straight down the trail, a good half of the hobgobbies were down and bloody, a few of the wounded trying to crawl away. Those still on their feet continued to come, showing their teeth between their thin lips as they snarled and raged, so infuriated by the human interlopers, and wanting blood so badly, that they continued heading fiercely, stupidly, straight into the bullet storm.

A few dropped down behind rocks on either side of the trail and tried to return fire, but the Gatling gun had them mostly cowering, unable to lift their heads.

Bam-bam-bam-bam-bam-bam-bam!

The hiccupping gun continued to tear through flesh, blow up dust, throw up sage branches, and hammer shards from rocks. Two well-placed bullets blew one of the ghouls' heads off its neck, which went tumbling in a geyser of snot-colored blood across the gravel, the body it had left kneeling as though in prayer, slowly lowering the Remington .44 in its quivering hand.

Zane added his Henry and LeMat to the fusillade, and when both guns pinged on vacant chambers, he emptied one of his Colts. Before he'd fired his last pistol bullet, the Gatling clicked empty. Hathaway had emptied his own rifle and two pistols and had leaped down off the boulder to reload behind it.

Through the sunlit smoke haze, Zane saw a hobgobbie poke its hatted head with its long, stringy hair out from behind a boulder. The hobgobbie gritted its tobacco-crusted teeth as it snapped off a shot. Before the one remaining ghoul could thumb his pistol's hammer back, Zane triggered his second Colt.

The ghoul's head snapped back as though he'd been hit in the face with a hammer. He dropped onto his back, flopped around, and gradually fell as still as all the others slouched beneath the wafting smoke, their pooling blood glistening like the skin of rotten lemons.

Angel rose from behind the hot Gatling, grabbing her rifle.

Hathaway looked down the slope from behind his boulder for a time, turning his head this way and that as he surveyed the carnage. Finally, he turned his broad, sweating, coffee-colored face with its black beard and wide brown eyes toward Zane and grinned.

"Looks like you got crossways with a hobgobbie camp."

"Somethin' like that." Zane started reloading and looked at Angel. "I thought you'd rode on."

Angel turned to him as she plucked shells from her cartridge belt and thumbed them through her Winchester's loading gate. "Ran into three other o' them demons along the trail. Drunk as lords, and when they saw me an' Al, they went into a frenzy and came at us shooting. They were heading this direction, so . . ."

She shrugged, jerked her charro jacket down at her waist and stared down the slope before her, one fist on her hip.

Zane rose slowly. He, too, was reloading his weapons, but his mind was elsewhere. "Bastards killed Alejandro," he said tightly, almost under his breath, wanting to kill every hobgobbie he could plant his sights on. "Just an old padre, wasn't botherin' no one."

"Yeah, they do that," Hathaway said with a fateful sigh. "Ghouls hate men o' the cloth in partic'lar."

The stocky scout wagged his bearded face sadly as he started down the slope to kick around among the bodies and to shoot any that had a glimmer of life left in them.

While Angel and Hathaway headed off to find a secure night camp, for the sun had dropped behind the western ridges, Zane returned to Padre Alejandro. He used his considerable strength to lift and twist the cross out of the ground. Then he pulled the spikes out of the priest's lifeless limbs, and wrapped the man in the altar cloth he'd found in the church.

It was nearly dark by the time the ghoul hunter, working bare-chested, sweating in spite of the cooling air, had dug the grave, gentled the blanket-wrapped priest into the dark hole, and covered him. He took extra time to erect a crude cross of pine branches and rawhide.

When he'd finished the chore of running down Charlie Hondo's bunch, he'd return and erect a chiseled stone. Doubtless the priest would scoff at such ostentation. Zane had never known anyone simpler or more self-effacing, but the padre would have to indulge the ghoul hunter. He could think of no words to say over the mounded dirt and the rocks he'd gathered to ward off predators. The stone would be his attempt at compensating the priest for the lack. Whether the old man wanted it or not, Padre Alejandro deserved something to mark his passing and the sanctified ground in which he would lie forever.

In a cellar in the padre's shack, Zane found the padre's cache of silver bullets. There were several hundred freshly milled slugs laid out in a bed of dried moss. Zane knew the padre had molded them for him, so he took the entire peach crate filled with the precious cartridges that likely would have cost him upward of a thousand dollars on the open market, if he'd been able to find any, as silver was always in short supply.

Nearly an hour later, he found Angel and Hathaway's camp in a dry arroyo sheathed in stone escarpments and cedars, a good half mile off Hondo's trail. The camp was relatively secure, if there was such a thing, from hobgobbies or the wandering bands of Indian swillers this country was known for, as many Arizona Apaches sought out the swillers' curse for the gift of everlasting life and the unearthly powers over the white man.

Angel killed a couple of jackrabbits with her shurikens and chopped them up with her silver Spanish dagger. Hathaway, an ex–camp cook, took over from there, throwing together a surprisingly flavorful stew from the rabbits and several handfuls of wild herbs and roots he'd gathered from the banks of the arroyo. They dined hungrily, washing the food down with whiskey-laced coffee.

When they'd cleaned their plates and brewed another pot of coffee, Angel offered to sew up Zane's bullet-burned right side.

The ghoul hunter reluctantly agreed. It wasn't a serious wound, but he could feel the sporadic discomfort of the oozing blood under his clothes.

"I'll be damned," Angel said, kneeling beside him and dabbing at the cut with a cloth she'd soaked from her canteen. "Looks like it's already started to heal."

"Wasn't much in the first place."

"I beg to differ. Looks like the slug ricocheted off a rib." She touched her finger to the bloody furrow. Zane felt only a slight numbness there, no pain. He shrugged but did not look at Angel, feeling the heat of her incredulous gaze on his face.

Hathaway refilled his coffee cup from the pot in the fire and glanced at Zane's side. "I'll be damned. It does look to be healin'." The scout chuckled deep in his chest and lifted his cup, taking a sip. "You must be part werewolf. Imagine that—a werewolf huntin' werewolves."

He chuckled again, pulled a blanket coat on over his bare arms. "I'll take the first watch from atop one o' them scarps over yonder. Who wants me to wake 'em in a few hours for the next hitch?"

Zane stared into the darkness beyond the throbbing firelight. "I'll take it."

"All right, then." Coffee in one hand, rifle in the other, Hathaway strode off in his drag-heeled, bull-legged fashion.

When he was gone, neither Zane nor Angel said anything while she finished cleaning the wound. She said when she'd threaded her needle, "Probably doesn't need this—looks like it'll be all healed up by morning, but I reckon I might as well finish what I started."

Then she pinched the skin along the furrow together, and began sewing the wound closed.

Zane stared into the darkness across the fire and sipped his whiskey-laced coffee, feeling nothing except for a gentle tug beneath his arm as she poked the needle through. When she finished, she lowered her head to cut the catgut with her teeth, then pressed her forehead against the ghoul hunter's shoulders.

She held her head there for a time. He felt the warmth of her skin against his. She wrapped her arms around his bare waist and pressed her forehead more firmly against his shoulder. She laced her fingers together, and squeezed him hard against her.

"Goddamn you, Uriah."

He felt a tug low in his belly. His blood surged. He turned to her, wrapped an arm around her, and lifted her chin. She stared back at him obliquely, lines cutting across her forehead, but she did not resist him when he pressed his lips to hers.

She rose a little on her haunches, pressing her lips firmly against his, opening them, lifting her arms from his waist to wrap them around his neck and squirm against him, mashing her chest against his. He felt the swell of her breasts behind the soft calfskin vest, and his heart beat faster. He was a little surprised when, driven by a hard desire, he drew her onto his lap and kissed her more passionately, and closed a hand over her right breast, kneading it gently through the vest, and still she did not resist him.

She groaned and placed her own hand over his.

Finally, she heaved herself to her knees and, staring at him with dewy eyes, quickly began untying the vest's rawhide drawstrings. Zane kicked out of his boots, waggled out of his buckskin breeches, and removed his own sweaty tunic and long handles.

He watched her stand and undress heatedly before him. Neither one said anything. Angel slowly revealed her delightfully rounded, full-breasted body to him, succulent hips swelling out from a belly nearly as taut as Zane's own. When she stood before him naked, she swept her hat off brusquely, and her hair fell in a sexy, dark red mess across her shoulders, red strands curling up from beneath her arms to lick at her swollen, pink-tipped orbs.

She slid her hair back from her cheeks and dropped to her knees before him, one hand pulling at his hard, jutting shaft, the other sliding through the thick, black, sweat-damp mop of his hair. She pushed him back against the ground, and straddled him hungrily, grunting, whispering, "Goddamn you, Uriah. . . ."

Chapter 22

. . . .

"HOW'D IT HAPPEN?"

Angel rose up and down on her knees for a time, straddling Zane, groaning and kneading the hard, bulging slabs of his pectorals. The firelight illuminated faint copper streaks in her hair. Her narrowed jade eyes smoldered at him as the firelight shunted across her naked body, her jostling breasts casting shadows across her belly and ribs.

He held her hips in his strong hands, moving as she moved, up and down, until she leaned down, pressed her breasts against his chest, and kissed him, moving her head and stabbing her tongue deep into his mouth. He gave a groan and rolled her over, then propped himself on his outstretched arms and hammered against her—hard, even thrusts.

He lifted his head, fought back the impulse to loose a howl. The blood ran hot in him.

She rolled her head from side to side, pulled at his hair,

tugged at his ears, his beard. She dug her heels into the backs of his legs, her knees flopping like wings, and closed her eyes and turned her head to one side. She arched her back, bucking up hard to meet his wild thrusts, closing her upper teeth over her lower lip, sobbing and groaning.

"Oh . . . Jesus . . . *God* . . . !"

They'd lain together enough times to know when the other was ready. She opened her eyes and stared up at him meaningfully as she wrapped her hands around his corded forearms, from which the veins stood out in sharp relief against his sweat-damp skin bronzed by the firelight. She frowned up at him, puzzled.

"Stop, Uriah," she whispered, caressing his arms with her hands.

He hadn't heard her above the thunder of the blood in his ears.

"Uriah!" she said, looking frightened now, lifting her head.

Zane forced himself to stop hammering against her. He ground his teeth and lowered his chin hard, clutching at the ground on either side of her, and withdrawing his pelvis from hers. It was like trying to stop a Baldwin locomotive on a steep downgrade under full steam.

She scuttled down until her head was below his belly, and he closed his eyes tightly, grinding his teeth, as she finished him with her mouth.

It took a long time. She writhed beneath his belly, making choking sounds.

He rolled over onto his back and she rested her head upon his chest.

"Jesus," she said raggedly, running her arm across her mouth and trying to catch her breath.

They lay there for a long time, entangled, Zane running his fingers through the silky strands of her hair, until he felt a wetness on his chest. He glanced down at her, saw tears dribbling out of her squeezed-shut eyes. One rolled down across the hooked scar on her cheek and into the hollow of his breastbone, showing gold in the firelight.

After a long time, she pushed off of him, slowly gained her feet, and gathered her clothes and myriad weapons including the silver Spanish sword. When she had them all in her arms, she set them down beside the fire, and, facing the flames, her back to Zane, she slowly dressed. When she had everything on except her boots and her hat, she tossed a piñon log on the fire, walked over to the other side of the blaze, and lay down in her blanket roll, resting her head back against her saddle.

Zane stood up and also dressed, before walking off in the brush beyond the fire to evacuate his bladder. He came back, refilled his coffee cup, splashed some whiskey into the hot brew, kicked out of his boots, and got out his hide makings sack. He lay back against his saddle with a weary sigh. Troughing a wheat paper between the first two fingers of his right hand, he dribbled chopped tobacco into it.

Angel's voice came quietly from the other side of the fire. "How did it happen?"

Zane didn't speak for a time as he slowly built the quirley. "You know that old stage robber Alden Woodyard?"

She nodded, staring up at the sky, not looking at him.

"After tracking him for five days north of Laramie, I ran him down in a box canyon in the Big Horns. Moved into his camp one night. There was a full moon. I shouldn't have been out there, but I wanted to run him to ground before he met up with the rest of his gang. He lured me in, leaped on me from a rock, and tore that hunk out of my back before I drilled a silver slug through his heart."

She didn't say anything for a long time. She just stared up at the night sky. The firelight played across her hair. The fire cracked and sputtered.

Zane sipped his coffee and whiskey, set the cup down, licked the edge of the wheat paper, and rolled it closed. He stuck the cylinder in his mouth, sealing it with his tongue.

"After this job, Uriah," she said in the same even tone as before, "I reckon we'll be forking trails for good."

She turned away from him and drew her blankets up across her shoulders.

"If that's what you want, Red."

Zane stared at the newly built quirley. Finally, he tossed it into the fire. The flames licked at it, causing white smoke to curl up from the cylinder. The fire consumed it, leaving only a line of gray ash beside the coffeepot.

Zane leaned back against his saddle once more and took another sip of his coffee. It tasted sour. He flipped the cup back over his shoulder, sending the coffee and whiskey splashing into the brush.

He lay back against his saddle and drew his hat down over his eyes.

Wet and naked, the bewitching Ravenna Gonzalez-Vara sat Indian-style on a flat stone slab above a steaming hot springs pool. She sat with her chin up, shoulders back, black hair behind her shoulders, eyes closed. Her invitingly fleshy, copper-colored belly moved in and out as she breathed.

A gold amulet in the shape of a hexagon and the size of a saucer hung from a rawhide cord around her neck. It lay with one edge tipped into her cleavage. Her full, dark breasts angled out slightly from each other, one a little larger than the other. The larger one had a faint brown birthmark along its bottom curve.

Charlie Hondo's loins sputtered and tingled as he watched from a niche in the rocks of this hidden canyon. He grinned, brushed a hand across his nose.

Steam bathed the Mexican witch, lifting all around her and causing her skin to glisten. There was a thin, warm trickle of water tumbling above her and onto the ancient stone trough behind her. The water slid darkly, steaming down to caress her buttocks and split and flow in two separate streams around her bent legs before continuing into the warm pool below the slab of rock she was perched on.

The water rattled like delicate wind chimes. It smelled of sulfur and moss.

Charlie thought he could smell the wild musk of the woman as well. His heart heaved. Warm fingers tickled his groin.

Moving stealthily on the balls of his boots, he stepped back into the niche and walked along the corridor of sandstone by which he'd stolen in here from the camp that he and the boys and Ravenna had set up late last night in this remote, unnamed sierra in north-central Arizona Territory. He came to a cut in the rock to his left and followed its circuitous route until it opened again just up the waterfall's bed from the meditating witch.

Warm, salty-smelling water tumbled onto the black volcanic rock to Charlie's left. He stepped out around it and into the trough of the falls, the water feeling hot as it closed over his boots. Ravenna sat about ten feet ahead of him, her back to him, her wet hair tumbling down her shoulders to nearly cover her plump, glistening buttocks.

Charlie stretched his lips back in devious delight as he stepped softly toward the woman, biting his lip with the effort of silence, lifting one foot at a time in the four-inch-deep black water. Humor rippled through him, and he had to pause a moment to choke it back down into his chest.

He continued forward. Ravenna was within four feet of him. He could see the pores in her skin, the droplets beading on her hair ends, tracing jagged routes across her shoulders and the backs of her arms.

Charlie held his arms out to both sides, crouching, cupping his hands, getting in position to grab the young, ravishing sorceress from behind, to grab her big breasts, scaring the holy hell out of her, and steal a wild kiss.

Ravenna was smiling, only Charlie couldn't see her face. She glanced behind her to see the javelina she'd conjured blinking up at her through Charlie Hondo's bright, horrified eyes.

It was a typical desert javelina, brown and gray, with a ridiculous-looking face that resembled that of a bear cub but with a long nose and flaring pink nostrils. The nostrils were really flaring now, the sides of the javelina that was now Charlie heaving as he breathed frantically, snorting his dismay at the sudden transformation.

Ravenna poked a finger to a corner of her mouth and tittered delightfully. "That'll teach you to sneak up on a girl saying her prayers to Elyhann!"

Charlie lowered his head and shook it wildly, as though to

rid himself of this ugly pig's body. His sides heaving faster and faster, he ran off squealing down the stone trough around the steaming pool, his little black, cloven hooves slipping and sliding on the slick rock.

He bulled forward into some manzanita grass and willows growing just beyond the spring and along the cut the runoff made through the middle of this canyon that slanted gradually down to the Salt River and then out of the mountains to the open Arizona desert beyond. He came back through the brush, splashed across the runoff creek, squealing and oinking madly, his eyes still the brown eyes of Charlie Hondo but now owning a horror that Ravenna doubted they'd ever shown before. Gold javelins of stark-raving terror shot from them as Charlie dashed up the ravine and into more brush on the stream's opposite side.

Ravenna threw her head back and laughed huskily with unabashed mirth, cupping her big breasts in her hands, as she watched the brush thrash and jostle, catching occasional glimpses of Charlie's pig head and curled tail above the weeds, willows, and black volcanic rocks.

Charlie arced away from Ravenna, then dashed back into the narrow ravine, splashed across the stream, and mounted the left-side bank, heading back in Ravenna's direction. When he reached the misty pool below her perch on the slab of rock, she touched the amulet with both her hands, muttered a phrase or two, and watched as the pig's front legs buckled. The javelina was suddenly Charlie again, lying belly down in the mud and moss and manzanita grass beside the pool.

Charlie's back rose and fell as he breathed. He pressed his cheek against the ground, grinding one of his hoop earrings into the mud, and blinked his wild eyes as though trying to reassure himself that he'd regained his human form. The cross tattoo on his right cheek shone spruce green against his terror-bleached skin.

Ravenna cradled her knees in her arms and loosed another volley of wicked, elated laughter.

"I'll put good money on the barrelhead that you'll never try that again!"

Charlie winced, pressed his hands to the ground on either side of him, and pushed himself up. He looked at Ravenna, his eyes hard with fury, teeth gritted, pale cheeks mottled red. Ravenna pointed at him and laughed all the harder, rocking back and forth on her naked bottom.

"You fuckin' bitch," Charlie bit out angrily, though instinctively knowing he had to restrain himself. If she could turn him into a javelina, she could turn him into a spider that she could crush under the heel of her hand.

And he had a feeling that if he pushed her at all, she'd be thrilled to do just that.

He got his knees beneath him and, drawing deep breaths of calming air, sat back on his heels. He ran a sleeve across his sweat-slick forehead. "Whew! You really had me going there."

"*Sí*," Ravenna said, her laughter slowly dying. "I had you running everywhere, Charlie." Suddenly, the laughter died and she looked at him coolly, narrowing one chocolate-brown eye. "I can do it again. Anytime."

"I thought you was tapped out."

"Too tapped out to conjure dragons, maybe. Too fatigued to let you boys turn into wolves just any old time. But any witch worth her salt can cast a spell like that in her sleep."

"Thanks for the warnin'."

Charlie heaved himself to his feet, grabbed his hat off a willow branch, pulled it down tight on his head, and strode off sulkily toward a wide crack in the canyon wall.

"Oh, come on, don't go sour on me, Charlie. I was only fooling around, just as you were, *mi amor!*"

"I didn't turn you into no pig," Charlie snapped, wheeling at the entrance of the defile that led back to the camp. "Hell, Ravenna, don't you know that during full moons, I *eat* pigs!"

"I apologize, *mi amor.*" Ravenna raised her eyebrows beseechingly. "Forgive me?" She drew her arms away from her breasts, lifted her chin, and threw her shoulders back. Alluringly, she said, "If you forgive me, you can have me. . . ."

Charlie would have none of it. He'd been scared shitless, and he wasn't used to the feeling. Didn't like it a bit. "Where we goin', anyways? You say we're getting close. Don't you think it's time you let me an' the boys know?"

"You'll know by the next full moon, Charlie."

"Goddamnit, Ravenna. Why's it such a big secret?"

"It is the biggest secret in all the world, Charlie. And not to be taken lightly. No offense, but if I tell you, you might blab it to the others. I know how you boys like to drink and carry on. We'll be laying in supplies in Tucson, and I don't want anyone there having any inkling about where we're headed."

"Me an' the boys don't like bein' kept in the dark by no . . ." Charlie let his voice trail off, frowning in frustration, averting his eyes.

"By whom?" Ravenna arched a severe brow. "By a girl? By a Mexican witch . . . ?"

She wagged an admonishing finger and clucked her tongue. "Never forget what I'm capable of, Charlie."

"Ah, hell." Charlie snorted, miffed, and stomped off down the rocky defile.

Ravenna laughed, funneled her hands around her mouth, and called, "I'll make it up to you soon, *mi amor!*"

Chapter 23

CUTTING THE TRAIL DUST IN TUCSON

Two weeks later, the dust-laden wooden sign leaning along one side of the stage and freight road and in the shadow of a tall, one-armed saguaro warned:

> BY ORDER OF THE TUCSON
> CITY COUNCIL ALL GOOLS
> WILL BE SHOT ON SITE!

Someone had scrawled in faded green paint below the main admonishment: *"Specially hobgobs!"*

"Now, that ain't no way to treat us ghouls that got jingle in our pockets," said Curly Joe Panabaker, riding directly behind Charlie and Ravenna, who headed up their small pack.

"Yeah," said Lucky Snodgrass indignantly. "Here we was,

aimin' on payin' for our trail supplies. Maybe we ought not be so damn nice, if'n they're gonna treat us like third-rate citizens!"

Ravenna chuckled. "I don't think they'd call us any kind of citizens, amigo."

"What I'd like to know is how they think they can pick a werewolf out of a townful of humans. They know and we know they can't, less'n there's a full moon, o' course."

Ravenna said, "Don't get cocky, Charlie. Word is probably out about your break from the pen, no? Telegrams have probably been flying all over the frontier—with your descriptions on them."

"Hell, you know there ain't no telegraph wire up longer than two days anywhere in the West without a ghoul of some sort rippin' it down." Charlie looked around with interest as he and the others rounded the trail and entered the outskirts of Tucson with its smelly stock pens and ancient adobe hovels from which the smell of spicy Mexican meat rose from brick chimneys. "Word of our escape from hell won't get out here for another month yet."

"Ah . . . Tucson." One-Eye sat up straight in the saddle, his lone dull brown eye sparkling beneath the brim of his shabby brown bowler hat. "Been a while since we been to a town, amigos. I say it's time to do a little stompin'." He glanced at a narrow, three-story building with FOUR ACES painted in arcing red letters over the high false façade. "And ruttin'," he added with a wolfish growl.

"Three days here at the most, boys." Ravenna looked around uneasily at the heavily armed men in skins and furs walking the boardwalks or slouching out front of quiet, dark Mexican cantinas or the more rollicking saloons. Bounty hunters, most likely.

"And we keep our heads down and stay out of trouble. A few drinks, a few girls, a little harmless fun."

She narrowed her eyes as she swept her admonishing gaze around the group. "But no trouble. Not even if it comes stalking. We avoid it at all costs. We are choir boys—remember that. We are the humble and meek and we give trouble of every color a wide berth. We have, as the gringos love to say, bigger fish to shoot."

"I think that's 'fry,' *chiquita*," Charlie corrected her, giving a snort as he ran his glance across a long, low-slung building on the south side of the pueblo's main street, which a board over the shake-shingled roof identified as a U.S. Bounty Office.

"Whatever," Ravenna said, as Charlie led them toward the Rincon Mountain Dance Hall and Beer Parlor on the street's right side, across a side street from a whitewashed Catholic church with a half-ruined wall around it. Several Mexicans in striped serapes and straw wagon-wheel sombreros lay atop the wall, hats tipped over their eyes. One had his arm hanging down the side of the wall, his brown hand still wrapped around the neck of a half-full tequila bottle. Another Mex lay slumped at his side against the wall's base, a brown cur sniffing around the pockets of his white cotton slacks.

Ravenna held back, looking up and down the street as the others drew rein at the hitchrack before which ten or twelve horses were lined up, the autumn-cool, late-afternoon sun shining on their backs.

"Come, *chiquita*," Charlie called to the witch as he swung down from the leather. "I'll let you buy the first round." He grinned, hitched up his blue wool cavalry trousers that showed the wear, tear, and campfire smoke of the long trek from

Colorado, and adjusted the black holster containing Warden Mondrick's .44.

"Me . . ." Ravenna said, narrowing her eyes at a building farther up the crooked main street. "I'm gonna have a long, hot bath. Scrub some o' the trail dust off my lovely body. I'll find you scalawags later."

"Ah, come on." Charlie beckoned to the black-haired sorceress. "One drink, and I'll join you!"

He grinned again.

Ravenna turned to him, one eye narrowed speculatively. She looked at the big, gaudily decorated building before her and from which came manic piano patter and the low rumble of male conversation. "I guess it couldn't hurt to see that you boys get our little sojourn here off on the right, quiet foot." Ravenna put her horse up to the hitchrack, swung down from the saddle, and tossed her reins over the tie rail. "And I sure could use some tequila and carne asada!"

"Now you're talkin'!" Charlie wrapped a long arm around the young woman's neck, leaning into her and glancing down her open vest as they followed the others up the porch steps and through the batwings. He'd forgiven the mercurial witch for changing him into a javelina under the waterfall. Or, at least, with the prospect of the treasure she was leading them to, he'd filed the transgression in the back of his mind for later.

"Welcome, gents . . . and, uh . . . senorita!" rumbled a jovial voice from the bar. The barman, a big, mustached, square-headed man in a white silk shirt, string tie, and paisley vest, was filling a schooner from a beer spigot. "Sit an' light a spell. Less'n you're spooks, that is. Don't allow 'em on the premises even if their pockets are loaded with silver!"

He tipped his head back and laughed as he swiped a flat stick across the frothy head of the beer schooner, sending a white spray of creamy foam shooting onto the floor behind the bar. He glanced at the plank sign nailed to a two-by-two ceiling beam about ten feet in front of the batwings. On it was crudely painted in a firm hand:

NO GOOLS ALLOWED.
IF YOUR A GOOL
THIS MEANS YOU!

Ravenna glanced at Charlie, who was still moving his lips and sounding out all the words, as he'd never learned to read above the third-grade level in his native tongue and was almost illiterate in English, as well.

"Like I said," announced the bartender, beckoning with a large, freckled arm revealed by a rolled-up shirtsleeve, "come on in an' sit a spell. I'll bring your drinks out in a minute!"

As the barman set the freshly poured beer on a tray and then carried the tray out from behind the bar, heading for one of the dozen or so tables, a good three-quarters of which were occupied by swarthy, bearded, sunburned frontiersmen of every stripe—mostly Americans—Charlie cut his perplexed gaze away from the sign, glanced at the other three men, and began tracing a zigzagging route toward an empty table toward the room's rear.

Ravenna remained in front of the batwings and jammed her thumbs behind her cartridge belt, a little apprehensive about the setup of the place. There seemed to be a lot of ghoul hunters in town, and that worried her. Not so much for herself—although she did have a sizable bounty on her own head in Arizona as well as New Mexico Territory and even western Texas. She was mainly worried about Charlie, One-Eye, Lucky, and Curly Joe. She didn't have the power to allow them to turn at will, so they couldn't turn until the next full moon, a week away. That meant they were relatively easy pickings for ghoul hunters.

But only if said ghoul hunters knew they were ghouls, that was. And Charlie himself had said it best—there were few ways to tell if one was a werewolf at any other time but the night of a full moon.

That thought relieved her apprehension somewhat.

Another one took its place, tying a little hitch in her belly. Werewolves and ghoul hunters were natural enemies. Could Ravenna's boys keep their heads when surrounded by the breed? Even after they'd had a few drinks and were hearing their wolves' howl?

Well, she'd never be able to get them out of here now. She doubted the crazy beasts realized how important it was they stay out of trouble, and what was at stake, all the power that was theirs for the taking once they got out of Tucson in one piece, with plenty of trail supplies, and reached the Lobo Negro Mountains three days southeast.

Deciding that she, a witch of her formidable powers, couldn't control three male wolves even in their human forms, she sauntered over to the bar, raking her spurred heels across the floorboards. She glanced at Charlie and the others just now doffing their hats and sagging into kicked-back chairs. Charlie eyed Ravenna with one brow arched questioningly.

She indicated with a toss of her head that she wanted to stand at the bar, then clutched her rump and grinned to signify she was sore from the long ride. She continued striding along the varnished mahogany counter with its brass footrail, past the half dozen men standing there chinning and drinking and casting lusty glances Ravenna's way.

Ignoring the leers she was so accustomed to, she drew up to the gap about two-thirds of the way down and was met there by a second bartender, a stocky, black-eyed gent with a nasty scar on his lower lip that was in contrast to his slicked-back and pomaded black hair. A citified half-breed, Ravenna reflected. Probably Pima or Apache.

Vaguely, she felt a little sorry for the man. She knew how it was to be an outcast, growing up as she had—a witch in the sprawling hacienda of a wealthy Mexican landowner who'd cast her out at an early age. Secretly coached by a half-breed peon witch whose family raised chickens and hay on her family's estate in southern Chihuahua, she'd finally been unable to suppress her powers. In a fit of pent-up rage, she'd turned her taunting older brother into a lobo who'd run away into the hills howling and yipping like a moon-crazed hyena, never to be seen again.

The half-breed gave Ravenna a dully inquisitive stare.

"Tequila," she said. "Put it up there with a beer, amigo."

While the Indian set about filling the witch's order, the jovial barman took the orders of Charlie and the boys. Ravenna threw back her first tequila, picked up her beer schooner, and turned to face the room, hooking a boot heel over the brass rail at the base of the bar behind her.

The jovial bartender hauled the tray of beer schooners and a whiskey bottle out to Charlie and the boys. He was the chatty sort, and as he passed around the beers and shot glasses and set the bottle on the table, he said, "You fellas don't have to worry about no ghouls in Tucson. No, sir!"

He turned to cant his head toward the rough-hewn men playing cards at the tables between Charlie's group and the door. "We got some o' the best ghoul hunters anywhere in the West right here in my very own saloon, and I'm proud to welcome Mr. Jesse James, his brother Frank, and their cousin Cole Younger to our fair territory."

He said this loudly enough to be heard above the patter of the scrawny little piano player in armbands and green eyeshade, smoking a loosely rolled quirley and hammering away at "Little Brown Jug."

A small-boned man with frosty blue eyes and a sparse blond mustache glanced toward Charlie and the boys and gave his chin a cordial dip. The man with the black beard beside him, a little bigger than Jesse James but with the same blue eyes, reached up with a sun-browned hand to pinch the brim of his battered felt sombrero. Cole Younger wore a tattered serape crisscrossed with bandoliers holding a good number of silver cartridges among the brass. There were six men with James and Younger, and the bartender proudly pointed them out, as well.

There were James Younger, Frank James, Bob Younger, Bill Chadwell, Clell Miller, and Charlie Pitts. These others barely acknowledged the introduction. They were a trail-seasoned, sour-faced lot, their hair and beards dusty and sweat-matted, and they were more interested in the stud poker they were playing than their ghoul-hunting fame.

"The only one who can compete with these boys for takin' swiller heads and wolf teeth and fer puttin' the fear o' god in the western hobgobbies is Uriah Zane his ownself." The barman said this to only Charlie's bunch, keeping his voice down. "But everyone knows Zane rides alone. Always has, likely always will.

He was in here once, wasn't all that sociable, but I reckon I never knew an overly sociable ghoul hunter. Odd breed."

The apron jerked his head covertly, meaningfully, toward the James and Younger bunch behind him.

"Hell," Lucky Snodgrass said, sneering over the beer he was lifting to his yellow-mustached lips, "everyone knows the Jameses and Youngers ain't nothin' but back-shootin', no-account robbers of small-town banks and slow-movin' trains. Hell, they'd shoot a hunk o' rock candy out of a child's fist."

Lucky snickered as he dipped his upper lip into his creamy beer foam.

The jovial barman looked suddenly stricken.

Someone cleared his throat loudly behind him. "What'd that sack o' burnin' ghoul shit say about me an' my boys?" Jesse James inquired, his blue eyes flat and mean.

Chapter 24

THE DEMISE OF THE JAMES GANG

The voice of steely-eyed Jesse James, while not lifted inordinately high, cut through the din of the Rincon Mountain Dance Hall and Beer Parlor like a razor-edged stiletto through hog tallow.

The low roar of conversation died suddenly. The little man playing the piano turned his head toward the James-Younger table, frowning through the smoke curling up from the quirley in his false teeth, and lifted his pale hands from the ivory keys. It was so quiet that Ravenna, still standing with her back to the bar, her belly tied in a half-hitch knot, could hear the piano keys' dwindling reverberations inside their drink-stained, bullet-scarred box.

The jovial barman standing between Charlie Hondo's table and the James-Younger table twisted around on his hips to stare, aghast, at Jesse, who sat slumped back in his chair. The Missourian held his pasteboards on the edge of the table in his left hand, his battered gray Stetson tipped back off his domed, sunburned forehead. The flap of his threadbare wool coat was pulled back behind the carved ivory grips of the .45 Peacemaker angled across his belly from the soft, brown leather holster on his left hip.

His pale blue eyes were menacingly dull as they stared across the fifteen feet toward Lucky Snodgrass, who sat slouched over his beer, both hands resting on the edge of his table, his eyes hard and cold, nostrils flaring. His long, dusty yellow ponytail curved down over his shoulder to disappear in his lap.

Charlie and the others wore similar expressions.

It was so quiet that Ravenna thought she could hear the jovial barman dribbling down his leg.

She broke the tense silence with, "Amigos! No, no, no, I think you misunderstand my friend Lucky over there. Lucky was only talking about that strange loner, big as a grizzly bear and twice as ornery—Uriah Zane!" She cast a cold smile at Lucky. "Wasn't that who you were talking about, Joe?"

She put just enough steel in her voice to get Lucky's attention, to communicate to the cork-headed fool the gravity of their situation and her previous admonishment to the boys to keep their noses clean here in Tucson.

"Yeah, that's what Joe said," Charlie said, all wide-eyed innocence in sharp contrast to the weirdly menacing tattoos on his cheeks. "He was talkin' about that loco Uriah Zane. Not you, Jesse, for Pete's sake." He chuffed ironically and lifted his beer to his lips.

"Yeah," Lucky said, fidgeting around with his own beer. "I meant that old coyote Zane." Softer now, really biting hard on his tongue, he added, "Didn't mean no offense to no one else . . . I reckon. . . ."

He threw back an entire whiskey shot and chased it with a long pull of his beer.

"There. See?" Ravenna said, swinging her hips as she sauntered over to where Jesse James still sat slouched down in his chair, his dangerous eyes still riveted on Lucky Snodgrass. "I tell you what—just so we can all get our friendly moods back, I will buy the next round for the James-Younger gang!" She pivoted, snapping a thumb above her head. "Apron, another round over here. Pronto! Anything they want! Add it to my tab. *Vámonos!*"

"Yes, ma'am! Yes, ma'am!" The jovial bartender, his face flushed deep russet, sweat glistening on his forehead, hurried around behind the counter and motioned for the half-breed apron to begin pouring and drawing fresh drinks. "Yes, ma'am, you got it! Whiskey and tequila all around for the James-Younger bunch! Really makes me proud to see them blessin' my humble establishment with their Yankee-killing, ghoul-huntin' presence. Yes, sir! Hurry up, there, Alfred. Pour them beers! No one gets thirsty in the Rincon, by God!"

When the James-Younger gang was all set up, the conversational din built up gradually again, the tone pitched with relief. The last thing anybody in the place wanted, least of all the jovial bartender, was a lead swap in such close, crowded confines.

The old man at the piano began hammering away at the ivories again, Charlie and the boys became distracted by their own conversation, and Ravenna herself breathed a sigh of relief as she turned to slouch over her beer and second tequila shot atop the bar. Soon, very soon, she would go over and lasso Charlie and the boys and haul them on out of the saloon and over to some quiet, side-street hotel.

"*Muchas gracias* for the drinks, senorita," a man's slightly slurred voice said behind Ravenna. She smelled horse sweat and whiskey. A finger poked her shoulder. "How 'bout you haul your pretty Mex self over to our table and join us?"

Ravenna cast a weary glance over her shoulder to see a ferret-faced young man in a bowler hat and a long, cream duster staring at her brightly. His eyes were spaced too far apart, and his nose sat oddly low between them, giving him the look of a moron. "Jesse's taken a shine to you, said he'd like an introduction."

The young man standing next to this one, a little shorter than the first and with a small knife scar on his knobby chin, chuckled, spraying spittle on his lower lip. "My brother Cole thinks you're just about the best-lookin' Mex piece o' ass he's seen in a month of Sundays!"

He rocked back on his undershot boot heels and nervously flicked one of his suspenders over and over again.

Ravenna couldn't help scowling at the pair. She recognized both from the James-Younger table, and she knew who they were. The first was Bill Chadwell. The other was Cole Younger's younger brother, James. She glanced behind them to see Jesse James, slouched casually as before, but staring between several standing men, casting his dully menacing, slightly jeering blue gaze at Ravenna. Cole Younger sat beside him, one stovepipe boot hiked up on a knee, his lips stretched drunkenly inside his shaggy black, tobacco-crusted beard.

"Tell senors James and Younger I am deeply flattered," Ravenna said huskily, unable to conceal her disdain for the arrogant Confederate ghoul hunters, "but I prefer to drink alone. Besides, I am leaving soon, on to better and bigger things—*comprende?*"

She blinked slowly and tossed her hair back from her face as she slumped forward over the bar once more. In the back bar mirror, behind pyramids of sparkling mugs and shot glasses, she saw Bill Chadwell's face flush. James Younger furrowed his dark brows and reached forward, grabbed the tail of her red sash, and jerked her around sharply.

"Don't turn your back on us, greaser bitch!"

"Yeah," said Chadwell, hardening his jaws, "we was talkin' to you on behalf of Mr. Jesse James his ownself!"

Ravenna's own face flushed. Miniature silver javelins of raw fury shot from between her narrowed eyelids.

Rage swept through her like a tidal wave, and before she knew it she'd muttered three words of a spell the peon witch had taught her long ago in Mexico. Bill Chadwell was suddenly gone, disappeared into thin air. Where his boots had been on the floor was now a yellow and green scorpion curling its striated tail with the venomous stinger at the end, and opening and closing its raised pincers.

James Younger looked around wildly. He dropped his eyes to the floor and stumbled back, lower jaw falling nearly to his chest. He made a choking sound and pointed at the scorpion.

"What have we here?" Ravenna said tightly, looking down at Bill Chadwell. "A goddamn scorpion in such a fine establishment?"

With that she stepped forward and rammed her left boot straight down, smashing Bill Chadwell under her copper-spurred heel. The scorpion crumpled under the red boot, blood and goo oozing out around the heel and staining the floor.

"She's a witch!" James Younger squealed, pointing at Ravenna with one hand and snagging one of the two Schofield pistols he wore in shoulder holsters inside his long denim jacket.

The piano fell silent once again, as did the crowd. All heads turned toward the commotion. James Younger whipped the Schofield up, raking the hammer back, and fired. Only his target was no longer before him. Younger's slug hammered into the side of the head of a bearded bounty hunter sitting at a table in Younger's line of fire.

As the man's head snapped sideways wildly, blood flying out his opposite ear to paint the two men sitting to the wounded bounty hunter's left, Younger gave another horrified yell and glanced down at the rangy mountain lion snarling and curling its tail in the same spot in which Ravenna had been standing only a second before.

Several startled bellows rose, the men sitting nearest the wildcat leaping to their feet and jumping back as Ravenna's angry cry swept through the room and she leaped off her back feet. She was a tan blur to most of the gents in the room as she rammed her lithe, dun, white-bellied body into James Younger, who triggered his pistol into the floor as Ravenna dug her fangs into the young border tough's throat, jerking her head from side to side, ripping and tearing. The young man's carotid arteries jetted hot, scarlet blood in all directions as the snarling lion rode him straight back down with a reverberating thud, causing the floor to lurch violently.

Thunder pealed as every man in the room not already standing bounded out of his chair and slapped leather, shouting. Charlie Hondo loosed his own version of a rebel yell as he and his three partners kicked their own chairs back and filled their fists with wood and iron, crouching as their pistols leaped and roared, flames stabbing toward the James-Younger table.

The James-Youngers were caught unawares, as they'd all

trained their pistols on the mountain lion, who, in the ten seconds that had elapsed since it killed James Younger, had bounded onto the back of Clell Miller, driving him into the floor beneath the James table.

Charlie Hondo's first shot blew Cole Younger's right earlobe off. Having bolted out of his chair and now aiming his Peacemaker and a short-barreled Remington toward the mountain lion killing Clell Miller under his table, Jesse James flinched and swung around toward Charlie. Hondo's second bullet slammed through Jesse's shoulder and punched him back into the table behind him.

As the mountain lion bounded out from under the James-Younger table, someone from another table triggered two shots at it, plunking one bullet into Frank James's knee while the other shattered the Missouri gorilla fighter's beer schooner, spraying glass and beer in all directions. James bent over, yowling and shooting the short, derby-hatted ghoul hunter who'd pinked his knee.

More pandemonium followed, the ghoul hunters shooting one another in the confusion while the mountain lion swept the room, dodging bullets and grabbing men's legs or arms and pulling them to the floor to rip their throats out beneath tables. The ghoul hunters were so confused as to whom exactly they *should* be shooting at, aside from the lion, that Charlie and the boys had a fairly easy time drilling one ghoul hunter after another, after making fast work of the James-Younger bunch, all of whom lay in bloody piles among overturned tables and chairs and blood-splattered cards and spilled ashtrays.

When most of the other men were down and powder smoke hung in an almost impenetrable haze from the rafters, Charlie started making his way to the front of the room, reloading one of his pistols quickly. "Come on, boys—I reckon we done wore out our welcome in the Rincon Beer Parlor!"

Lucky was down on one knee behind the bullet-shaped stove in the room's center, having just reloaded his own pistols, and was rolling the cylinder of one across his forearm, looking around in sparkle-eyed delight. He echoed Charlie's rebel yell and shot a wounded man climbing to his knees on the room's right side, then ran after the others, following Charlie to the front of the room and out the batwings.

"Come on, darlin'!" Charlie shouted back into the room from over the doors. "You cleaned up right well. Yessiree, indeed you did!"

He laughed as Ravenna bounded toward him, leaping sleekly over the only three tables still standing upright, and followed Charlie on out of the saloon. Only it wasn't the mountain lion leaping across the front gallery but the lovely black-haired witch herself, cursing shrilly in Spanish as the end of her red sash trailed out behind her.

"*Mierda!*"

"Best you learn to control that bean-eater temper, darlin'!"

"I think you're right, *mi amor*. But I have to admit to enjoying myself back there!"

"You still want that bath?" Charlie asked her as he untied his horse and swung into the leather.

"*Sí*, but I guess a creek will have to do!"

She leaped into the saddle of her own mount and jerked her gelding away from the hitchrack. Boot scrapes sounded from across the gallery. The jovial barman, no longer looking so jovial covered in blood, pushed through the batwings wielding a double-barreled shotgun.

"Monster bast-*arrrds!*"

He leveled the shotgun. Holding their horses' reins taut in their left hands, Charlie and Ravenna fired the pistols in their right hands. The bloody barman screamed as he triggered both barrels of his shotgun into the gallery's roof and danced back into the saloon, where he fell with a thud.

Charlie and the boys and Ravenna looked around warily. Men were moving toward them from up and down the street, crouched over rifles or extending pistols.

"Which way, *chiquita?*" Charlie said. "I'm feelin' a mite crowded."

Ravenna looked around, saw a gap between two buildings behind her. "South!"

Her gelding whinnied as she wheeled it around and shot it through the gap, the others galloping behind her, Lucky and One-Eye triggering a couple of rounds at men cautiously approaching along the main street. They thundered down the gap, weaved around several stock pens and piles of stacked mesquite wood, and hammered off into the saguaro- and greasewood-stippled desert, their hoof thuds dwindling behind them.

Back at the Rincon Beer Parlor, gun smoke sifted out over the still batwings and across the gallery, as though a fire smoldered inside. A face appeared in the smoke over the doors. Two pale blue eyes shone against ridged, sandy brows beneath a domed, windburned forehead. The man was hatless, his thin, light brown hair sitting close against his bony skull.

Jesse James staggered through the batwings. Holding himself tensely, bleeding from a shoulder wound and a leg wound and several grazes, he stumbled out to the edge of the gallery. His knees buckled, and he slammed onto the gallery floor. Kneeling there, bleeding, his face bleached and bland except for one eye twitching, he stared into the gap between buildings through which the gang of ghouls that had cut down his gang had disappeared.

"You got a reckonin' comin', ghouls," he muttered, gritting his teeth till his jaws cracked. "You . . . you ain't seen the last o' Jesse Woodson James!"

Chapter 25

. . . .

THE LITTLE MAN IN THE BONEYARD

"Goddamn you, you green-livered cur—drop that boot! Drop it this instant, you hear?"

The enraged admonition rumbled inside a shed on the left side of Tucson's crooked main drag. Hearing it, Uriah Zane reined General Lee to a halt before the long, disjointed, mud-brick and wood-frame building of which the side shed was a part. A shingle identified the sprawling dump as H. A. DEROSSO'S CABINET MAKING AND UNDERTAKING, with a smaller sign below that read: NO INJUNS SERVED HERE. SEE MIRO ESTACADO AT THE BLACKSMITH SHOP.

The voice inside the shed cursed sharply just as a yellow-and-brown mutt hurled itself through the one-foot gap in the shed's sliding door. The dog gave a little cry as the boot caught on the door and slipped from the cur's jaws to lie in the dust just outside the shed. Undeterred, the cur picked up the boot, and, as a potbellied, stoop-shouldered older man in a shabby canvas hat poked his head out the gap in the door, the thieving beast took off at a dead sprint past Zane, Angel, and Al Hathaway, heading at a slant across the main drag.

The potbellied man, possibly in his late sixties, though he could have been older, sucked in his gut, shuffled sideways out the door, and shook his fist toward the cur, shouting, "That's Cole Younger's boot, you son of a bitch! You bring it back here pronto and I maybe won't fill your ass full o' double-ought buck!"

The cur didn't slow its step but ran beneath a ranch supply wagon parked in front of a general merchandise store. He ran out the other side of the wagon and cut into a break between the general store and a tonsorial parlor, disappearing down the gap, leaving only a smear of sun-coppered dust behind him.

"Goddamn!" cried the potbellied oldster, whose face was nearly as black as the cur's stolen boot, though he was obviously a white man. He wore a red-and-black-checked shirt under a greasy deerskin vest that hung down to his bony knees. "Where'm I gonna find another boot to match the other'n?"

Angel studied the oldster. "Did you say that was Cole Younger's boot?"

"That's what I said, all right." The old man stared after the cur, his eyes still sharp with fury. "Got him all laid out inside, all dressed up and ready for plantin' in the suit Jesse picked out his ownself—*minus one fucking boot!*"

He cut his tan, fury-bright eyes to Angel and flushed with chagrin. "Sorry, there, young lady. Please pardon my blue tongue."

"Ah, it ain't nothing I haven't heard before when a cur was caught stealin' a dead man's boot. Under similar circumstances, I'd probably indulge in an epithet or two, myself."

The old man's eyes sparked as he stared fondly up at the redhead. "I'm Hank DeRosso, owner of this fine establishment behind me. Some call me an artisan. Soon to be a dog killer." His shoulders jerked as he wheezed a short laugh. "Who might you be, young lady, and any chance you're lookin' to settle down here in Tucson? Maybe git yourself hitched? I never been married, but . . ." He winked. "I reckon it ain't never too late to give her a shot!"

Angel laughed. "I'm Angel Coffin. These two polecats are Uriah Zane and Al Hathaway. Unfortunately, we're here on business, Mr. DeRosso. Otherwise, I could do worse than hitch my star to a man with his own business."

Uriah was staring up the street, toward the Rincon Dance Hall and Beer Parlor, against the front gallery of which several open coffins leaned. The watering hole was a block away, but the coffins appeared to have dead men inside, some with placards hanging around their necks. "What was that old train robber Cole Younger doin' in Tucson?"

"Him and Jesse and the boys come out to hunt wolves up in the White Tanks. There's an especially large bounty on 'em since a railroad's surveyin' track through that range into California, and the track layers and rock breakers been droppin' like june bugs on a goose pond."

"And likely runnin' from the law," Angel added. "The bounties on those fellas' heads is as big as that on the wolves they hunt."

"All I can tell you," said Hank DeRosso, "is we need all the ghoul hunters we can get. Especially after what happened day before yesterday to Cole and Frank James and nearly the whole damn James-Younger gang, 'ceptin' Jesse hisself. And half a

dozen other ghoul hunters and two deputy town marshals." He
shook his head, baffled. "How Jesse ever survived them wounds
o' his, I'll never know. Reckon he must have some ghoul in him
his ownself."

Hathaway spat chaw on a rock in the street and gave the man
a pointed look as he ran the back of his buckskin glove across
his mouth. "Charlie Hondo leave his callin' card, did he?"

"Charlie Hondo?"

"Four men ride into town day before yesterday?" Zane asked,
studying the coffins tilted against the Rincon House. "With a
pretty Mex gal?"

"Shit," the oldster said. "How'd you know?"

"I'm clairvoyant." Zane gigged General Lee ahead, starting
up the street. The others fell in behind him, and they angled
over toward where the coffins were lined up against the Rincon
House.

There were five open coffins, each containing a woeful-
looking dead man. All five of the men were naked. Bullet holes
showed in their chests and bellies and elsewhere, like round, gray
discs. The blood had been cleaned away. Likely, their clothes
had been too torn and bloody to bury them in. One had had an
eye shot out. Another had two bullet holes in his forehead. A
placard hung around the first man slouched in a coffin nearest
the beer parlor's front steps.

The placard read: DO YOU KNOW THESE MEN? An arrow
pointed to the right, indicating the four others.

A living, breathing man sat on the steps of the Rincon
House, holding a frothy beer schooner on his lone knee. His
other leg was wooden, and it ended in a peg where his foot
should have been. He was middle-aged, and he wore an eye patch.

He was drawing deep on a long, black cigar as he eyed the three newcomers sitting their horses near the coffins.

"Them's the five we can't identify. Unknown ghoul hunters in these parts. Probably here to hunt the White Tanks, just like Cole and Jesse James was."

Zane said, "How many others killed?"

"Shit, damn near fifteen men. Including Nevada Lewis, owner of the Rincon. Half-breed's runnin' it now. He's one of only three who survived the maulin' and shootin', 'cause he was smart and kept his head down behind the bar. The others probably won't make it."

"What do you mean mawlin'?" Angel inquired.

"That Mex bitch turned herself into a wildcat. Went wild as hell with the fires stoked." The one-legged man drew deep on the cigar and let the smoke out his nostrils, running a grimy thumbnail down the several-days' growth of beard on his pale cheeks. "The men with her opened up with their six-shooters. Coulda heard the din as far away as Phoenix or Fort Bowie."

"Did the men change?" Zane asked, looking past the Rincon Beer Parlor across the street to a cemetery flanking the church. There were several men digging graves among the titled gravestones and sage, while another man sat in a wheelchair in the minimal shade cast by a large saguaro.

"No, they didn't change. What—you think they were ghouls, too? This was day before yesterday, not *night* before yesterday. Won't be a full moon again for four nights, praise Jesus and Jezebel."

Zane glanced at Angel. "Well, they're still not changin'," she said. "That's good." She turned to the one-legged man. "Which way did they head?"

He pointed his cigar toward the gap between buildings on the south side of the main street. "Through there. A passel of hunters went out after 'em yesterday, led up by Sheriff McQueen his ownself. The town marshal lost both his deputies, who were also his sons, in the bloodbath. Pretty broke up about it. He took a couple bottles and two old Civil War pistols, and lit out for the Santa Catalinas. Doubt we'll ever see ole Carney again . . . poor bastard. If he don't drink himself on over the divide, he'll likely blow his brains out. Them boys was all he had."

Zane cast his gaze back behind the old Catholic church. "Is that Jesse out at the cemetery?"

The one-legged man turned to look, then turned forward again, nodding and taking another drag off his cigar. "Poor bastard's overseein' the buryin' of his brother, Frank. He don't normally drink, but he took a couple beers with him."

"Didn't know the Jameses were Catholic," Angel said dryly.

The one-legged man only shrugged. "Only cemetery we got."

Zane glanced at Angel and Hathaway, then swung down from General Lee's back. He tossed his reins to the scout. "You wanna stable our mounts? I'm gonna go powwow with Jesse."

"Sure thing," Hathaway said.

Zane slid his rifle from his saddle sheath, set it on his shoulder, and walked on around the corner of the Rincon toward the cemetery. He walked on past the half-ruined adobe wall that surrounded the old Spanish church that had likely been erected a hundred years ago, and began striding up the hill over which the boneyard sprawled among greasewood, bleached rocks, and Spanish bayonet. Some of the stones had been carved in the 1700s, and their edges had been weathered by time. Some of the names and years had eroded away completely, leaving flat faces of gray rock.

Zane walked up toward the crest of the hill, where two men were digging a grave with their shirts off. Their shovels clattered and scraped against the rocky earth. They were breathing hard and sweating, hat brims shading their faces.

Jesse James sat up the hill about fifteen feet, near the saguaro, though now its shade had angled away from him. Even with his left arm in a sling and a bandage around his right thigh, he was a tough-looking little man in a gray Stetson with a braided rawhide band. The hat appeared almost too big for his head. His face looked carefully chiseled from granite with its grave, deep-set eyes, delicate nose, and long, jutting jaws. The lines were clean and hard and gave the man an air of knotted-up power and barely bridled rage.

He had an open beer bottle clamped between his thighs. Another beer bottle, unopened, was wedged between his right leg and the arm of his wheelchair. Between his thin lips smoldered a quirley emanating the sweet smell of marijuana. His chin was dipped downward, eyes on the lined pad on which he was writing in pencil.

Zane walked up on his left side and, glancing at the pad, saw that the tough-nut gorilla border dog had a fine cursive hand. Almost girlishly slanted and looping.

Zane was six feet away from the chair when, not turning his head toward the newcomer, Jesse said quietly as though speaking to himself, "Uriah Zane."

Zane stopped, looked at the two men digging the grave, then at the sealed coffin sitting beside the mounded, red-brown dirt. "Sorry to hear about your loss, Jesse. Frank was a good hunter. One of the best."

"A good bank robber, too." Jesse turned to smirk at Zane

towering over him. His pale blue eyes were rheumy and red from the beer and Mexican marijuana. "Wouldn't you say, Uriah?"

"I reckon he was, at that. Leastways, he earned a fancy price on his head."

"You was too good for all o' that, weren't you?" Jesse's eyes turned accusing though somehow they did not lose their bemused cast as well. "No train robbin' for you . . . even if it was Yankee money you was stealin'."

"I didn't come here to discuss our differences, Jesse. After the War, some of us who survived went one way, others another. You're a good ghoul hunter, as Frank was, and while I wish you'd concentrate more on the ghouls and less on robbing innocent folks of their hard-earned savings, I wish you all the best." Zane pinched his hat brim and started to turn away.

"Innocent folks?"

Zane glanced over his shoulder at the little man in the wheelchair. "It was the government that turned those ghouls loose on the South, Jesse. Not the citizens. Lincoln's dead. Grant's wallowing around inside a bottle somewhere in Tennessee."

"The government is its citizens, Uriah—don't you know that?"

"Like I said, sorry for your loss."

Zane had walked a good ten feet back down the hill, his Henry rifle resting on his shoulder, when Jesse said, "They was Hell's Angels, weren't they? And that *puta* bitch . . . she was that witch from Chihuahua, Ravenna somethin' or other."

Zane kept walking.

"I'll be ridin' with you, Uriah, when you set out after them ghouls."

"No, you won't."

Zane kept walking, the tough soles of his high-topped moccasins crunching gravel and brushing against shrubs.

Behind him, Jesse sighed. "I'm gonna change your mind, Uriah."

"Doubt it."

Zane kept walking as Jesse chuckled softly beneath the *snick*s of the shovels digging Frank's grave.

Chapter 26

. . . .

THE BEAST IN THE CELLAR

Zane dined on hot, spicy Mexican food in a little, no-name eatery in an adobe shack near the flophouse he always threw down in when he visited Tucson and where he and Angel and Hathaway had each taken a room after stabling their mounts. The trio of ghoul hunters ate without speaking, fatigued from the long pull down from Colorado.

Afterward, they left gold coins on the table and headed on back to the Santa Catalina Inn, where they muttered their intentions of rising at dawn and heading out before sunrise. Zane went into his musty room furnished simply with a few sticks of crude furniture and a crucifix over the lumpy bed with its corn-shuck mattress and moisture-stained pillow.

He opened a shutter to the cool, desert air, taking a deep breath of the sage and the perfume-like fragrance of burning piñon pine and mesquite. Standing at the window, hearing the mournful strains of a mandolin twanging in some smoky cantina and the love moans of a soiled dove in the whorehouse that slumped on the other side of this dark side street, its shaded windows showing pink lamplight, Zane kicked out of his boots and stripped down to his balbriggans, which stretched across his broad-shouldered frame like buckskin soaked in a creek, then dried and shrunk in the hot sun.

He took another lungful of the fortifying desert air, lifting his chest so that the long underwear top drew even tighter against his shoulders. Then he turned the sheet and quilt back and eased into the bed, resting his head against the pillow and drawing the covers up to his chin.

He leaned over and blew out the candle on the bedside table. He closed his eyes, drew another slow, deep breath, and released it. He beckoned sleep, called for it, finally gritted his teeth and ordered it to come.

Like a rotten cur, it ran in the opposite direction.

For some reason, every muscle in his body leaped and writhed beneath his skin. His mind was a restless, twisted tangle of random, half-formed images flashing like the sun off a looking glass.

Finally, he threw the bedcovers back, dropped his feet to the floor. He'd go out and have a few drinks in the first watering hole he came to, maybe goose a few whores, and get his mind settled down. Then he'd return to the Santa Catalina, get a few hours of restful sleep, and be ready to ride at first light.

He dressed, left his rifle in his room with his other gear, and strode off down the hall lit by a single, smoky bracket lamp. Behind the doors off both sides of the corridor, he could hear men snoring, one whimpering childlike. He stole down the creaky, uncarpeted stairs with their rickety railing, walked past the hotel's middle-aged proprietor sleeping behind his desk with a *Policeman's Gazette* spread open across his chest, gold spectacles hanging down his nose, and headed out into the night.

Several pockets of lamplight shone up and down the main street, casting saddled horses tied to hitchracks in ghostly silhouette. The air was still and cool, the sky alive with stars, the desert around the ancient pueblo so quiet that Zane could hear coyotes calling from miles away.

He walked east along the street, following its meandering, widening, and narrowing course between the desert-blistered buildings. After thirty or forty yards, following the mandolin strains, he stopped and drew a lungful of air. The breath spread his ribs, opened his chest and belly, loosened the knotted muscles along his spine.

Maybe he didn't need a drink, after all. Maybe he just needed a walk to limber his legs and more of this light, cool, desert-perfumed air to nudge him off toward sleep.

He swung around and headed in the opposite direction, intending to walk a ways out of town where it was especially quiet and he could calm his racing thoughts in solitude. He passed the church that hulked up darkly against the shimmering stars that appeared as close as the many small crystals in a chandelier he'd once seen hanging in a Leadville opera house.

He came to the shaggy end of town and kept walking along the road that shone violet under the sky that as yet had no moon. The shrubs and rocks stood out in silhouette, the edges of the branches bathed in a deep purple luminescence. Zane stretched his stride, breathing deeply, the oxygen making him feel lighter, calmer. The blood flowed warm, loosening his muscles. His mood lightened.

He was beginning to enjoy the night, all the sounds he could hear, the brief blaze of a shooting star arcing across the northwestern horizon, shedding sparks before it disappeared behind a jagged-edged sierra. A coyote howled in the far distance. Nearer, he could hear a small pack snorting around an arroyo.

As he continued walking, he swung his head from left to right, scanning the terrain before him. As far as he could tell, the desert nearby was scored with no arroyo. It was dishpan flat all around him for a good half mile, before a low rise lifted like rumpled velvet in the north and began the swell of the foothills climbing toward the Santa Catalinas and the high, triangle-topped bulge of Mount Lemmon.

Zane stopped.

The coyotes continued to yip and snarl. There was a low, frantic peeping. They'd brought a deer down, and the deer was in its death throes while the coyotes finished it and fought among themselves over the warm blood and fresh, hot meat.

But where in the hell were they?

A dark, shaggy line shone to the west and slightly left of the wagon trail he was following. Could that be the arroyo? It had to be a half mile away.

No. His heart chugged softly in his ears as he stared at the mesquites and willows lining the distant wash. The cut was a good mile away. It appeared nearer only because he could see it so well, clearly enough to pick out the silhouette of the mountain lion stalking belly down amid the brush lining the wash. He could see the whiplike curl of its tail as it stole up on the coyotes.

Suddenly, the cat gave a shrill, snarling cry. The echoes rolled menacingly. Brush crackled raucously. Several coyotes yipped.

Their padded feet thudded off down the arroyo, abandoning the now-dead deer to the more formidable stalker.

The wildcat disappeared in the darkness of the cut, but one last snarl sliced across the silent night, chasing its own diminishing echoes.

Zane felt his lower jaw drop. Fear pricked at him like a chill hand under his collar. His senses were alive as snakes in a den. He could not only hear the howl of a wolf on Mount Lemmon now, but he realized that the soft snicking sound he'd been hearing for the past few minutes was a snake slithering along the ground to the north, maybe fifty yards away, maybe heading for a pack rat's den it had checked out earlier that day and had marked as a good place for a meal.

He looked up. The stars throbbed and glowed as though on the other end of a sharp lens. They were so clear that seeing them now made Zane's head ache, as though someone were flashing a railroad lantern in his face.

As though chained deep in a cold, dark cellar, the wolf in the ghoul hunter stirred. It paced to the end of the chain and back, sniffing and snorting at the crack under the door, growling and mewling deep in its throat. Angry. Frustrated.

Wanting more than anything to be free to hunt, stalk, and kill . . .

Zane had chained the beast and locked the cellar door. But for how long could he keep it in there? What would happen during the next full moon, or the next, or the one after that? Would it finally break its chain and burst through the door?

Would he become like Charlie Hondo and the rest of the Hell's Angels he'd come west all those years ago to hunt?

Closing his eyes against the magnified vision, clamping his

hands over his ears to quell the night sounds of predators and prey—the tearing and frantic screaming and the salty smell of blood—he wheeled and began striding back toward Tucson. He opened his eyes. The dim lights spilling out of the cantinas and saloons beckoned him. His heart beat faster but more hopefully now.

He'd get a drink and try to distract himself from the keenness of his savage senses, the barely contained will to unleash them, to follow them, and turn himself loose upon the night.

He dropped his hands to his sides, ground his teeth against the sounds that began slithering into his brain once more, making him feel dizzy and overloaded and causing his knees to grow spongy, his heart to beat faster and faster, his breath to grow shallow and weak.

His hands sweated in the chill air. His feet burned in his moccasins.

For a moment, he thought he'd pass out.

He kept walking.

As he passed the church, the padding of many canine feet sounded. He glanced down the side street between the church and the Rincon Beer Parlor that was dark now in the wake of the massacre.

Up the hill on which the cemetery sprawled, he heard frantic panting and scratching and saw the silhouettes of several shaggy wolves scrambling around the boneyard while one hunkered forward and dug, tearing at the soil with its front paws. It stopped digging, ran around, mewled and whined in frustration, then resumed digging once more.

Zane's nostrils filled with the sweet, wild scent of the carrion-stalking pack. The fetor struck his belly like pig slop, and his stomach turned, nearly heaving up its contents.

If a full moon had been rising, would he have been able to keep his wolf in its cellar?

No, somehow he had to kill it. He had to find a way to kill the beast or surely it would free itself, and it would be Uriah Zane forever chained and locked in that cellar while a madman ran loose upon the frontier.

He quickened his pace, stopped at the first cantina he came to, no more than a long, low adobe box with PULQUERIA scrawled in black paint over its deep casement door, above which a bead curtain hung, clicking and clacking in a slight breeze that had risen, bringing even more scents—so many it was hard to identify a single one—to the ghoul hunter's nostrils.

He bulled through the curtain, the beads clattering back into place behind him, loud as the thudding of shod hooves in his ears. His knees and hands shaking, he moved forward, sagged into an empty chair that sat back against the cracked adobe wall. A small, square table of half-cut cottonwood logs sat to the left of the chair. He rested an elbow on the table and entwined his hands together, mashing their heels against each other to steady himself.

He'd thought he'd been through all this months ago, during the first several full moons after he'd first been bit. It was happening again with nearly as much force as it had happened then.

He knew why.

It was happening because he'd become keenly conscious of the wolf inside him—maybe partly because of the savagery he'd seen in the Hell's Angels, maybe partly because of what they'd done here in Tucson day before yesterday—and he was steeling himself against it.

What he needed to do—and he did not know where the realization suddenly came from—was to ignore it. To ride it out. To not fight the sensations. He hadn't been fighting them before. He'd merely used the heightened senses to his best advantage. Now he was fighting them again in the same way he'd first fought them until he'd learned the key: to let go and distract himself, to have enough confidence in his own humanness to keep the wolf under lock and key without an overwhelming effort.

Without dwelling on the temptation he felt to turn the wolf loose . . .

The strains of the mandolin flooded Zane's senses. He welcomed the distracting music and looked around until he saw the player—a plump Mexican girl in an ornate Mexican basque. She was round-faced and sleepy-eyed, and she sat in a chair beside the bar made of crude cottonwood planks and resting on beer kegs. Two large crock jugs stood atop the bar, and Zane could smell the pulque inside one—a milky liquor made from the fermented juice of the century plant. In the other was *bacanora*, brewed from the agave plant, and a form of mezcal.

"*Bacanora*," he told the big-eared, thin-haired barman staring over the plank board at him, while the girl continued strumming the mandolin. While the barman was old and craggy, Zane could see the hint of his features in the girl, probably his daughter.

The barman, dressed in a white shirt, filthy apron, baggy green slacks, and rope-soled sandals, reached for the dipper handle poking up from the *bacanora* crock. Zane looked around the room, which spun and tilted slightly, and saw a milky-eyed man with close-cropped gray hair sitting at a table just beyond Zane's, staring blindly toward Zane and grinning toothlessly.

His small brown hands with nails thick as seashells were wrapped around a wooden cup.

Three men played craps on the floor toward the back of the cantina, and two other, younger men dressed in the gaudy attire of vaqueros sprawled in chairs near a smoky charcoal brazier. They smiled shiny-eyed at the opposite wall, one waving a hand lazily to the strains of the mandolin.

Beneath the girl's hide-bottom chair, only partly visible behind the pleats and folds of her black, gold-embroidered crinoline dress, the cur that had stolen Cole Younger's boot lay curled, nose to tail, sound asleep.

The barman limped out from behind the bar and set a stone mug on the table before Zane. With a shaky right hand, the ghoul hunter lifted the cup to his lips and drank the glass down in four deep swallows, the powerful hooch that tasted a little like skimmed milk and grapefruit juice searing his tonsils and lighting a welcome fire in his chest and belly.

The heat rose from his gut and flooded into his face, and he felt suddenly as though he were ensconced in warm wool during a raging blizzard.

"Another."

The barman turned from the bar, arching one thin, dark brow dubiously. The man lifted a shoulder, retrieved Zane's mug, and refilled it from the same crock as before. He set it on Zane's table and watched while the ghoul hunter took a sip. Zane put the cup down and smiled up at the man.

"Nectar of the fucking gods, eh, amigo?"

He fished some coins out of his shirt pocket, placed them one by one in the man's open palm, and waved him away.

He sat back in his chair and welcomed the warmth that

washed through him—up and down and sideways, reaching as far up as his hair ends, as far down as his toes.

The girl began to sing an old Spanish ballad, *"Había hace tiempo un muchacho para mí en Chihihuaha,"* and the ghoul hunter sagged farther back in his chair, setting his hat on the table and letting his head rest against the wall.

He sighed.

A warm, relieved smile stretched his mouth. Bittersweet tears filled his eyes as he listened to the lonesome song of unrequited love in Mexico, of a girl who drowned herself in a well because the boy she loved had eyes only for her more beautiful sister, and he indulged himself without feeling foolish.

He probably looked foolish, lounging there, teary-eyed, but he didn't feel anything but sorrow for the poor girl who'd drowned herself.

He listened to the ballad and then to two more, his soul dangling from every note. He'd never felt more alone—even during those long nights he'd first started fighting the wolf inside him—but the strong Mexican liquor filed off the edges of the loneliness. He finished the pungent but deadening brew, then heaved himself unsteadily to his feet. He shambled over to the girl with the mandolin and dropped a copper dollar into the coffee tin sitting beside her atop the bar.

She gave him a cordial nod as she strummed and sang.

He bowed lavishly, doffing his hat and sweeping it down before him. *"Muchas gracias, senorita. Para uno tan joven, usted canta maravillosamente sobre angustia."* For one so young, you sing beautifully of heartbreak.

He set his hat on his head, turned, and staggered out of the cantina, retracing his steps back to the second floor of the Santa

Catalina Inn. He glanced at Angel's door directly across from his own.

No sounds in there. At least, none that he could hear. She was likely asleep. His heart started to tighten, and he floated away from it. Vaguely, behind the curtain of drunkenness that had dropped down over his senses, numbing them, he made a mental note to remind the marshal that if they were still riding together during the next full moon, she'd need to keep her guns filled with silver, and a watchful eye on her partner.

He chuckled. Angel wouldn't need reminding.

He went into his own room and was finally drifting off into a welcome slumber when someone rapped loudly on his door.

"Zane! Zane! You in there, Zane?"

The ghoul hunter jerked his head up from his pillow and reached for the LeMat. He flicked the hammer over the shotgun shell and aimed the piece at the door. "Holy Christ! Who the fuck is it?"

"It's Jesse. Open up! We gotta talk, Zane!"

Chapter 27

. . . .

JESSE'S DREAM

In his balbriggans and still holding his heavy, cocked LeMat, Zane threw the door open and stood barefoot, staring down at the wheelchair-bound, wiry little creature in the too-big hat, pale blue eyes still sparkling crazily, as they had been earlier in the day.

The outlaw/ghoul hunter was no longer drinking or smoking, but he hadn't quit long ago. He reeked of both alcohol and marijuana. He was dressed in a long, gray duster, and pistols jutted up from holsters on his hips. He held a Spencer repeater across his bony knees with his good hand, the left one still in a sling.

"We done talked at the boneyard, Jesse," Zane said, voice raspy from the sleep he'd been drifting into.

"Hear me, damn you," Jesse said, narrowing his eyes menacingly, his delicate face flushing, veins bulging in his temples. "You're gonna need me when you go after them ghouls."

"I doubt it."

"I know where they're headed, Uriah." Jesse's lips shaped a slow smile. He let that sink in, and then he added, "Seen the place in a dream last night. And it's still right here."

He lifted his right hand from the carbine's breech and set a long, slender index finger against his right temple. "You don't got time to track 'em, 'cause they're racin' the full moon, four nights away. And now they'll be coverin' their trail. Won't take no chances."

He lifted his chin to glance out the window behind Zane, where the milky wash of a three-quarter moon was brushing Tucson's rooftops. "You need me to lead you to where they're goin'."

"Bullshit." Zane started to close the door.

Jesse wheeled himself forward and stuck a boot out to stop it. "Don't you do me that way. I know where they're headed, goddamnit, and you need me to show you. My men are dead, and I need you, Uriah, though I'll likely rue this night for sayin' it. But you need me, too."

"I won't ride with you, Jesse."

Zane had been invited to join the James-Younger gang years ago, just after the War, when they'd all found themselves together in Kansas. Zane had declined then, because the gang was a pack of angry killers led by a demented, kill-crazy hillbilly in Jesse James. The War had given him a good excuse to kill and rob banks, but even without the War, his severe visage would be adorning wanted dodgers throughout the West. That was just who Jesse was. It was also Cole Younger and even Jesse's late brother, Frank, to some extent, though Frank might not have been as het up without the War and the Hell's Angels giving him a cause.

"Don't be a fool, Uriah. You an' me fought on the same side. We're still fightin' on the same side." Jesse made his red-rimmed eyes bulge crazily. "And I got the gift. Handed down by my grandmammy. Second sight." His eyes danced as though there were lights behind them. "And I seen where them killers o' Frank and our Confederate brethren are headed, Uriah."

He cackled like an old woman, sitting there shaking in his chair. Just then Zane smelled cigar smoke and saw one of the men who'd been digging Frank's grave standing in the shadows near the end of the hall, near the stairs. He stood with one hand against the wall behind him, smoking desultorily, waiting to take his crazy benefactor back down the stairs.

Across the hall, Angel's door opened. The marshal stepped out in a striped nightshirt that hung to her bare knees. She had a pistol in her hand, and as she moved out into the hall, she aimed it at the back of Jesse's head, loudly ratcheting the hammer back.

The Missourian had heard the door latch click and the hinges squawk, and now he turned to see the redhead bearing down on him, and he grinned. "Well, if it ain't the lovely Marshal Coffin."

"Sorry for your losses, Jesse, but I reckon I'll be lockin' you up in the local hoosegow. Pick you up on my way back to Denver. Several rail lines will be very happy to see you hanged."

Zane sighed in frustration. "Forget it, Angel."

She furled a skeptical brow. "How's that?"

"The crazy bastard's pullin' out with us tomorrow."

Zane stepped back into his room and closed the door.

* * *

The next day, at high noon, the hunting party, including Jesse James, riding his black-socked buckskin, was angling southwest of Tucson, the direction in which the outlaw from Missouri said they were heading. The tracks made by both the Hell's Angels and the posse that had followed them out from town bore this out.

It was a cool, sunny day, though high, thin clouds moving in from California threatened rain later. Al Hathaway, who was riding ahead, checked his mule down suddenly and rose in his stirrups to inspect the trail, swinging his head slowly from left to right and back again.

"What is it?" Zane asked.

Hathaway said nothing. He swung heavily down from the mule's back, dropped the reins, and walked ahead a ways, where the trail narrowed between two piles of cracked and sun-bleached granite heaved up from the earth's volcanic bowels eons ago. Chin dipped, he swerved off the trail's left side where a thin corridor in the rocks rose up a low shoulder along an outcropping. He walked forty yards to the top of the shoulder, then turned to stare back down where Zane, Angel, and Jesse James waited astride their horses.

"They came this way, swingin' back east. The posse from town was still followin' 'em."

"Nope." Jesse shook his head.

He no longer wore the sling but kept his left arm sort of hanging gingerly at his side, gloved hand resting on his thigh. He'd changed the bandage on his right thigh that morning before they'd left, and so far no blood spotted it. A tough little Missouri devil, Zane silently opined.

"What do you mean, 'no'?" Hathaway asked, indignant. "I got eyes; I can see their trail."

"They mighta gone that way for a time, but they would have swung back west. They were just tryin' to shake the posse and anyone else trailin' 'em—includin' us. I told you fellas . . . and ladies . . . I know where they're goin'. There's no need to waste time scourin' for sign!"

He booted his buckskin ahead between the scarps and disappeared behind a bend in the trail, his dust sifting behind him.

Sitting to Zane's right, hands crossed on her saddle horn, Angel gave the ghoul hunter a pointed look. "How can you be so sure he really does know where the Angels are heading? He's crazier'n a tree full of owls, Uriah."

"That's sorta how I know." More to the point, the wolf in Zane sensed the medium in Jesse. Saw it in his eyes. He'd seen it before in the Southern hill folk, many of whom practiced the art of clairvoyance and witch doctoring and all manner of magic, black and otherwise. Besides, Jesse hadn't been studying the trail at all, but he seemed very confident about the path he'd chosen south of Tucson.

When Hathaway had stepped into his saddle, he gave Zane a skeptical glance before shuttling it to Angel, who shrugged. With a grunt, Hathaway touched heels to his mule's flanks, and Zane and Angel followed the scout on up the trail a half mile before they spotted Jesse squatting atop a hill to the right side of the trail. His buckskin lazily foraged short, green grass spiking among the black rocks.

Jesse looked at the trio below him and jerked his head, beckoning. "Take a look, friends."

Zane dismounted, dropped his reins, and started up the hill. Angel and Hathaway glanced at each other dubiously once more, then stepped down out of their saddles. They followed Zane up the hill to where Jesse knelt, staring off toward the southwest. He pointed toward a series of rocky, sun-blasted sierras rearing up against the western horizon—long, toothy-tipped ranges that appeared as dark and foreboding as the mountains on the moon.

"See that second range there, a little higher than the first with that high peak in the middle?"

Zane tipped his hat brim down a notch and squinted, following Jesse's finger. "I see it."

"That's the Lobo Negros. From a different angle—from the angle I saw in my dream of two nights ago—that high peak there looks like the head of a giant, snarling wolf, both ears sticking straight up in the air."

"And that's where you think the Angels are headed?" Angel said.

Jesse nodded.

"Since you know so much about where they're headed from this dream of yourn," Hathaway said, "you must have some idea why they're headed thataway."

"Nope, can't help you there, Mr. Hathaway. I got the powers of seein'. Not readin' what's in a man's—or, most 'specially, a wolf's—heart. But that's where they're headed, and if they keep movin' as fast as they was through here, they'll be in the heart of them mountains in three nights."

"The night of the full moon," Angel said, staring pensively off at the dark, volcanic range dappled in sunlight and shadows cast by the high clouds. She glanced quickly at Zane and away again.

A hunting hawk screeched in the far distance, though in Zane's ears it sounded no farther away than their horses.

"Let's shake a leg," he said, and walked back down the rise.

The others followed, approaching their mounts.

Angel turned to Jesse. She had her rifle on her shoulder. "James, you an' me need to get somethin' straight, because it's been gallin' me ever since we left Tucson."

The Missouri outlaw turned to her with that lascivious grin he reserved especially for the buxom, redheaded deputy marshal. "How can I help, Miss Coffin?"

Her hands and arms moving in a blur, she swept her rifle off her shoulder and rammed the butt hard into the outlaw's belly. Jesse gave a great, pained *whoosh* of expelled air and dropped to his knees, kicking up a dust cloud.

"What . . . in Christ . . . ?" he grunted, making a face while pressing the heels of both his hands to his battered midsection.

"That ain't much, but that's for all the trains you robbed and all the people, including badge toters, you killed over these years since the War. And that's my promise to you that when our mission here is over, you'll be accompanyin' me back to Denver in cuffs and shackles."

She spat into the trail beside the grunting, panting Jesse, gave his dislodged hat a kick, and turned toward her horse.

"Feel better?" Zane inquired.

"I do."

As Angel mounted her horse and Hathaway shook his head, choking back snickers, Zane crouched over the damaged outlaw and grabbed one of his arms. "You all right, there, Jesse?"

He helped the man to his feet and gave him his hat.

"Law, law," Jesse said, shaking his head as if to clear the cobwebs, limping over to his horse, "she is a caution!"

* * *

They camped that night about seventy miles southwest of Tucson, having made good time and seeing enough of the Hell's Angels' sign as well as that of the posse behind them to convince them all, including Angel, that the outlaw was indeed leading them in the right direction—pretty much on a cross-country beeline toward the Lobo Negros.

They rose well before dawn and traveled by the light of the large moon still high in the western sky and shedding nearly as much light as the dawn sun would. They followed arroyos and shallow canyons, crossed two low jogs of dun-brown hills, and found a bowl in the hills where Apaches had once camped, the jacales still standing and waiting for the wandering hunters and warriors to return. Five horses had been picketed nearby, and there was a pile of fresh ashes in the middle of the camp.

Without a doubt, Hondo's group had camped here.

The posse from Tucson had followed about three hours later but did not camp. As it turned out, they would never camp again, for as Zane's party headed into a deep, narrow canyon between two shelving escarpments of cracked sandstone boulders, they found seven of the nine posse riders and their horses lying smashed to bloody pulps beneath the rocks and boulders that had been loosed from one of the ridges.

The killings had occurred about a day ago, judging by the state of the carcasses after the carrion eaters had been at them. They were still at them. The canyon was aswarm with quarreling buzzards and coyotes that pranced among the rocks on the sides of the ridges, tongues hanging, eyes bright with the feeding frenzy. They'd likely been hard at work in the canyon bottom, fighting with the buzzards, before they'd heard the approach of the four riders and scrambled away.

The buzzards were more persistent. Some refused to leave the bodies, flapping their ragged, dusty black wings in challenge, or flying awkwardly onto boulders nearby to bark and curse the interlopers, their proprietary eyes sharp and wicked.

No one said anything as they weaved their horses around the dead men and their dead mounts and the boulders now nearly jamming the canyon. Zane's casket-carrying coffin scraped against the rocks, occasionally getting hung up until Zane clucked to General Lee and nudged it free. He was riding point, the others riding Indian-file behind him, when he jerked back on the palomino's reins, slid his cross-draw pistol from its holster, and raised the piece, clicking back the hammer.

He loosened his trigger finger. A man sat atop a flat-topped boulder with his back to the scarp behind him. His legs were stretched straight out before him, the badly worn, pointed toes of his boots tipped slightly to each side. He was dressed in dusty denims and a canvas coat.

His head had been hacked off of his shoulders.

The head was now resting in his lap, cradled in his arms as though its owner was afraid he might lose it.

Chapter 28

. . . .

THE WINGED DEMON RETURNS

The eyes of the disembodied head, still wide in horror, stared out over Zane as though at the dead man's own killers among the rocks on the other side of the canyon. The head's thick, chapped lips were stretched back from scraggly teeth. He was missing one eyetooth. He wore a three-day growth of black beard and a deep gash below his left eye.

He also wore a dusty, faded-yellow Stetson with the front brim pinned to the crown. Several buzzards and a lone hawk circled above the corpse. One buzzard was perched atop the man's shoulders, probing the gap where the man's head had been and where now only blood and viscera shone. The bird turned its ugly eyes on Zane and gave a challenging squawk, splaying one wing and shifting its weight from one foot to the other.

"Mother of God," Hathaway said behind Zane.

"No, it's Day Summerville," said Jesse. "Ghoul hunter from over Nevada way." He clucked fatefully. "Told me as he was leavin' the Rincon just before that *puta* bitch came in and turned into a mountain lion that he was fixin' to settle down, go back home to Winnemucca, and get himself hitched to a half-Mojave gal with big, pillowy teats."

The Missourian spat a runny quid against the face of the boulder on which Day Summerville sat.

Zane nudged General Lee ahead, and they rode down the twisting corridor and up a steep grade where the walls drew back and they were suddenly out on a broad flat once more, heading for the cut in the mountain range that would take them to the next valley and the Lobo Negros beyond.

They came to an old lava field with what appeared to be an ancient Indian trail cut through it, angling toward the Negros rearing blackly and jaggedly in the west. It appeared the only route through the field of sharp-edged and jumbled boulders that had likely spewed from the top of the Negros millions of years ago, when the volcanic cones had blown their proverbial stacks. Zane put General Lee onto the trail, looking around cautiously, caressing the trigger of his Henry repeater that he held across his saddlebow. His crossbow and quivers hung from lanyards down his saddle skirt.

When they approached a keyhole-like notch in a low ridge, Zane checked General Lee down again sharply and grimaced. The others rode up around him, following his gaze to the man tied to a gnarled paloverde along the right side of the trail, just before the trail entered the tunnel-like canyon.

The man was naked and sun-seared a bright, blazing pink. His hands were tied behind the tree, as were his ankles. He'd been cut up bad—long, deep, torturous slices. It was hard to tell for all the blood, but he appeared to be missing his privates, and he'd been gutted.

"Well, well, well—what have we here?" Angel said grimly. "Another warning to anyone dusting those killers' trail?"

"Looks that way, sweet Marshal," Jesse said. "If you need comforting, I'd like to be the first to volunteer my services."

"Shut up, James."

"Hold on." Zane swung down from General Lee's back

"What is it?" Hathaway said.

"Thought I seen him move."

The big ghoul hunter tramped up the steep, short trail to the ledge of sand and rocks upon which the paloverde grew, its thin, slender leaves flashing silver in the breeze, which also blew the tied man's straw-yellow, coarse blond hair about his forehead, his chin tipped to his thin, bloody chest.

Zane stood before the man, whose age it was impossible to tell. He reeked heavily of blood and viscera and urine. He'd been cut up bad, but most of the cuts except the one that had disemboweled him were only an inch or so deep. He was about five and a half feet tall, and Zane could see chin whiskers a shade darker than his hair, though he couldn't see much else about his face until he reached up with his right hand and used his index finger to shove the man's head back against the tree.

The head jerked. The skinny, blood-matted chest rose slightly. The eyes fluttered, opened to slits. They were cobalt blue and dark and pain-racked.

"Pl . . . please," he rasped, barely loudly enough for Zane to hear. "Kill me . . . !"

Zane grimaced and took one involuntary step back. He

turned to Angel, who sat her paint beside General Lee. "Cross-bow!" A gunshot would have been heard for miles around.

She reached over and grabbed his bow, nocked an arrow to it, and tossed the weapon up to Zane. He grabbed it one-handed, aimed, and drilled the silver-tipped shaft through the man's chest and into the tree behind him. The missile crunched through the man's breastbone. The fletched tip quivered.

The man's head shook as though he'd caught a sudden chill, coarse hair sliding this way and that across his eyes. His chin dipped one last time to his chest.

"Those fucking killers," said Hathaway. "I sure can't wait to drill some forty-four slugs through those bastards' cold, black hearts." He cast his molasses-eyed gaze at Zane. "What was the point of that? Huh? Will you tell me? I know 'Paches do it, but . . ." He let his voice trail off in bitter frustration.

"They did it for the same reason the Apaches do it," Zane said, long-striding down the slope and lashing the crossbow to his saddle. "To scare the hell out of us, make us think hard about following. Which means," he added, peering through the keyhole notch, "that we must be damn close to the Angels' destination. Best proceed with extra caution."

He swung back into the leather and nudged General Lee ahead once more, Angel falling in behind the bouncing, rattling casket, Hathaway behind her, and Jesse bringing up the rear. As the Missouri outlaw entered the keyhole notch, he lifted his Spencer's barrel to scratch his cheeks, his pale eyes bright with eager anticipation. To Zane glancing back at him, he almost looked as though he were about to break out in hysterical laughter.

Zane turned his head forward again as General Lee carried

him out the other side of the keyhole and they found themselves in another canyon cut into the side of a steep slope rising to the left and straight ahead, on the canyon's other side. A narrow trail hugged the side of the slope to Zane's left. The trail followed the rim of the canyon to the other side, then switchbacked up the far side to the edge of a massive block of steeply shelving sandstone crowning the ridge crest.

Zane gigged the palo on into the broad canyon, saw several steep, rocky hills around him, between him and the mountain's far side. Another trail snaked off across the canyon floor to Zane's right, rising and falling out of sight for a time before reappearing in the far-northeastern distance, curling around the base of the steep ridge and disappearing around its side.

Nearby, a roadrunner made a red flash as it darted out from behind a low, rocky knoll covered in greasewood, and crossed the trail before disappearing into a patch of Spanish bayonet and rocks on the other side.

Zane swung down from General Lee's back. Hathaway dismounted his mule, and the two strode around, looking for spoor. Hathaway crouched, grabbed a chunk of horse dung, and sniffed it.

"Rained last night here, likely compromised the Angels' sign. Musta come through here, though, as I found a couple horse apples like this one along our backtrail a ways."

"Split up," Zane said, remounting and turning General Lee down the canyon floor to the right.

Hathaway followed him. Angel turned to follow the trail hugging the slope and switchbacking up the far ridge, and Jesse reluctantly followed the marshal. "Don't see why I have to follow her," he groused, "when she could so easily shoot me out of my saddle and say I was beggin' for it."

"Wouldn't put it past her," Zane agreed.

"What the hell's that?" Hathaway said behind him.

Zane had heard it, too—a heavy *whooshing* that sounded all too familiar, and which caused a cold hand to reach into Zane's belly and twist his stomach hard. He looked up. A winged creature, little larger than a golden eagle from this distance, curved around the far-right side of the ridge crest and began descending. Quickly, it grew larger, its large wings flapping slowly, heavily, long tail curling out behind it like a rudder.

"Ah, no," Zane complained as the dragon rushed toward them.

He glanced behind him at Angel and Jesse following the trail along the side of the canyon. "Take cover! Our winged friend is back!" As Angel and Jesse looked toward where the big ghoul hunter had been pointing, Zane pointed down canyon ahead of him and to his right, where a pile of cabin-sized boulders all jumbled together offered the only cover for him and Hathaway.

"Come on, Al—let's head for them rocks!"

Hathaway glanced once more at the dragon that was now within two hundred yards and winging toward him and Zane fast, eyes blazing like sunlit gold. "I'll race ye!"

Zane pulled General Lee off the trail and down the grade toward the boulders. Hathaway's mule brayed indignantly and thumped along toward Zane on the ghoul hunter's left. They gained the rocks at nearly the same time, leaping down from their saddles. Quickly, they led their mounts into a narrow notch between the boulders and the southern ridge, tying them both to spindly shrubs.

Zane ran back and grabbed his Gatling gun and a cartridge belt out of the casket. Hathaway was climbing up the rocks, breathing hard and hauling himself up one boulder at a time.

Zane climbed frantically up behind him. The *whooshing* was growing louder. The big beast's wings were creaking and flapping like giant flags.

As Zane scrambled up into the rocks that afforded plenty of niches to hide from the dragon's flames, he saw the beast itself as it bore down on the escarpment, its gold eyes blinking slowly, fiercely, flames beginning to spiral out of its mouth and nostrils. Zane shoved Hathaway into a notch between two of the stacked boulders. As he threw himself into the same notch, he felt the rush of heat behind him, heard the beast's enraged bugling. Belly down in the gravel between two slab-sided boulders, his Gatling beside him, he saw the orange bursts of flame hammering just outside his and Hathaway's hiding place.

Fifty feet below, General Lee whinnied shrilly though the horse was likely safe in his and the mule's deep, well-protected gap. The mule brayed raucously.

Outside the notch, flames leaped and coiled. Tendrils licked a couple of feet into the gap, like living things trying to reach Zane and the Army scout. They disappeared as suddenly as they'd appeared, leaving only smoke and the heavy smell of charred rock and foliage.

Zane looked at Hathaway. The scout's eyes were large as he stared back out of the notch. He'd lost his hat, and sweat trickled down his dark forehead and bearded cheeks. "That hydrophobic polecat with wings nearly cooked us like spitted jackrabbits!"

Zane grabbed the Gatling gun. He caught a glimpse of the bandolier he'd slung around his neck and shoulder, and cursed. He'd meant to grab a bandolier of silver, but in his haste he'd grabbed one with lead slugs. What the hell, he thought. Dragons weren't his trade. He had no idea if any kind of slug would kill one.

Sliding the big gun behind him, he scrambled back out of the notch.

"Best stay in here!" Hathaway warned. "You ain't never gonna kill it even with that bullet belcher!"

Outside of the notch, Zane rose to his knees and perused the sky. The dragon was just then winging over the southern ridge, over and beyond the keyhole through which he and the others had entered the canyon. A second later, it disappeared on the ridge's other side.

Most likely, it would be back.

Zane shouldered the Gatling gun and began crawling up the boulders above him, grabbing the edges of the rocks and hoisting himself, grunting and groaning and using his legs to push, his arms to pull. Finally, he gained the top rock that was slightly slanted but that offered a good view of the canyon and the ridges all around.

He glanced to his left, saw the dragon banking steeply in the southwest and beginning to wing back toward him. He couldn't see either Angel or Jesse. A limestone knob jutted out of the western ridge, with towers and parapets of wind-sculpted rock. Likely they'd holed up in there.

Quickly, keeping an eye on the fast-approaching dragon, Zane set up the tripod, spreading the wooden legs and mounting the gun atop the platform. He twisted the locking nut in place and rammed a cartridge belt into the cylinder, hearing the satisfying hollow click of the first cartridge slipping neatly into the breech.

Zane swung the gun to the west and crouched low, aiming

over the barrel. Gatling guns sacrificed distance and accuracy for the volume of shots and power they expelled in a short amount of time. He had to wait for the critter to get in close enough to do some damage, but not so close it would turn Zane into a roasted coffee bean before he could kill it.

If bullets of any kind could even kill such a hellish monstrosity . . .

The dragon winged toward him, black smoke curling from its nostrils. The wings flapped, making their sinewy sounds, like unoiled door hinges. A bugling cry rose from the long, down-canted snout, and the gold eyes pulsated, drilling straight across the hundred-yard gap now between itself and its quarry.

"Ugliest damn bird I ever seen," Zane muttered through gritted teeth as he began turning the wooden crank furiously.

Chapter 29

. . . .

DRAGON SLAYER

The Gatling fairly exploded, leaping on its legs as the roaring canister spit smoke and fire at the great beast closing on it fast. Echoes hammered off the surrounding peaks.

Bam-bam-bam-bam-bam-bam-bam-bam-bam!

Zane cursed as the beast kept coming. The bullets seemed to bounce off its nose and forehead and even the two golden eyes. Determined, Zane kept cranking as the dragon winged in, dangerously close.

Bam-bam-bam-bam-bam-bam-bam-bam-bam!

"Get down!" Hathaway shouted from below, the scout's voice barely audible above the beast's angry wails and the whoosh of its giant wings. As it drew within thirty yards, the smoke curling from its nostrils, there was an orange flash and then fire began jetting from its nose and mouth. Zane had already grabbed the Gatling gun and fairly hurled himself over the side of the crag, his boot slipping on a stone ledge below. As the fire leaped like an orange blanket onto the slanted rock he'd just vacated, he rolled off the ledge and hit the boulder below it hard on his left shoulder, the Gatling crashing down beside him.

The air left the ghoul hunter's lungs in one massive grunt. He blinked rapidly.

As his vision cleared, he saw the dragon sort of twist and pivot in the air. Unsteadily? Hard to tell. Now it banked sharply left, heading toward the tall northern ridge mantled far above the beast with the sandstone caprock. The dragon continued to bank, still rising and then gradually dropping as it turned away from the ridge and careened toward the limestone knob where Zane figured Angel and Jesse were hunkered.

Apparently, the beast was going to make another try for Zane.

The ghoul hunter, buoyed by the possibility he'd done some damage to the winged ghoul and wanting to give it another shot, shouldered the battered gun and heaved himself back up the rocks to the slanted, scorched boulder at the crag's top. The rock beneath his moccasin souls was hot. He could feel the heat through his buckskins as he knelt and spread the tripod's legs once more.

He turned the canister toward the west, where the winged beast was just now banking against the lower edge of the northern ridge's caprock and sinking back down toward the canyon.

"Come on, you devil," Zane said. "Let's do-si-do around the old oak tree one more time! *Whaddaya say!*"

The dragon dropped down over an edge of the limestone knob. As it dropped lower, one wing brushing the side of a stone parapet, a slender figure appeared suddenly atop that same rock formation. Just as suddenly, the figure kicked out away from the rock, scissoring its legs, its hat tumbling down its back, and leaped onto the dragon's back and dropped belly down against the scaly hide.

The sun flashed off bloodred hair streaming out in the wind.

Zane lifted his head from the Gatling's canister and blinked, awestruck. "Crazy bitch!"

As the dragon angled toward Zane, the winged beast tipped to one side and then the other, its golden eyes not looking as bright as before. If a dragon could look confused, this one looked that way, as if detecting a weight on its back but unable to comprehend what it was or where it had come from. The dragon, in its confusion, tipped northward and slightly off Zane's course. As it did, the ghoul hunter watched in horror as the redhead atop the beast's back climbed up behind the massive, green head.

"Angel, for Christ's sakes," Zane shouted, lunging to his feet and cupping his hands around his mouth. "Get down from there, you cork-headed fool!"

Balancing on her knees, red hair streaming out in the wind, Angel unsheathed her long, silver Spanish sword from the scabbard hanging down her right, leather-clad leg, just behind one of her holstered six-guns. The beast was still angling slightly away from Zane, between him and the northern cliff wall.

As it came within fifty yards, he watched, lower jaw hanging, as Angel rose up on her knees and raised the down-angled sword in both her gloved hands. She and the dragon were so close to him now, the dragon suddenly seeming oblivious to him, that he saw Angel's green eyes open wide in determination and her fine jaws draw taut as she thrust downward with both hands.

The sword plunged into a ring of what appeared relatively

soft tissue between the beast's head and neck. Angel threw herself down and forward, heaving with all her weight on the handle and burying the blade nearly hilt deep. As she did, and as she and the winged beast flew past Zane, whom the strong wind of the massive wings blew back on his butt, the dragon threw his head back and grimaced and loosed a high-pitched, snarling wail that bounced like thunder off the near rims.

Beneath the wail and the rush of the wind, Zane could hear Angel screaming, "Die, you son of a bitch! *Die!*"

Her scream as well as the dragon's wail dwindled as the beast flew off to Zane's right and pitched steeply groundward. For a few seconds, it looked as though the dragon would plunge headfirst into the canyon bottom.

Zane's heart was like a turnip in his throat.

The beast tipped slightly to one side of a low pile of boulders from which several cedars grew, then gave another defiant wail and, with a violent thrash of his tail, righted himself and hammered the air with his wings.

He gained altitude. Because of the distance and the shadows on that side of the canyon, Zane could no longer see Angel as the dragon climbed, launching himself north toward the steep ridge looming there. High and higher he climbed, growing smaller and smaller against the runneled and crenellated side of the sandstone cliff pocked here and there with talus slides.

Gradually, he closed on the cliff, rising toward the bulging sandstone cap.

That he wasn't going to make it became clear as Zane saw the ridge fairly swallow the giant beast a half second before the dragon crashed headlong into the sheer rock wall. Where the giant's body once had been, now a great burst of orange flames roiled outward from the cliff, consuming the still-flicking, green-and-yellow tail.

A second after the beast had smashed into the cliff, the thunder of what sounded like a barrel of dynamite detonating reached the ghoul hunter's ears. At the same time, through the roiling flames bursting outward and down from the side of the cliff, Zane saw bits and pieces of the body, including its wings, free-falling toward the canyon bottom. He couldn't help watching for a slender figure clad in leather and with long, red hair. . . .

As the torn hulk of the dead beast continued falling and burning and smoking, Zane left the Gatling gun where it was and, wheeling, began climbing, half leaping and half falling down the side of the escarpment. He was halfway down when he saw Hathaway standing on a ledge of rock and leaning outward to stare toward the north cliff face. The scout looked at Zane, his eyes and mouth big as he said, "What the hell happened?"

"Fool girl killed herself," was all Zane could say, breathless, as he continued dropping down the escarpment, skipping from one boulder to another.

Ten feet from the ground, he leaped the rest of the way, landing flat-footed, spreading his arms for balance, and took off running around the side of the scarp, lifting his knees and arms high, moccasins crunching brush and gravel and pummeling sage and low cedars. He didn't know where he was running exactly—generally, toward the dragon, but as he ran he turned his head this way and that, hoping to find Angel alive somewhere among the rocks and brush littering the canyon floor.

But the brunt of his attention was fixed upslope, where the great burning hulk of the dragon was just now tumbling in pieces both large and small to the base of the cliff face, burning among the strewn boulders. He ran hard, mindless of his aching lungs and burning chest. A big chunk of the dragon teetered at the base of the cliff, then tumbled toward him, and as it burned and rolled awkwardly down the slope, he could see that it was one of the demon's wings. Rolling and burning behind the wing was the tip of the tail.

He ran to his right, avoiding the burning appendages by several yards. The scorching heat of the burning carcass growing intensely before him, like that of a vast blacksmith's forge, and knowing he could go no farther without being burned himself, he stopped suddenly, fifty yards from the cliff. He leaned forward, hands to his thighs, wheezing as he sucked breaths into his aching lungs and stared in horror at the several leaping fires.

"Red," he said, managing only a raking whisper. "For Christ's sake, Red, why in the hell'd you make such a dunderheaded play?"

Brush crackled behind him. He froze, staring straight ahead, pricking his ears.

"Damn," a familiar voice said among the crackling weeds and crunching gravel. "Anyone got a drink? This dragon-slayin' is a mite hard on a girl."

Zane wheeled, wide-eyed.

Angel stood about thirty yards downslope from him, her hair a dusty, weed- and seed-flecked mess about her bare shoulders. Her leather vest was twisted low and to one side, causing one large breast to bulge up farther than the other. Generally, she was dirty and disheveled, and her scarred face was scraped and bruised, as were her long, bare arms, the knees of her leather pants torn. But she was all in one piece.

And she was alive.

With a great burst of raw energy mixed with overwhelming emotion, Zane cursed and ran down the slope to her. He wrapped his big arms around her in a savage bear hug, lifted her two feet off the ground, and swung her in a complete circle before setting her back down. "Goddamn, you crazy redhead, I thought for sure you'd bought the ranch and the whole damn remuda!"

He wrapped his arms around her neck and planted a hard kiss on her cheek. He placed his hands on her shoulders and held her away from him, looking her up and down to make sure she was all right.

"How in the hell did you make it out of that? You a cat or somethin'?"

Pale and exhausted, Angel blew a strand of hair out of her face and hooked a thumb over her right shoulder. "I sorta rolled off the side of that critter when I figured it was about to crash. Skidded down a few of the trees sticking out from that scarp yonder, and landed in a patch of buckbrush."

She wrinkled her nose and looked up the slope toward where the dragon continued to burn. "Contrary to the fairy tales we all read as sprouts, those dragons are repugnant damn critters. Close up, they smell like rotten fish."

She spat in disgust and ran the back of a gloved hand across her mouth.

Zane wrapped an arm around her shoulders from behind, and turned her around. Hathaway was leading both General Lee and his mule toward Angel and the ghoul hunter. From across the canyon, Jesse James was galloping atop his buckskin while leading Angel's paint, pumping a fist in the air and howling madly.

"Come on," Zane said. "I'll buy ya a drink."

"I could use one."

They walked several yards along the canyon bottom.

"Look at that," Angel said, glancing at the sky over the southern ridge. "Damn near a full moon."

Zane looked at the big, pale orb, large as a watch face in the sky fading toward a dusky gray green, and nearly full except for a loss of definition along its lower left side. Like the edge of an old, worn nickel. In twenty-four hours, that blurred edge would be clearly defined.

"Well, look at that," Zane said, dropping his arm away from the redhead's shoulder. "I do believe you're right, Red."

Chapter 30

. . . .

FULL MOON RISING

Hathaway's resonant voice was close in Zane's ear. "Dawn, Uriah. Rise and shine."

Zane opened his eyes as the scout went over and crouched beside Angel's still form on the other side of the campfire that was a low mound of umber coals. The ghoul hunter perused the sky touched with periwinkle blue between the jutting, black velvet peaks in the east. No sign of the moon, of course.

That damn moon.

He shook the thought from his mind. He'd beaten the wolf. The only reason he felt it stirring inside him again was because he'd started doubting himself after being so repulsed by the Hell's Angels. He'd beaten it back for nearly a year, and he'd even almost stopped thinking about it. He couldn't think about it today, either. He had plenty of other problems on his mind, the biggest being the need to run down the Hell's Angels and their Mexican witch guide before they accomplished whatever hellish task they intended here in the Lobo Negros.

What Elaina Baranova had told Zane made him think that the stakes were higher than he could ever imagine. . . .

He yawned, sat up, ran his hands back through his tangled mane of black hair, and looked around at the horses picketed nearby. Zane's party had set up camp near the scarp from which the ghoul hunter had fired on the dragon, as it had been too late to continue their trek. Besides, Angel needed rest after her ordeal, which she'd worn well despite her scrapes and bruises.

To his right, Hathaway crouched over the figure of Jesse James lying curled on his side, head resting on the elbow bent beneath him, softly snoring beneath his two wool Army blankets. Cautiously, Hathaway clamped a foot down on the gun and holster lying near Jesse, then nudged the Missourian's shoulder with the butt of his Winchester.

As expected, the outlaw jerked with a start, throwing one hand out toward the six-shooter jutting from the holster around which the cartridge belt was coiled. His hand grabbed the top of Hathaway's low-heeled cavalry boot. He froze, looked up slowly, a little chagrined, to see the dark face peering down at him.

Jesse smiled sheepishly.

"That's the lurch of a wanted man," Angel observed as she knelt, rolling up her blankets. "Don't worry, James—you won't be wanted much longer."

"Oh, I'll always be wanted, Marshal. By good-lookin' women, 'specially. Always have been."

"You flatter yourself."

"Someone has to." Jesse yawned and stretched.

Zane rolled his own blankets quickly and tied the roll closed with rawhide straps he'd sewn into the wool. He glanced at Jesse, who'd crawled toward the fire with his empty cup and used a leather swatch to lift the coffeepot from a flat rock in the coals and shake it.

"Well, you got us to the Lobo Negros, Jesse," Zane said with reluctant gratitude. "You got some vision about where we trail from here?"

Jesse poured the scorched, smoking brew into his tin cup, then sat back on his butt, looking over the cup's rim toward the northern ridge where the dead dragon had finally stopped smoldering though the rotten-fish stench remained. "Hell, I ain't no witch. Now, my granny could lead you right to where the Hell's Angels are right now. Me—I didn't get that much of the gift. I just seen the wolf's head cappin' that peak there." He lifted his chin to inspect the ridge towering over them, capped in weathered sandstone.

Zane followed Jesse's gaze. "I don't see the head."

"It's back farther. Can't see it from this angle. Juts up from the other side of this here ridge, forms a ridge all its own. I been keepin' a watch on it as we approached the range."

Jesse blew on his coffee, sipped, and shook his head. "Them killers is gonna rue the day they killed my brother, Frank . . . Cole . . . all the others." Tears of rage and grief glistened in the outlaw's pale eyes. "Them's all the family I have except a few stashed here and there in the hills back home—all beaten an' broken by the massacre o' Lincoln's"—he gritted his teeth—"mercenaries."

"Well, you'll get your chance at what's left of those mercenaries," Zane said, donning his hat and adding a few chunks of piñon to the fire. "Just don't forget who your enemies are. Might cause me to make the same mistake."

"I scouted north last night, before good dark." Hathaway had emptied the coffeepot and was adding fresh water from his canteen. "Found a coupla piles of horse apples them spooks didn't bother to hide."

"Probably figured the dragon would keep their backtrail clear of shadowers," Angel said, tossing a pouch of Arbuckles' to the scout, who caught it against his chest.

"I 'spect we won't have much trouble followin' 'em. From what I seen, just north of here there ain't too many trail options. Rough country, all up and down, steep ridges of sandstone and granite. Not much water, neither. Just a few trails between narrow canyons. Devil's playground kind of place."

"Well, hell," Zane said, grabbing his rifle and blanket roll and walking toward their picketed mounts. "No reason to burn daylight here, then."

"There ain't much daylight to speak of, Uriah." Angel sat back against her saddle, watching him.

Zane glanced toward the lilac sky showing between black ridges in the east, then continued striding toward the horses, casting a look in the direction the full moon would rise. "There's enough."

Behind him, Hathaway glanced at Angel and shrugged. As he began pouring the coffee water back into his canteen, he sighed. "I reckon we can brew a pot later, when we stop to rest the hosses."

"What's his hurry?" Jesse wanted to know as he sipped the last of the brewed coffee without chagrin, glancing over his shoulder as Zane walked away. "Might have poor luck, trailin' in the dark."

Angel kicked dirt on the fire, then lifted one of her six-guns from its holster. "I reckon Uriah's got it right," she said, also casting an uneasy glance toward where the full moon would rise. "There'll be light enough soon." She rolled the cylinder across her forearm, imagining each of the silver slugs nestled in their chambers, then sheathed the piece, grabbed her rifle, saddlebags, and bedroll, and strode off toward the horses.

Only a few hours ahead rode the Hell's Angels and Ravenna Gonzalez-Vara. At midmorning, riding along a narrow, crooked, steep-walled canyon, Ravenna glanced at the sky.

"Chico, where are you, damnit?" She noted the wary tone in her voice and didn't like it.

Riding to her left, the other three riding single-file behind, Charlie said, "What's the matter, *chiquita*?"

"Chico. I haven't seen him since just after I managed to conjure him again finally. And I had a dark dream last night."

"About the dragon?"

"*Sí.* I think so. I don't like it that he's not near."

"Thought he was supposed to be out interceptin' folks who might be shadowin' us."

"*Sí, sí.* But I should see him. I conjured him. I can call him back when I have the power. I have the power now, and I called him back this morning, after my dream. To reassure myself that . . ."

The horses' shod hooves clacked on the stony canyon floor. A hawk sat on a small thumb of rock protruding from the two-thousand-foot cliff on the right side of the canyon, the raptor's head turning slowly, tracking the four men and the black-haired woman walking their horses along the rocky trail partly shaded by the eastern ridge blocking the climbing sun.

"To reassure yourself what?" She offered Charlie a cockeyed grin. "You think somethin' might have happened to that winged demon? I don't think so, *chiquita*. When you conjured him, you outdone yourself and any witch I ever known here or in the Old Country."

Ravenna lowered her glance from the rims of the canyon walls and turned her head forward once more. She frowned darkly, not a customary expression for her. It worried Charlie a little, and he laughed to cover it. "Come on, *chiquita*. Chico's fine. Maybe he's taking siesta."

"*Sí.*" Ravenna rode along, brooding, worried. "That's probably it, Charlie." She cast her anxious glance to the right, where an old, massive rockslide formed a jagged hill against the north wall of the canyon, starting just below a great gap in the wall, where an earthquake had likely caused the cliff to bulge and drop.

"Whoa."

Ravenna stopped her gelding and threw up a hand for the others to follow suit as she perused the massive slide, pulling her nickering horse's head up, the bit clacking in its teeth.

"Now what is it?" Charlie was impatient, edgy. "Goddamn, girl, you're startin' to make me nervous, and I don't *get* nervous."

"I saw a flash up there in those rocks. Might have been a rifle."

The others turned to follow her stricken gaze.

"You sure?" Charlie asked.

"Of course I'm sure. You think I'm seeing things?"

"I don't know," Charlie said. "You're worried about a fuck-ing dragon it'd take a whole ton of dynamite to put a dent in. . . ."

"Fuck you, Charlie!"

Snarling, she rammed the dull points of her spurs into her gelding's flanks and galloped thirty yards to the base of the canyon's north wall. While the mount was still moving, she leaped off the horse's back and onto one of the boulders compris-ing the rockslide. Cocking her Winchester one-handed, swinging the barrel up and down, she leaped like a mountain goat up the slide, picking her way quickly, black hair dancing across her shoulders and flashing in the golden sunlight flooding that side of the canyon.

She climbed a hundred feet up the slide, leaped onto a high, narrow boulder and down the other side, into a niche among the rocks. She dropped to a knee and scoured the niche's floor.

Recent boot tracks scored the floury dirt. There was some-thing else. Ravenna reached down, picked up the half-smoked cigar butt, and held it up to her face. She rolled it between her fingers.

Still warm. And store-bought.

Ravenna dropped the butt, rose, and unholstered her ivory-gripped Remington. She followed the prints back down the canyon along the slide, until they disappeared among the tum-bled boulders. She stared out over the side of the slide, seeing nothing but more rock. Whoever had been here a few minutes ago was gone.

She holstered the pistol and retraced her steps back down the slide to the canyon floor. As she walked out to where her horse stood, ground-tied, she glanced over at Charlie, Lucky, One-Eye, and Curly Joe. They were all staring tensely up canyon, all unsheathing their rifles, except Curly Joe. Now Curly Joe unsheathed his saddle-ring carbine and whistled softly through his crooked teeth.

Ravenna swung up onto her gelding's back and neck-reined the horse around to face up canyon. She stiffened in her saddle, that recent dark expression returning as she saw the six riders approaching from fifty yards away, angling out away from a bend in the north canyon wall. They were little, dark men with long, black hair, in breechclouts and deerskin vests and high-topped deerskin moccasins. They were like living shadows astride horses.

They carried nocked bows in their wiry, muscular arms, holding them out flat in front of them while also holding their mounts' braided hide reins. Swords of what appeared to be gold dangled from beaded sashes encircling their waists.

The riders were so incredibly tattooed it was hard to distinguish anything else about their features. All their horses—rugged, short-legged mustangs—were also marked with tribal designs, with painted rings around their eyes and talisman designs unfamiliar to Ravenna etched across their breasts.

The witch was vaguely confused. Whoever had left the cigar stub in the rocks had not been one of the natives approaching her group now. These men wouldn't buy their tobacco in any store. Were she and Charlie being stalked by a white man as well as by these natives?

Charlie glanced wryly at Ravenna. "You didn't say there'd be 'Paches out here, *chiquita*." His voice echoed loudly off the stone walls.

"Those aren't Apaches, Charlie." Ravenna's voice was pitched low with alarm. Fire flared in her veins as dream visions flashed behind her eyes.

She jerked a savage look at the wolf pack leader. "We must kill them now, Charlie," she screamed. *"Kill them now!"*

Chapter 31

. . . .

THE LOST TRIBE
AND A VOICE ON THE WIND

A chill wind blew from down canyon against Zane's back, blowing his sombrero forward. Clamping the hat down low on his head, he turned to squint behind him along the narrow, steep-walled corridor of striated granite, basalt, and sandstone, the jagged-edged rim poking like gnarled witch's fingers at a sky tan with windblown dust. The dust swirled toward him along the canyon floor.

"Lousy luck," he said. "This wind's gonna rub out the Angels' sign."

"Don't need it."

Zane turned to Hathaway, who was staring off the canyon's right side. The short, stocky man dismounted and led his mule over to a boulder leaning against the canyon's southern wall. He squatted beside the boulder and placed his gloved right hand against the side of the rock.

"What is it?" Angel asked, lifting her voice above the wind's keening.

"Wolf's head carved in this rock!"

Zane and Angel both swung down from their saddles and walked over to stand near Hathaway. Jesse did not dismount, as his leg was hurting, but he gigged his buckskin over. The scout was running his right index finger along a crude wolf's head about the size of a man's open palm chiseled into the lower-middle section of the boulder. "I seen one a while back, figured it was just some kind o' rock painting like you see all over the Southwest. But now I reckon it was somethin' more."

"Prospectors often use such signs to lead the way back to a remote digging," Zane said. "In case they can't remember where it is exactly, or they lose their maps."

"Sorta like Hansel and Gretel layin' out breadcrumbs," Jesse said.

"You think that's what this is?" Angel asked. "A prospector's signpost?"

Hathaway straightened, pulled his hat brim down snug on his head. "I reckon we'll know if we keep heading down this canyon and find another one."

They mounted up and continued along the canyon, the building wind blowing their horses' tails between their hind legs and keeping a nearly constant curtain of grit and tumbleweeds ensconcing the riders. Where the canyon corridor forked, the three riders scrutinized the cliff walls.

"There," Zane said, reining General Lee toward the north canyon wall, nearest the right fork in the corridor.

Another wolf's head had been chiseled into the granite and limestone. It was fainter than the other one but still recognizable—a definite signpost. Zane gigged General Lee along the right corridor, the others falling in behind him, Angel riding to his left. Riding to Hathaway's right, Jesse yelled, "Anyone else feel like someone's watchin' us?"

Zane glanced back at the Missourian riding crouched in his saddle and tightening his jaws against the gale.

"You see somethin', Jesse?"

"In your head or elsewhere?" Angel added with a faintly wry note.

"Nah." Jesse glanced over his left shoulder, then swung his head forward again. "I just got a creepy-crawly feelin' between my shoulders, like someone's starin' a bull's-eye on my back." He managed to turn it into a joke, grinning at Angel. "Used to think it was one Marshal James Coffin. Couldn't be him now, though, could it? Not in the daylight!" He stretched his lips wider, showing his small yellow teeth.

Zane glanced at Angel. Even through the windblown grit, and even though she tried hard to hide it, he could see the injured look in her eyes. And the rage. He felt it himself, and before he fully realized what he was doing, he'd drawn the Colt Navy from his cross-draw holster. The click of the hammer was nearly drowned by the wind.

He aimed the pistol at Jesse's face. "I do believe you've outworn your welcome, James. Time to ride on over the divide with Cole and Frank an' the boys."

"Hold on!" Angel rode over and nudged Zane's right arm down. "I'll fight my own battles, mister. And we're going to need all the guns we have against the Angels. If he makes it through the battle, I want the pleasure of watching him hang."

She reined Cisco around and gigged him on up the right-forking canyon. Hathaway cast his white-ringed gaze between Zane and Jesse. "Boys, boys, boys . . ."

Zane depressed the Colt's hammer and slid it back into its holster. As Hathaway gigged his mule after Angel, Zane held his hard gaze on that of Jesse James, whose pale eyes had grown uncustomarily apprehensive when he'd seen the big pistol bearing down on him.

"You keep riding her," the ghoul hunter warned the Missouri outlaw, "and not even she's gonna be able to save your worthless hide."

Jesse frowned, tipped his head to one side. "You an' her . . . ?"

"She goes her way; I go mine." Zane nudged his hat brim down once more, reined General Lee around, and put the big palomino into a trot along the right-forking canyon trail.

Not far ahead, Angel's and Hathway's mounts stood riderless in the middle of the corridor. Angel and the scout were crouched over what looked like rubble from a collapsed cutbank littering the canyon's right side.

Zane rode over, was about to ask what had caught their interest, when he saw a bloody, brown, tattooed arm sticking out of the rubble. Beyond, a brown eyebrow peered up from its bed of loose, red dust and clay. Hathaway was looking into a horseshoe-shaped alcove cut into the canyon wall just beyond the collapsed cutbank.

He wandered around for a time, Angel following him, her red hair blowing wildly in the wind. Zane walked into the alcove, saw a few more bodies hastily tossed among the boulders that littered the alcove's floor.

"Three more," Angel said. "With the four someone tried to bury under the bank there, that makes six."

"Six who?" Zane crouched over one of the bodies—a young man wedged between two boulders, where he likely wouldn't be easily seen by someone passing through the main canyon. He wore crude deerskins with dyed designs that Zane had never seen. On the top of each of the young man's moccasins was a red wolf's head about as big around as a gold eagle coin.

"I was gonna say 'Paches," Hathaway said. "But I ain't never seen Apaches painted so." He stood over Zane, fists on his hips, and shook his head slowly. "I seen several of them wolf heads. One over there had it tattoed on his chest. Never heard of no 'Pache, Pima, Papago, Navajo, or Yaquis tribe with such a totem as that—just like the wolf heads we seen in the canyon yonder."

"Whoever they are," Zane said, "I see no firearms of any kind on 'em. Some bows and arrows." He brushed dust away from the leg of the young brave before him, uncovering a long, slender sheath with an engraved gold handle jutting up against the youth's sharp hip bone. He wrapped his hand around the handle and drew the sword, staring in wide-eyed awe at the solid gold, razor-edged blade.

All up and down the length of the blade had been etched the figures of wolves engaged in hunting or mauling various creatures—rabbits, deer, mountain lions, bears, and, most fascinating of all, faintly comical caricatures of fleeing humans.

"Here's another one," Angel said, holding the blade she'd found in both hands, staring down at it in wonder.

Jesse had dismounted when he'd seen the gold and was pulling up another sword from the dirt and gravel of the collapsed cutbank, grunting against the pain in his wounded thigh. He ran his hands down the blade he'd found, his eyes fairly dancing as he scrubbed away the grit and saw the pure, glistening gold beneath.

He shook his head and laughed. "Frank, this breaks my heart." Tears beaded in his eye corners. "It purely breaks my heart, brother, that you and Cole and the boys ain't here to see this."

Zane lowered the golden sword, and willed himself to let it drop back down where he'd found it. Even at such a dire time, gold had an intoxicating effect. One sword would probably be worth as much bounty money as he'd earned in the past five years.

"Leave 'em." He slapped his hands together. "We got more important work ahead of us."

"Leave gold?" Jesse laughed, tears now streaking the dust on his cheeks. "I don't think so! I'm gonna take me one of these here pigstickers in case we don't make it back this way. You know how much this is worth?"

"Think about Frank and Cole, Jesse," Angel said, knowing the way to the emotional Confederate's heart. "How would they feel—you droolin' over gold when their killers are still pounding the trail?"

Jesse looked at her, blinked the tears away, squinting against the dust blowing in under his hat brim. Angrily, he held the blade out before him in both hands. "You got a nasty side, Marshal." He dropped the sword, swung away as though it caused him great pain, and grabbed his buckskin's reins.

He'd just swung up into the leather when Zane, also walking toward his mount, Angel and Hathaway behind him, saw the outlaw flinch. In the grit haze kicked up by the wind, he thought he saw something sticking out of Jesse's back, just below his right shoulder. Jesse stiffened and lifted his chin, gritting his teeth.

"Gnah!"

His cry was obscured by the wind.

Zane froze. It saved his life. An arrow whistled through the air about six inches in front of his face and clattered against the rocks to his right. He jerked a look to his left where several horseback riders were galloping up the canyon toward him—five dark little men with long, black hair, all triggering arrows expertly as they rode. More arrows clattered among the rocks, while another slammed into the side of Hathaway's mule. The beast immediately began pitching and braying indignantly, though Zane had seen the arrow bounce off its stirrup and clatter onto the canyon floor.

"Company!" Zane shouted, palming both his Colt Navies, dropping to one knee, and beginning to trigger each pistol in turn.

He dropped one of the Indians with his first shot, as the brave leaped off his galloping mount—a lucky shot that sent the warrior spinning and cartwheeling to the ground, whooping wildly. The others commenced yowling then, as well, and Zane dropped another just as the man triggered an arrow that sliced just past the ghoul hunter's left cheek.

His bullet plunked through the brave's upper arm. As he reached for it with his other hand, dropping his bow, either Angel's or Hathaway's bullet plowed into the side of his head, blowing him back off his heels and laying him out, quivering. The fusillade of bullets was too much for the natives. The two survivors of the attack ran back down the canyon, one pausing only to trigger one more arrow before wheeling and sprinting off after the others and their fleeing, buck-kicking mustangs.

Zane holstered both his empty pistols and ran over to grab Jesse as the outlaw sagged dangerously backward and sideways over his skitter-stepping buckskin's right hip. Wrapping both arms around the outlaw, he pulled him easily out of the saddle; the wiry Missourian couldn't have weighed much more than a slightly hefty woman.

As Hathaway walked a ways down canyon to make sure their attackers were gone, Zane set Jesse down against the cliff wall, the outlaw grunting against the pain of the arrow fletched with brown and black hawk feathers protruding from his right shoulder, the stone point sticking out his back. Blood stained his denim jacket and duster.

"Leave it to a goddamn redskin to fill me with misery!" Jesse cried, kicking against the pain. "Pull the goddamn thing out, Zane! Pull it out!"

"If you'll hold still, I will."

Zane shoved one of the man's fumbling, flailing hands down, then with his own hand grabbed the six inches of arrow protruding out the man's back. With his other hand, he grabbed the front to hold it steady, then broke off the back part with a dull crack.

"Ahh!" Jesse kicked his legs and tightened every muscle. "Christ, could you give me some warnin'? We might have our differences, Uriah, but we're brothers of the Confederacy, fer cryin' out loud!"

Zane kept a firm hold on the front of the arrow and jerked it forward. It slid out smoothly, blood dribbling out from the hole it left in the outlaw's shoulder. Crouched on the other side of Jesse, Angel immediately stuffed the outlaw's own neckerchief into the hole, clamping it down hard.

Jesse said, "Oh, mercy!" His eyes closed, and his head sagged to one side as he lost consciousness.

A voice rose on the wind. "Confederates?"

There was a pause during which Zane thought the voice must have been a trick of the wind itself. He and Angel looked around, frowning.

The disembodied shout came again, louder this time, as though its owner was moving nearer from the opposite wall of the canyon. It was a man's voice, shrill with exasperation.

"Did you say 'Confederates'?"

Chapter 32

JERICHO TURNIPSEED

Zane straightened tensely, quickly thumbing cartridges from his shell belt into one of his Colts. A figure appeared on the far side of the canyon, materializing out of the blowing grit as he ran a sort of shambling, stumbling run, open fur coat slipping down his shoulders.

He held an old, rusted trapdoor Springfield carbine in one hand, barrel up. The gun was held together with wire and rawhide. He was tall and thin, and at first Zane thought he had no hat, but then he saw it dangling down between the man's shoulders, blowing in the wind.

Zane flipped his Colt's loading gate closed and spun the cylinder, holding the pistol halfway out from his belly, half threatening. "Hold it there!"

The man stopped about ten feet away. He had a long face and a bulging forehead. Thin, curly brown hair lay sparsely atop his head, blowing wildly. His eyes were yellow brown, incredulous. He held the rifle and his other hand out to each side in supplication. "I'm friendly if you folks are. I got me a good set of ears, and I thought someone mentioned Confederates!"

"Some of us are." Zane glanced at Angel, who stood a few feet to his left, caressing the .45 on her right hip with one hand, squinting into the grit at the raggedly clad stranger. A prospector, Zane thought. Desert rat. There was a bright, crazy cast to his brown eyes. No sane man would approach a party of strangers this far out in the high and rocky without considerably more caution than this gent had showed.

The man grinned and, ignoring Zane's uncocked Colt aimed at his belly, walked slowly forward. "Uriah Zane!"

Zane scowled, trying to place the man. A name came to him, swirling up from the gale of his distant past. "Jericho?"

The man laughed and clamped a hand thick and hairy as a bear's paw on the ghoul hunter's shoulder. "You remember after all these years!"

"For Christ's sakes—I figured you and your boys were all dead in the War."

"We'll talk later." Jericho looked both ways along the canyon, glanced from Zane to Angel and then to Jesse sitting unconscious, head to his shoulder, against the canyon wall. He gave a start when he saw Al Hathaway walk out of the windblown grit and hesitate, raising his rifle in both his hands and studying the stranger uncertainly.

"He's one of us," Zane said.

"Come on, then. Bring your injured friend there and you're horses. Ain't much time. There's more guardians where those there came from." He glanced out to where the dead Indian lay sprawled as though dropped from the sky. "And they'll be some piss-burned when they see how many they done lost in the past couple hours. They ain't a large tribe to begin with!"

In the corner of his left eye, Zane saw Angel glance at him apprehensively. He had to admit that while he'd grown up knowing Jericho Turnipseed as a good, God-fearing Carolinian who'd sharecropped on Zane's family's plantation before the War, in which Jericho and his three sons had proudly enlisted, he hadn't seen the man since sixty-one, nearly fifteen years ago.

Men changed in less time than that, and the years had not been kind to his old friend, whose shoulders were stooped, legs skinny and bowed, eyes a little foggy. But Zane didn't see that he had much choice in the matter.

"It's all right," Zane told Angel, then swung around and hauled the unconscious Jesse James up and over his shoulder.

While Angel and Hathaway hurried out to grab the reins of their horses, the scout holding the bridle of Jesse's mount while Zane eased the unconscious Missourian over the buckskin's saddle, Jericho walked out into the canyon, holding his rifle up high across his chest as he shuttled his gaze up canyon and down, on the lookout for more—what had he'd called the dark-skinned warriors?

Guardians?

When Zane had Jesse secured, he led both the Missourian's horse and General Lee behind Jericho, who hop-skipped to the opposite canyon wall. Zane was ten feet from the wall when he saw that the wall was not solid. A crescent of thick rock jutted out from one side. Jericho beckoned to Zane and the others, then disappeared behind the crescent.

Zane stopped, frowning.

Jericho poked his head out behind the seven-foot-high wing of crenellated sandstone. "It's all right. Wide enough for your horses. I bring mine and a wagon through here all the time!"

He pulled his head back behind the rock again, and Zane looked behind it to see that there was a crooked corridor back there, twisting into the side of the cliff wall, wide enough for a couple of horses. He pulled the skittish General Lee around through the half-open door of sorts, having to throw a shoulder into the casket-carrying Gatling gun to position it correctly to slip through without catching its wheels.

When General Lee was inside and moving freely, the wheels clattering behind him, Zane led Jesse's buckskin in behind him. Angel and Hathaway both followed, leading their own mounts, the mule braying raucously at the foreignness of this inner sanctum.

"Hold on," Jericho called from ahead, unseen in the darkness.

There was a scraping sound, the clatter of what sounded like a lantern mantle. A light grew slowly until Zane could make out the bull's-eye lantern in Jericho's waving hand, see the dusky silhouette of the Southerner below and beside it. "Everyone all right?"

"Now that we have some light," Angel said, her tone nonplussed.

Jericho laughed as though at a joke. "Yeah, it's dark in here. Lighter farther in, but we'll stop when it's widened out a little. I call that my smoking parlor!"

Jericho laughed again, turned, and continued limping forward along the twelve-foot-wide corridor. There were rocks along both sides, and Zane stumbled over them, unable to see much but deadheading on the lantern swinging high before

General Lee, whom the ghoul hunter kept moving with frequent slaps to the palomino's behind.

When the corridor turned abruptly, Jericho waited until the others behind him could see the lantern before he continued forward, swinging the lamp from side to side like a signaling brakeman. More light ebbed into the chasm from chutes and funnels that opened onto the sky far above the mountain they were apparently inside. The sandstone and limestone seemed to glow the same soft red as Jericho's lamp.

They'd walked maybe fifty yards into the mountain when the right side of the corridor drew back and formed a room of sorts about twenty feet wide by fifteen feet deep and lit from above by two cracks in the ceiling. There was a fire ring in which low flames licked and a coffeepot chugged and gurgled. A rickety ladder-back chair sat near the fire ring, and a dried and cracked cartridge belt hung from the chair back, its Army-issue holster containing an old cap-and-ball pistol, the walnut grips cracked and worn.

There was an old farm wagon here, as well. Its end faced the far wall, tongue drooping forward. It was half-filled with sweet-smelling hay recently cured. Near the wagon, a stocky, cream-and-brown burro was grazing on a pile of hay mounded between its forefeet and the wagon.

A wooden bucket of water sat beside the hay mound. General Lee snorted when he saw the burro. The burro switched its tail in greeting. As Hathaway pulled his mule into the room, the mule lifted a shrill, angry bray as it studied the burro gravely, twitching its ears and stomping a front hoof.

"That's Jeff Davis." Jericho stepped aside to let the men, woman, horses, and mule pass into the room. "He won't hurt you, mule. He likes company whenever he can get it, and he don't get it much around here. That's a good thing."

Zane was helping Jesse, who was coming around now and grunting through gritted teeth, down from his buckskin. As Zane led the outlaw over to the chair, he glanced at Jericho. "Those Injuns outside," he said. "Who . . . ?"

"They wasn't no Injuns like those you ever seen, Uriah. They're an old tribe, far as I can tell. Maybe an ancestor race of the Yaqui or Apache. I been here for fifteen years, and I never seen a single one stray more than five miles from this mountain range. They stay here in these mountains and canyons—some of the biggest, emptiest country in the Southwest—to guard this here mountain. Against what, I don't know. I'm the only white man I seen here in twelve years!" He chuckled.

"Why do they need to guard a mountain?" Angel asked as she unbuckled her paint's latigo strap.

"I can't answer that question just yet."

"Why not?" asked Hathaway, who was also unbuckling his mule's belly strap.

All four were dusty and sweaty, as though they'd soaked in an alkali hole, then rolled in the dirt. Their faces were sun- and windburned, with pale circles around their eyes where their brows and hat brims offered shade. Zane's and Hathaway's beards were adobe-colored. As a group they looked like desert nomads, and they were all slouched slightly under the weight of their fatigue.

"'Cause I don't know you well enough." Jericho squatted down beside his fire, dug a fat cigar out of his coat pocket, and looked at Jesse. "He don't look so good."

"I been better," Jesse said, his chest rising and falling sharply as he breathed. "Been worse, too. You didn't happen to see five renegades out there in the canyon, didja? That's who we're after. You can have your damn mountain."

"I seen 'em," Jericho said, scraping a stove match to life on his thumbnail. His voice was low and brooding. "They're trouble—I saw that. They picked up the wolf trail. First white men I ever seen in these mountains—leastways since I come here nigh on ten years ago now. You folks are the second bunch. When I heard you was Confederates, I decided I might have to trust you to help me keep them others away. Then I seen Uriah"—his face brightened as he glanced at the big ghoul hunter kneeling beside the fire and passing a blade of one of his bowie knives over the flames—"and my heart grew light."

Uriah looked at his old friend. "Where's that trail of wolf heads lead, Jericho?"

"It . . ." Turnipseed looked at the others, all of whom had turned to him now with keen interest. "It leads to treasure."

Uriah looked at the glowing blade in his hand. "I sorta figured. What kind of treasure? If you have a mine, Jericho, we ain't interested."

"You trust all these folks, Uriah?"

"All?" Zane set the knife down, slipped another bone-handled bowie from a sheath tucked inside his left moccasin top, and began cutting Jesse's shirt away from his shoulder, tearing the material as he sawed through it. "I reckon you could say that."

Jesse looked up at him and grinned.

Zane exchanged the unheated knife for the glowing one and pressed it against the entrance wound in the Missourian's breast. The knife sputtered as it seared the bloody, torn skin. Fetid smoke wafted. Jesse screamed, tipped his head back, and his eyes fluttered closed. Out again. Angel came over and held the outlaw up in his chair while Uriah cauterized the exit wound.

"Clean through," the ghoul hunter said. "That oughta do him. It's hard to kill a snake."

"Him a Confederate?" Jericho asked.

"He calls himself one."

"What about the Negro?"

Jericho glanced at Hathaway, who stood back near his burro, fists on his hips, looking skeptically back at the desert rat. "I notice he's wearing a Yankee hat. What I have to say, the deal I have to make, Uriah, is not one I take lightly. I've been sitting on it for a long time, waiting . . . wondering what I oughta do. Wondering how I can get the treasure to the Southern folks who need it most, so we can rebuild our country, make it better and more beautiful and gallant than before."

Zane cleaned the burned blood from his knife on Jesse's shirt, sheathed it, then dropped to his butt and wrapped his arms around his knees. Angel sat on the other side of Jesse from Uriah and began reloading one of her pistols.

Zane said, "Like I said, Jericho, we ain't interested in treasure. We're interested in those four men and that Mexican woman who rode into that canyon ahead of us. They're ghouls—the leaders of the very same pack of wolves who attacked our soldiers at Gettysburg. The Hell's Angels. Their leader is Charlie Hondo. I don't know why they're here, but we have to catch 'em and kill 'em. We'll need to get back after 'em soon."

"No point in goin' back out there." Jericho jerked his head in the direction they'd come through the cavern.

Angel said, "You mean because of the guardians?"

"No." Jericho removed the stogie from his long yellow teeth, blew a wobbly smoke ring, and stared at it cross-eyed. "Them you're after will be in *here* soon enough."

Chapter 33

. . . .

CITY OF THE WEREWOLVES

Zane, Angel, and Hathaway stared at Turnipseed, expressionless. Jesse groaned in his sleep.

Hathaway stepped forward slowly, scowling, closing one hand over the Colt Army .44 holstered on his right hip. "Excuse me, there, Mr. Turnipseed, but did you say them ghouls'll be *here* soon?" With his other hand he pointed at the floor.

"Well, not right here. But they'll be in the city soon. Them wolf pictures'll take 'em to the main entrance, on the other side of the canyon."

"City?" said Angel, arching a brow as though she were beginning to think the old desert rat might be a little touched.

Turnipseed puffed his cigar. "I done sat on the secret long enough, I reckon. Just couldn't bring myself to tell no one about it. Oh, I brought out a little of the gold now and then—bits and pieces of a wall or the shavings from a bell. Just to keep myself in hooch and see-gars and dry goods and the like."

They all continued to stare at him. He shuttled his rheumy gaze around at his dubious visitors and laughed.

He shook his head. "You've never seen the like. I'll show you . . . as long as y'all swear to keep it a secret till we can figure out a way to use that treasure to build up the Confederate Army once more. See, there's enough gold down there"—he jerked the cigar over his shoulder—"to rebuild the South bigger and stronger than it ever was. Leave the so-called Union once and for all, squash that high-an'-mighty President Sherman like the damn bug that he is, and leave the North in burnin' ruin!"

Zane felt a twinge of unease. And sadness.

Turnipseed had been out here living in these mountains alone since the end of the War—the massacre that had claimed his entire family. But the seclusion hadn't healed his wounds, only made them fester. Like so much of the rest of the South, he was living in a dreamworld built on the desire for revenge. Zane didn't agree with that desire. The only way the country could heal was if all of its citizens drew their horns in and vowed to learn from the mistakes of the past—including the gigantic mistake made by Abraham Lincoln and his cabinet.

"For the last time, we don't care about the gold," Angel told him. "The gold is all yours to do with as you see fit, Mr. Turnipseed. We just want the Hell's Angels."

Turnipseed slid his glance around skeptically. Gradually, his expression changed to one of deep incredulity. "You just wait till you see what I'm talkin' about, young lady."

With that, he used his thumbnail to file the coal off his cigar, letting the ashes roll into the crackling fire, then heaved himself to his feet, his stiff knees popping. He grabbed his Springfield carbine, slung it over his shoulder, glanced once more at Zane, then walked out of this broad place in the cavern.

Zane touched his pistols, including the LeMat in its shoulder holster. He decided to leave his crossbow with General Lee, then slid his Henry from its saddle boot. He'd leave the Gatling gun here, as well, since they were after only five ghouls and the sidearms and rifle should suffice. He opened the casket's lid, however, and grabbed a bandolier filled with the silver he'd found at Padre Alejandro's.

Angel and Hathaway had already followed Turnipseed out of the room. He could hear their boots clacking on the stone floor. Zane hooked the bandolier over his shoulder and started after them.

"Hold on." Jesse's voice echoed behind him.

Zane turned. The Missouri outlaw was heaving himself up from his chair. "Stay there, Jesse. You're in no shape to tangle with Charlie Hondo. I'll bring you the bastard's head."

Jesse winced, gave up the struggle, and sagged back once more in the creaky chair. He gave a ragged sigh. Zane headed on out of the room and strode down a broad corridor that presumably led deeper into the mountain. The floor angled downward. The corridor was lit dully by occasional shafts of light dribbling down natural flues in the ceiling.

He caught up with Angel, who was walking behind Turnipseed and Hathaway. Without looking at him, she said, "What time is it?"

Zane started to reach for his pocket watch, then stopped and looked at her. She stared straight ahead, her face expressionless. "Don't worry. I'm well aware of the lunar cycle."

They walked several yards, following Turnipseed and Hathaway, the floor continuing to slant downward, the walls gradually falling back to each side, widening the corridor.

"If it should happen," Zane said just loudly enough for Angel to hear, "I not only expect you to cap a silver bullet on me, but I'll want you to."

"Not when you've changed, you won't," she said.

"You might not see it in me." He grabbed her arm, stopped her, and jerked her around to face him. "But I will, Red."

She looked at him bitterly but with a sadness in her eyes, as well. "Glad to help, Uriah."

She jerked her arm free and continued striding along the corridor.

The floor leveled but the walls continued to slide away to each side. Light grew ahead of them, as though the cave were opening up to the world outside, falling away behind them. It did, in a manner of speaking. What lay beyond the cave was a broad canyon with walls nearly two thousand feet high in places. Lush grass and palm trees and sycamores and shrubs grew along the canyon bottom, across which a stream threaded.

Zane was only peripherally aware of the growth and the stream.

He and the others had exited the cave onto a rocky slope some thirty or forty feet above the canyon, and now they all stood there staring aghast at the veritable city that sprawled before them—as large as or larger than Denver. But no dusty cow town, this.

Zane's heart fluttered as his eyes tried to convince his brain that what he was seeing—a city made almost entirely of giant, gold-domed buildings set upon cobbled streets—was real and not just a figment of his fatigued imagination.

The wind made a distant rushing sound above the canyon. Threads of it made it to the canyon floor, but it was only a breeze down here, stirring the mineral smell of the stream with the lush smell of the flora. Palms lined the stream as it came in from Zane's right near the other side of the canyon and disappeared behind the buildings. The palm trees fluttered in the breeze, occasional dead leaves tumbling lazily.

Zane noted with dread that the light angling down the canyon wall was striated and pink and orange—the light of late afternoon or early evening. The full moon would be up early, just after sunset. They didn't have much time.

"I'll be damned," Angel said, staring at the towering, turreted, many-tiered structures. She pointed to a near dome of a building set behind a vast wall. "Is that what it looks like?"

"If it looks like gold," said Turnipseed.

As Angel, Zane, and Hathaway followed the man down what appeared an old wagon trail, wheels ruts still scoring the rock of the canyon floor, Zane's eyes swept the terrain around him. Nearly everywhere were ruins of one type or another. Whatever structures they once had been—probably barns and stables, maybe some supply sheds—they'd been constructed of stone or brick, and now they were overgrown with brush including greasewood and sagebrush and green patches of grama and galleta grass.

Zane stopped at the wall surrounding the giant, domed building nearest the canyon's south wall. He used his gloved hand to scrape the thick dust and grime from the bricks and blinked in surprise. What lay beneath the dust was more gold. Gold bricks.

Even the walls of this giant fortress had been constructed of gold!

As he looked around at the other near buildings—there must have been more than a hundred such structures lined up along several cobbled streets—he saw that the sand, dust, grime, and bird shit of centuries covered the walls, lay piled along the foundations. A thought occurred to him, making his head light, and he turned to Turnipseed, who stood grinning at the amazed expressions on his visitors' faces.

"Are all these buildings built of gold?" Zane asked, unable to wrap his mind around the idea of nearly an entire city constructed of one gold brick after another, making up thousands of such bricks, maybe hundreds of thousands.

"As far as I can tell," Turnipseed said. "In some places, even the streets are paved in gold. They're just buried under centuries' worth of dust."

"How'd you find this place, Mistuh Turnipseed?" Hathaway asked, his eyes wide, jaw slack, in his dark brown face.

Turnipseed chuckled. "I was out prospectin' with a supply wagon and mule when I found the range. Wandered into it by the same route you folks did, and started followin' them wolf heads. When the guardians attacked me, I run down that very corridor we just took . . . and found . . . all this."

"Who built it?" Angel was walking around, looking up in hushed awe.

"Don't know. There ain't nothin' here that tells—leastways, nothin' that I've ever found. And I've been through every building, over every inch of this canyon. I can tell you one thing, though. They were mighty keen on the wolf. They have statues of wolves. Even temples to wolves, and pictures etched in gold."

A chill rippled through Zane. As it did, a realization rolled through him, as well, though he was reluctant to put words to it. There was a whisper in the back of his mind, so soft that he probably wouldn't have heard it had he not been listening for it:

Eurico.

Demon offspring of Elyhann.

Eurico, the Lord of Darkness.

"What do you suppose Charlie Hondo hopes to find here?" Hathaway was down on his knees, staring at a patch of gold in the wall before him, caressing the shiny, unadulterated surface with the tip of his right index finger. "You think it's the gold? Like maybe that witch leadin' him an' the others found a map or some such?"

"Not sure," Zane said, though he was sure but somehow reluctant to voice it, as if voicing his suspicion would give it more credence. "But we'd best split up and start looking for him. It'll be dark soon."

Eurico. They were searching for the grave of Eurico, the Lord of Darkness. Long-dead apple of the demon-god Elyhann's eye.

And they'd better not find it. . . .

"It will at that," Angel said, following his glance toward the rim of the canyon, where the sky was beginning to turn green, the sunlight angling over the ridges now touched with saffron and copper. Shadows bled down the funnels and talus slides of the steep western slope.

Zane turned to Jericho. "The guardians ever venture in here?"

"Not since I've been here. Figure it must be against their religion or somethin'. Maybe it's off-limits to them. They're only here to protect it."

"They must know about you."

"Oh, they do, but they won't come in here after me. I live in the canyon, mostly. I mostly leave here at night to hunt, 'ceptin' when I'm checkin' my rattlesnake traps. That's what I was doin' when I spied them Angels and that Mex gal, saw 'em throw down on the guardians."

Turnipseed wrinkled his nose and raked a glance around the surrounding ridges. "I travel to Tucson for supplies couple times a year. Always come and go at night, and the guardians don't do much at night. Hole up purty tight in their little brush-hut villages scattered around the mountains. Almost like they're afraid of the dark."

To Angel and Hathaway, Zane said, "Let's start looking around. Be careful. If you see Charlie's bunch, fire a shot or two. I'll do the same. No one tries to take 'em down alone." Zane set his rifle on his shoulder. "Why don't you stay here, Jericho? Fire a shot if you see anything. Don't confront 'em. Remember, they're the worst of the ghouls."

"Will do, Uriah." The old desert rat smiled weakly. "Sure is good to see ya again. Awful about . . . back home . . . ain't it?"

"Yeah."

Zane swung away and began heading toward the stream that seemed to bisect the city from west to east. Angel and Hathaway drifted off among the towering buildings, their eyes still amazed at the city they'd found here.

Looking beyond the rooftops toward the ridges, Zane saw that while the city itself was large and extravagantly constructed, the canyon was vast. And likely nearly totally sealed off from the outside world—both naturally sealed, and sealed by the lost race of Stone Age warriors who might have lived here through the ages, one generation after another, fed by admonishment through legend and religion that it was their duty to protect this sacred place.

Eurico's home.

The home of his race of werewolves who had likely ruled the continent. And now, most likely, the home of Eurico's final resting place.

No one had ever found this one until Jericho had stumbled upon it by accident.

Zane followed the stream into the heart of the city. It was hard to watch for Charlie and the other Angels and Ravenna. The magnificent buildings seemed to whisper to him from down the centuries. They towered over him, still and dusty with the silence of expired eons. Window casements and doors gaped at him like the eye sockets and empty mouths of grinning skulls.

The only sound was the distant whine of the wind combing the cliff tops and the faint crackling of occasional tumbleweeds or breeze-ruffled palm fronds. Pigeons cooed and warbled, perched along roof edges and window ledges. Here and there in the dust covering the cobbles were Jericho's hobnailed boot prints and the tracks of small, scurrying animals—pack rats, rabbits, mice, and quail. Near a low, squat structure, he saw the week-old tracks of a hunting bobcat.

Uriah strode slowly down the broad main thoroughfare, the façades of what must have been shops, saloons, and brothels on his left and beyond the verdant, trickling stream on his right. The buildings were of all shapes and sizes, all made of gold. Occasionally, he stopped to peer in an empty window, but the buildings, so extravagant on the outsides, were as hollow as caves within.

Once in a while, he saw a golden statue of a wolf or the figures of wolves in all states of being—hunting, sleeping, fornicating—etched into walls. An anxiousness bit at him. It was like electricity from a near lightning storm leaching into his bones, plucking his nerves. As if from another world, he could hear a howling in his ears. Half-formed visions of werewolves flashed behind his retinas—dark nights of slaughter. Even bright days of slaughter during certain seasons. And then the return to this canyon, this city of gold.

Their home.

Where they lived with their living god who allowed them to shapeshift even during the day.

His pulse beat faster and faster. He pressed his hand to a gold casement. The gold fairly vibrated beneath his flesh. Silver had made them sick. But gold had given them strength. That was why they'd built an entire city of it.

The gold in the city was giving Zane strength, as well. The wolf in him stirred. He cast a wary eye at the sky and drew back from the window casement.

Something ripped his hat from his head and pinged loudly off the gold casement to his left.

A rifle screeched shrilly.

A man laughed and howled. "Uriah Zane!" The booming voice echoed madly. "Fancy meetin' you here, pard!"

Chapter 34

. . . .

STREET FIGHT

Zane jerked around and pressed his back to the front of the building he'd been looking in. In a window across the stream-bisected street, a man stood aiming a Winchester at him.

Smoke and flames stabbed from the rifle's maw. At the same time that Zane flung himself forward and the bullet slammed into the front of the building behind him, ricocheting wildly, the rifle's hammering report reached his ears.

Zane rolled off his right shoulder and, staying low, sprinted into the palms and willows lining the creek.

Dust blew up in front of him, and the rifle roared twice, sounding hollow inside the building from which the Hell's Angel was shooting. Zane pressed his shoulder against the front of the palm he was crouched behind, swung his rifle around the tree, and aimed hastily toward the window as the shooter drew back away from it.

Zane fired three silver rounds quickly, the ejected casings winging back over his shoulder and pinging onto the gravel. He racked another cartridge into the Henry's breech, glad more than ever that the Henry firearms company had had the wherewithal to design a sixteen-shot long gun, and sprang out from behind the palm. He ran into the stream, splashing over the sandy, gravelly bed, the gold-colored water flying up against his thighs and knees.

Gaining the opposite bank, he sprinted up it, through a heavy line of willows, stopped, and fired three more shots toward the large, square window in the building beyond.

One bullet ricocheted off the gold façade. Two more screeched on through the window and hammered off the walls or support pillars beyond.

Racking another cartridge, Zane bounded off his heels and began sprinting once more. He looked around carefully, knowing he could be running into a trap. Seeing no other Hell's Angels around him, or the venomous witch who had guided them, herself led by Elyhann, he slammed his back against the building's grimed front and slid a cautious glance through the window.

He caught a brief glimpse of a man with a long yellow ponytail leaping out a window on the other side of the hall-like structure. Zane snaked the Henry through his own window and fired a single round that merely blew grit and grime from the foot-thick casing. The shooter disappeared, running toward the building's rear.

Behind Zane, water splashed. He whipped around, cocking the Henry and extending it straight out from his right hip. He eased the tension on his trigger finger when he saw Angel and

Hathaway running across the stream behind him, about ten yards apart.

"Be careful!" the ghoul hunter yelled. "Might be a trap." He gestured for the two to head on up the fast-darkening street, then slipped around the side of the building and strode quickly down the gap between it and another hulking structure, toward the rear.

When he reached the back of the building from which the man with the ponytail had ambushed him, Zane slowed. He stepped out into the open behind the buildings on either side of him. Something hot ripped into his right cheek, just beneath his eye, then hammered the corner of the building to his right. Zane lunged forward and dove into a stone trough of some kind—probably part of some elaborate sewer or freshwater system—as at least three rifles thundered before him. The slugs tore into the lip of the stone trough and into the shrubs lining it, throwing torn sage and rabbit brush branches every which way, spitting rocks.

When the shooting died, Zane lifted his head to see one shooter standing crouched atop a ruined rock wall about thirty yards ahead and to his left. One more was crouched at the base of the wall the first man was shooting from, while another stood atop a boulder perched on a low ridge straight ahead of Zane.

As the rifles exploded once more, all three shooters howling and yipping devilishly, Zane ducked his head behind the lip of the stone trough, gritting his teeth as the bullets hammered into the ground above, spitting more dust, branches, and rocks into the trough.

When the shooting tapered off, Zane whipped his rifle up but held fire. He looked toward where the ghoul whom he'd recognized as One-Eye Langtry had been standing atop the boulder. The ghoul had disappeared. The others had disappeared as well.

To Zane's left and up the rocky, ruin-stippled slope, spurs chinged. He heard the thudding clacks of boots running on stone, and saw the three bushwhacking ghouls dashing along the base of the far ridge as they ran deeper into the canyon.

Rifles barked to Zane's hard left and from about twenty and thirty yards away. Angel and Hathaway were both down on their knees behind a ruined wall overgrown with ancient vines, firing toward the base of the ridge as they slid their rifles left, tracking the fleeing wolves.

Zane scrambled out of the draw and ran over to where both Hathaway and Angel knelt behind the wall, reloading.

"Only three," Zane said. "Must've been looking for us."

He knelt down near Angel, pressed his back to the ruined wall, and slipped the loading tube up from beneath the Henry's barrel. Quickly, automatically, while gazing through the ruins and the brush between him and the base of the ridge, he slid silver cartridges from his bandolier and punched them down into the loading tube.

Angel gave an angry grunt as she racked a shell into her Winchester's breech. "Ravenna must've missed her dragon, figured she had someone behind her."

Hathaway said, "Or maybe they heard our shots when we threw down on them guardians, as Turnipseed calls 'em."

"Well," Zane said, "they know we're here . . . and don't like it."

"Where do you suppose Charlie and the witch are?"

"Lookin' for what they came here for. That's why only the

lesser three in the pack came after us. They'll likely try another bushwack so's we don't interrupt Charlie and his sweet Mexican darlin'. I got a feelin' they're hearin' ole Eurico's howl."

Angel frowned at Zane, genuinely puzzled, more than a little worried. "Who's Eurico?"

"I'll tell you later." Zane shook his head and rose a little higher to stare off through the ruins. "But that they're here now and the moon's full is no coincidence."

"The moon'll be up in an hour or so," Hathaway said, "if I got the calendar right, an' I usually do. Somethin' big's gonna happen here, tonight, with that moon on the rise. I can feel it in my blood."

Zane shuttled his glance between Hathaway and Angel. "The other three haven't given up—they'll try to circle around us. I'm gonna head up this slope a ways, try to cut their sign, stay behind 'em. You two split up again and gradually move down canyon. We'll likely run into 'em again soon. We have to get those three out of our way, 'cause they'll do everything in their power to keep us from getting to Charlie and Ravenna."

Zane broke away from the others, running at a crouch up the slope, weaving among the ruined outbuildings and cisterns where the city had probably stored its water during the dry months. He walked a hundred yards, following the clear sign of the three running ghouls until they split up, one angling straight back into the city, one angling up canyon, the other continuing along the base of the slope.

Zane glanced at the sky. The light was almost gone. Heavy shadows plunged down the canyon walls, and the air was growing cold. Zane's heartbeat quickened. He squeezed his rifle in his hands as, on one knee where the tracks of the three ghouls had split up, he gazed off over the darkening city.

Where would Charlie and Ravenna find Eurico?

He crossed the stream and headed back into the city, where he promptly lost the tracks of the ghoul he'd been following. The man must have followed the stream either up or down canyon. Zane didn't want to take the time to backtrack and look for him. He had to concentrate on Charlie and Ravenna. The moon would be up soon, and it was those two he needed to kill first.

A half hour later, as he prowled a back alley and silently willed the moon to slow its ascent, there was the spatter of belching rifles. He broke into a run, leaving the alley and finding himself in a broad street between more golden ruins that were dark gray now in the thickening darkness. The rifles crashed from up the dusty, cobbled street down which a breeze now kicked up tumbleweeds and brought the dank odors of the canyon.

Three rifles flashed above street level on the right side, while an answering gun barked in a shaded portico on the left. Just then a man screamed and dove forward out of a balcony on the right. Zane made out a black eye patch as One-Eye turned a somersault and dropped his rifle, his body thudding to the street, kicking up dust.

The other two ghouls, one firing from a rooftop, the other triggering lead from a third-floor window, stopped firing. In the street, One-Eye arched his back and groaned. A rifle flashed and barked from the shaded portico, and One-Eye's head jerked sharply to one side, dark blood jetting into the street.

Zane sprinted to the street's left side. The other two shooters opened up once more, hammering the building fronts around Zane. The ghoul hunter felt the burn of a bullet across his right thigh as he threw himself into the shaded portico behind four gold pillars, the base of each suspended on a long-clawed wolf's paw.

Zane flung himself back against the front of a building, saw Hathaway lying on his side a few feet away, one bloody leg stretched out before him, the knee bent slightly. The man's left hand was clamped over the bloody wound just above the knee. His other hand held his rifle.

"How bad?" Zane asked, edging a look around one of the support columns toward the rooftops on the other side of the street.

"Just pinched me but I can't straighten my leg."

"Where's Red?"

"She was up the street when they bushwhacked us. Last I seen she ducked back into an alley." Hathaway looked at Zane gravely. "She might be hit."

As two bullets smashed into the cobbles around him, Zane dashed up to one of the support columns and snaked his Henry around the side. He triggered two shots at the shooter to the left, who gave a yelp and dropped flat atop the opposite roof. His hat poked up from the level of the roof, and Zane triggered another shot.

The hat flipped up off the Angel's head and disappeared.

The ghoul gave an angry howl. "For that, amigo," he shouted tightly, belly down against the roof, "I'll be takin' your hat just as soon as you have no more use for it! Won't be long."

Meanwhile, the other Angel, to the right of the first, was continuing to pound Zane and Hathaway's position with lead. The slugs barked against the front of Zane's column as well as the one covering the scout.

Zane turned his body and slid a glance out around his column's right side. He saw the silhouette of the shooter and the man's rifle in the second-story window. Orange flames jabbed from the Winchester's barrel, and Zane drew his head back behind the column. The shooter's slug hammered the side of the column, ricocheting against the building behind him and Hathaway. The screech of the slug was deafening.

There was another shot. This one sounded more like a *crack* than the thundering rifle shots—a pistol shot. A man screamed hollowly. The scream echoed inside the building across the street.

A familiar voice added its shouted echo to that of the scream. "That's for Frank and Cole, you mangy, yellow-livered coyote!"

Lines cut across Zane's forehead. "Jesse, that you?"

Zane looked around the pillar, saw Curly Joe slouched beside the empty window, one arm slung over the broad gold ledge. His hat was off, and he was facing toward Zane's right, where a figure just now leaped through a window between the joined buildings and into the same building that Curly Joe was crouched in.

The new figure, Jesse James, aiming two pistols out in front of him, stumbled in front of another window. Jesse's pistols cracked and leaped in his hands. Curly Joe's head snapped back, and he dropped down beneath the window.

Jesse walked over to Curly Joe's window, looking down before turning his head toward Zane. He threw an arm out in a wave, then slumped forward and to one side with the effort, grabbing the shoulder that the guardian's arrow had pierced. "At least I got one of the spineless damn killers!" he bellowed. "I got one of 'em, by God, and Frank's smilin' in his Catholic grave!"

Zane saw movement on the roof to the left of the building

Jesse was in. He raised his Henry, trying to draw a bead on the figure running from the building's rear toward the front, taking long, leaping strides. The ghoul gave a shrill cry and bounded off his heels, throwing his rifle out to one side as he launched himself over the street.

Zane lunged out from behind the pillar, desperately trying to plant a bead on the airborne wolf. He triggered the Henry, but the ghoul arced up and over the street and disappeared above the roofline of the building behind Zane and Hathaway.

In a pain-pinched voice, the scout said, "Did he do what I thought he just done?"

"Yep."

The ghoul had felt the gold—probably also the full moon—as Zane was feeling the otherworldly influences himself. It made him light-headed and electric, fairly bursting with energy.

"I'll be back, Al!" Zane leaned his rifle against the side of the pillar and ran around the corner of the building and down the side about twenty feet, until he saw a second-story window directly above him.

He did not hesitate, but set his heels, bent his knees, and sprang straight up off his feet. He gave a great groan as he closed his hands over the gold, grime-encrusted ledge, and was surprised that he could so easily hoist himself up with his arms and swing his feet over the ledge and through the window.

He got his feet beneath him and landed at a crouch. The ghoul before him, who'd been heading toward a stairway at the back of the empty, pillared room, likely intending to get behind Zane and Hathaway, was as surprised by Zane's burst of strength as Zane was himself.

He swung around with an exasperated grunt, the flaps of his

yellow duster winging out to his sides, and pressed the stock of his Winchester against his hip. The gun roared, flashing in the nearly night-dark room. The slug hammered the wall behind Zane as the ghoul hunter flung himself forward and dug his LeMat out of its shoulder holster. Rolling up off his shoulder, he aimed the revolver quickly and pulled the trigger, detonating the twelve-gauge shotgun cartridge beneath the main barrel.

The fierce hogleg thundered and leaped in the ghoul hunter's hand. The wad of silver dimes he'd filled the cartridge with tore through Lucky's chest, lifting the ghoul a foot in the air and punching him six feet straight back before he hit the floor hard and lay, limbs akimbo, snarling and quivering. Zane flipped the latch-like switch on the side of the versatile weapon and fired two silver .45 rounds through the dying ghoul's forehead, putting him away for all eternity.

Zane turned to a front window and barked a curse. The full moon was up. As large as a dinner plate, it fairly throbbed with pearl light. With anxious eyes, Zane followed the trail it would take across the city. His gaze held on a high, cylindrical tower about two hundred yards away and capped with a snarling wolf's head mounted at the edge of the domed ceiling and limned in the milky lunar wash.

From the direction of the tower, a woman's terrified scream rolled over the hulking buildings.

Zane's spine tensed as he stared across the night. He ground his fingers into the window ledge. *"Red!"*

Chapter 35

. . . .

WOLF MOON

A half hour before Zane blew Lucky Snodgrass to hell with his LeMat, Angel had stepped through the low, arched door at the base of the cylindrical tower with the wolf's head perched atop its dome several hundred feet in the air.

She'd seen the tower just as she and Hathaway had been ambushed in the street. Somehow realizing that Charlie Hondo and Ravenna were in the tower, Angel traced a circuitous route to the bizarre structure. She'd known Al had been hit—she'd taken a graze to her upper right arm, herself—but saw that he'd been able to pull himself to relative safety in the alcove.

The moon was climbing, and Angel knew she had precious little time to stop the wolf leader and the witch before they attained whatever dark power they were after. She had to abandon Al for now and go after them.

Now she stared into the dank dimness before her, where

stone steps spiraled up the tower into musty darkness. She pricked her ears to listen, but there was only a ringing silence in the cavernous cylinder punctuated by the increased shooting along the street behind her.

She knew that Charlie and Ravenna were in here. When she'd first set eyes on the building with that snarling wolf's head capping it, she'd known it had to be the place they'd been heading for. The three other ghouls had placed themselves on the rooftops nearby to keep the hunting party away from it.

She started up the steps, and immediately the darkness and the close confines, the chipped stone steps rising steeply before and behind her, made her feel as though a giant fist were closing around her. Claustrophobia tugged against her, making her legs stiff. When she'd climbed what she'd figured to be about sixty feet, however, the light from the full moon pushed through small, diamond-shaped notches carved into the walls about two feet apart from one another. The stairs appeared in the milky half-light, forever rising, forever falling away behind her.

Gradually as she climbed, voices emanated from somewhere above. At first they sounded like little more than a vibration in the golden walls. Little by little, however, the vibrations separated, became two distinct sounds, and as she continued to climb she could make out a man's voice and a woman's voice. Mostly the woman's. Ravenna seemed to be doing most of the talking.

"Chatty bitch," Angel muttered to herself—a lame attempt at dulling the myriad fears clinging to her like thorns.

It was soon only Ravenna's voice that Angel was hearing. The witch was chanting loudly, her voice growing louder and louder so that Angel could plainly hear the echoes now. She was speaking in Spanish, and Angel could hear only bits and pieces of what the witch was chanting—something about many years passing, the full moon, a new age beginning for the wolf people.

Angel quickened her pace. She stopped when the moonlight revealed the steps opening onto a flat surface, the walls falling away. Lifting her Winchester fully loaded with silver, Angel continued up the steps, walking slowly now on the balls of her boots, and stepped onto the floor above. She found herself in a vast circular room lit via the diamond-shaped ports in the walls by moonlight.

Two torches flared, fixed in brackets against the walls on the other side of the room, which was three steps below Angel, who remained hidden in the shadows against the wall behind her, near the stairs. Angel squinted to see more clearly in the dawn-like light, and then she frowned.

On the far side of the circular room sat a giant, golden chair. It was a throne with two golden wolf's heads rising from the back, two giant wolf feet serving as front legs. Sitting in the chair was Charlie Hondo. The ghoul was tense and stiff, arms resting on the chair arms, and he stared straight ahead, expressionless, eyes wide, as though he were in a trance. The gold hoop rings dangling from his ears shone like silver in the angling moonlight.

He looked pale and wiry, sitting there in that big chair in his cavalry blues that were a size too tight for him, the pants too short. He looked ridiculous, his long hair mussed, several days of beard growth darkening his jaw, the two blasphemous tattoos on his sunburned cheeks. The man—or god—for whom the throne had been built must have been three times Charlie Hondo's size.

Behind him and a little to his right stood Ravenna de Onis

y Gonzalez-Vara in black leather, with red boots and a red sash blowing out away from her in a breeze that Angel could not feel. The witch held what appeared to be an eight-sided amulet above her head. It, too, was made of gold. She had her eyes raised toward a round hole in the domed roof filled with the blue black of the moonlit sky. Through the diamond-shaped ports in the dome, Angel could see the moon rising on an interception course with that hole in the dome.

Angel stepped forward to the edge of the wall shadows and raised her Winchester, drawing the hammer back. Her hands inside her gloves were hot and sweaty. Her heart thudded. Drawing a deep, slow breath, she planted the carbine's sights on Charlie's chest.

Something peeped sharply nearby. Startled, Angel lowered the rifle a few inches and looked down. A rat stood on the sunken main floor, staring up at Angel, twitching its whiskers and wiry tail.

Ravenna broke off her chanting and raised her voice more loudly as she said in English, "You don't think I know you're there?" She laughed wickedly, still holding the amulet above her head.

Angel pressed her cheek against the Winchester's stock, narrowing one eye as she slid the sights over Charlie's chest, the ghoul staring at her now, eyes sharp but his face otherwise still expressionless. Again, Ravenna laughed, making Angel's hands jerk as she tried to slide the bead at the end of the carbine's barrel into the V-notch above the breech.

A cat wailed sharply, the snarling cry filling Angel's ears. Her hands jerked, and she nudged the rifle up, the gun exploding and the slug slamming into one of the wolf heads rising above Charlie Hondo's pale, bony shoulders.

The cat—it couldn't be a cat!—wailed again. Angel saw something large move toward her from where the rat had been standing a few feet before and below her. The gray, yellow-eyed mountain lion lunged up the three steps, showing its long, curved fangs, and began to leap toward Angel as the marshal stepped back and swung around, ejecting the spent cartridge and throwing a fresh one into the chamber.

The cat was a gray blur bounding up off its springlike hind feet. Angel screamed as she lowered the carbine's barrel, pressing it hard against the cat's chest and squeezing the trigger, the explosion muffled by the great feline's powerful body.

The cat slammed into Angel, pinned her arms down to her sides. She dropped the Winchester, heard it clatter to the gold-cobbled floor a half second before she hit the floor on her back and shoulders, slamming her head down so hard that everything went black and silent. The clack of boot heels grew louder in her ears, and she opened her eyes to see the great cat staring glassily down at her, its forehead pressed against hers.

Its glassy, dark brown eyes rolled around a little in their sockets, and the jaws spasmed. Angel felt the hot blood spilling out of the hole she'd drilled in the beast's chest, soaking her vest and running down between her breasts to her belly.

Ravenna reached down, grabbed the back of the dying cat's neck, and pulled it off of Angel, who drew a deep breath and closed her right hand over one of her pistols.

"Did you kill my dragon, too, you fucking bitch?" Ravenna's shrill voice echoed sharply off the gold walls and the dome, the round hole in which was growing brighter and brighter. "It was you, wasn't it? I know it was you. I just now saw it! Dragons do not materialize out of thin air without some effort on the part of the conjurer, you know!"

"Here," Angel said, flicking the keeper thong free from her Colt's hammer and sliding the piece out of its holster. "Let me make it up to you."

She jerked the gun up and began clicking the hammer back, but she did not get the barrel leveled on Ravenna before the witch slammed her bare foot hard against the underside of Angel's wrist. The pistol flew up out of Angel's hand, hit the floor behind her with a sharp thud, and slid back into the shadows.

Ravenna leveled an ivory-gripped Remington at Angel's head and cocked it, smiling. "Get up. You're interrupting us and the Lord of Darkness, who stirs even as I speak, and you're piss-burning me bad!"

Angel lifted her head, wincing, and looked around the witch toward Charlie, who sat as before, stiff and tense, trancelike. He was staring toward Angel, the moonlight sharp in his otherwise flat eyes.

"But I won't kill you," Ravenna said, reaching down and pulling Angel's other pistol from its holster and tossing it away with the other one. She removed the ivory-gripped stiletto strapped to the marshal's right calf, tossed it away, then ripped two whang strings from Angel's leather pants. "No, I am going to make you watch the transformation. If you do not die of fright, you will die by Eurico's fangs and claws!"

She kicked Angel onto her belly and drove a knee into the base of her back, pinning her to the floor. The witch was stronger than she looked, and the braining Angel had taken made it impossible for her to fight. Her limbs were weak, and she was seeing double, her ears ringing madly. As Ravenna tied Angel's wrists behind her back with the whang strings, the witch leaned down and whispered sensuously into Angel's right ear.

"Or maybe we should make you one of us, eh? A girl such as you would be a formidable wolf in Eurico's pack. He and I might be honored to have you running along beside us in our war against the quivering mortals!"

"Don't bet on it!"

Angel gave a clipped cry as Ravenna grabbed her hair and jerked her to her feet. Angel got her boots beneath her and kept them moving as Ravenna pulled her savagely across the floor by her hair. Angel watched with keen frustration as her rifle faded into the distance behind her. Only vaguely did she notice that the dead wildcat was gone and that in its place lay the rat, nearly torn in half by Angel's silver bullet.

She fought at the leather ties to no avail. She couldn't move her hands at all, and she felt the numbness as the blood flow was pinched.

Ravenna dropped her about fifteen yards in front of Charlie, still seated in the large golden throne. Angel sprawled belly down, grunting and cursing, then lifted her head and sank back against her heels, struggling in vain against the leather ties cutting into her wrists.

"Now, watch and quake, you miserable, mortal slut! Ely-hann promised that if I brought Charlie here and replaced his soul with Eurico's, I'd share his Lord of Darkness powers." Ravenna laughed heartily. "I guess that would make me the Queen of Darkness, wouldn't it?" Ravenna, chuckling, set down her gun, picked up the amulet, and resumed her position flanking Charlie, who now stood grinning drunkenly, wolfishly, down at Angel.

Ravenna resumed chanting, thrusting her tan breasts out from behind her revealing leather vest and raising her eyes once more toward the ever-brightening ceiling. After several minutes, a circular gold dais rose up out of the floor with a hollow scraping sound. In the middle of the dais lay what appeared to be an oblong, light blue vase.

A giant red heart lay inside the vase, throbbing.

With each throb, the organ grew redder and redder until it fairly glowed. It seemed to be growing, as well, threatening to burst out of the vase.

"The immortal heart of the Lord of Darkness!" Ravenna squealed, staring down brightly at the ever-brightening heart. "Oh, Charlie!"

Angel cast her horrified gaze at the hole in the dome. The huge moon had edged inside the hole. Angel wasn't sure if it was only her battered brain registering things that weren't there, but the moon appeared to throb with each beat of the red heart on the pedestal between her and Charlie Hondo.

Charlie's eyes also rose toward the moon.

His chest began to expand, as though he were drawing a deep breath. The leer faded from his lips, and now an expression of magisterial awe and wonder shaped itself there. A similar expression brushed across Ravenna's regal features, and slowly, holding the amulet in front of her breasts, she dropped down to her knees beside Charlie. She placed her right hand on his thigh and held her gaze on the hole in the ceiling quickly filling with the pulsating moon.

"Oh . . ." Ravenna wheezed in hushed awe. ". . . *Charlie* . . . !"

Angel felt her own heart beating with every throb of the heart in the blue vase. She continued to struggle fiercely against the leather stays, until she finally tore her right hand free, scraping off a good bit of skin in the process. She glanced up again at the ceiling, and a cold sweat oozed from every pore.

She was too late.

The hole in the dome was completely white.

Before her, the heart in the vase was gone.

Charlie's chest was red, and it throbbed. Ravenna's chest was also red and throbbing.

Both of them were growing larger and larger as thick brown hair began sprouting on their suddenly naked bodies, their hands and feet broadening and extending into paws. Their skulls thickened, ears rising, eyes sinking, noses enlarging and extending. In seconds, they were both more wolf than human, and Angel was scuttling back on her rump, digging into the pouches sewn inside her cartridge belt with quaking hands.

Ravenna's eyes glowed as red as her chest. Charlie's eyes glowed even brighter.

Ravenna opened her mouth and showed her white fangs, stepping toward Angel on her four paws, what could only be a smile shaping itself on her mouth, in her glowing eyes.

"Son of a *bitch*!" Angel's fingers closed over the silver shuriken nestling in the pouch. Quelling her fear, she gave herself over to her training and whipped her arm back behind her before flinging it forward and loosing the five-pointed silver star.

Ravenna howled miserably as the disc thumped into her chest, burying itself so deep that the tip of only one point showed through the thick matting of dark brown fur. Blood oozed out around it. The she-wolf snarled and yipped and clawed at her chest with both paws, running in circles.

At the same time, the wolf that had been Charlie Hondo only fifteen seconds before tipped his head back and loosed a howl that filled the cavernous, round room like the yowls of a thousand wolf demons at once. The tooth-gnashing din slammed against both sides of Angel's head like giant fists.

The room shook before her, the floor bounding beneath her.

Charlie jumped up out of the chair, stood on his hind feet for a half second before diving forward, hackles raised, knifelike fangs bared, front paws with their terrible black claws swiping at the air. Something moved behind Angel, and then she felt a hot rush of air across the back of her neck as the thing leaped over her from behind and crashed headlong into Charlie Hondo.

Chapter 36

. . . .

THE WRATH OF ELYHANN

The wolf that had leaped over Angel hammered Charlie Hondo backward onto the dais, knocking the vase onto the floor, where it did not break, and sunk its teeth in Hondo's neck, the enraged growls and slathering snarls of the second beast joining with Hondo's own screams to set up a shrill ringing in Angel's ears.

The din as well as the appearance out of nowhere of the second beast sent her into further shock, and it wasn't before the two wolves had rolled off the dais and had risen onto their back feet, snarling and digging at each other's neck with their fangs, that she realized the second wolf was Uriah. Only the hazel eyes were his. The rest of the wolf was long and rangy and hump-backed and nearly the same black and charcoal color as Hondo.

But whereas Hondo fought with a savage defensiveness, Uriah fought with a dominant, mindless rage, his hazel eyes turning yellow red and throbbing with primal fury. Hondo had the

334 ......PETER BRANDVOLD

strength some awakened black god had given him, and it was enough to withstand Uriah's ferocious, selfless attack.

The two fought entangled and leaping around the large, round room for a long time, without sign of either tiring, until at least a bucketful of blood had washed across the golden floor. Angel looked at her rifle, but it was too far away, and the two were fighting between her and the Winchester. Besides, even if she could reach the gun, there was a chance she'd hit Uriah with one of her silver bullets.

Frustrated sobs racked her, and she pressed her hands to her temples as if to clear the horrible vision of the two fighting beasts from her head, and the horrifying yips and snarls and tearing growls from her ears. Finally, after fifteen minutes of savage fighting, the wolves separated, facing each other, breathing hard, their hot breath frosting in the air above their heads. Their eyes pulsated.

The moon had moved away from the circle in the domed ceiling, and its liquid white light angled onto the two beasts as if to isolate them in an otherworldly incandescence.

Their dark bodies were massive, their fur standing on end across their humped necks. The moonlight limned the ends of their fur coats like bristles. Blood black as ink pooled beneath them on the gold-cobbled floor. Their bellies sagged, shoulders slumped.

Finally, the wolf with the pulsating hazel eyes glanced at Angel, then drew a deep breath, gave a terrific howl that seemed to nearly implode the tower, and leaped off its back legs. It dug its teeth into Hondo's already bloody neck, drove the ghoul to the floor, and, with one last decisive slash of its razor-edged fangs, tore the rest of Hondo's throat out.

It tore the entire neck out.

Whipping his head up, Uriah cast the ghoul's large, hairy skull high and far across the room to land in the dim reaches and bounce, roll, and thump against an unseen wall. Blood geysered from the gaping hole between Charlie's shoulders.

The wolf that was Uriah Zane stared into the darkness of the room. Finally, his head and shoulders sagged. He slumped to the floor with a ragged sigh and rolled onto his side. His blood-matted side rose and fell heavily.

Angel stood and walked over to him, dropped to her knees by his side. In the time it had taken her to make the short trek, he'd assumed his human form once more, his clothes torn, blood leaking from a dozen different deep wounds. His chest rose and fell shallowly, and his eyes were closed.

Angel placed a hand on his shoulder. "Uriah."

He didn't move.

"Uriah," she said, clearing the phlegm from her throat and jerking his shoulder. "Heal yourself, Uriah. You have the power."

Zane's eyes opened. He stared blindly for a time, and then he turned his head to her and rolled onto his back. He swallowed, licked his lips. "Finish me."

Angel shook her head. "No."

"Go ahead."

"You saved me. Now heal yourself, you bastard."

Zane shook his head. "Leave me, then."

Beneath Angel's knees, the floor vibrated. The vibration grew into a rumbling quiver. She looked up. Dust sifted down from the domed ceiling. The rumbling grew gradually from all across the night-cloaked, moon-bathed city.

"Get out of here," Zane told her.

"No." Again, she shook her head, tears rolling down her cheeks. She grabbed the collar of his buckskin shirt in her fists and jerked his head up off the floor. "Not without you, god-damnit."

Zane closed his eyes. His body lay absolutely still for a time, and Angel thought he was dead. She placed a hand on his chest, felt the insistent beat of his heart. She ran her eyes across his body.

His clothes were still torn, but the bleeding appeared to have stopped. After several more minutes, during which the vibrations grew louder and more violent, Zane opened his eyes and stared up at Angel. "Sure wish you'd make up your mind," he rasped. "First you wanna drill me with a silver bullet; then you refuse."

"Get your ass up," she said. "I think we've made someone angry."

"Wouldn't be the first time."

She looked around, blinking dust from her lashes as it sifted down from the ceiling. Now chunks of gold were beginning to fall, as well, hitting the floor with loud crashes.

She grabbed his hand in both of hers and, rising, pulled. "Can you stand?"

"Think so."

He let her help him to his feet and wrap his right arm around her neck. Together, Angel crouching beneath his considerable weight, feeling the weak trembling in his spent body, they made their way toward the stairs, Angel pausing only to grab her Winchester.

By the time they'd reached the bottom of the tower, Zane was strong enough to walk on his own. He saw the others—Jesse James, Al Hathaway, and Jericho Turnipseed—milling around

DUST OF THE DAMNED.......337

outside the tower, the wounded James and Hathaway leaning on their rifles. They all looked shocked and miserable, glancing around at the slowly crumbling city, the pillars cracking and crashing and golden objects tumbling from roofs.

"What the hell happened up there?" Jericho shouted above the din.

"All hell broke loose," Angel said. "But I think we got the gates closed. For now."

Tenderly, Zane limped forward and beckoned to the stunned crowd behind him. "Best pull our picket pins, fog it out of this place."

"The gold!" Jericho shouted, turning slow, shambling circles, his eyes on the crumbling roofs.

Leaning on his rifle, Hathaway gave the prospector a shove toward Zane, who was limping back the way they'd come. "Come on, fool, or you're gonna be buried with your precious gold!"

"It's all Zane's fault," said Jesse James, looking around and shaking his head. "You can't take that no-account Carolinan nowhere he won't cause trouble!"

"My gold!" the prospector continued to scream in disbelief, face tipped to the moonlit sky against which the city slowly shook loose and fell. "I waited so long!" He bawled like a baby as he stumbled after the others, hands raised as if to hold the domed city of gold in place. "Oh, merciful Jesus, *noooo!*"

They managed to retrieve their gear and horses and hightail it out of the cavern before the brunt of the earthquake struck.

They couldn't see the effects as they galloped their rested

mounts back the way they'd come, back past the dead guardians and finally out onto the western flats. But they could hear the loud rumbling and crashing, like enormous, distant cannons, of the canyon walls caving in on the city.

By the time they were miles away, the light from the sagging moon shone only a pale, dusty streak in the sky where the mountain shaped like a wolf's head had once been. The streak resembled stardust wafting from a damned, destroyed world. No one spoke for the rest of the night as they continued to ride northwest and away from the tantrum of Elyhann, who had been waiting for Charlie Hondo only to watch him die in the god's temple, the demon's hope for a master race of werewolves snuffed for the present.

At dawn, they made camp and slept at the base of a low escarpment near which a tiny spring trickled. At midmorning, they saddled their horses, filled their canteens, mounted up, and continued riding, swinging northward toward Tucson, where they'd seek medical help for their wounded. As they left the escarpment, Zane glanced back at the mountain. Dust continued to waft, forming a thin cloud over the vanished peak and lower ridges around it. Nearer, a line of dark riders threaded toward him through the chaparral on small, rangy ponies.

Zane told the others to go on ahead, and gigged General Lee up a hillock near the old Spanish trading trail the others were following. He positioned the wheeled coffin in a gap in the rocks crowning the hill. Quickly, he set up the Gatling gun on its tripod and squatted behind it in the open coffin.

When the dozen or so guardians rode into view around another outcropping and galloped to within fifty yards of Zane, the ghoul hunter triggered the Gatling gun, shattering the midmorning silence with the machine's staccato bellow. The slugs blew up a line of dust in the sand in front of the riders, who reined their ponies to sudden stops, jerking back on the rawhide reins and looking around wildly, dark eyes frightened.

The lead, tattooed rider turned his head toward Zane and the smoking Gatling gun. He yelled something in his guttural tongue, and he and the other riders swung their ponies around and galloped back in the direction from which they'd come. Their dust rose, sifting slowly. Gradually, their hoof thuds dwindled.

Nearby, a shod hoof rang off a stone, and Zane turned to see Angel riding up behind him, staring after the fading line of natives from beneath the crown of her dark brown Stetson.

"Can't help feeling sorry for them," she said. "A whole race born to protect a city. Now the city's gone. No wonder they're angry."

Zane sighed and leaped out of the Gatling's casket. He returned the gun to its bed among the silver and other ghoul-hunting paraphernalia, and closed the lid. He swung up onto General Lee's back and booted the gold stallion down the hill, stopping beside Angel. She was looking at him obliquely.

"You all right?" she asked.

Zane lifted his hat, ran a hand back through his long, black, sweat-damp hair. He stared after Turnipseed, Hathaway, and Jesse James continuing to ride northward along the faint trail angling through the chaparral.

"Damn dangerous—don't you think?" he asked.

"What?"

"Doin' what you did. Or *not* doin' it. Might only be makin' more trouble for yourself later." Zane tilted a glance at the bright, brassy sky. "Next full moon . . ."

Angel leaned toward him, wrapped an arm around his neck, and kissed him. "I reckon I'll take my chances." She kissed him again. "Come on. I'll race you to Tucson and a long bath in a tubful of whiskey!"

She reined her paint around and booted the horse into a ground-eating gallop. Zane glanced once more behind him at the thinning dust cloud over the vanished mountain, then gigged General Lee into a lunging lope behind the marshal as she smiled back over her shoulder at him, through a wave of wine-red hair.